COLLECTING STICKS

COLLECTING STICKS

Joe Decie

JONATHAN CAPE / LONDON

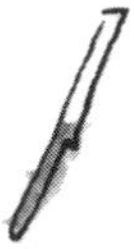

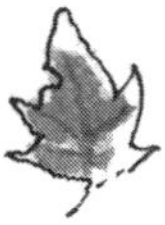

FOR STEPH AND SAM

THANKS TO: JOHN MARTZ, STEPHEN COLLINS, DANIEL LOCKE, JULIE TATE, DAN BERRY, DUSTIN HARBIN, HANNAH BERRY, JULIA GFRÖRER, ROSS TEPEREK, AILEEN McEVOY

COLLECTING STICKS WAS SUPPORTED USING PUBLIC FUNDING BY THE NATIONAL LOTTERY THROUGH ARTS COUNCIL ENGLAND. EARLY DEVELOPMENT OF THIS PROJECT WAS FUNDED BY A CONTRIBUTION FROM LAKES INTERNATIONAL COMIC ART FESTIVAL

LOTTERY FUNDED

Supported using public funding by ARTS COUNCIL ENGLAND

THE LAKES INTERNATIONAL COMIC ART FESTIVAL

PROLOGUE

GLASTONBURY FESTIVAL 2003

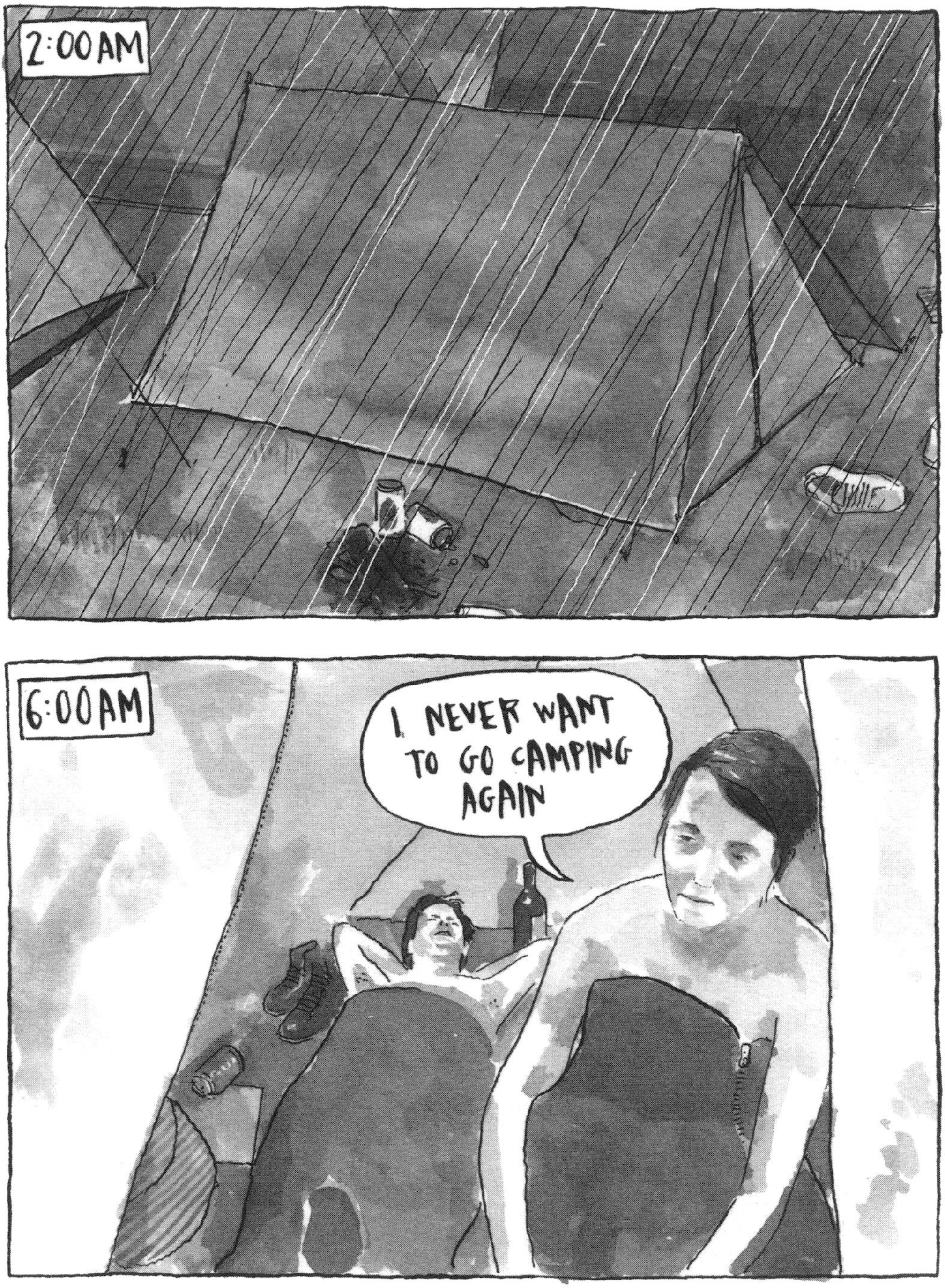
2:00AM
6:00AM
I NEVER WANT TO GO CAMPING AGAIN

OH DEAR

ANOTHER PROLOGUE

CORNWALL 2012

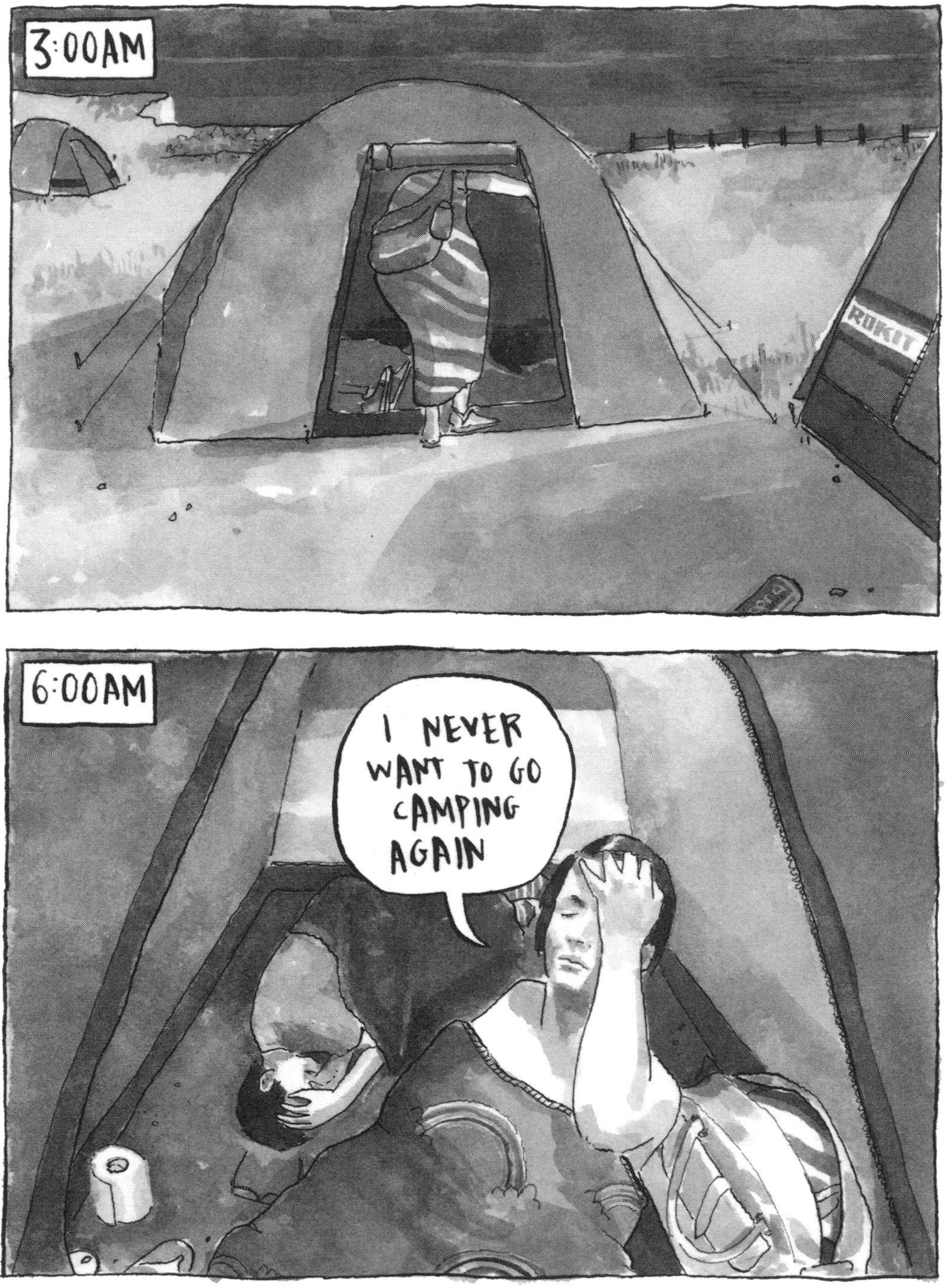
3:00AM
ROKIT
6:00AM
I NEVER WANT TO GO CAMPING AGAIN

AHH WELL

COLLECTING STICKS

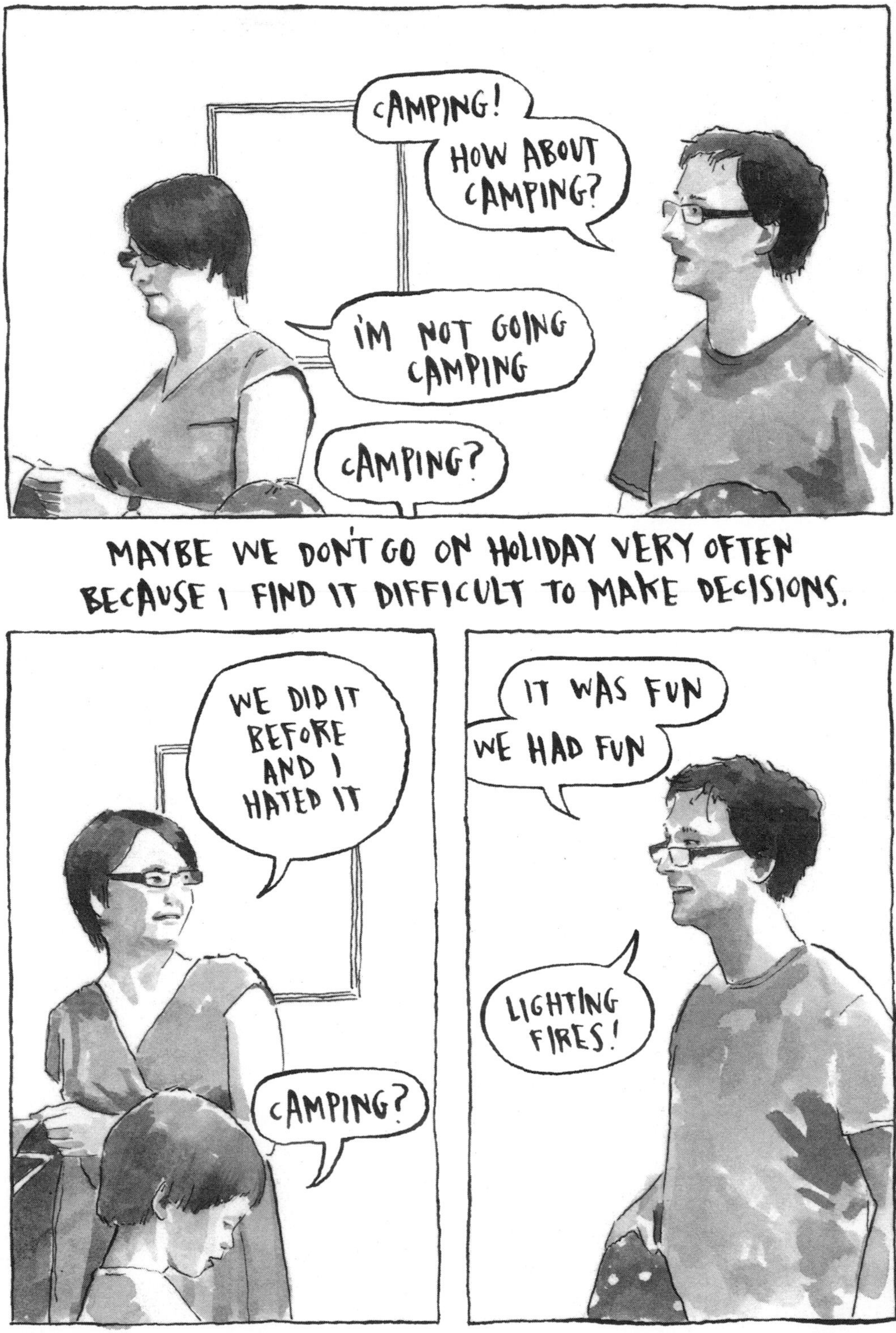
CAMPING!
HOW ABOUT CAMPING?
I'M NOT GOING CAMPING
CAMPING?
MAYBE WE DON'T GO ON HOLIDAY VERY OFTEN BECAUSE I FIND IT DIFFICULT TO MAKE DECISIONS.
WE DID IT BEFORE AND I HATED IT
CAMPING?
IT WAS FUN
WE HAD FUN
LIGHTING FIRES!

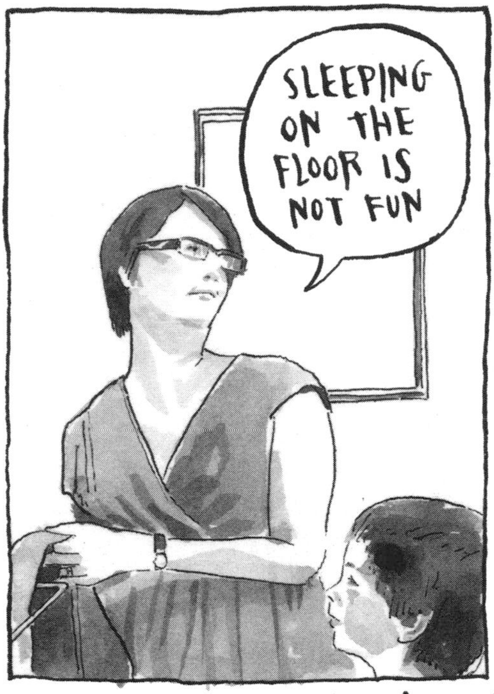
SLEEPING ON THE FLOOR IS NOT FUN

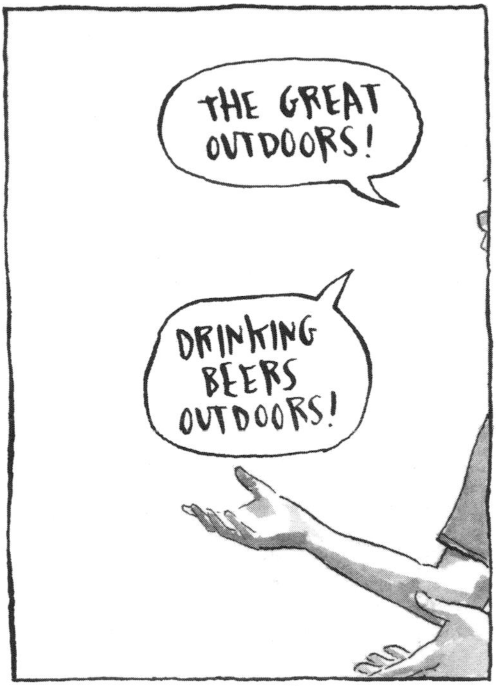
THE GREAT OUTDOORS!
DRINKING BEERS OUTDOORS!

OR BECAUSE THE DECISIONS I DO MAKE,

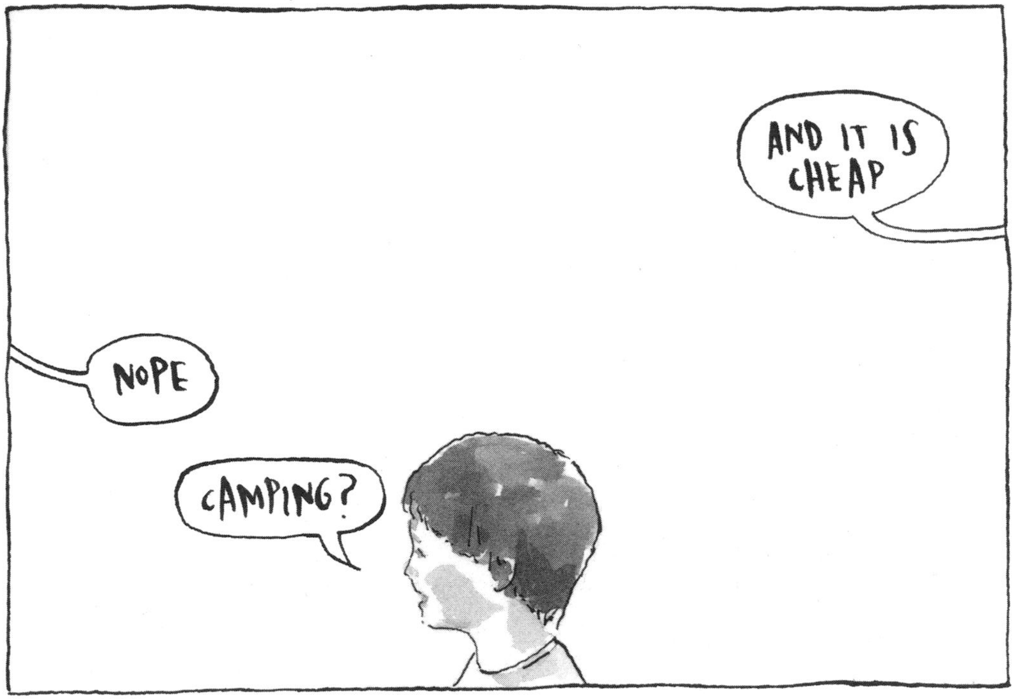
AND IT IS CHEAP
NOPE
CAMPING?

THEY ARE OFTEN WRONG DECISIONS.

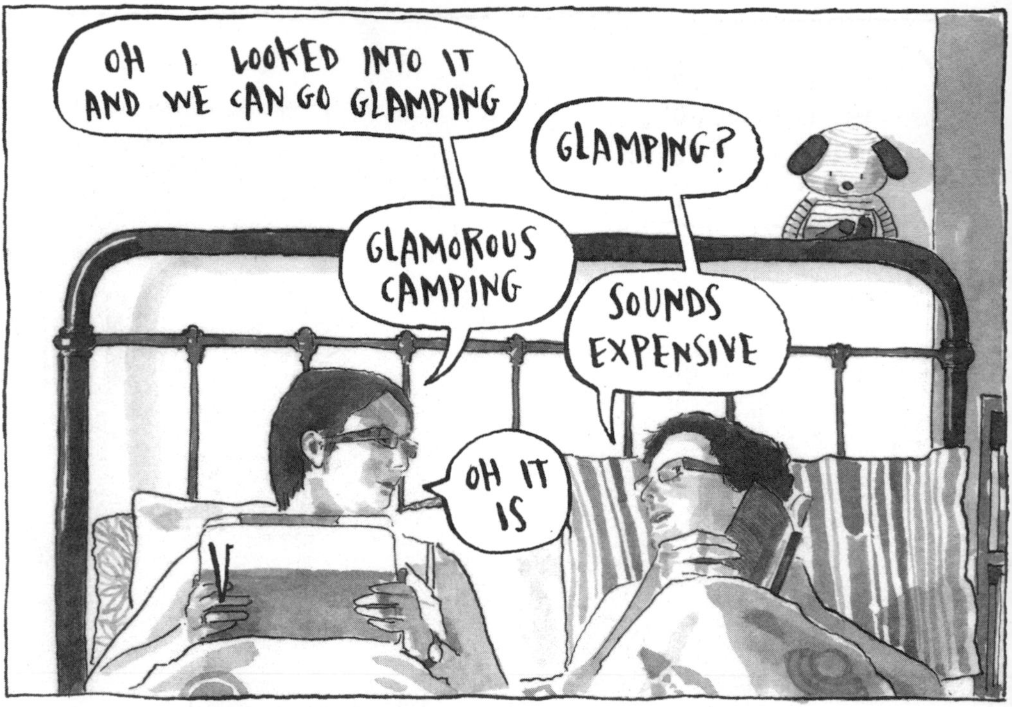
OH I LOOKED INTO IT AND WE CAN GO GLAMPING
GLAMPING?
GLAMOROUS CAMPING
SOUNDS EXPENSIVE
OH IT IS

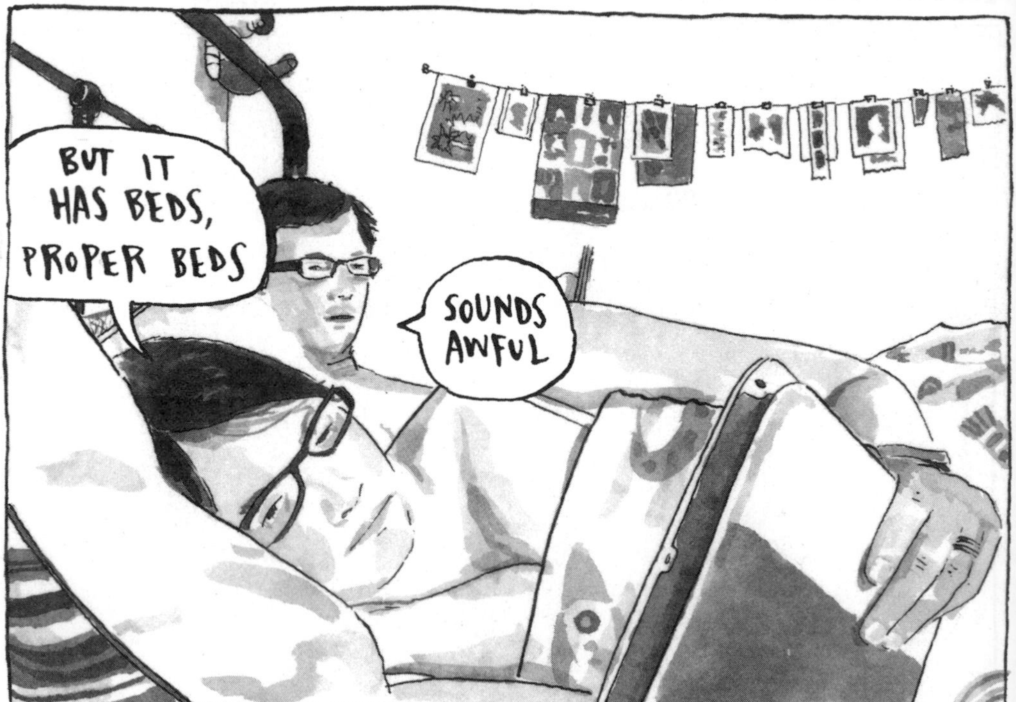
BUT IT HAS BEDS, PROPER BEDS
SOUNDS AWFUL

LUCKILY STEPH, SHE'S BETTER AT THIS THAN ME.

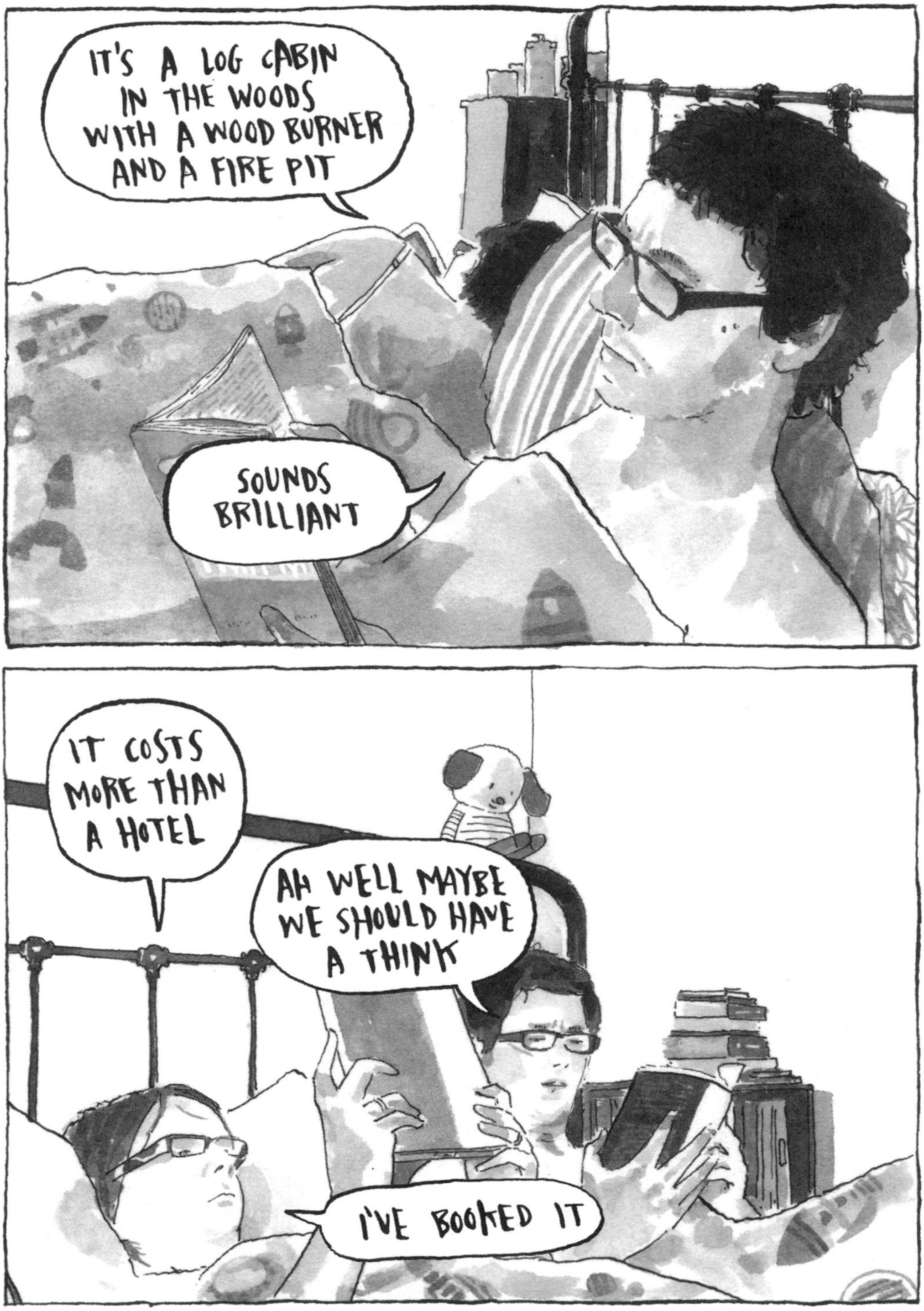
IT'S A LOG CABIN IN THE WOODS WITH A WOOD BURNER AND A FIRE PIT
SOUNDS BRILLIANT
IT COSTS MORE THAN A HOTEL
AH WELL MAYBE WE SHOULD HAVE A THINK
I'VE BOOKED IT

SHE CAN MAKE DECISIONS.

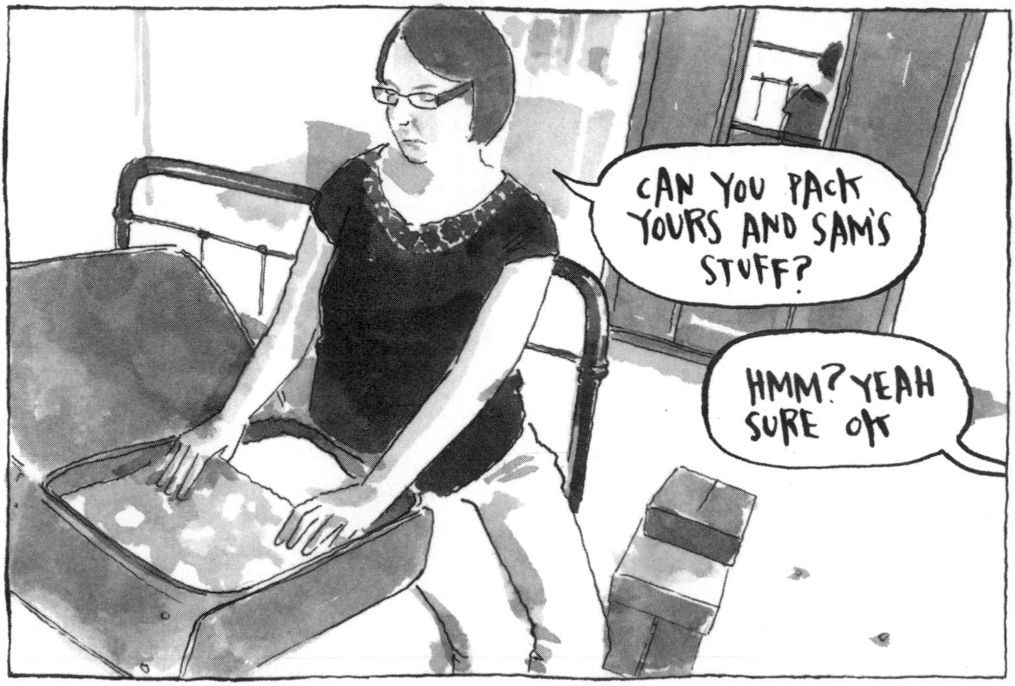
CAN YOU PACK YOURS AND SAM'S STUFF?
HMM? YEAH SURE OK

WHAT I LACK IN DECISION-MAKING...

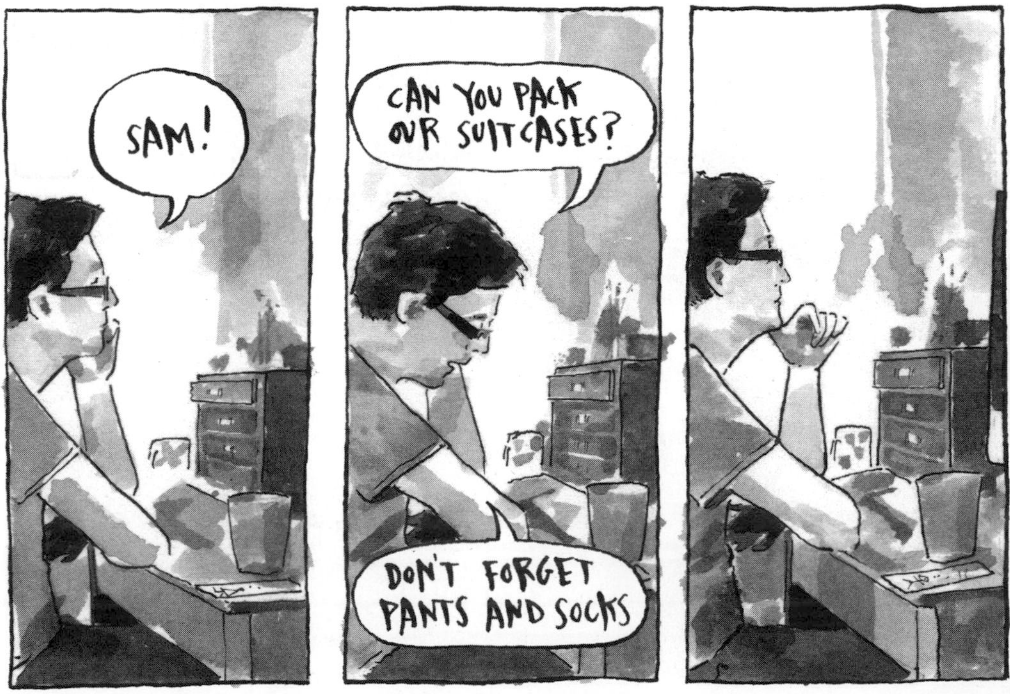
SAM!
CAN YOU PACK OUR SUITCASES?
DON'T FORGET PANTS AND SOCKS

...I MORE THAN MAKE UP FOR IN ENTHUSIASM AND "GET UP AND GO"

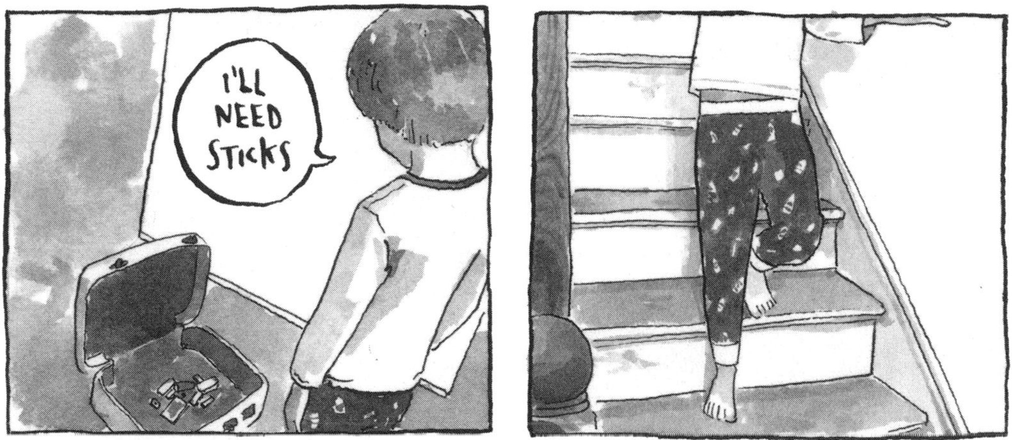
I'LL NEED STICKS

PLUS I ENCOURAGE THE BOY TO GET INVOLVED.

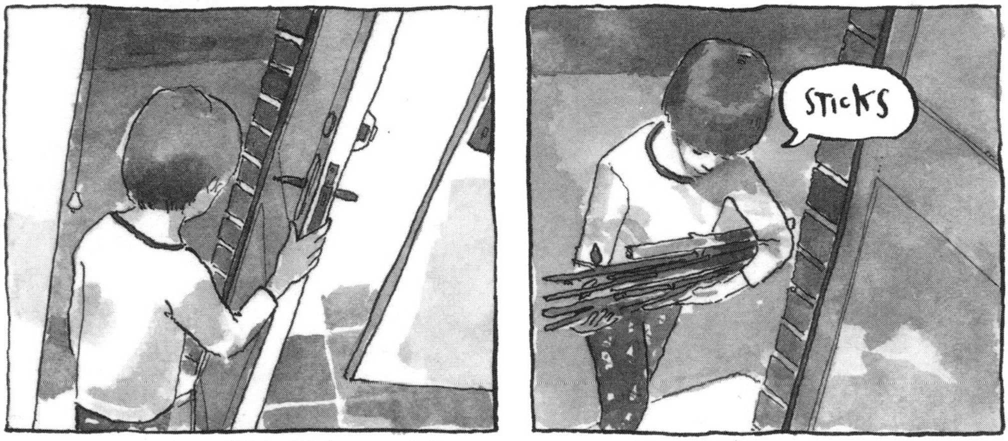
STICKS

WE CAN ALL LEARN FROM HIS MISTAKES

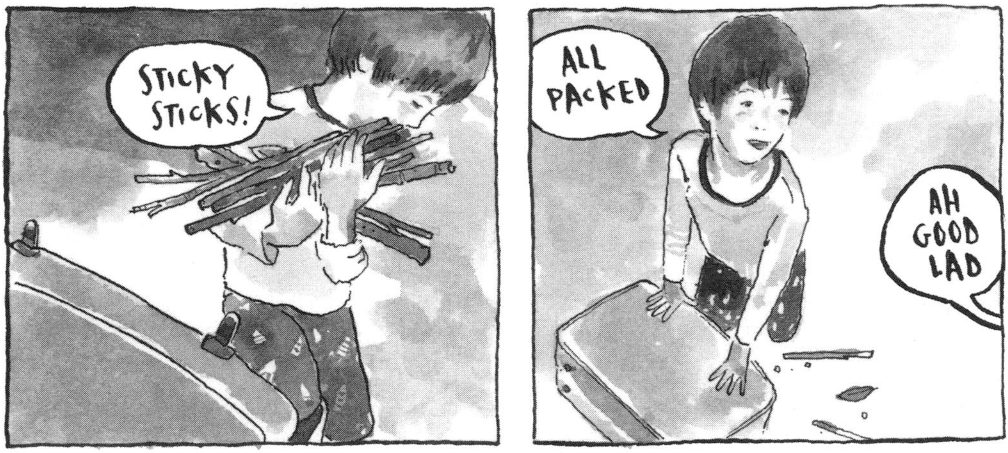
STICKY STICKS!
ALL PACKED
AH GOOD LAD

OR SOMETHING.

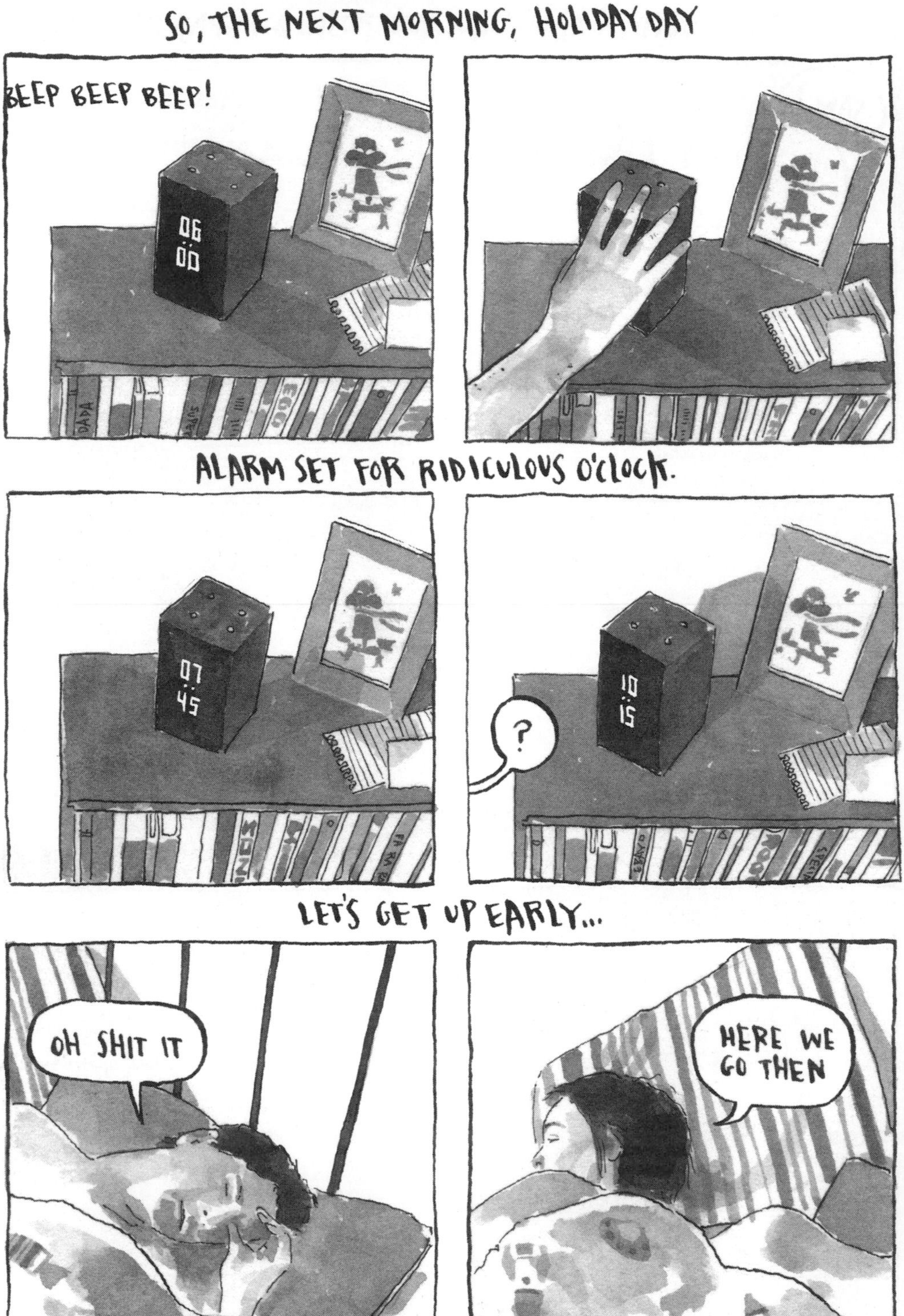
SO, THE NEXT MORNING, HOLIDAY DAY
BEEP BEEP BEEP!
06:00
ALARM SET FOR RIDICULOUS O'CLOCK.
07:45
10:15
?
LET'S GET UP EARLY...
OH SHIT IT
HERE WE GO THEN

..."TO AVOID A PANICKED AND RUSHED DEPARTURE"

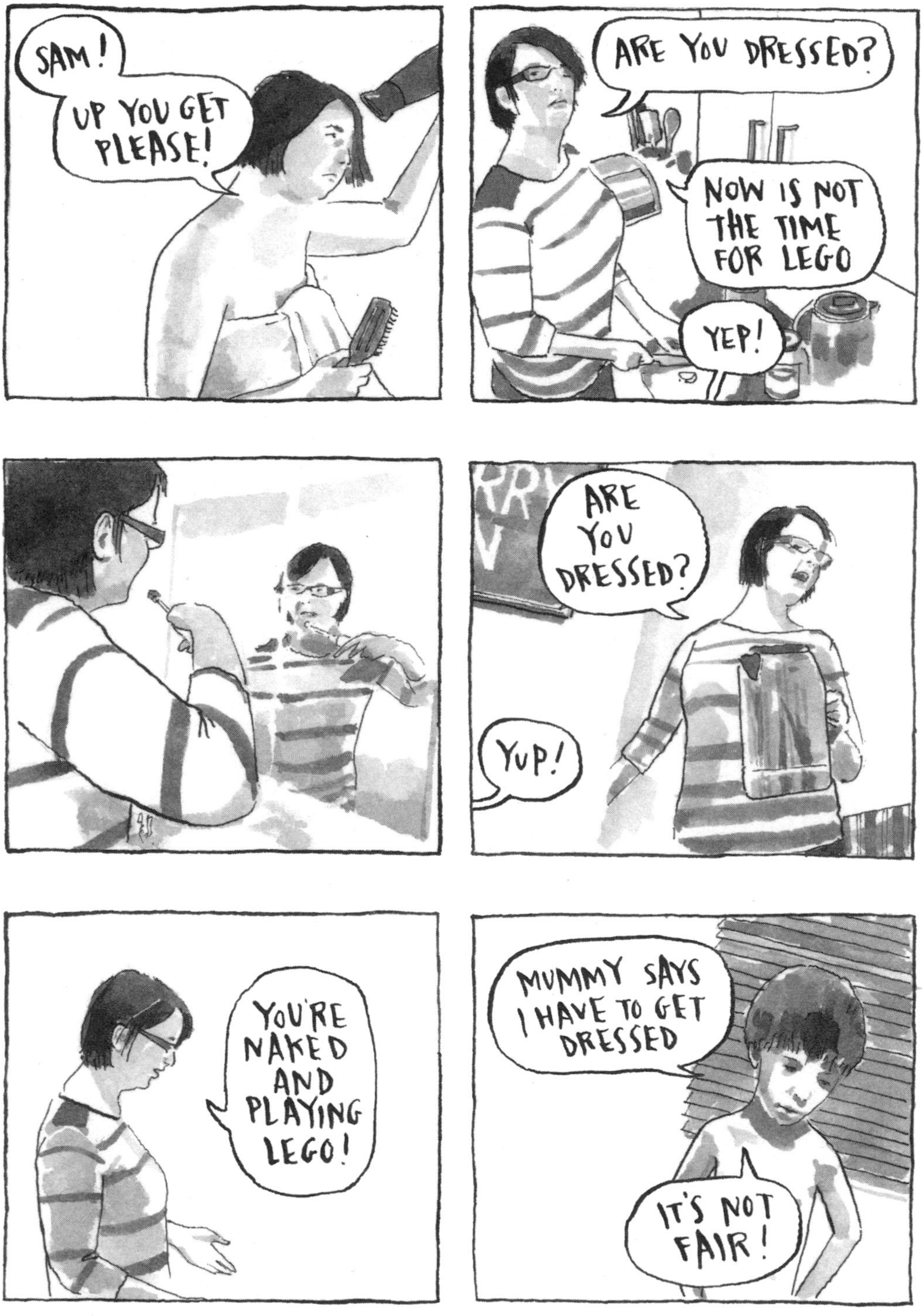
SAM!
UP YOU GET PLEASE!
ARE YOU DRESSED?
NOW IS NOT THE TIME FOR LEGO
YEP!
ARE YOU DRESSED?
YUP!
YOU'RE NAKED AND PLAYING LEGO!
MUMMY SAYS I HAVE TO GET DRESSED
IT'S NOT FAIR!

BEFORE WE HEAD OFF I HAVE TO
COMPLETE MY CRIPPLING LIST OF OCD CHECKS

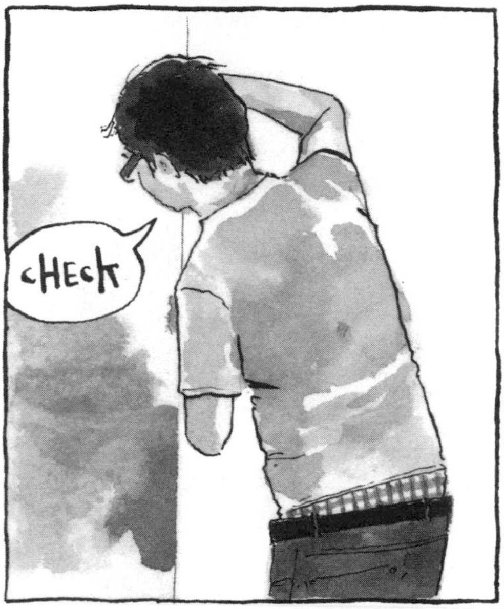
CHECK

BATHROOM TAPS OFF
(NO ONE'S HAD A BATH TODAY)

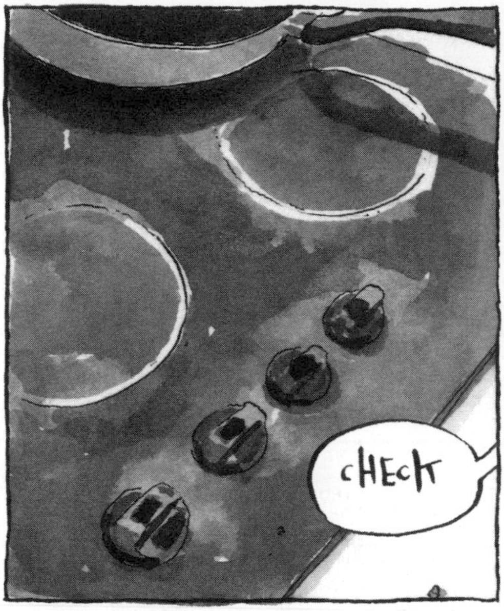
CHECK

OVEN OFF
(NOBODY'S COOKED TODAY)

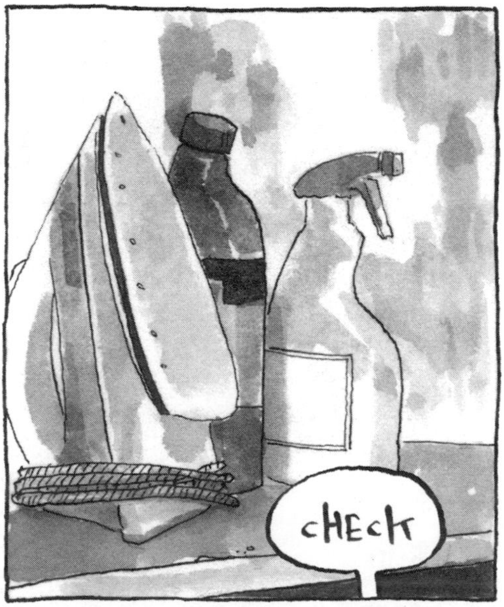
CHECK

IRON IS UNPLUGGED
(NOT USED IN MONTHS)

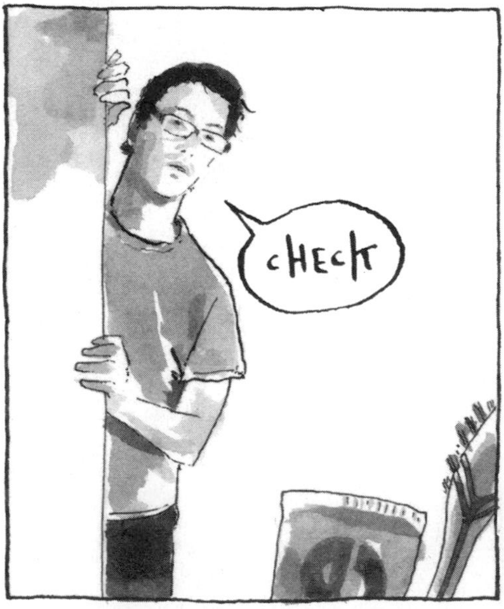
CHECK

BATHROOM TAPS
(STILL AS THEY WERE)

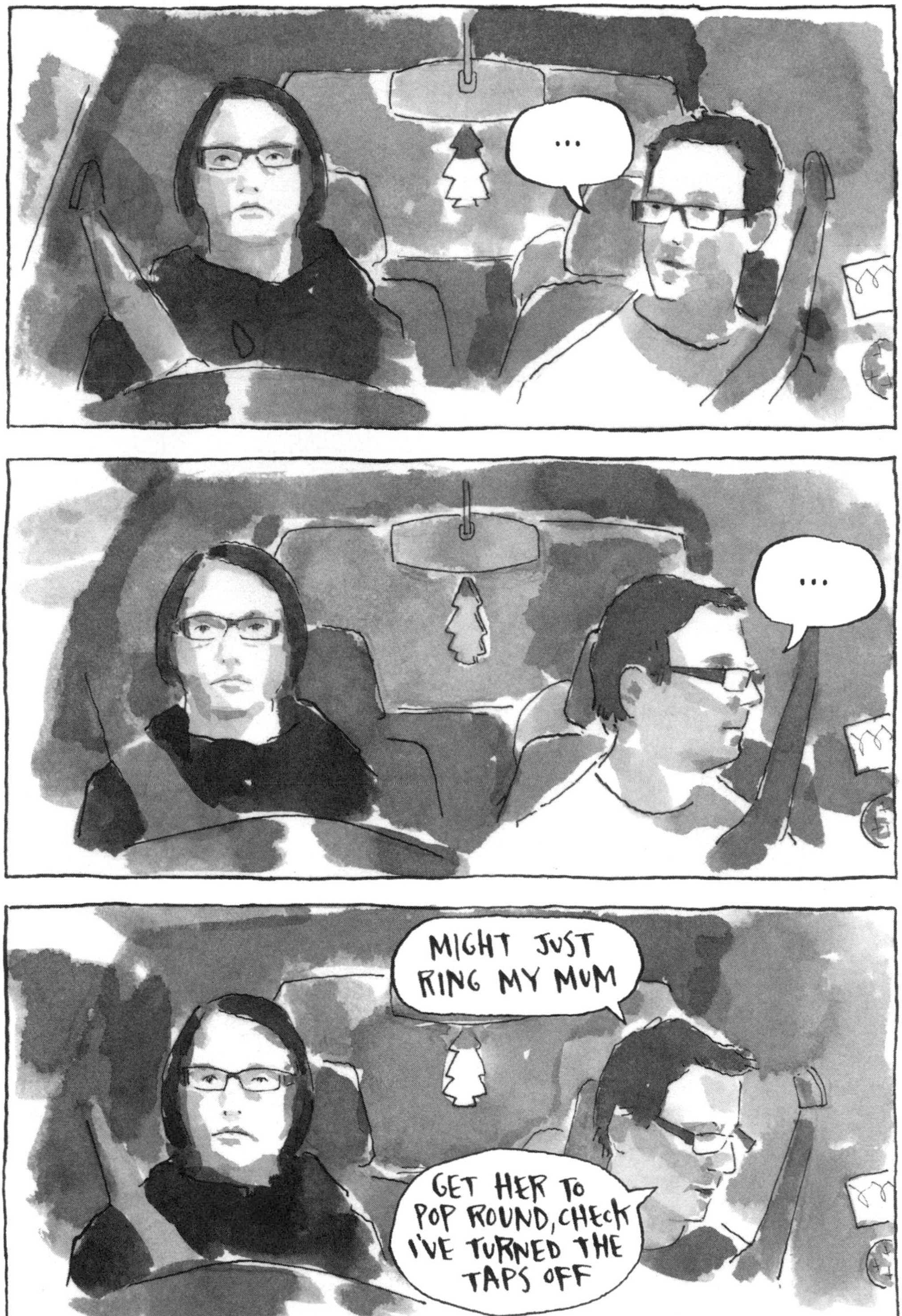
...
...
MIGHT JUST RING MY MUM
GET HER TO POP ROUND, CHECK I'VE TURNED THE TAPS OFF

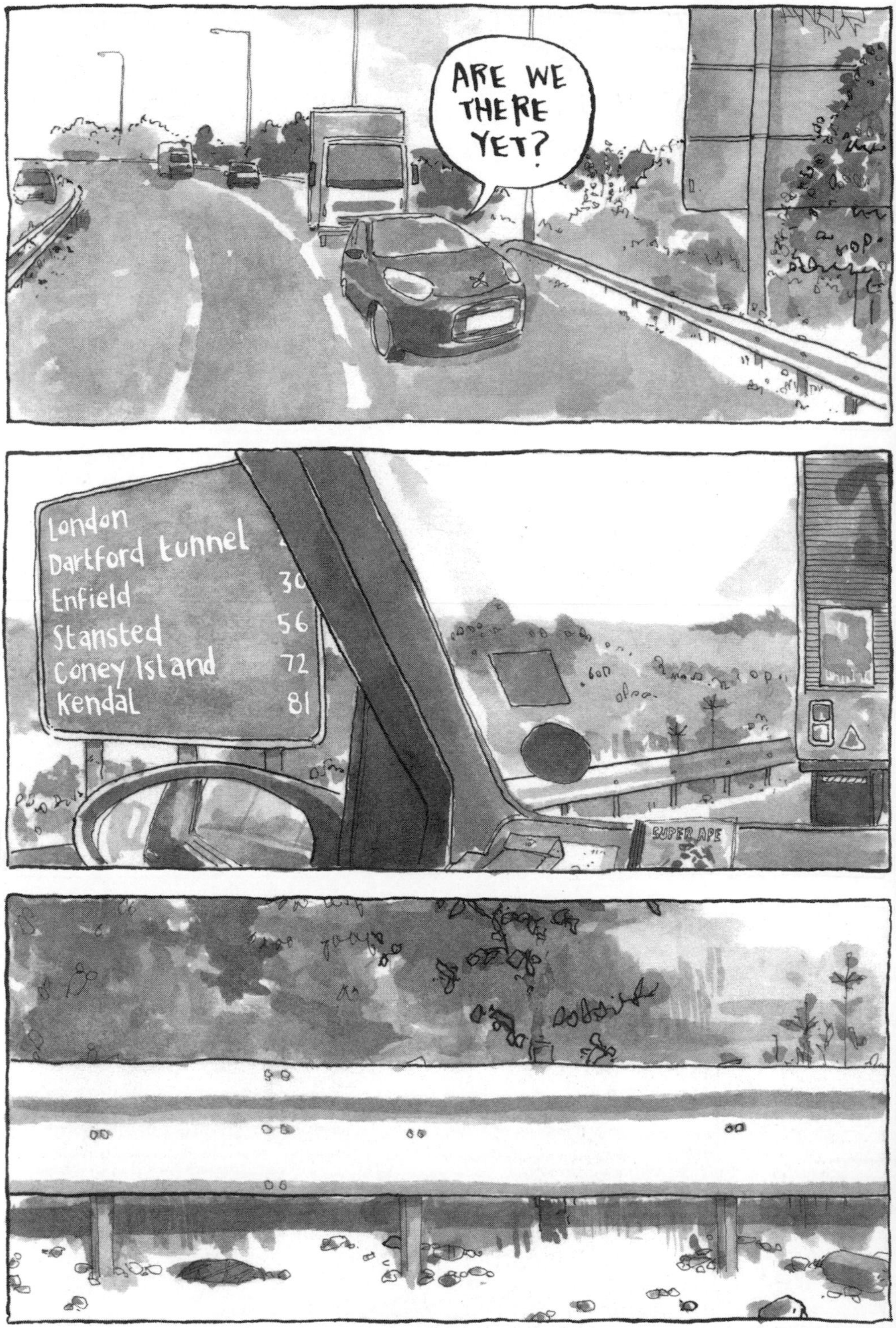
ARE WE THERE YET?
London
Dartford tunnel
Enfield
Stansted 56
Coney Island 72
Kendal 81
SUPER APE

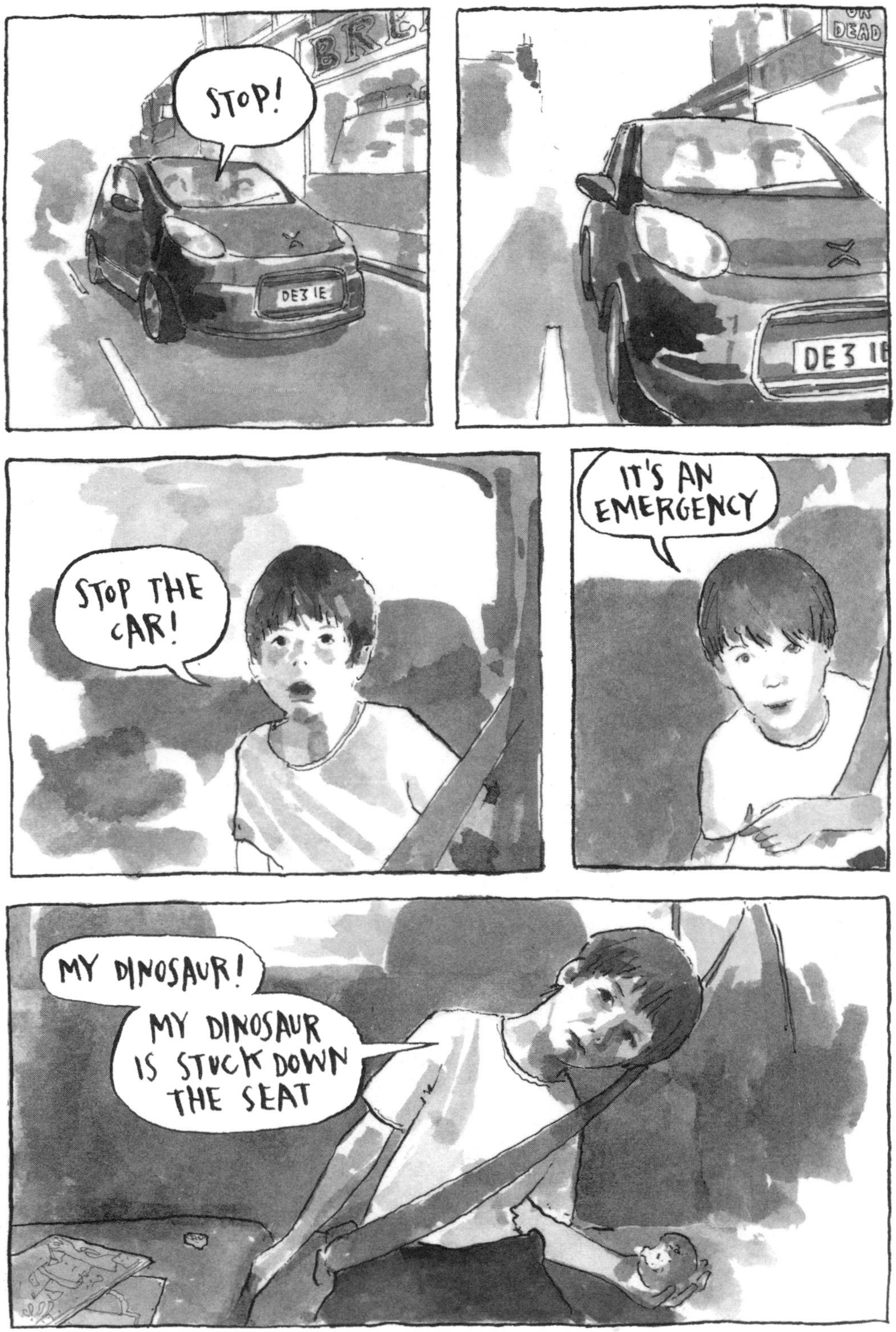
STOP!
DE3 IE
DE3 IE
STOP THE CAR!
IT'S AN EMERGENCY
MY DINOSAUR!
MY DINOSAUR IS STUCK DOWN THE SEAT

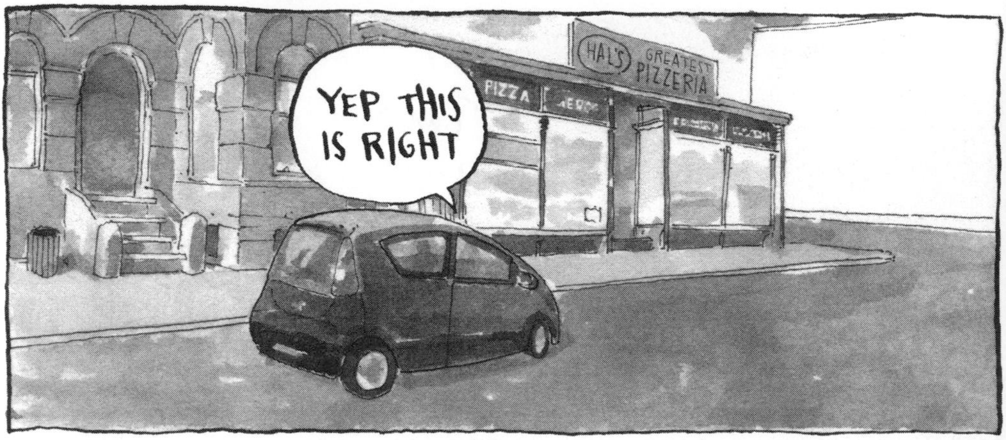
HAL'S GREATEST PIZZERIA
PIZZA
YEP THIS IS RIGHT

I AM...

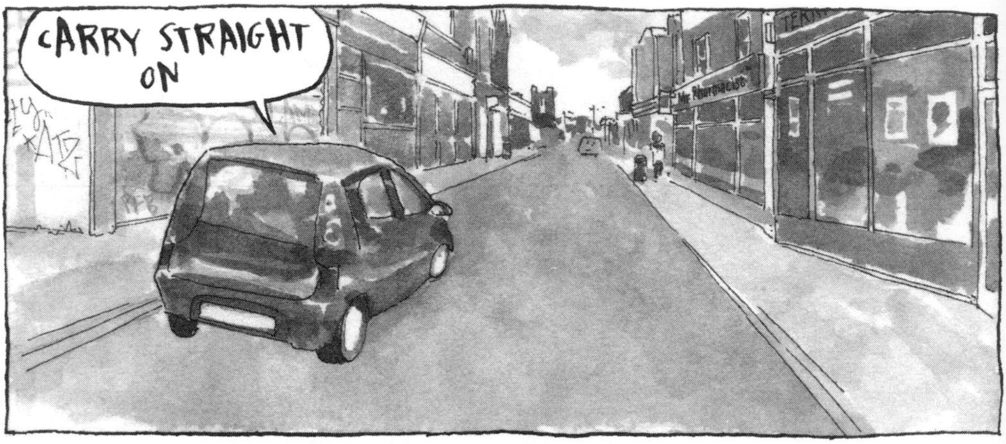
CARRY STRAIGHT ON

...AN EXCELLENT...

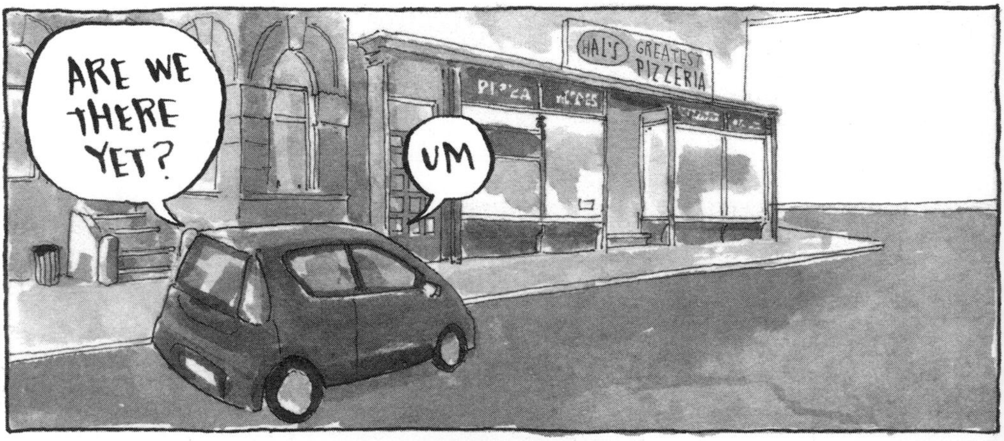
HAL'S GREATEST PIZZERIA
ARE WE THERE YET?
UM

...NAVIGATOR

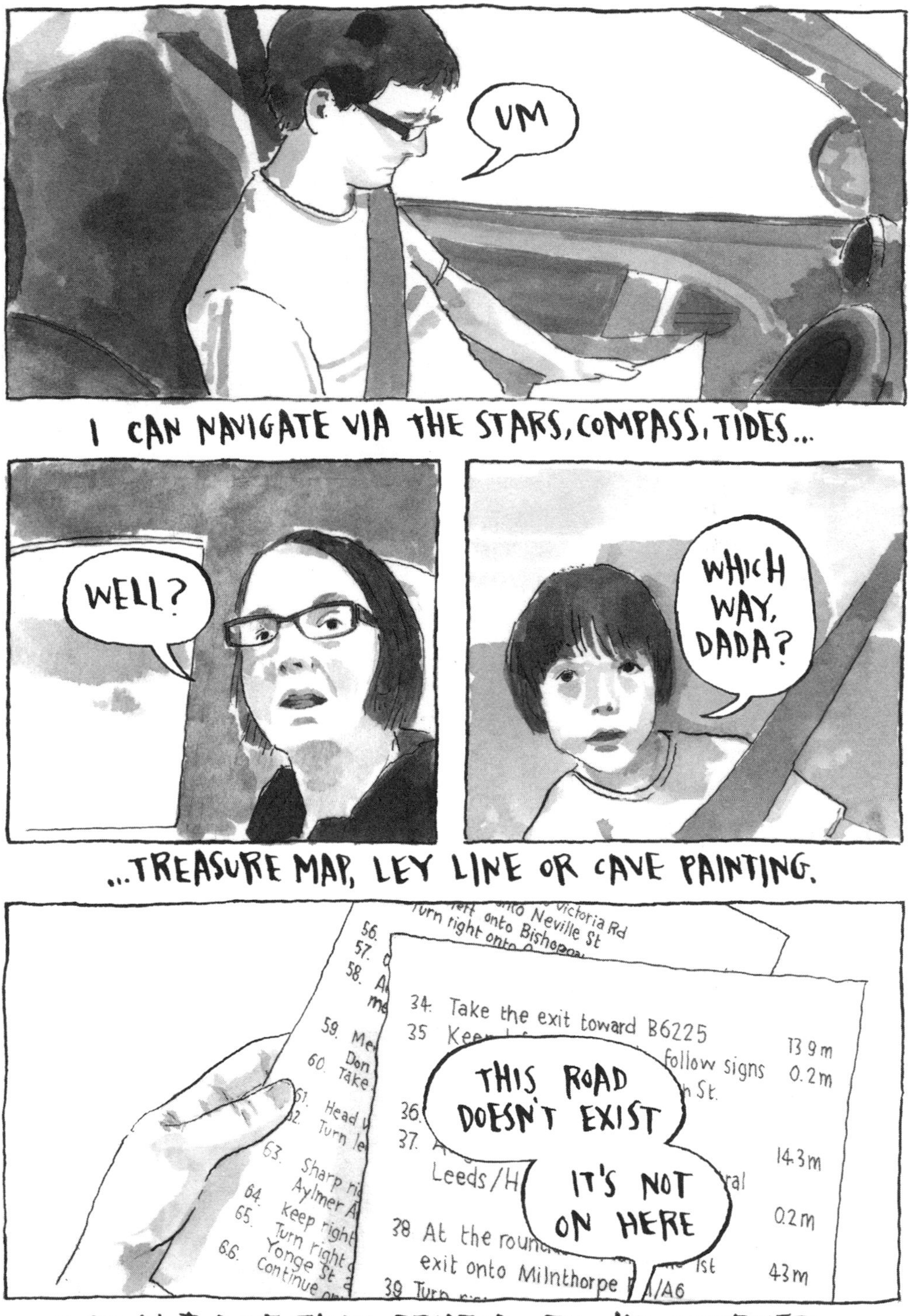
UM
I CAN NAVIGATE VIA THE STARS, COMPASS, TIDES...
WELL?
WHICH WAY, DADA?
...TREASURE MAP, LEY LINE OR CAVE PAINTING.
onto Neville St
Turn right onto
34. Take the exit toward B6225
13.9m
follow signs
0.2m
14.3m
Leeds/H
0.2m
38 At the round
exit onto Milnthorpe
43m
THIS ROAD DOESN'T EXIST
IT'S NOT ON HERE
JUST NOT DIRECTIONS PRINTED OFF THE INTERNET.

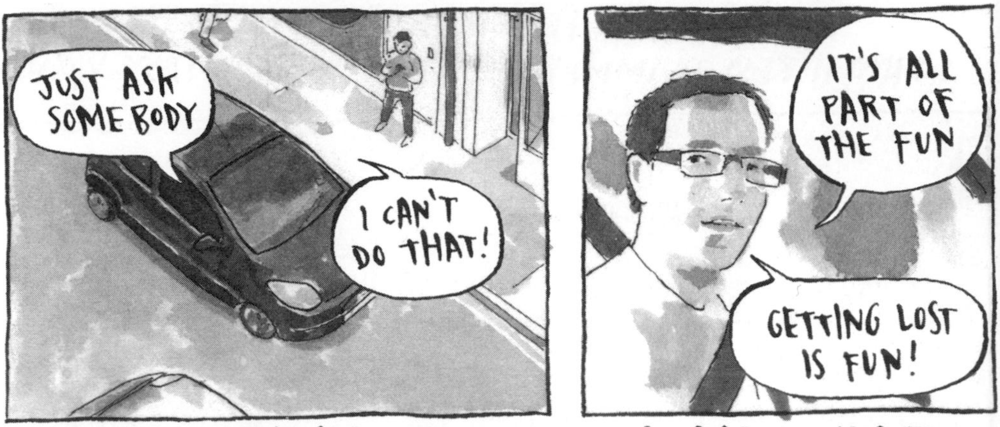
JUST ASK SOMEBODY
I CAN'T DO THAT!
IT'S ALL PART OF THE FUN
GETTING LOST IS FUN!

ASKING A STRANGER FOR DIRECTIONS IS ADMITTING TO THAT STRANGER THAT I HAVE NO NAVIGATION SKILLS.

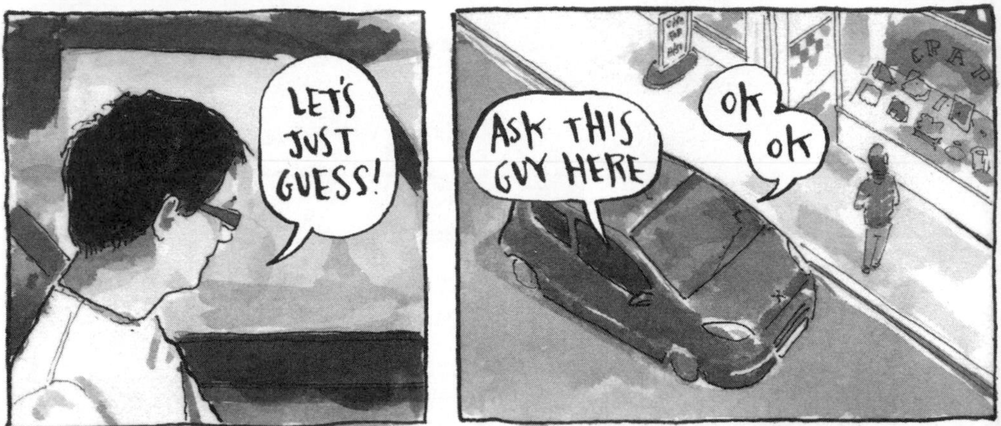
LET'S JUST GUESS!
ASK THIS GUY HERE
OK OK

AND STRANGERS ARE THE PEOPLE I TRY TO IMPRESS MOST.

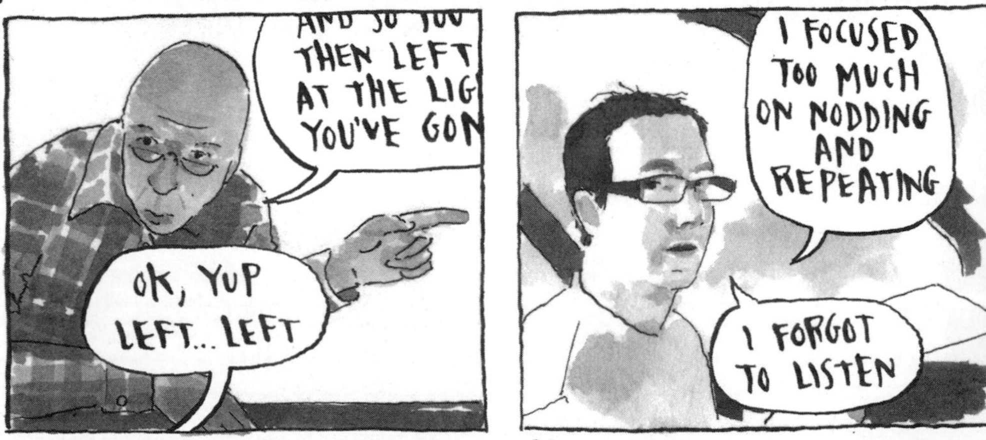
THEN LEFT AT THE LIG YOU'VE GON
OK, YUP LEFT... LEFT
I FOCUSED TOO MUCH ON NODDING AND REPEATING
I FORGOT TO LISTEN

NAVIGATION I'M GOOD AT. SOCIAL INTERACTION, LESS SO.

LIKE ANY SANE PERSON, IN TIMES OF STRESS
I FIND IT BEST TO IMMERSE MYSELF IN A FANTASY WORLD

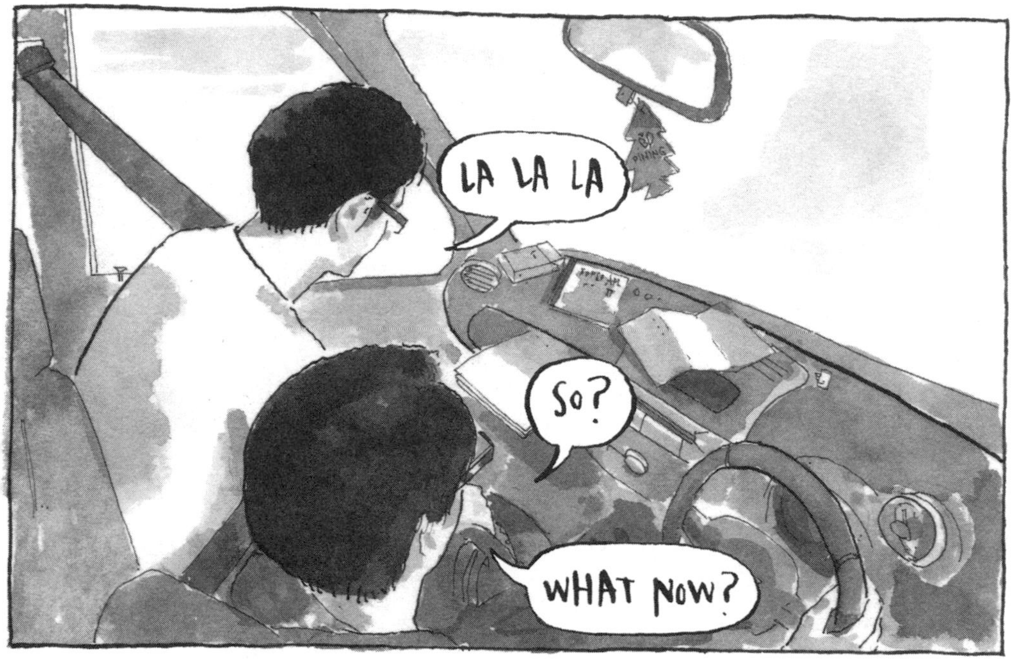
LA LA LA
SO?
WHAT NOW?

AND AS LUCK WOULD HAVE IT,
I'VE PREPARED FOR JUST THIS OCCASION.

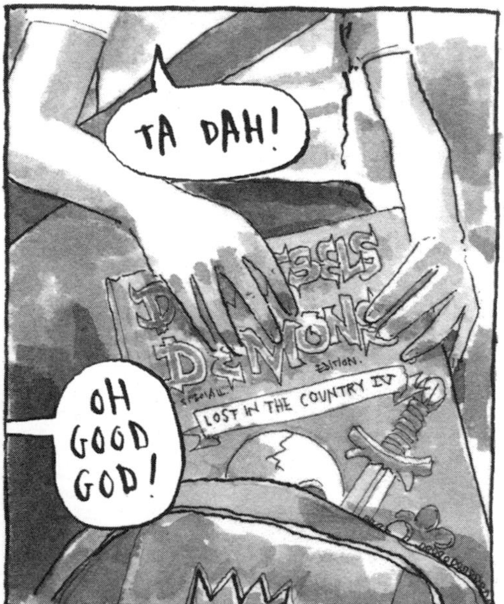
TA DAH!
LOST IN THE COUNTRY IV
OH GOOD GOD!

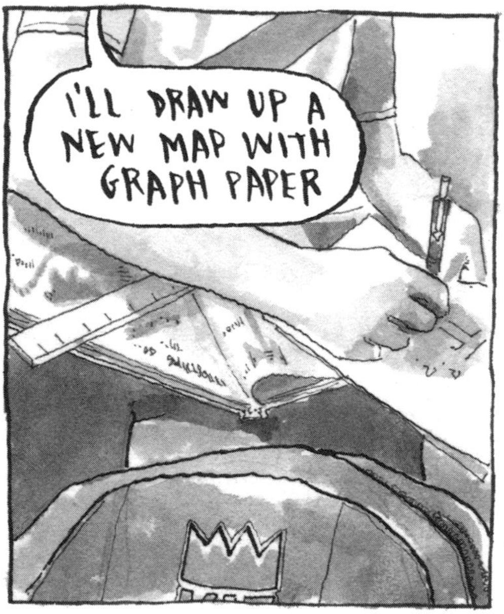
I'LL DRAW UP A NEW MAP WITH GRAPH PAPER

LET THE DICE DECIDE OUR FATE! THE SKILFUL ROLL OF A D-20 TO POINT US IN THE RIGHT DIRECTION!

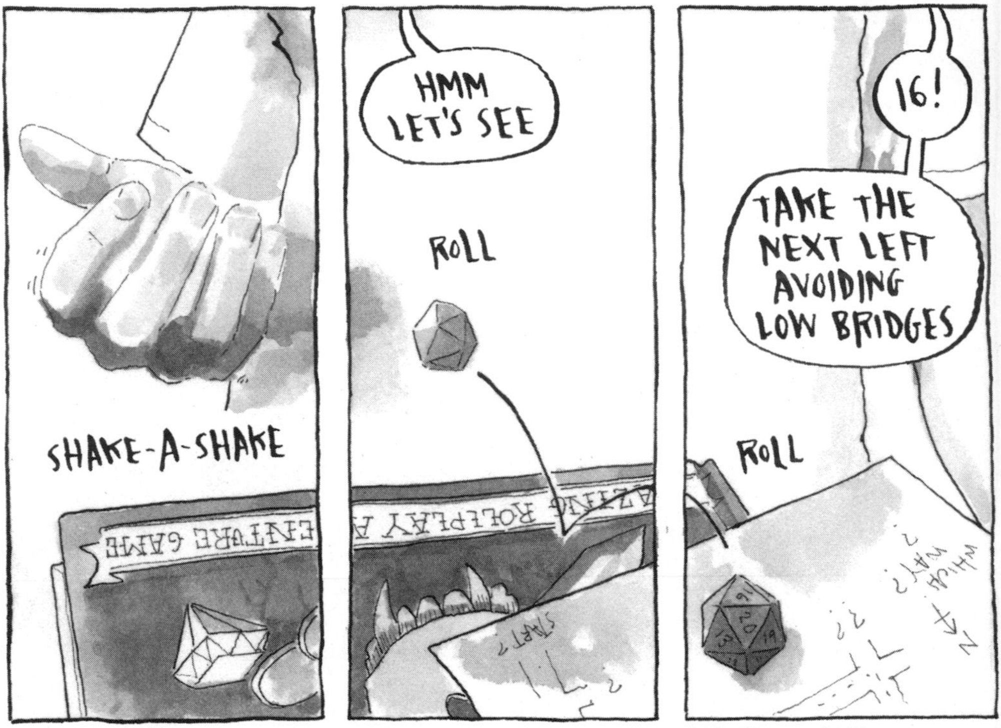
SHAKE-A-SHAKE
HMM LET'S SEE
ROLL
16!
TAKE THE NEXT LEFT AVOIDING LOW BRIDGES
ROLL

AND IT WORKS! WELL, IT WOULD HAVE DONE, HAD STEPH NOT DECIDED TO RING THE CAMPSITE INSTEAD.

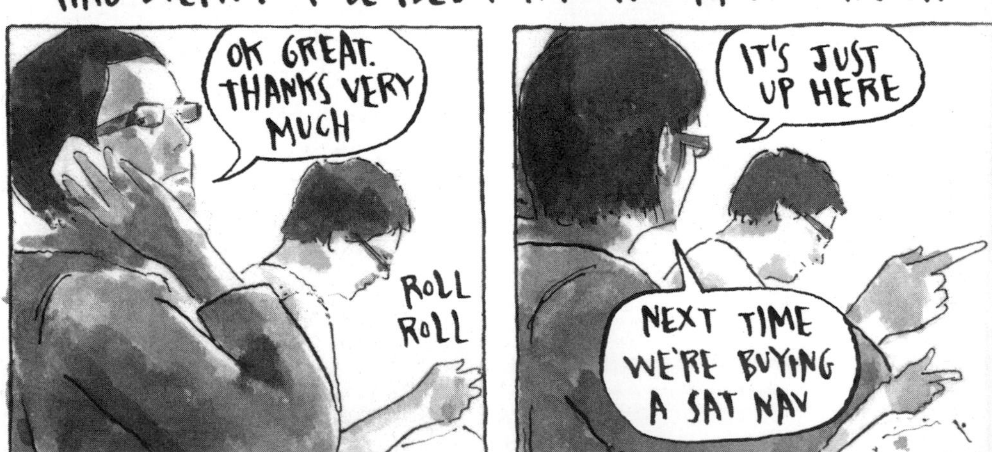
OK GREAT. THANKS VERY MUCH
ROLL ROLL
IT'S JUST UP HERE
NEXT TIME WE'RE BUYING A SAT NAV

TELEPHONES EH?
TURNS OUT IT WAS JUST OVER THE NEXT PAGE ...

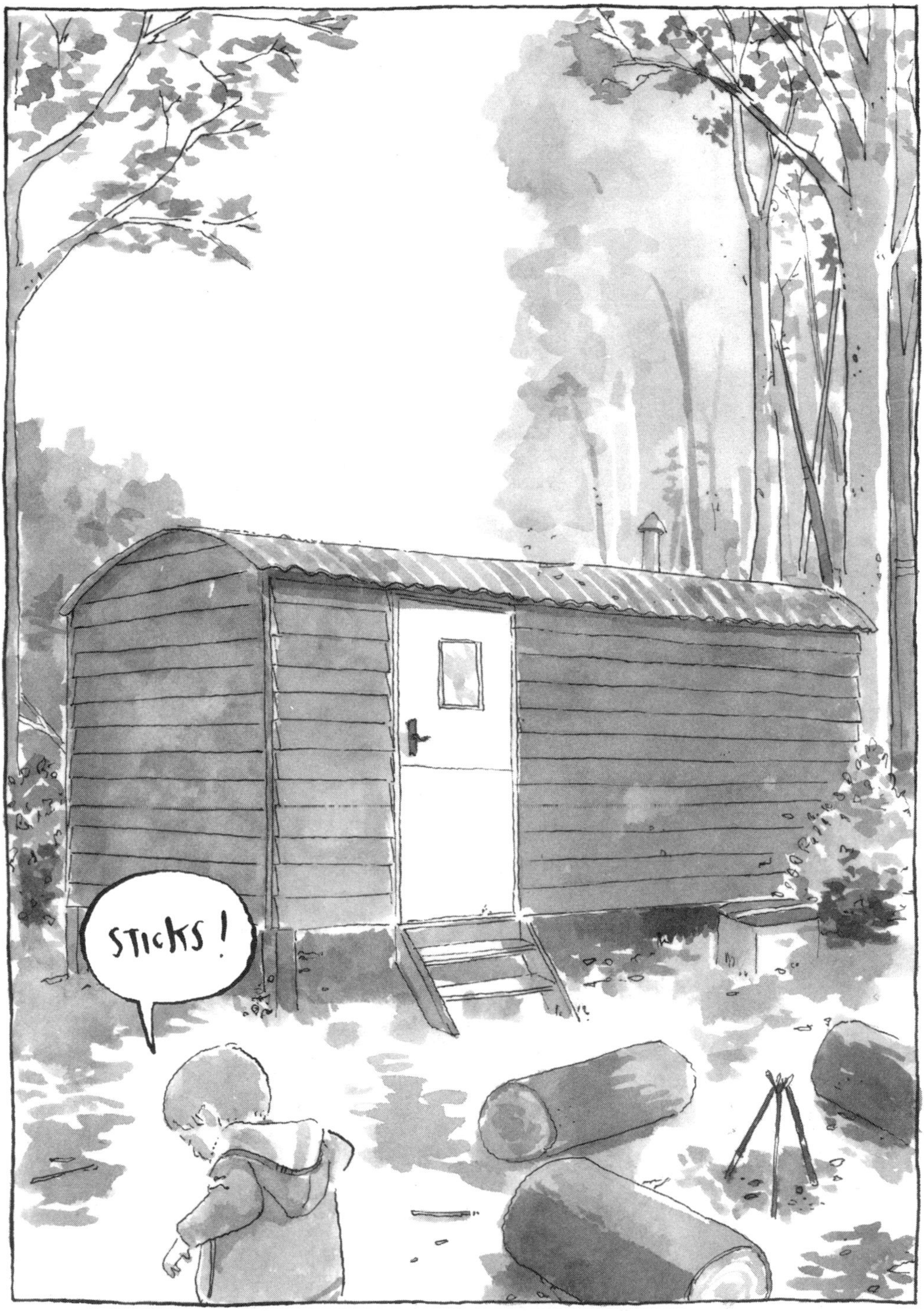
STICKS!

PRETTY DAMN IDYLLIC, RIGHT?

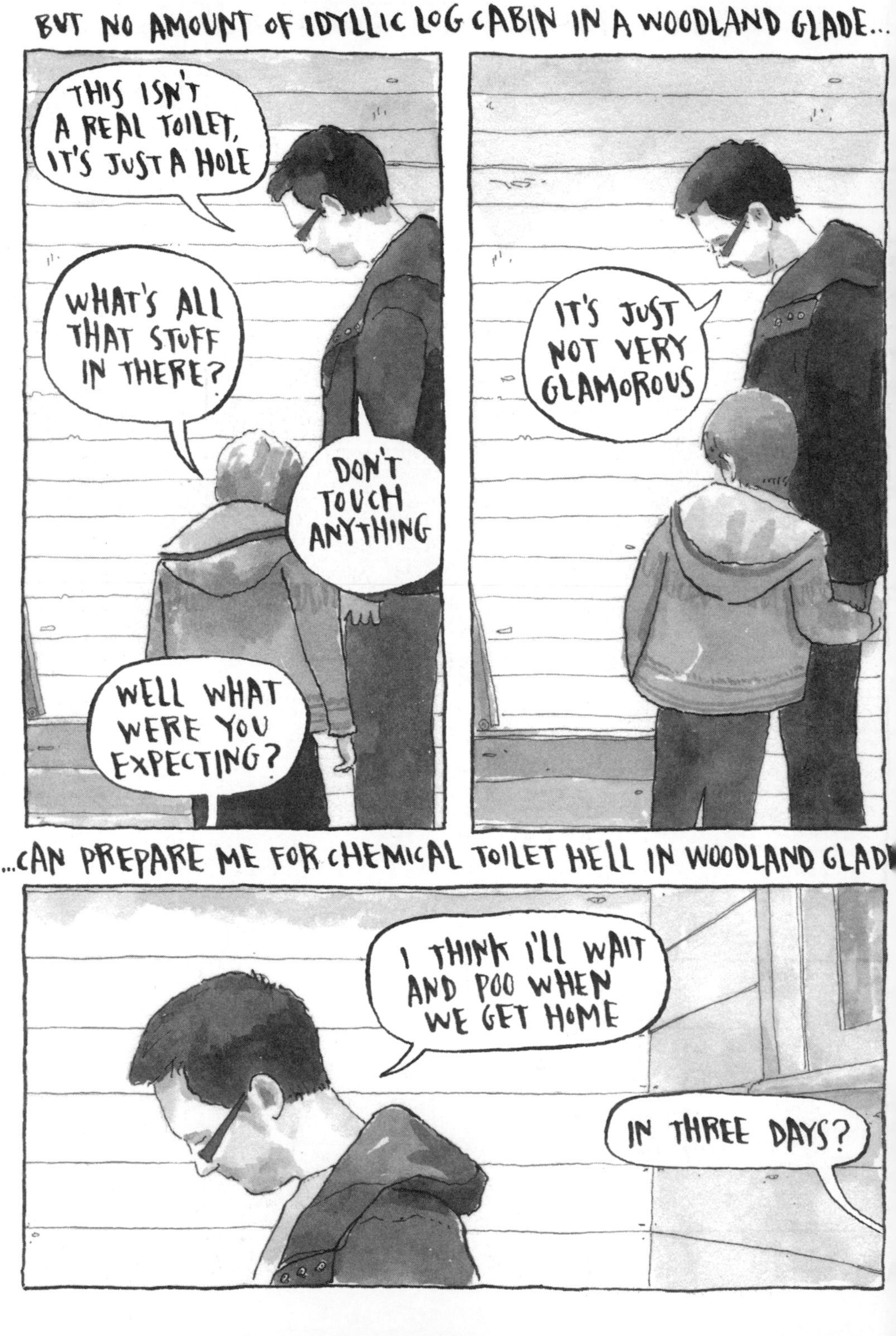
BUT NO AMOUNT OF IDYLLIC LOG CABIN IN A WOODLAND GLADE...
THIS ISN'T A REAL TOILET, IT'S JUST A HOLE
WHAT'S ALL THAT STUFF IN THERE?
DON'T TOUCH ANYTHING
WELL WHAT WERE YOU EXPECTING?
IT'S JUST NOT VERY GLAMOROUS
...CAN PREPARE ME FOR CHEMICAL TOILET HELL IN WOODLAND GLAD
I THINK I'LL WAIT AND POO WHEN WE GET HOME
IN THREE DAYS?

I DON'T CARE FOR THE COMFORTS OF HOME.

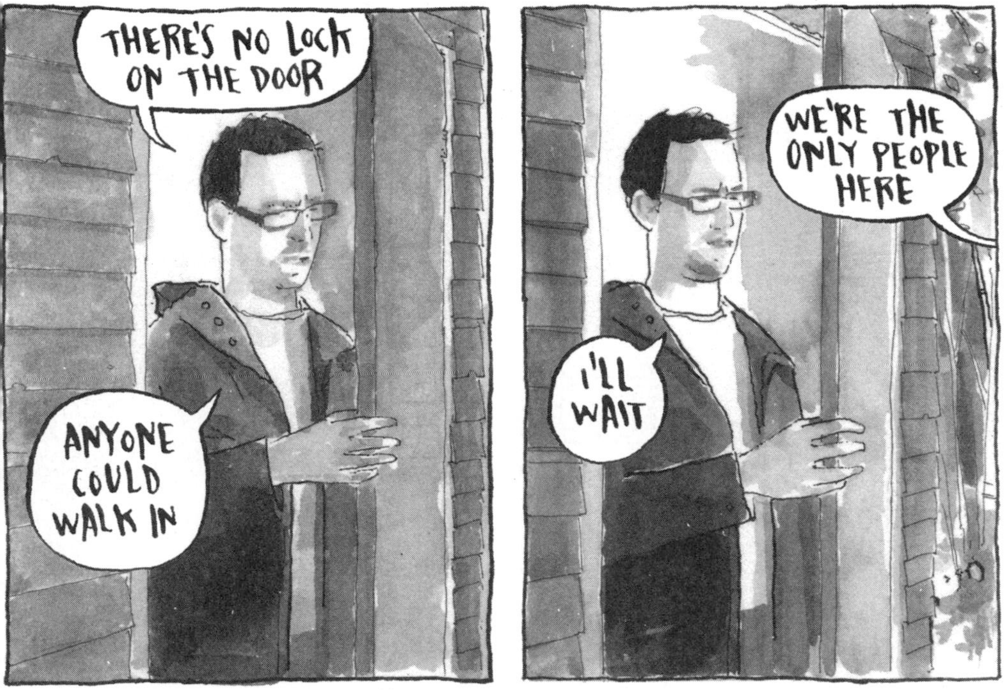
THERE'S NO LOCK ON THE DOOR
ANYONE COULD WALK IN
WE'RE THE ONLY PEOPLE HERE
I'LL WAIT

HONESTLY, I CAN ROUGH IT.

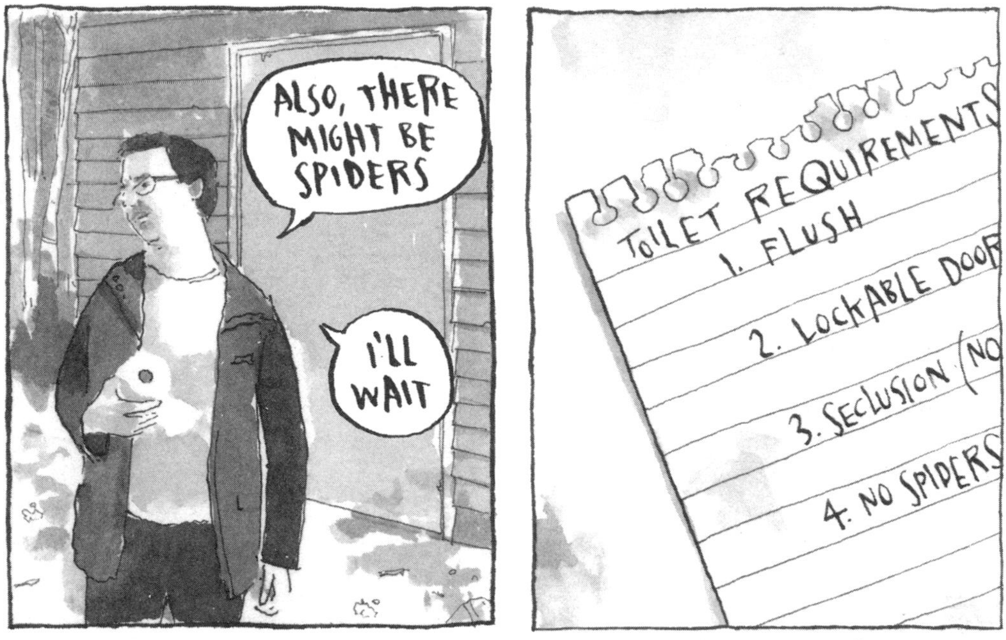
ALSO, THERE MIGHT BE SPIDERS
I'LL WAIT
TOILET REQUIREMENTS
1. FLUSH
2. LOCKABLE DOOR
3. SECLUSION (NO
4. NO SPIDERS

I JUST HAVE CERTAIN TOILET REQUIREMENTS. BASIC REQUIREMENTS.

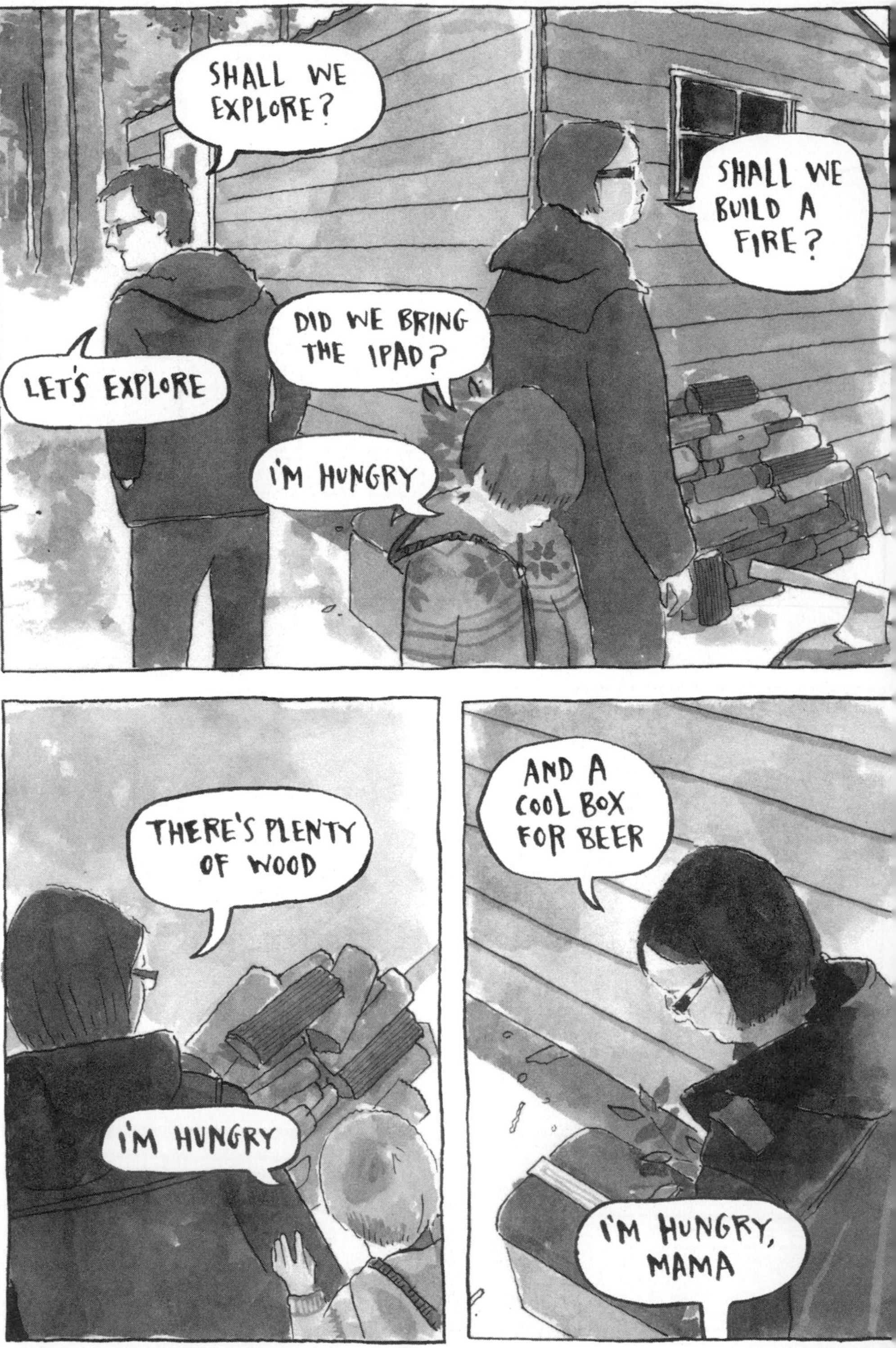
SHALL WE EXPLORE?
SHALL WE BUILD A FIRE?
LET'S EXPLORE
DID WE BRING THE IPAD?
I'M HUNGRY
THERE'S PLENTY OF WOOD
I'M HUNGRY
AND A COOL BOX FOR BEER
I'M HUNGRY, MAMA

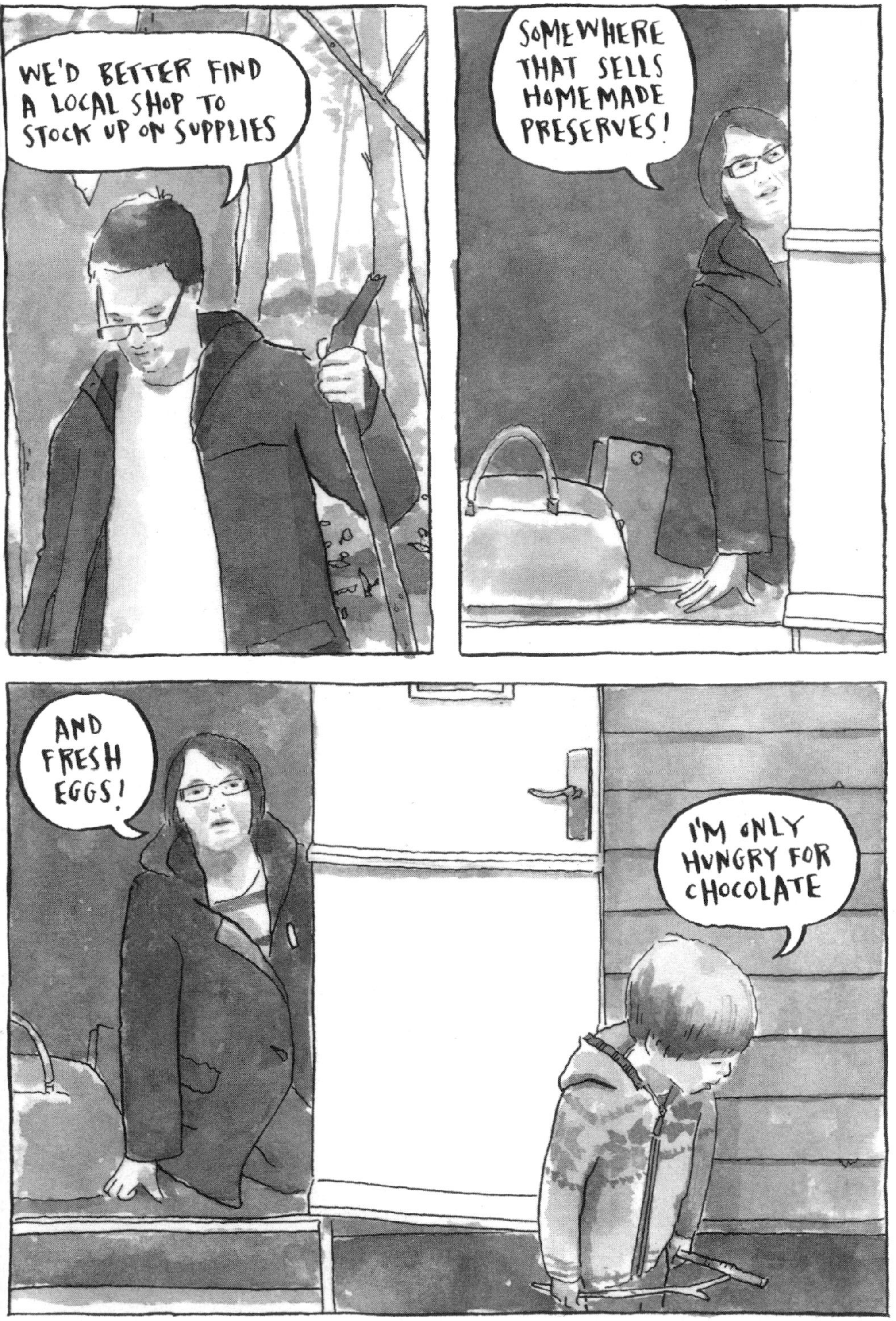
WE'D BETTER FIND A LOCAL SHOP TO STOCK UP ON SUPPLIES
SOMEWHERE THAT SELLS HOMEMADE PRESERVES!
AND FRESH EGGS!
I'M ONLY HUNGRY FOR CHOCOLATE

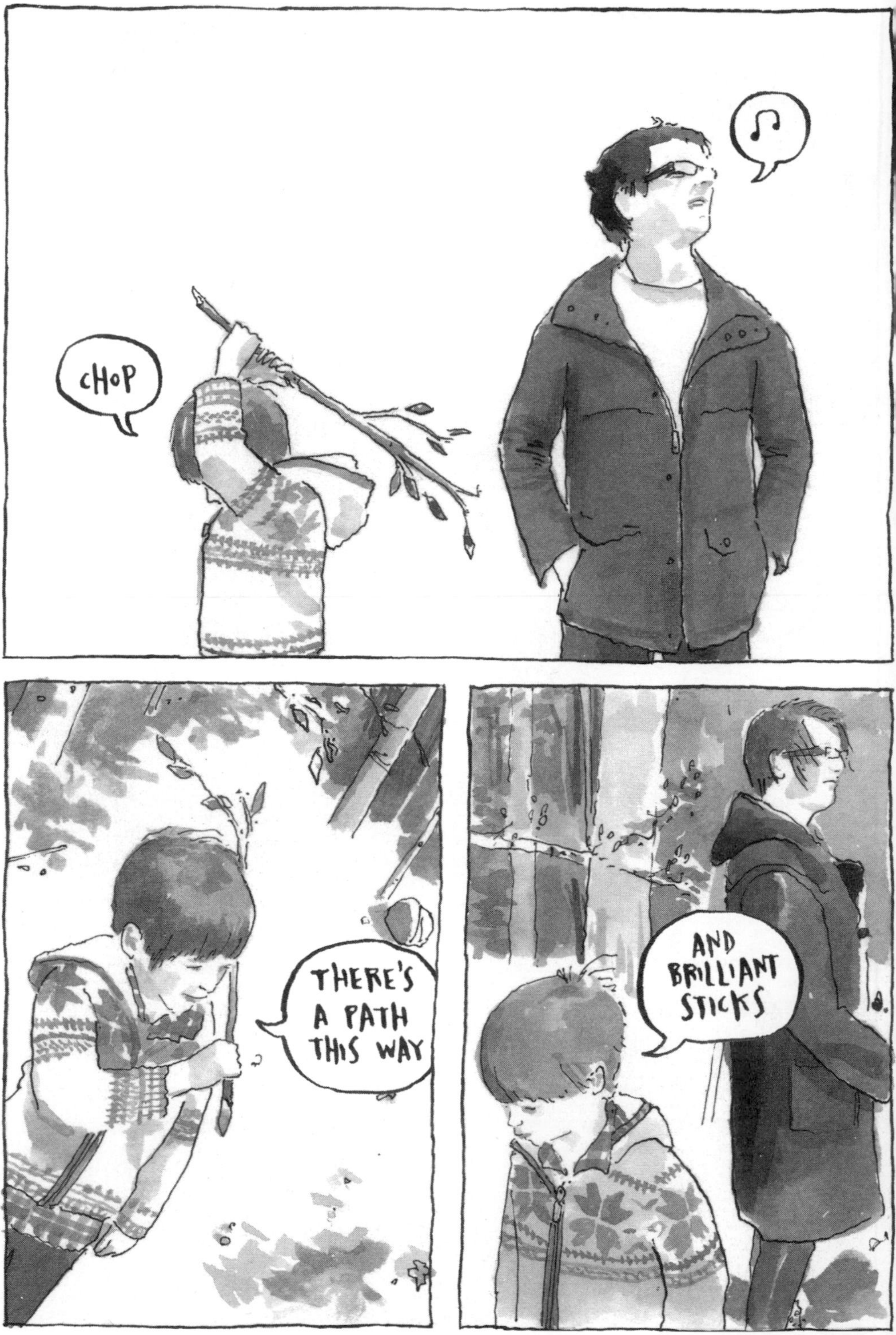
♪
CHOP
THERE'S A PATH THIS WAY
AND BRILLIANT STICKS

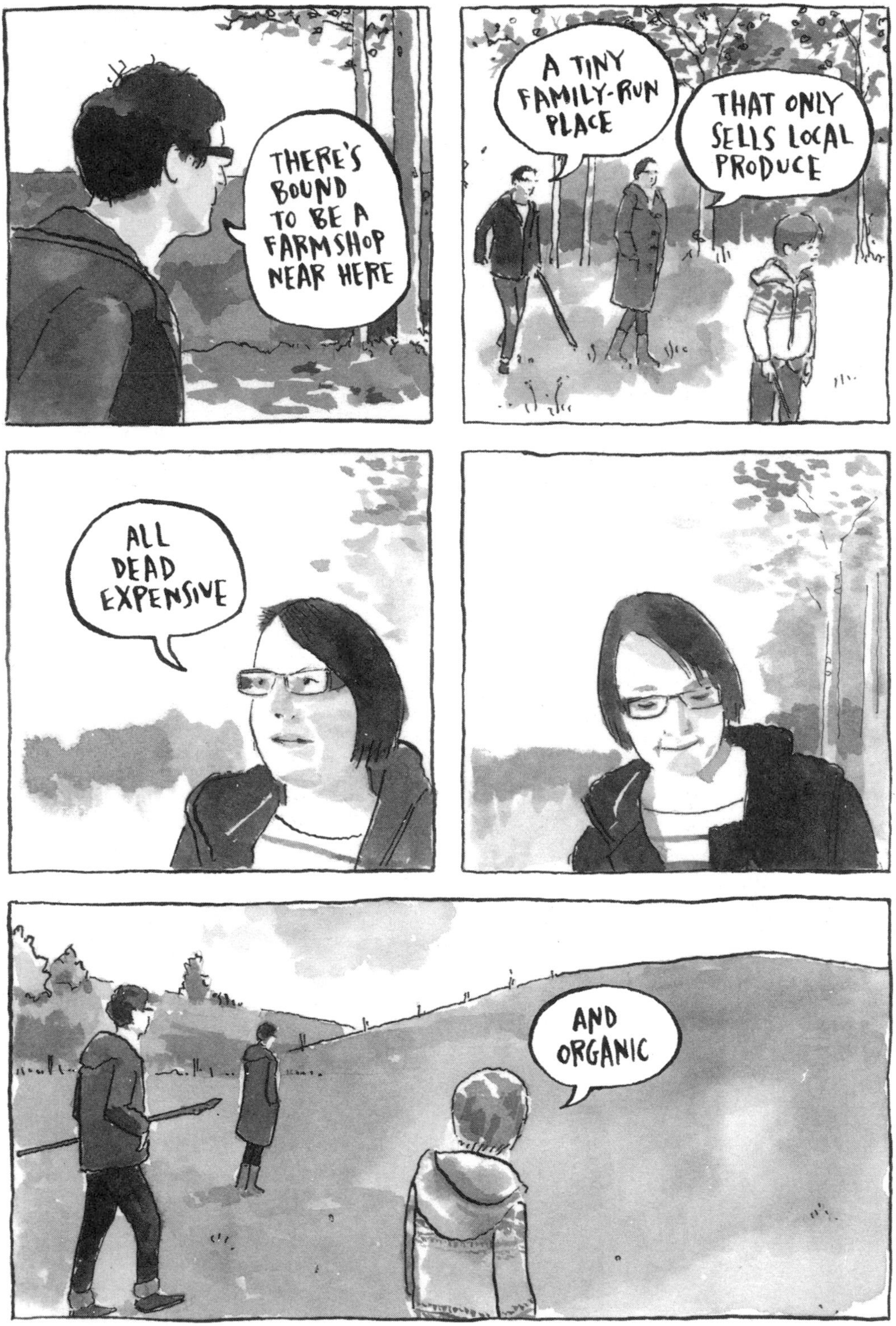
THERE'S BOUND TO BE A FARMSHOP NEAR HERE
A TINY FAMILY-RUN PLACE
THAT ONLY SELLS LOCAL PRODUCE
ALL DEAD EXPENSIVE
AND ORGANIC

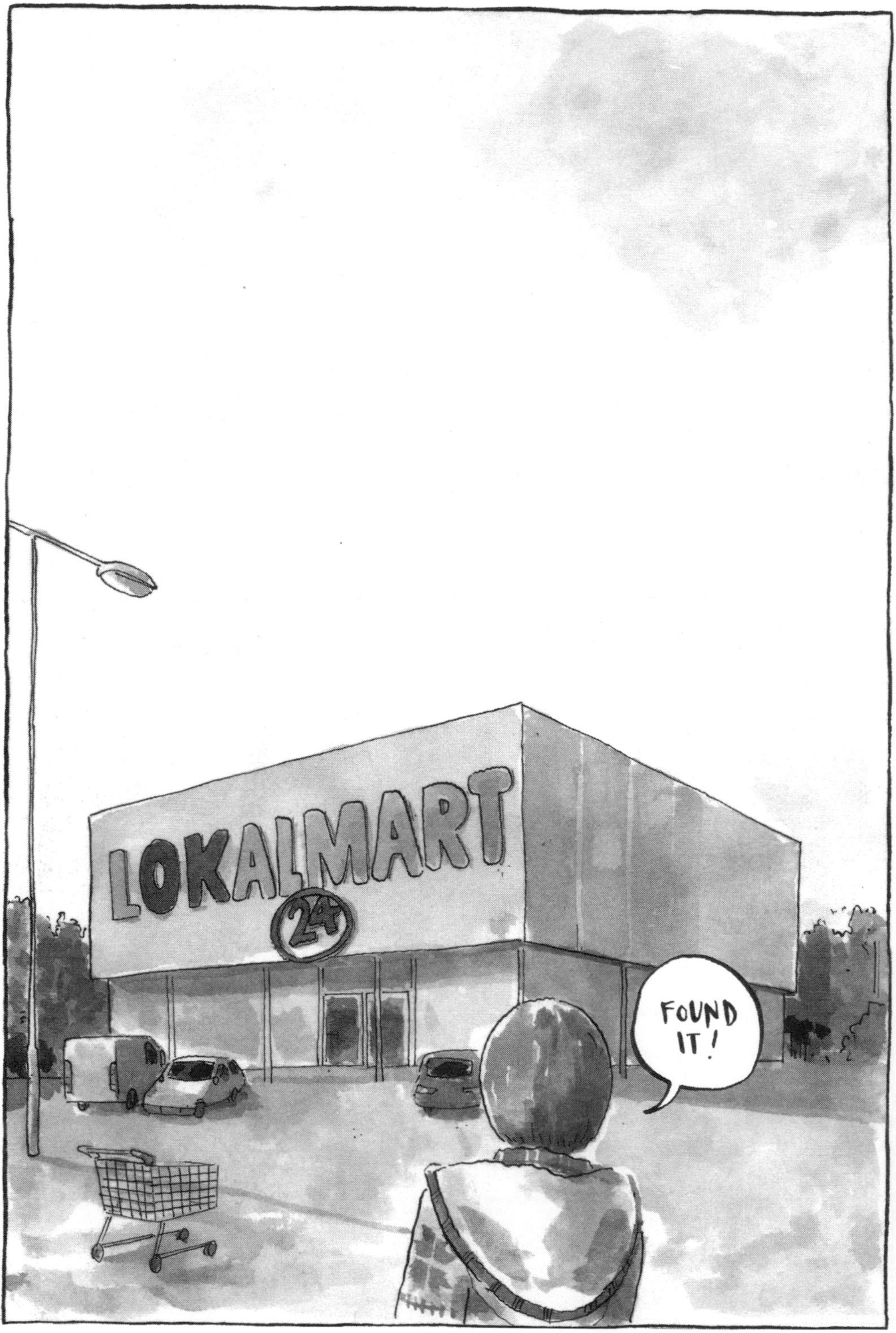
LOKALMART
24
FOUND IT!

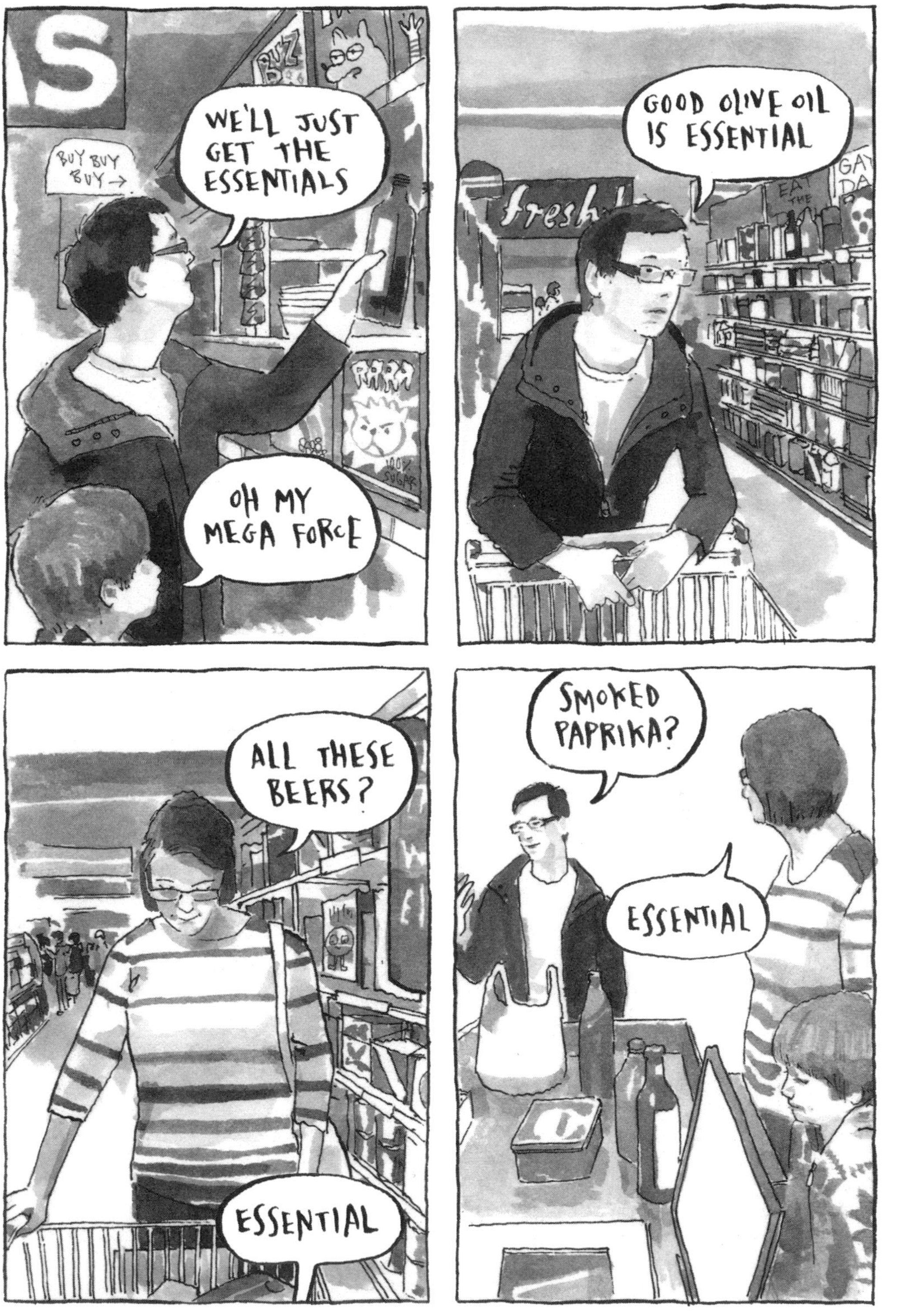
BUY BUY BUY →
WE'LL JUST GET THE ESSENTIALS
OH MY MEGA FORCE
100% SUGAR
fresh
EAT THE
GOOD OLIVE OIL IS ESSENTIAL
ALL THESE BEERS?
ESSENTIAL
SMOKED PAPRIKA?
ESSENTIAL

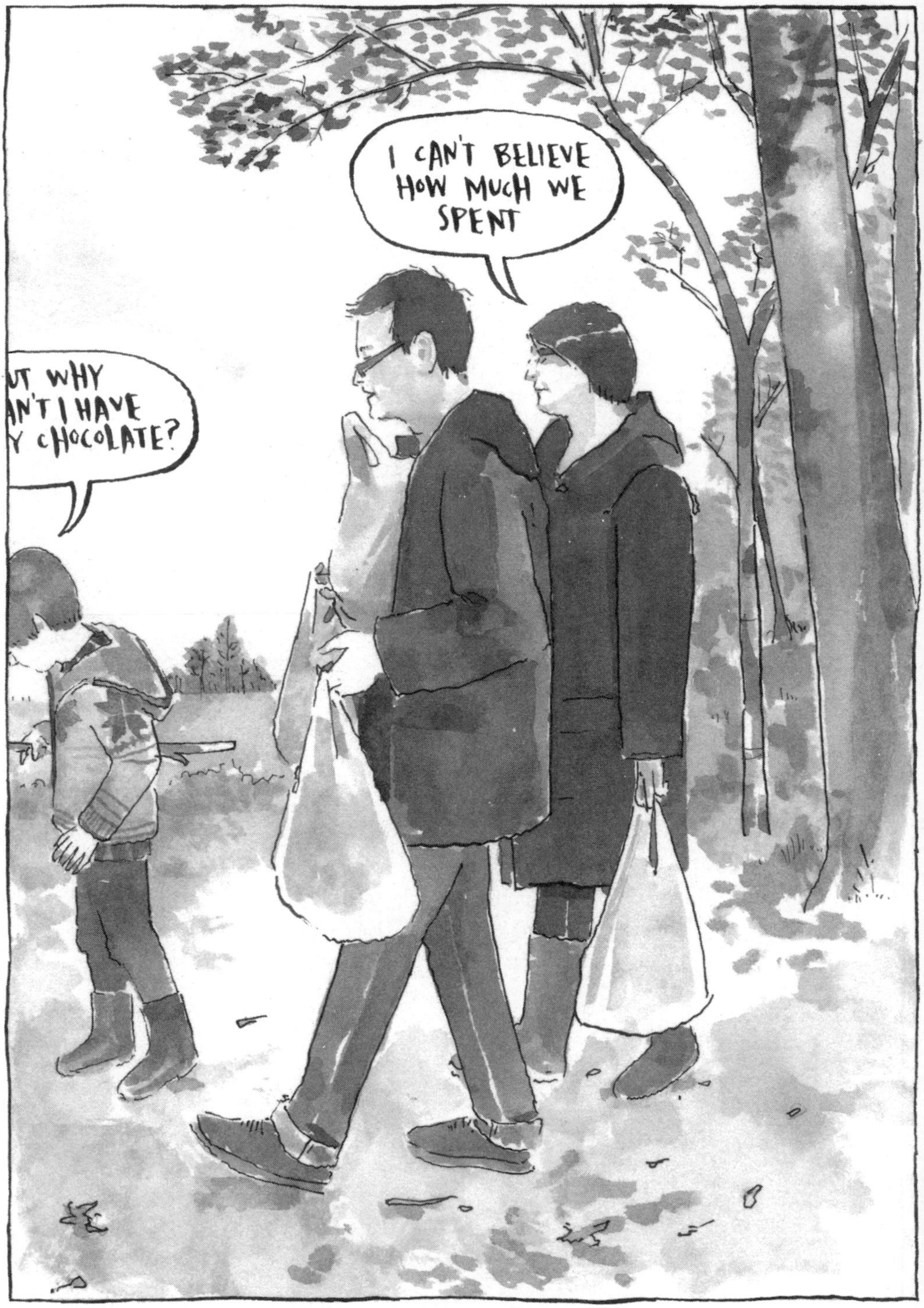
UT WHY
AN'T I HAVE
Y CHOCOLATE?
I CAN'T BELIEVE
HOW MUCH WE
SPENT

WE ARE NATURAL SURVIVALISTS

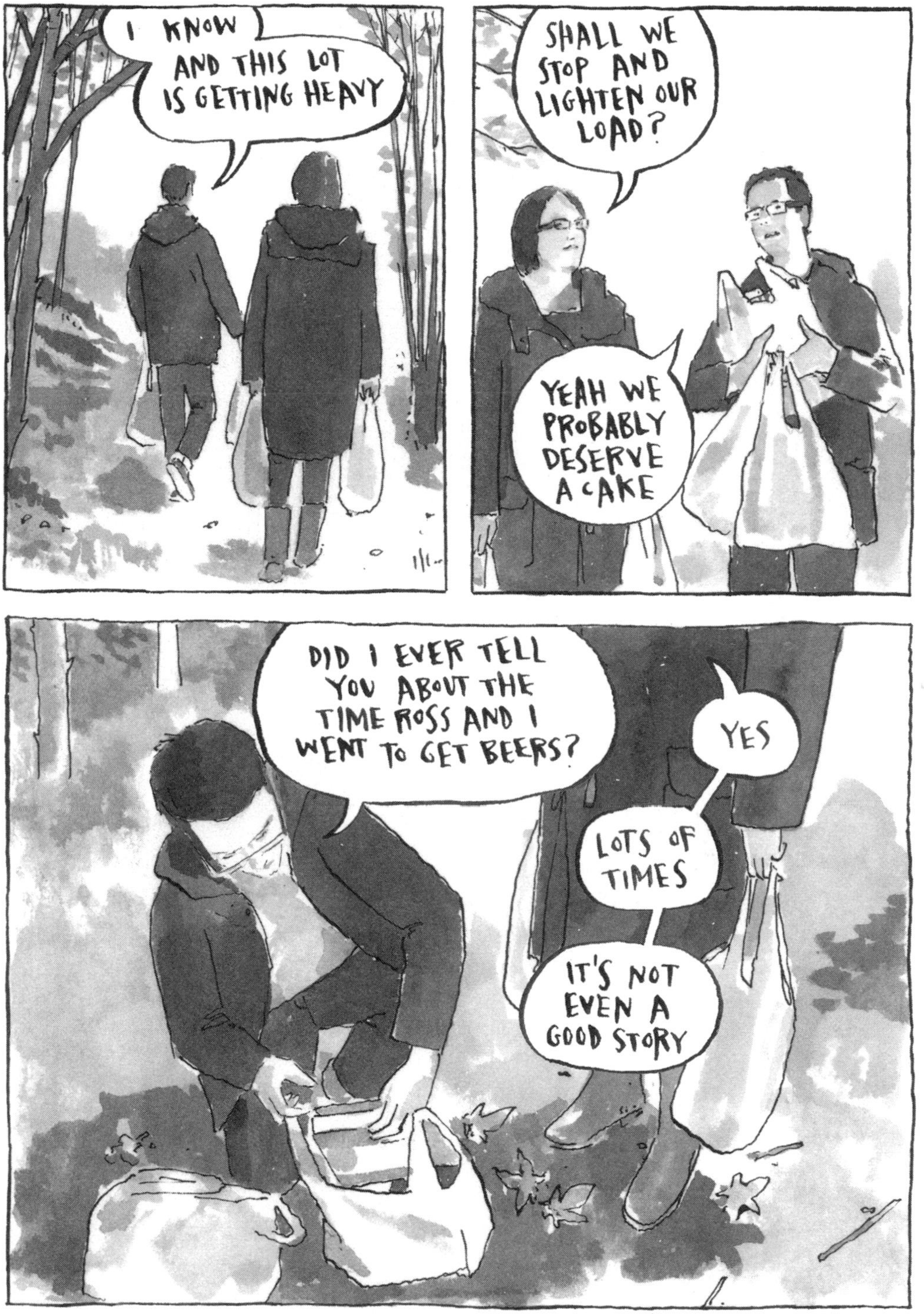
I KNOW
AND THIS LOT IS GETTING HEAVY
SHALL WE STOP AND LIGHTEN OUR LOAD?
YEAH WE PROBABLY DESERVE A CAKE
DID I EVER TELL YOU ABOUT THE TIME ROSS AND I WENT TO GET BEERS?
YES
LOTS OF TIMES
IT'S NOT EVEN A GOOD STORY

DID I EVER TELL YOU THAT STORY? I DON'T THINK I DID...

I THINK IT WAS 98 OR 99, MY OLD FRIEND ROSS AND I HAD SEEN A GREAT DEAL ON CASES OF BEER AT SAFEWAY.

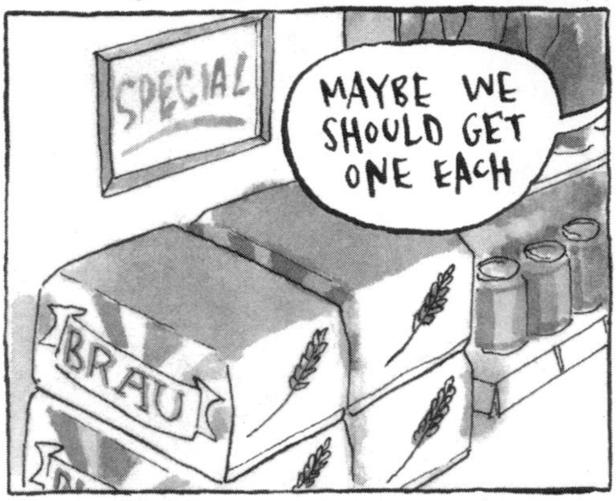
SPECIAL
MAYBE WE SHOULD GET ONE EACH
BRAU

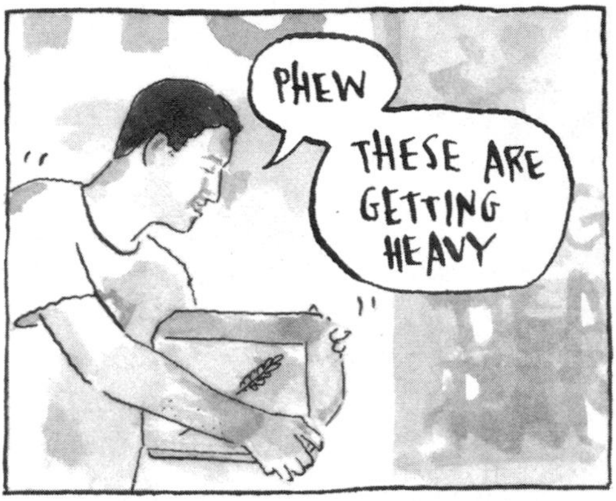
PHEW
THESE ARE GETTING HEAVY

IT WAS A GLORIOUS HOT SUMMER, WITH ZERO RESPONSIBILITIES.

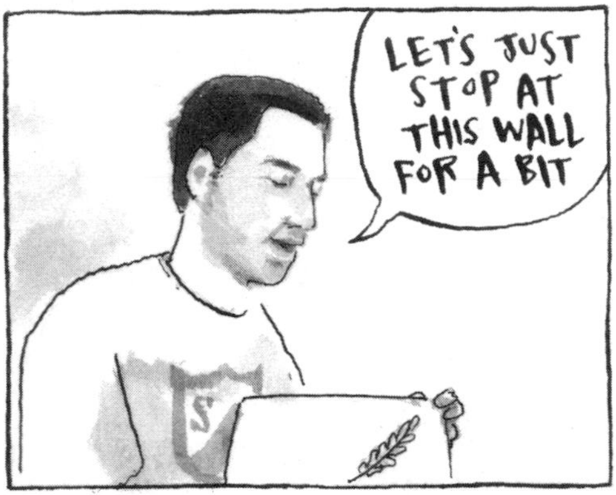
LET'S JUST STOP AT THIS WALL FOR A BIT

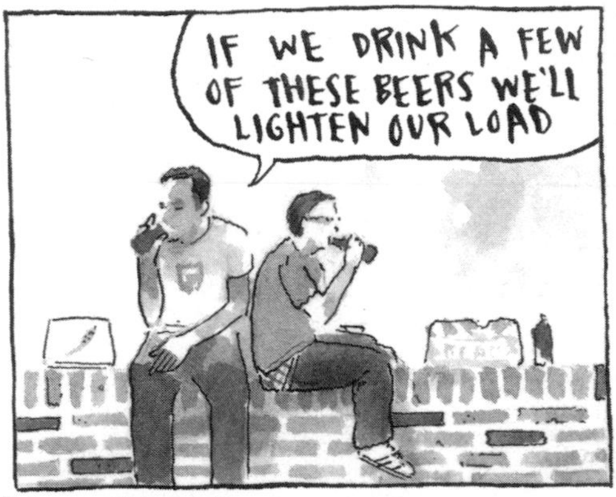
IF WE DRINK A FEW OF THESE BEERS WE'LL LIGHTEN OUR LOAD

WE WERE SAT ON THAT BUSY ROAD FOR MOST OF THE AFTERNOON, WORKING OUR WAY THROUGH THOSE BEERS.

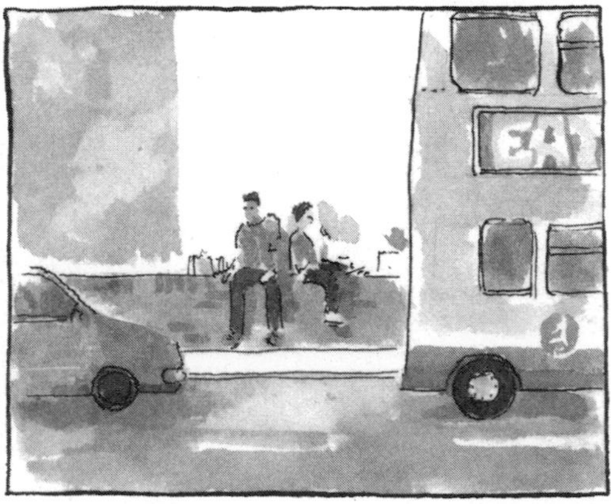
EAT

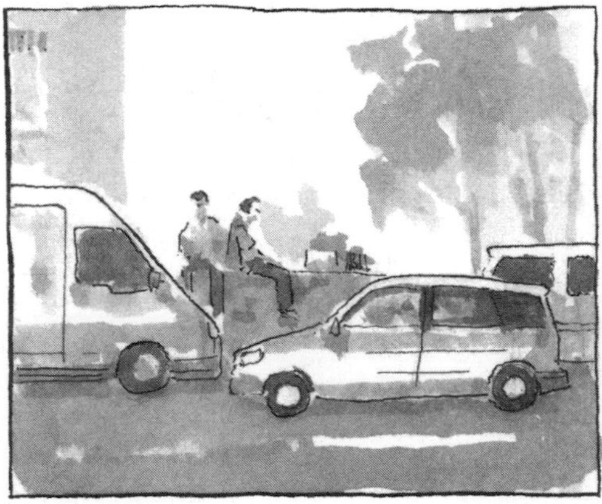

STEPH'S RIGHT, IT'S NOT A GOOD STORY. OH WELL.

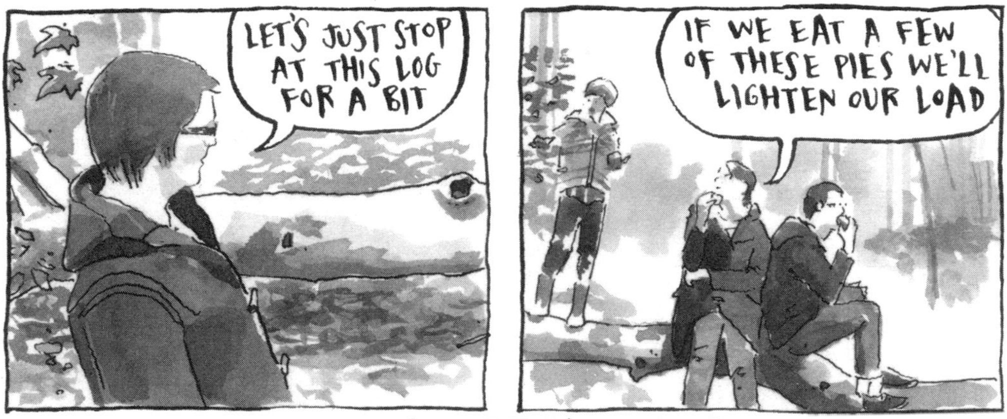
LET'S JUST STOP AT THIS LOG FOR A BIT
IF WE EAT A FEW OF THESE PIES WE'LL LIGHTEN OUR LOAD

CONTRARY TO POPULAR BELIEF,
PROVISIONS SHOULD BE EATEN AT THE FIRST OPPORTUNITY.

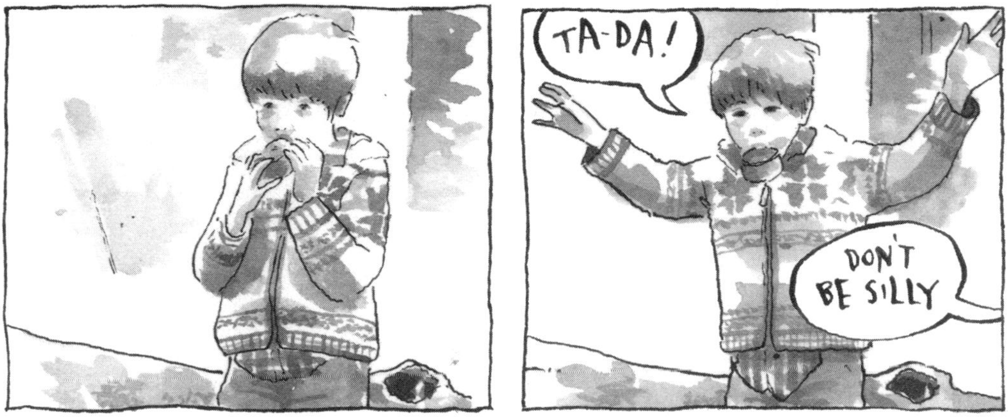
TA-DA!
DON'T BE SILLY

AND LUNCH IN THE WOODS...

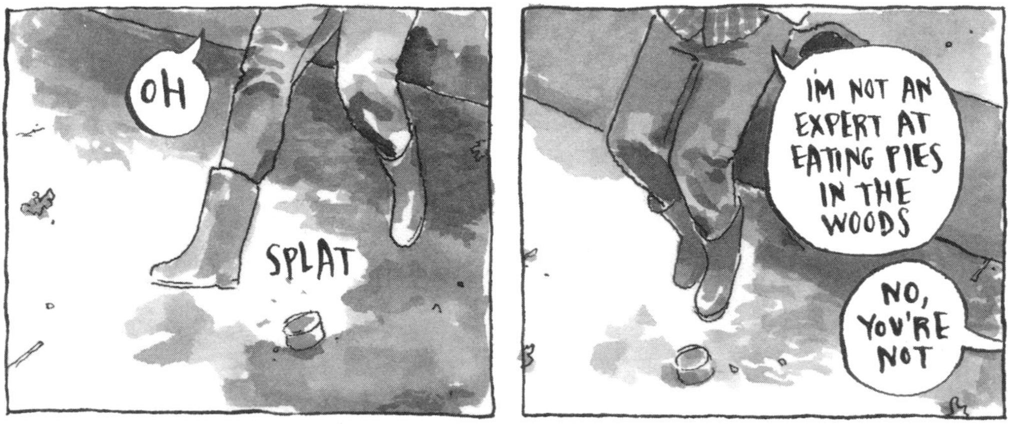
OH
SPLAT
I'M NOT AN EXPERT AT EATING PIES IN THE WOODS
NO, YOU'RE NOT

...BEATS LUNCH NOT IN THE WOODS. PROBABLY.

WE THINK ABOUT FOOD ALL THE TIME AT HOME TOO.
BUT HERE IT'S ABOUT SURVIVAL.

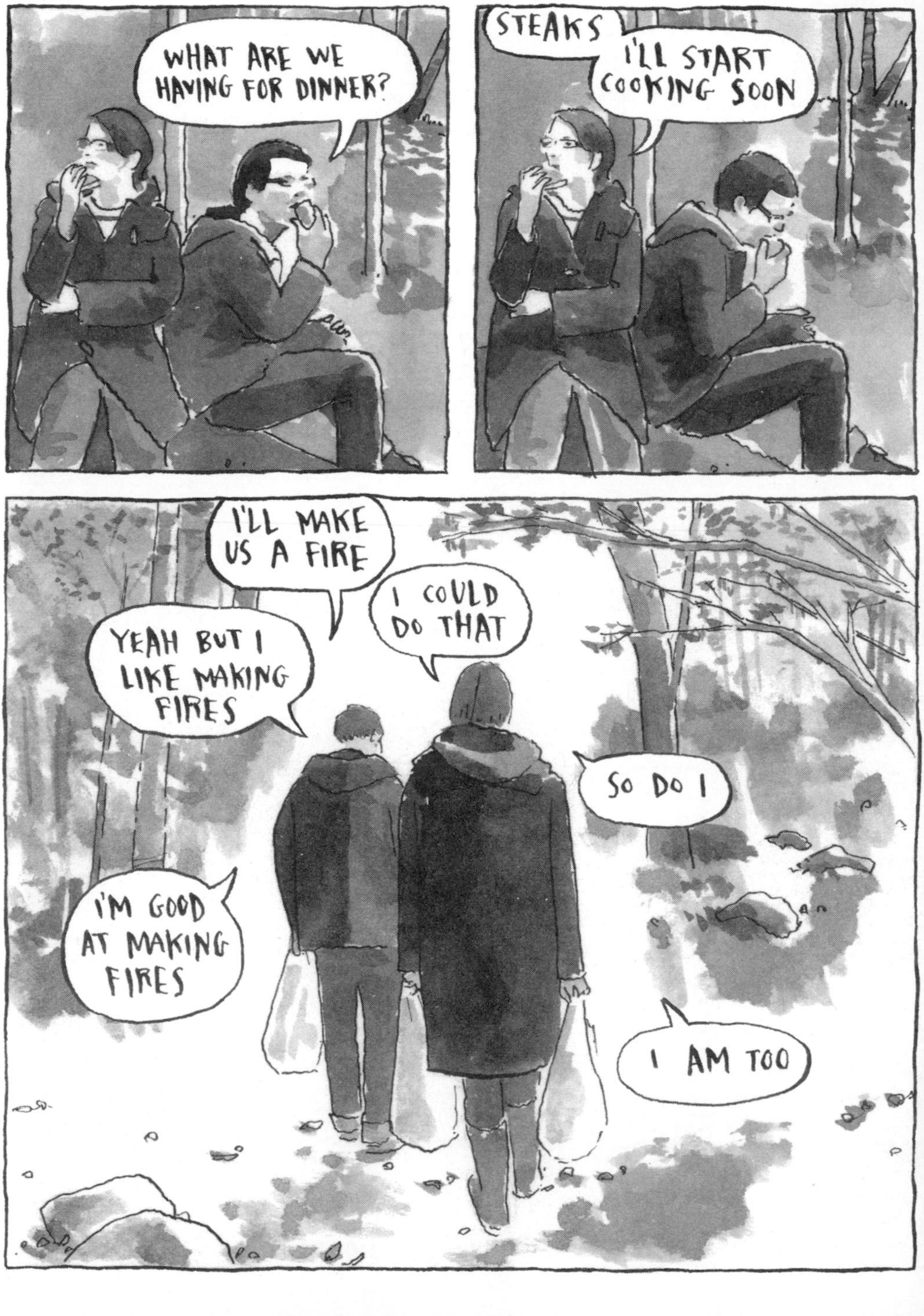
WHAT ARE WE HAVING FOR DINNER?
STEAKS
I'LL START COOKING SOON
I'LL MAKE US A FIRE
I COULD DO THAT
YEAH BUT I LIKE MAKING FIRES
SO DO I
I'M GOOD AT MAKING FIRES
I AM TOO

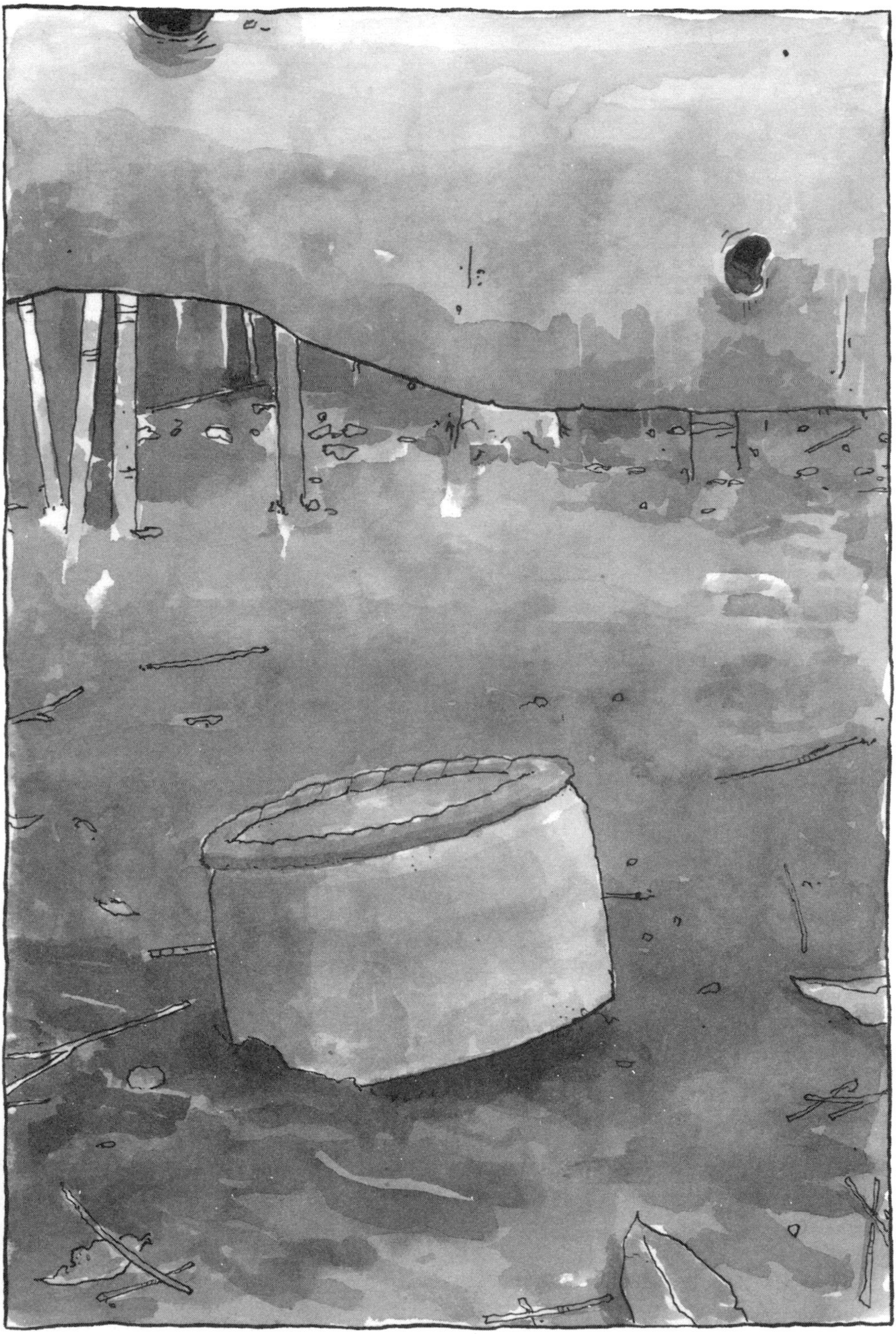

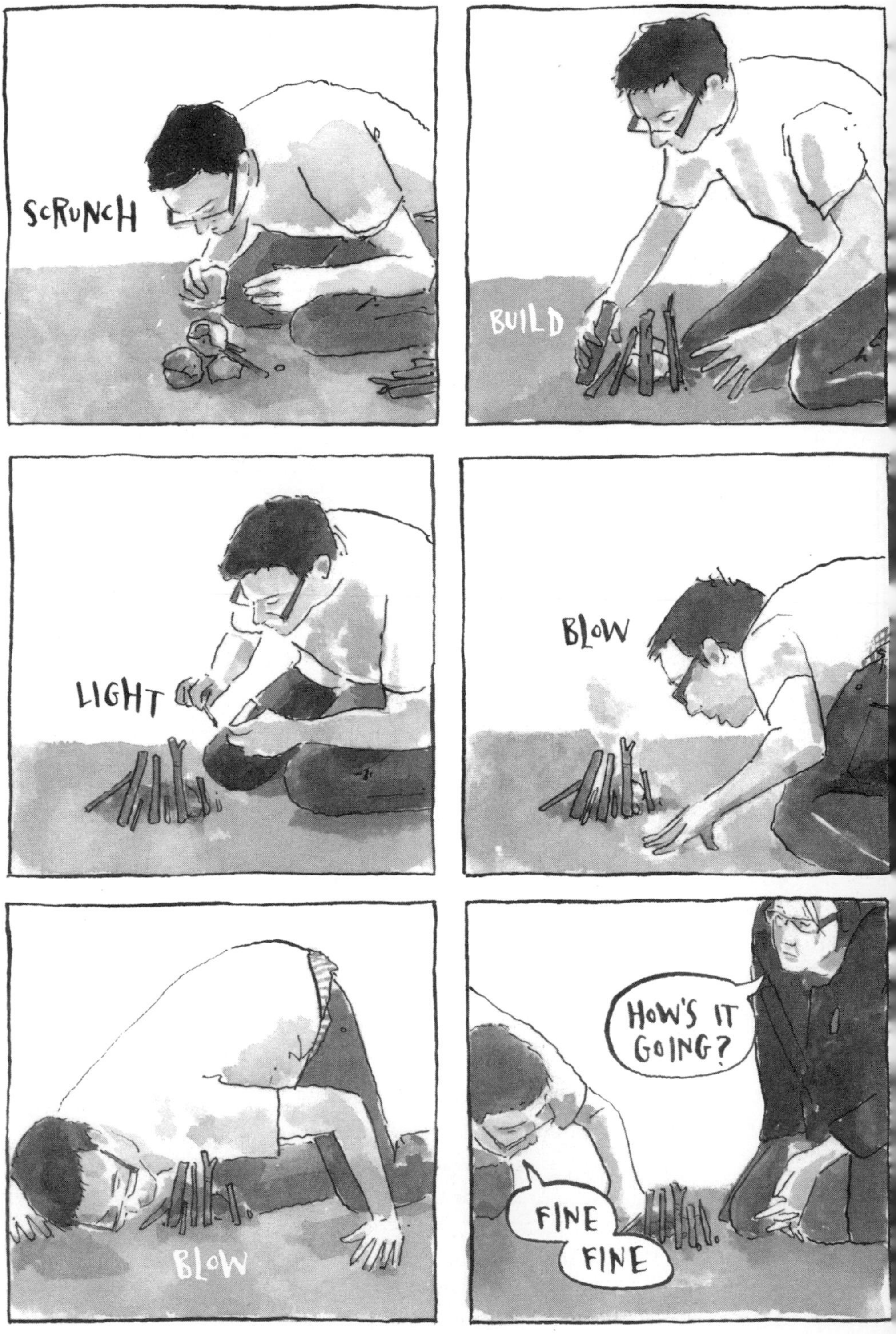
SCRUNCH
BUILD
LIGHT
BLOW
BLOW
HOW'S IT GOING?
FINE FINE

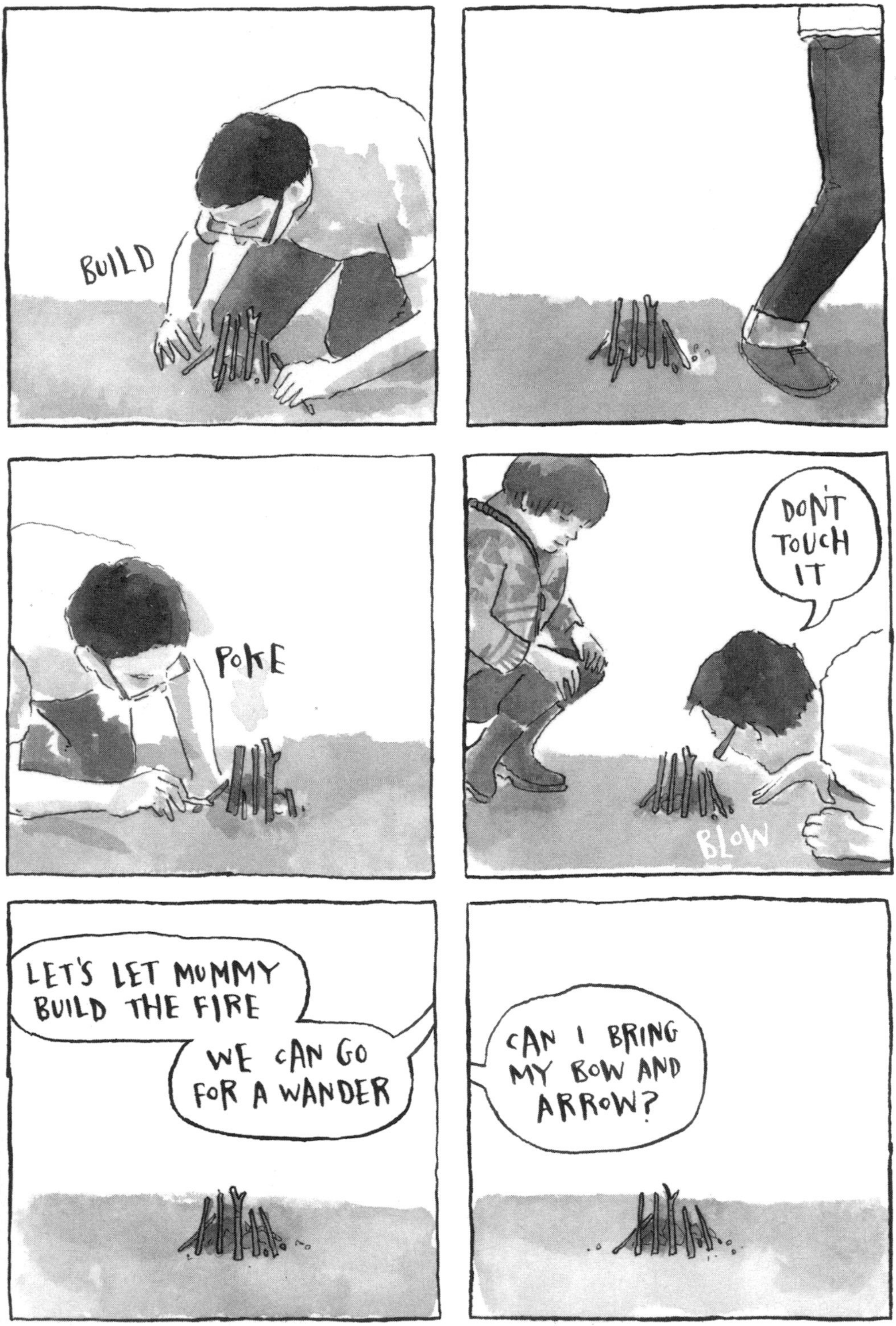
BUILD
POKE
DON'T TOUCH IT
BLOW
LET'S LET MUMMY BUILD THE FIRE
WE CAN GO FOR A WANDER
CAN I BRING MY BOW AND ARROW?

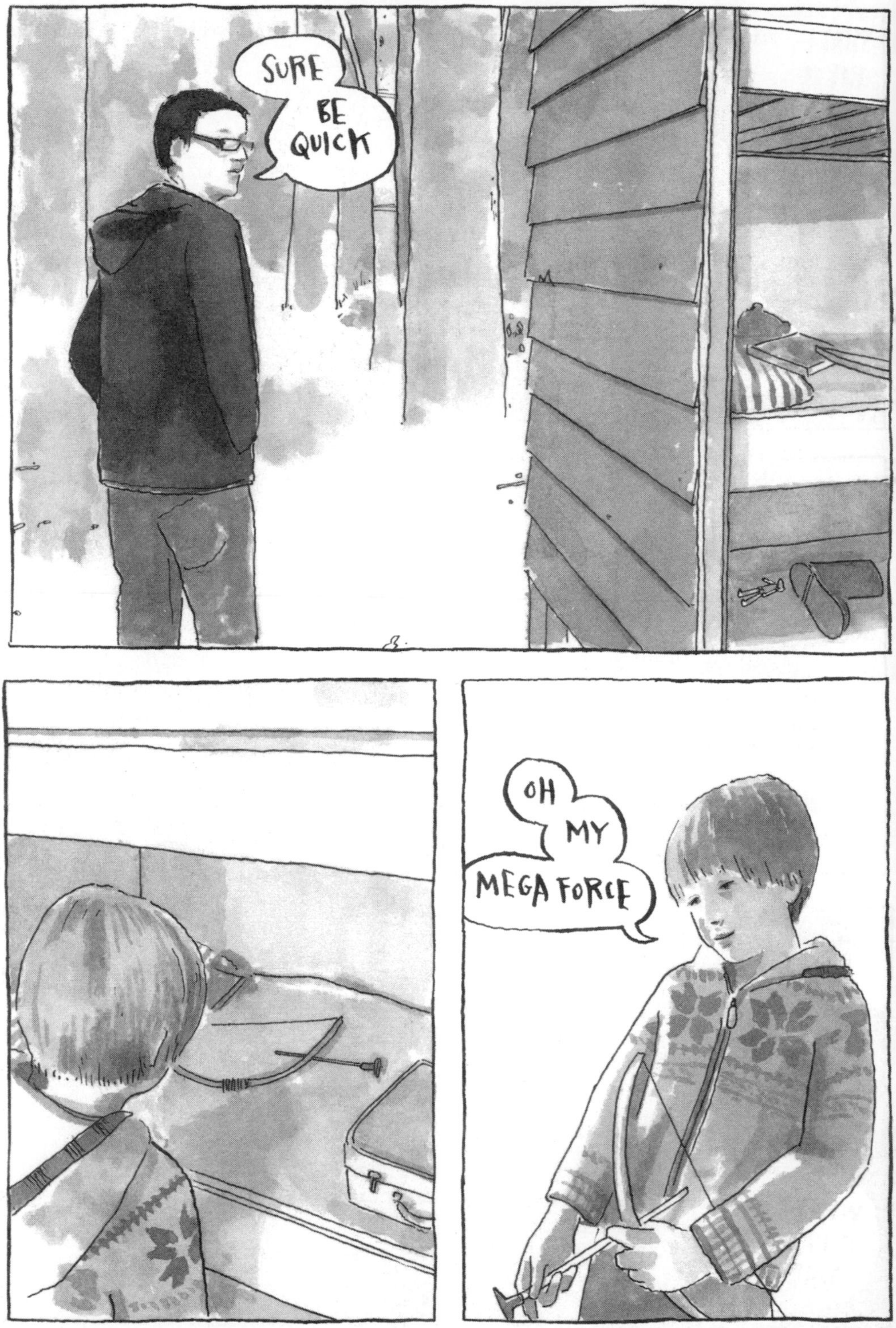
SURE
BE QUICK
OH MY MEGA FORCE

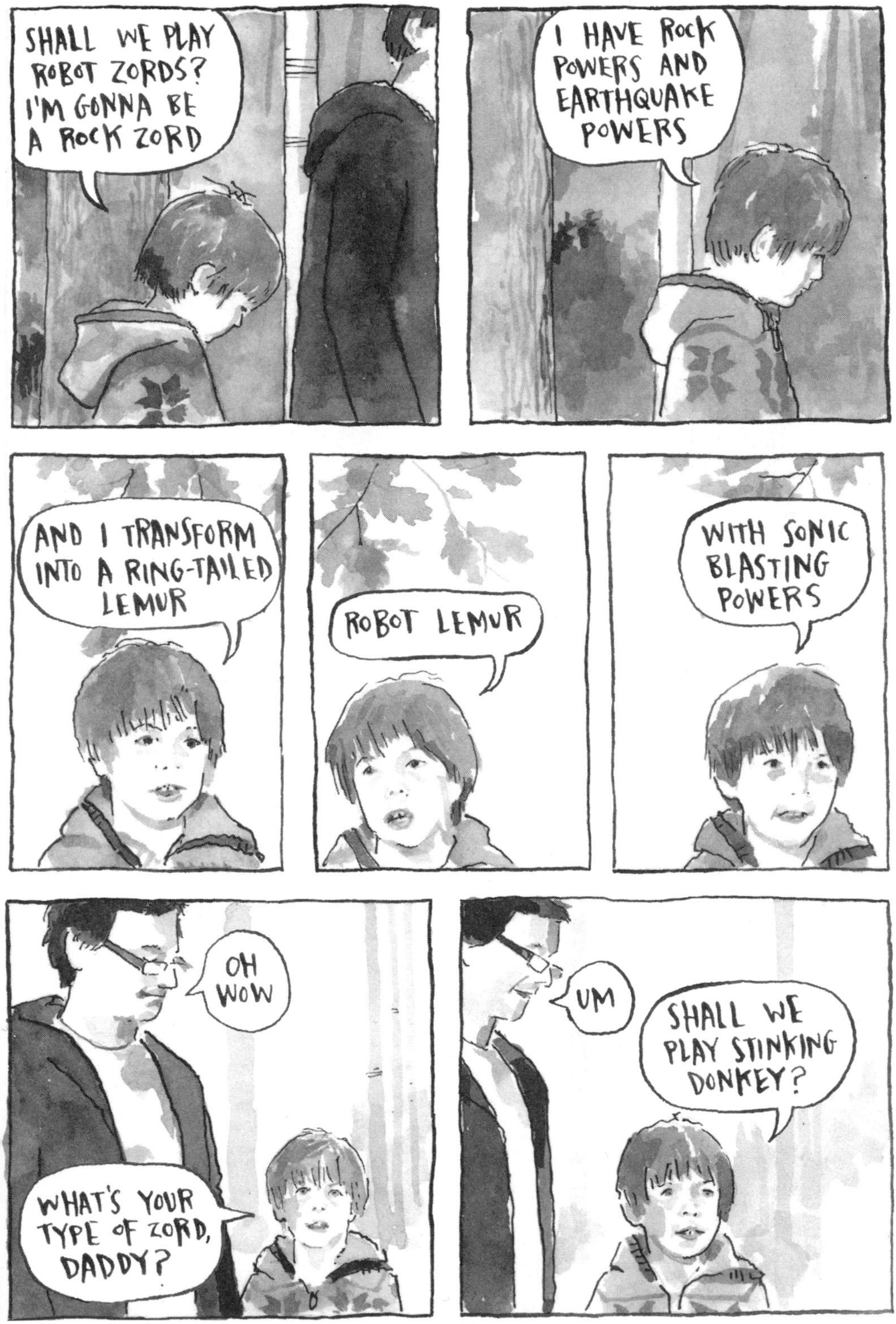
SHALL WE PLAY ROBOT ZORDS? I'M GONNA BE A ROCK ZORD
I HAVE ROCK POWERS AND EARTHQUAKE POWERS
AND I TRANSFORM INTO A RING-TAILED LEMUR
ROBOT LEMUR
WITH SONIC BLASTING POWERS
OH WOW
WHAT'S YOUR TYPE OF ZORD, DADDY?
UM
SHALL WE PLAY STINKING DONKEY?

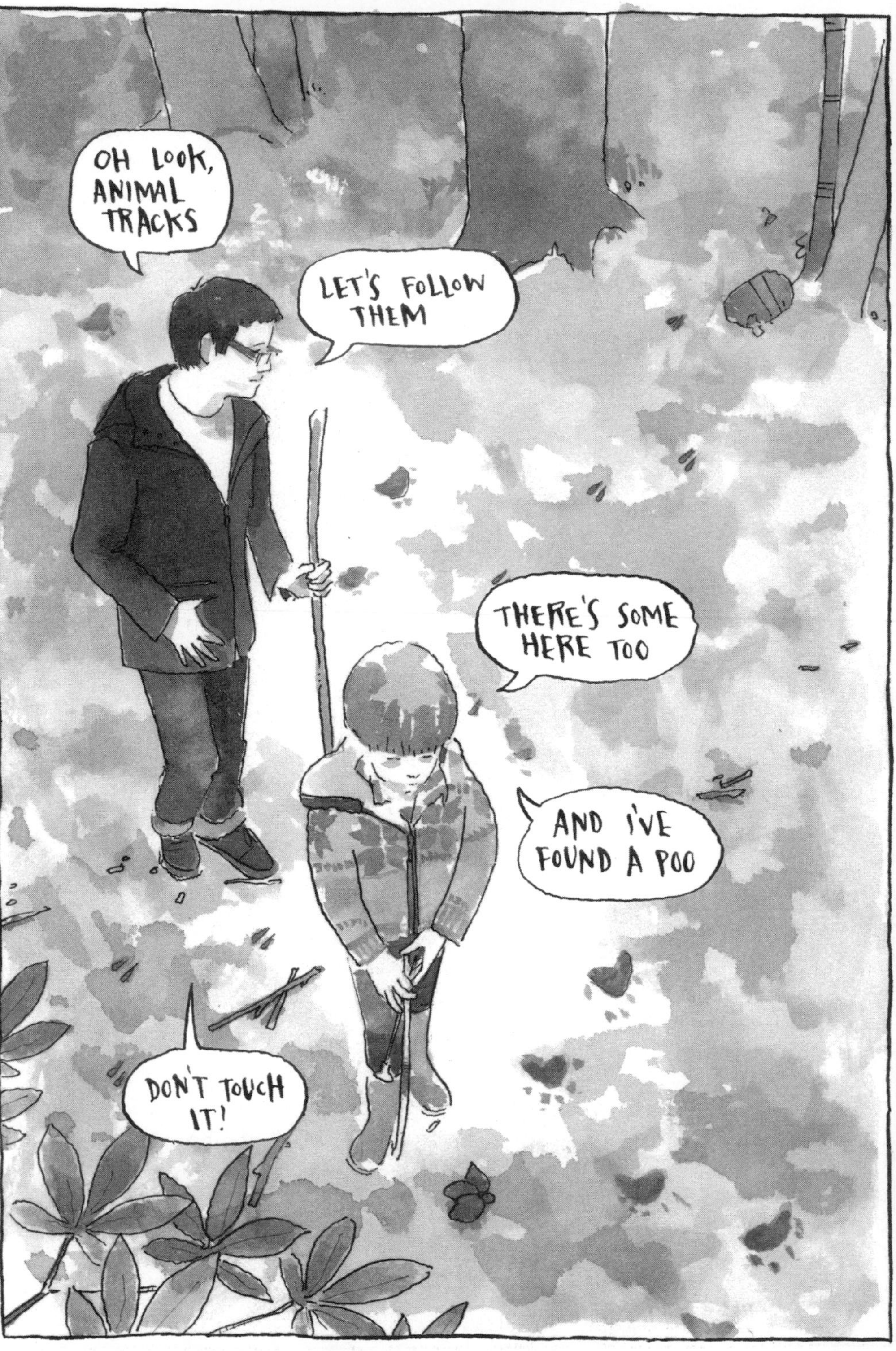
OH LOOK, ANIMAL TRACKS
LET'S FOLLOW THEM
THERE'S SOME HERE TOO
AND I'VE FOUND A POO
DON'T TOUCH IT!

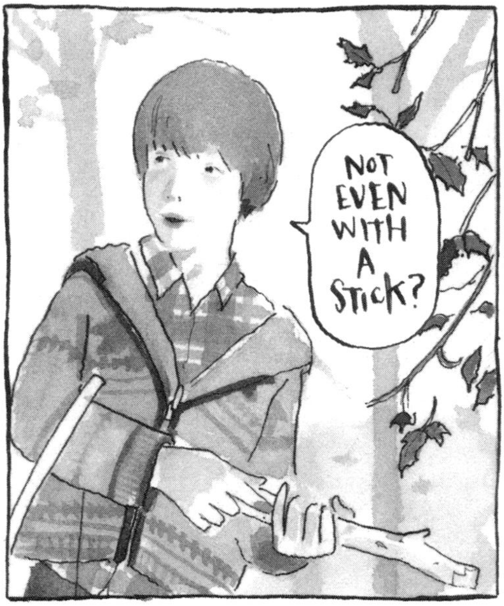
NOT EVEN WITH A STICK?

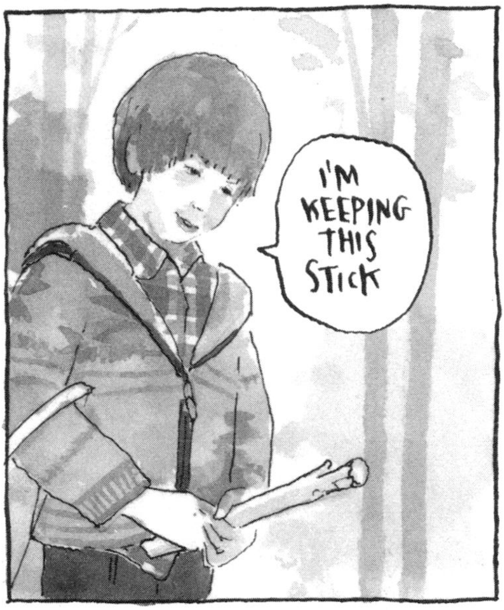
I'M KEEPING THIS STICK

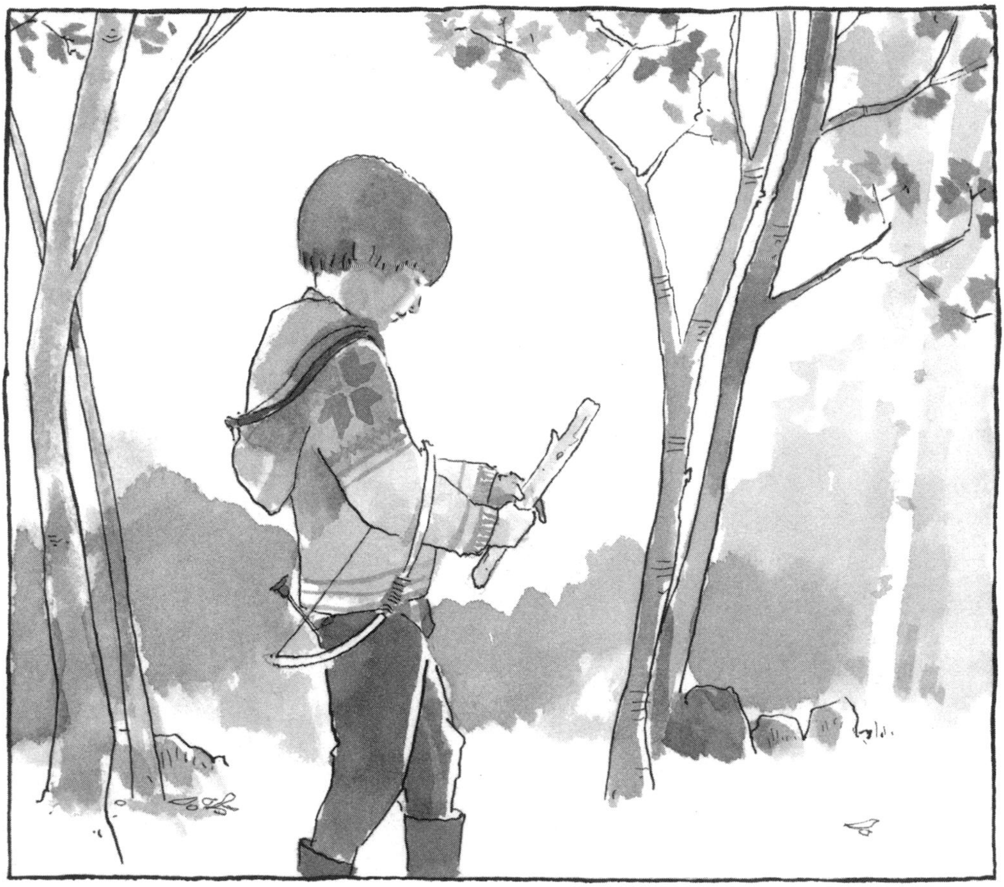

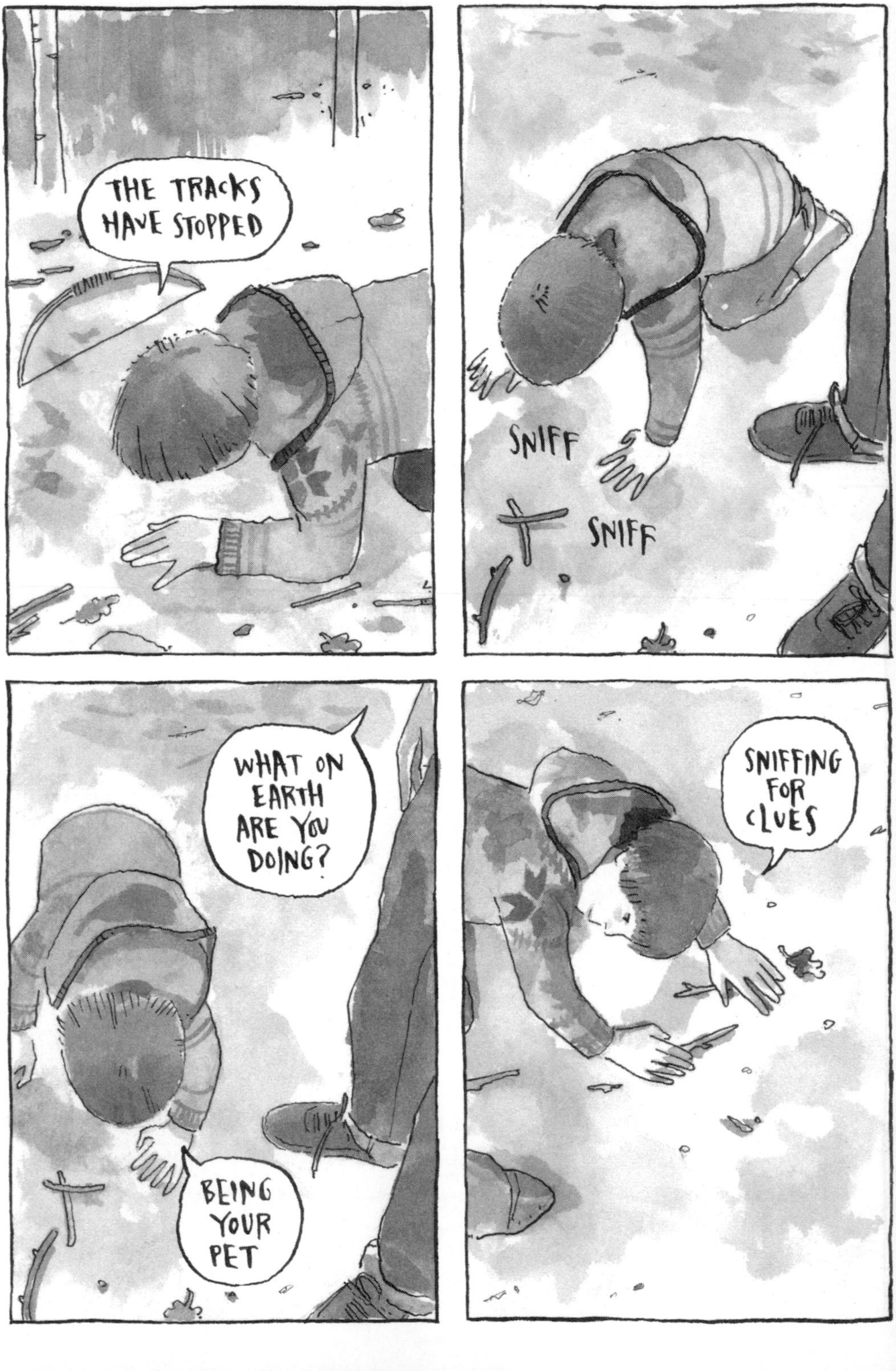
THE TRACKS HAVE STOPPED
SNIFF
SNIFF
WHAT ON EARTH ARE YOU DOING?
BEING YOUR PET
SNIFFING FOR CLUES

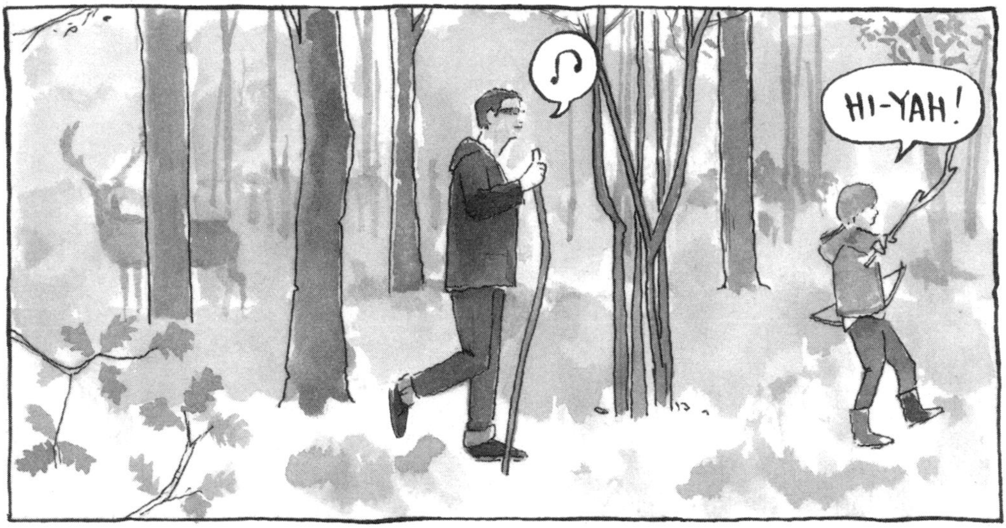

HI-YAH!

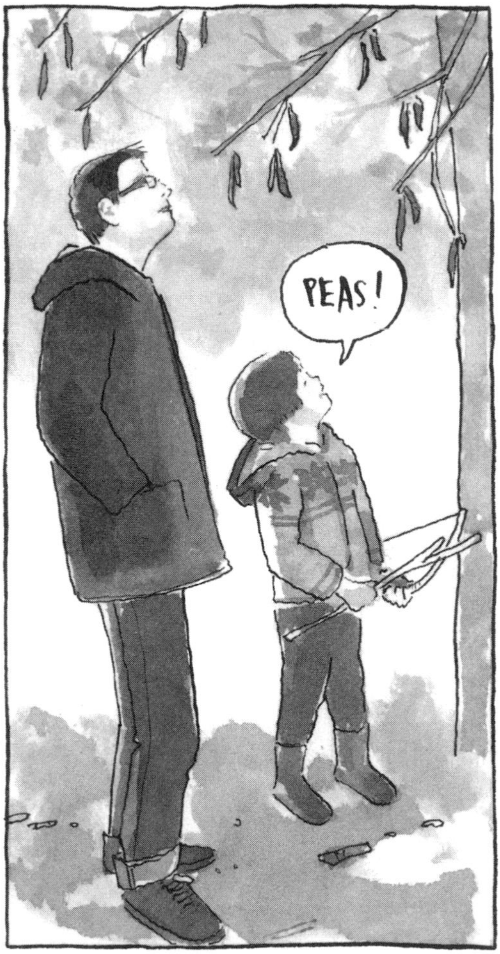

PEAS!

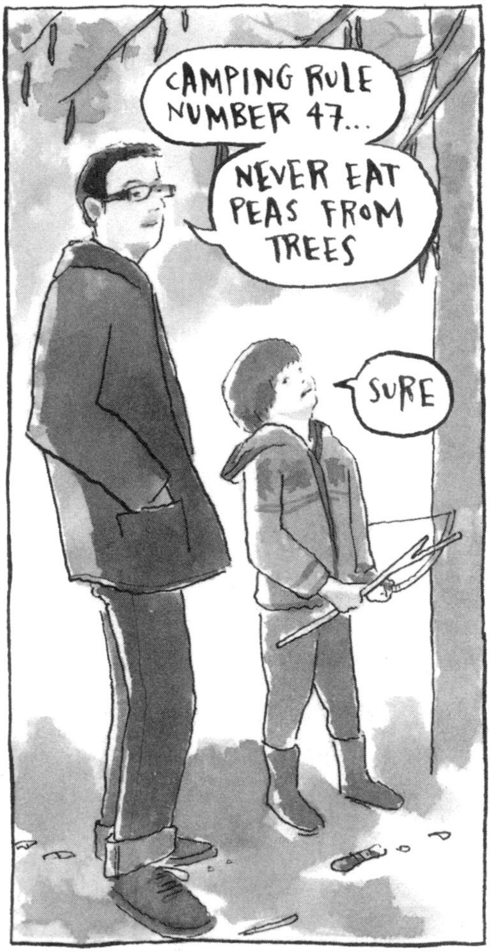

CAMPING RULE NUMBER 47...
NEVER EAT PEAS FROM TREES
SURE

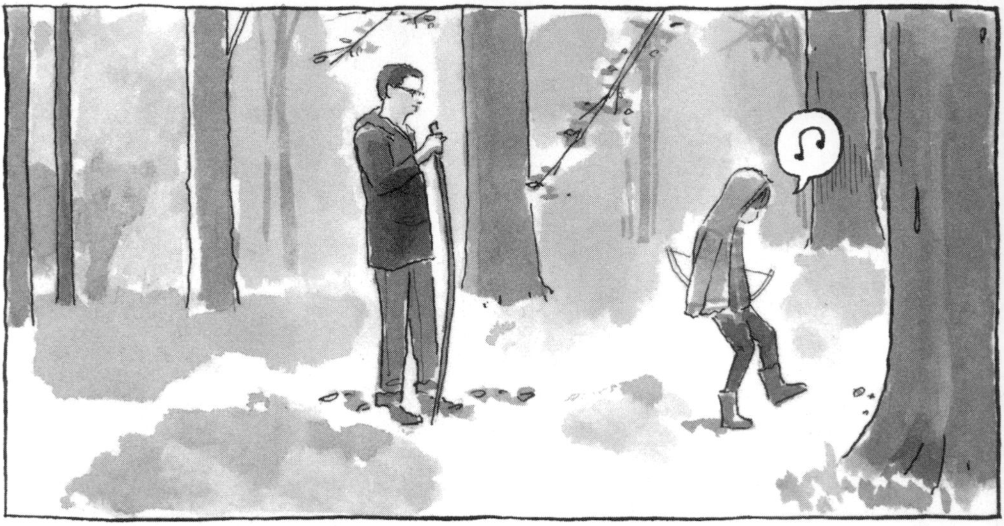

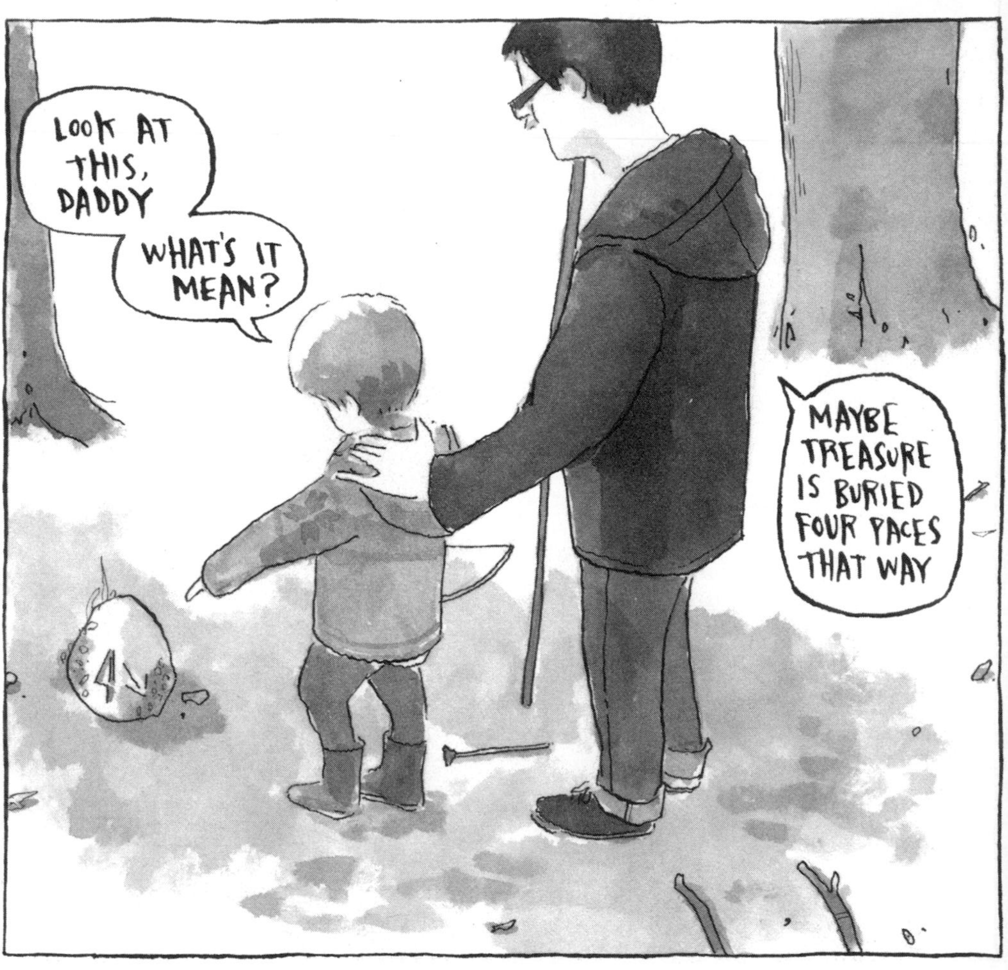
LOOK AT THIS, DADDY
WHAT'S IT MEAN?
MAYBE TREASURE IS BURIED FOUR PACES THAT WAY

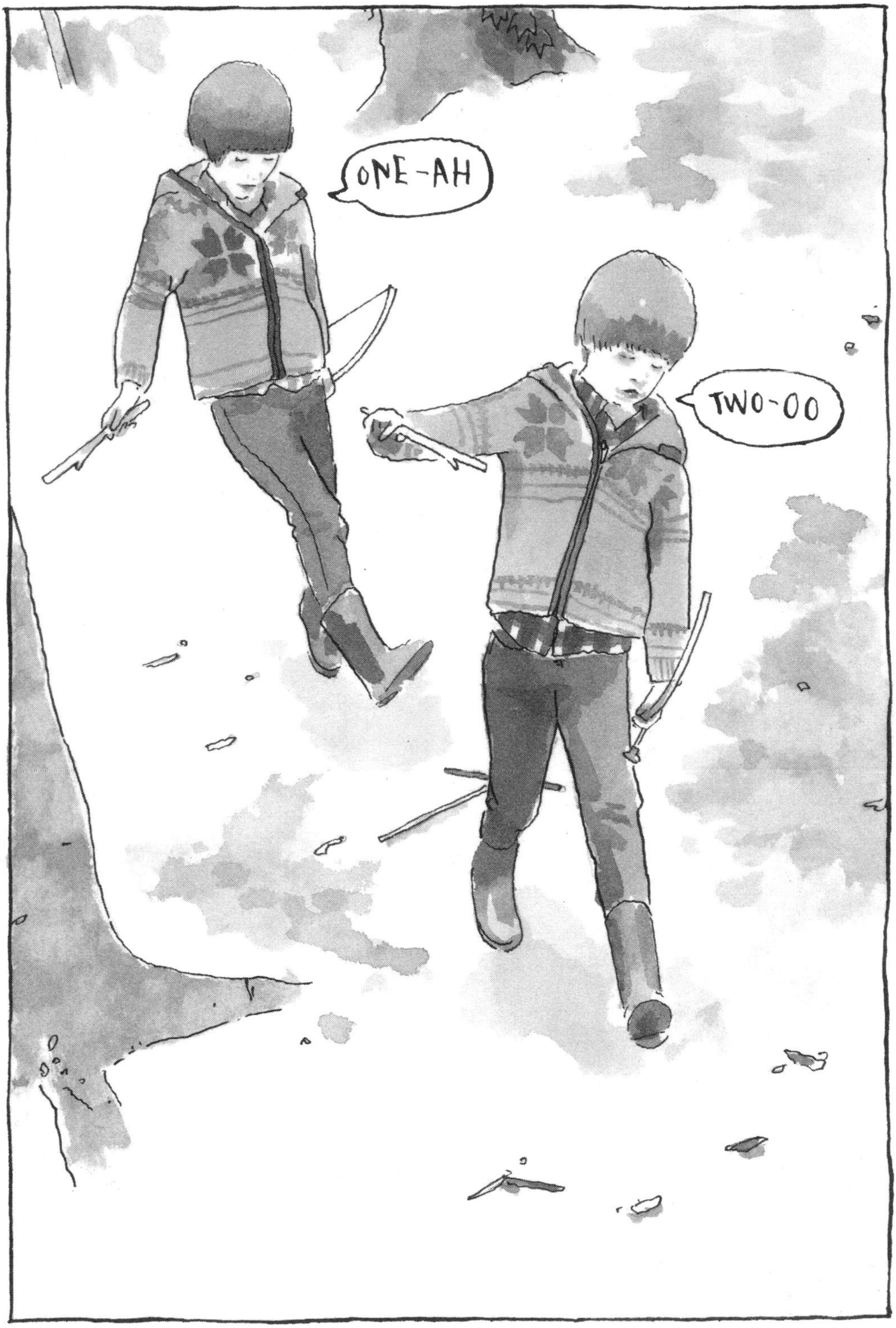
ONE-AH
TWO-OO

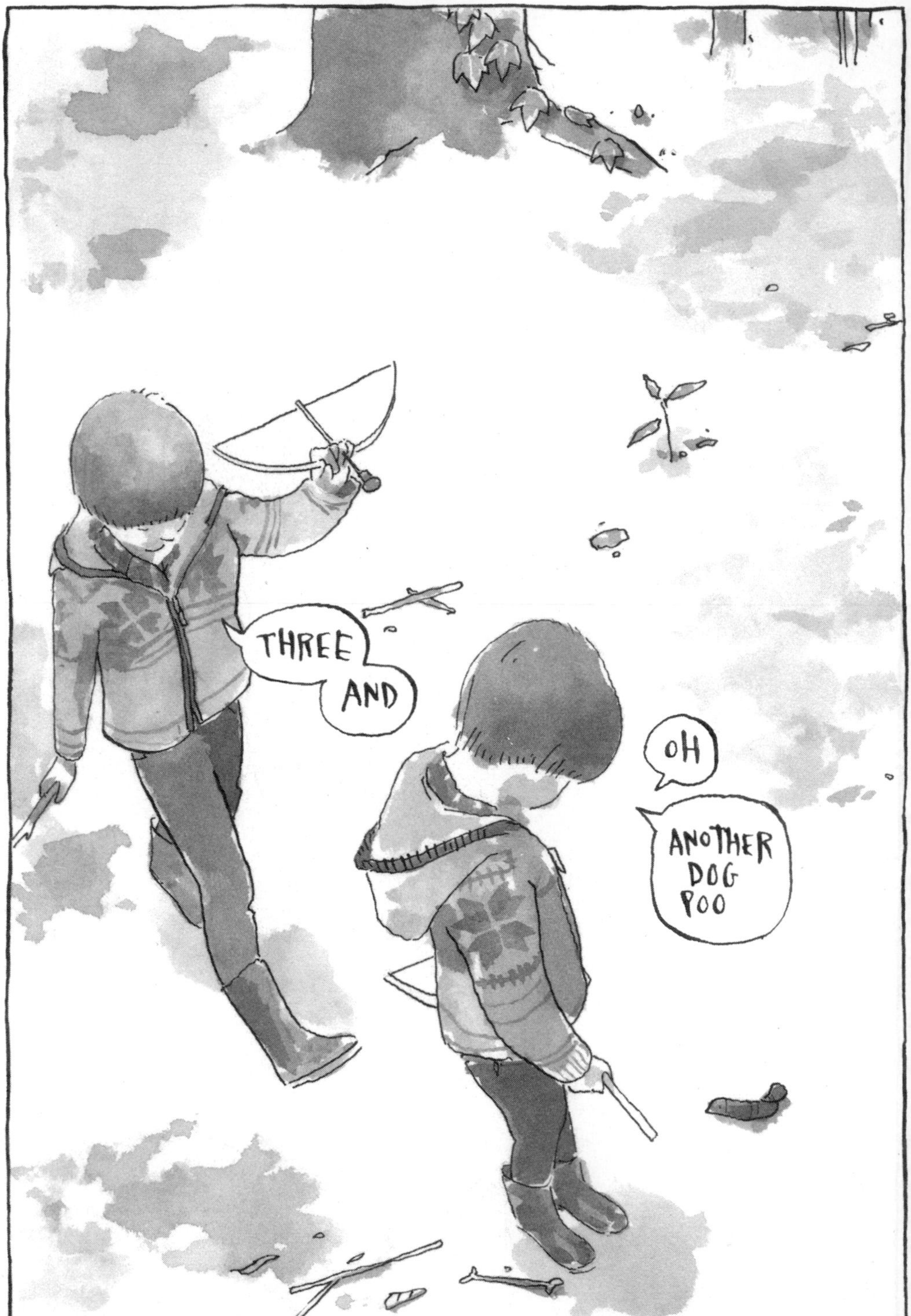
THREE AND
OH
ANOTHER DOG POO

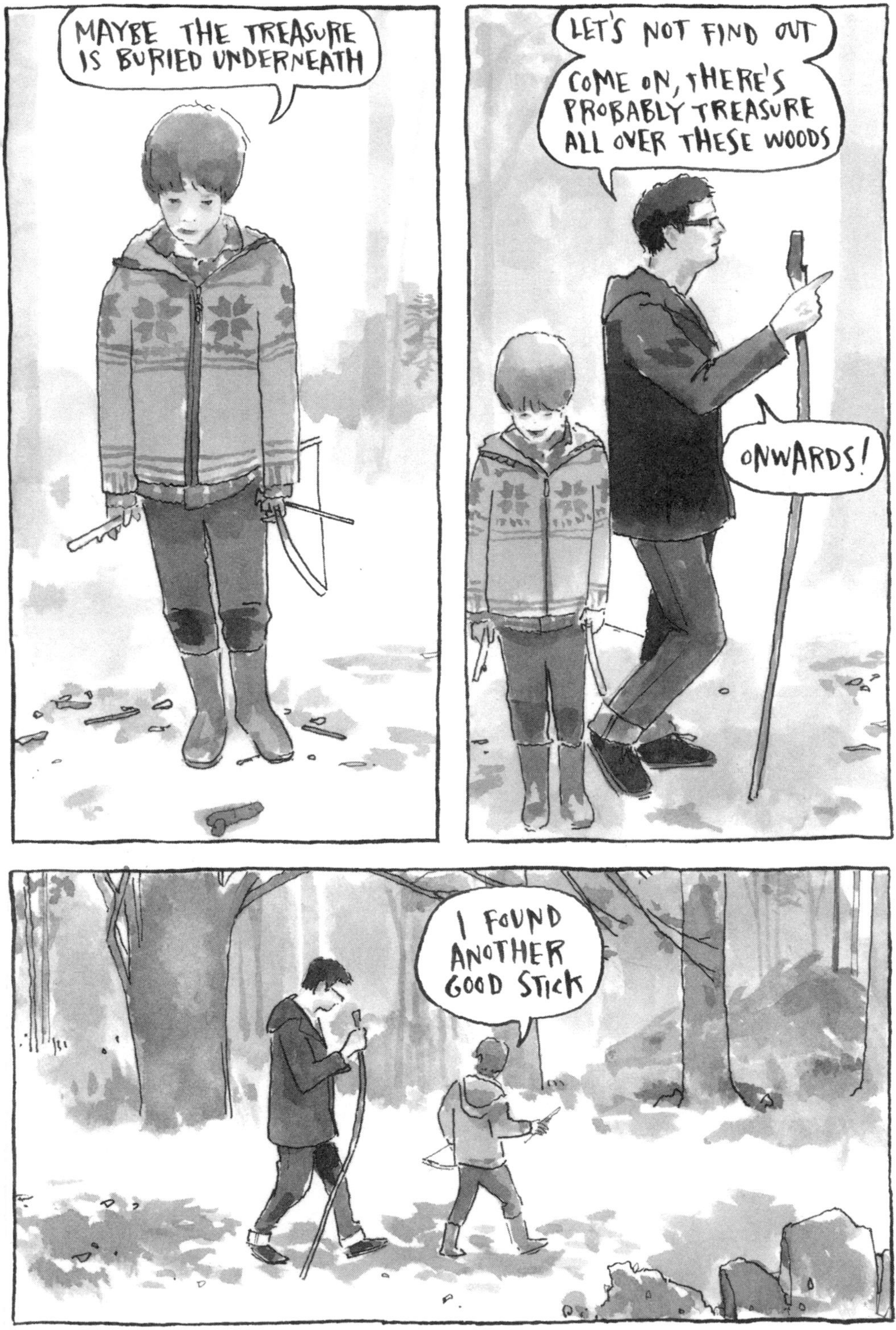
MAYBE THE TREASURE IS BURIED UNDERNEATH
LET'S NOT FIND OUT
COME ON, THERE'S PROBABLY TREASURE ALL OVER THESE WOODS
ONWARDS!
I FOUND ANOTHER GOOD STICK

AFTER SEVERAL HOURS SEARCHING
WE DO FIND SOME PARTIALLY BURIED TREASURE...

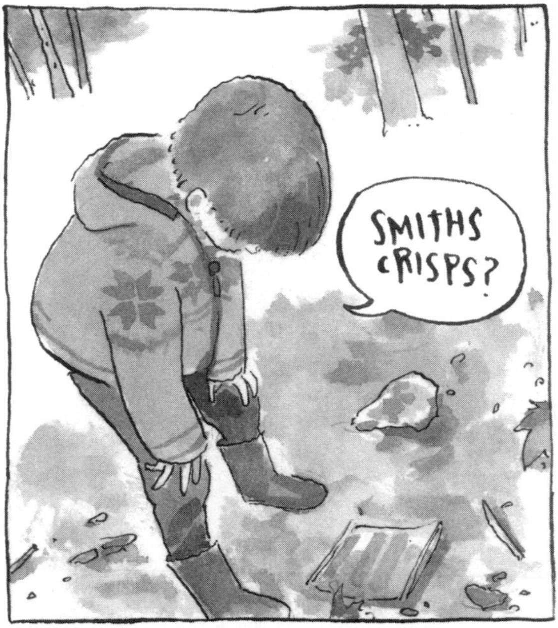
SMITHS CRISPS?

VERY OLD CRISP PACKET...

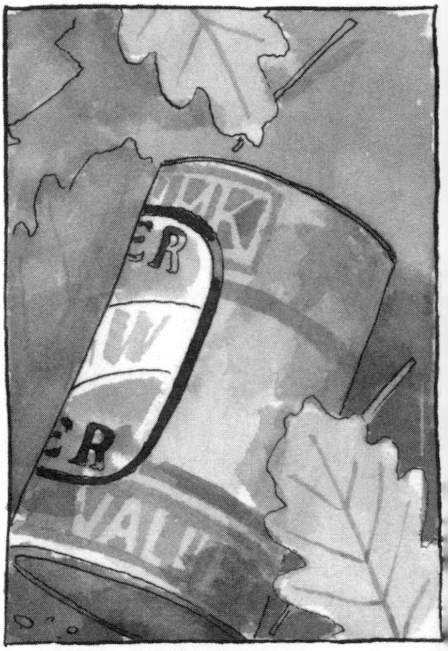

...AND A "VINTAGE" BEER CAN.

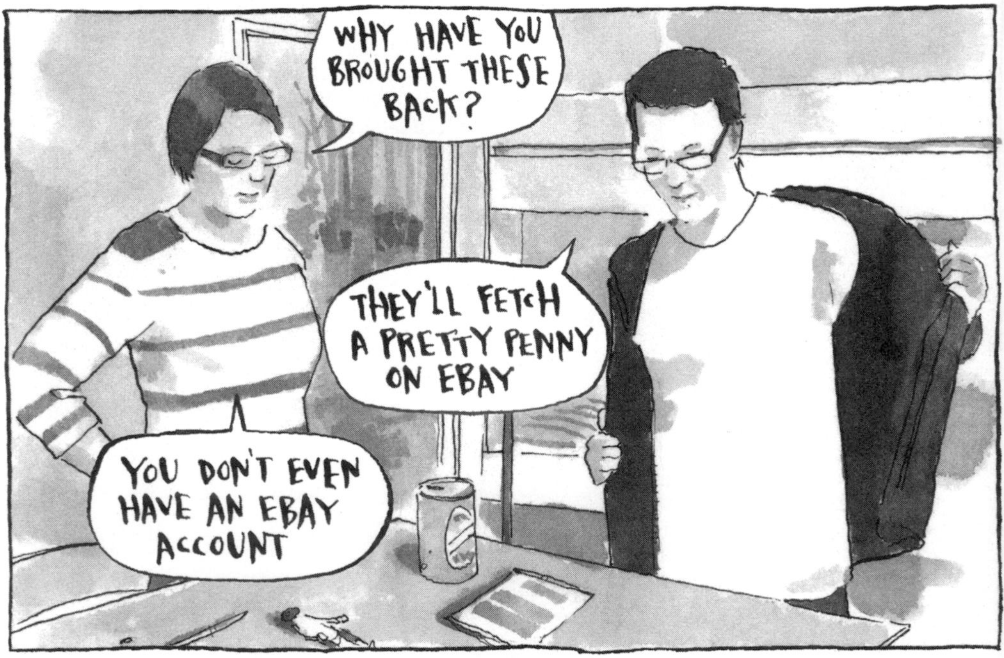
WHY HAVE YOU BROUGHT THESE BACK?
THEY'LL FETCH A PRETTY PENNY ON EBAY
YOU DON'T EVEN HAVE AN EBAY ACCOUNT

TRUE...

BUT I DO LOVE COLLECTING JUNK
WITH THE AIM OF ONE DAY SELLING IT ALL FOR MEGABUCKS.

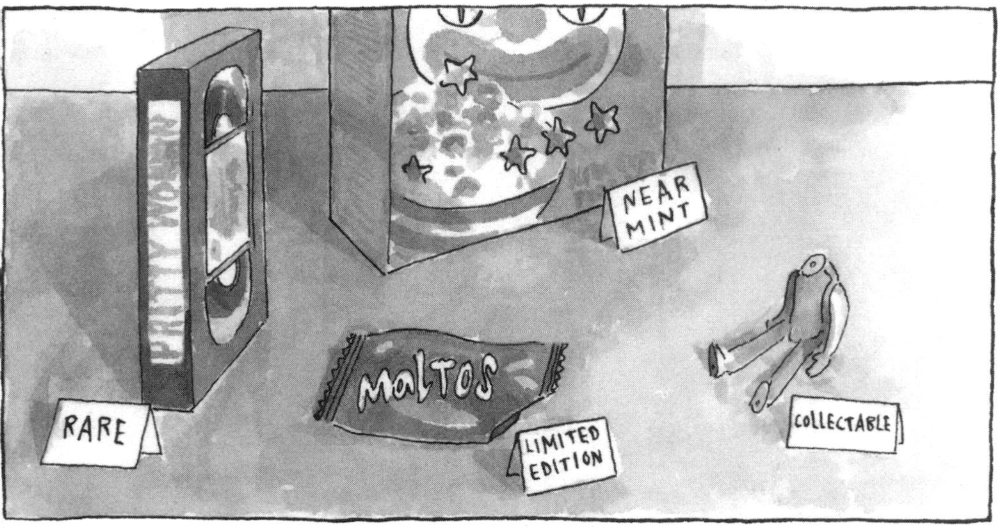
NEAR MINT
MALTOS
RARE
LIMITED EDITION
COLLECTABLE

MAYBE. OR MAYBE I JUST LOVE STUFF.

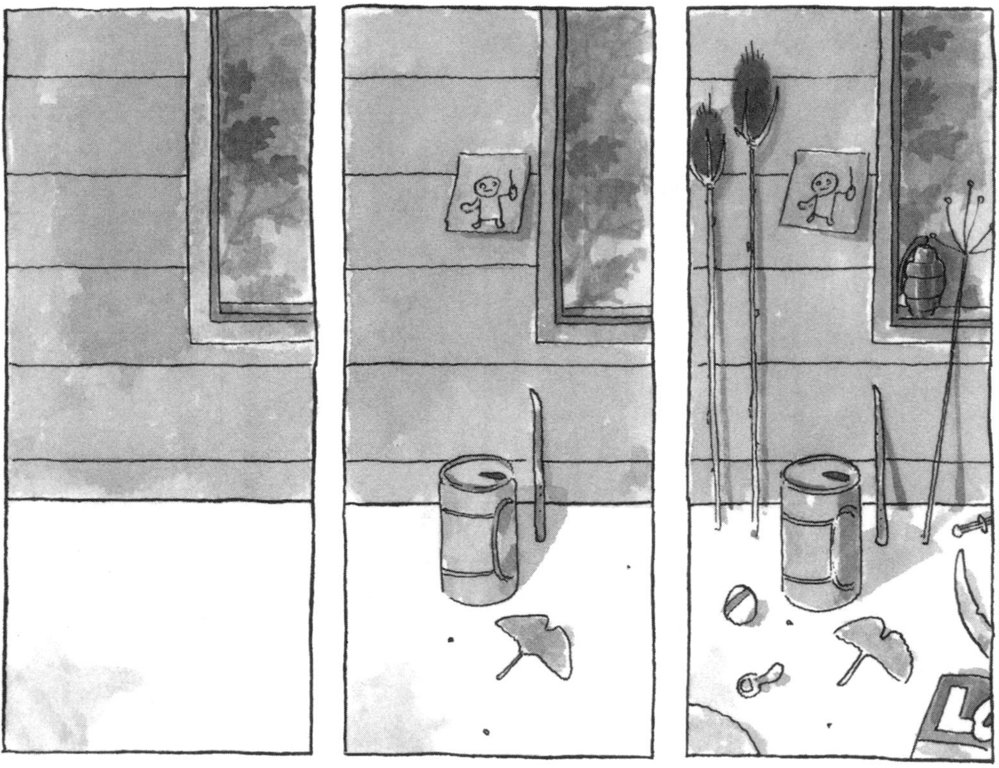

GIVE ME SURFACES AND I WILL CLUTTER THEM.

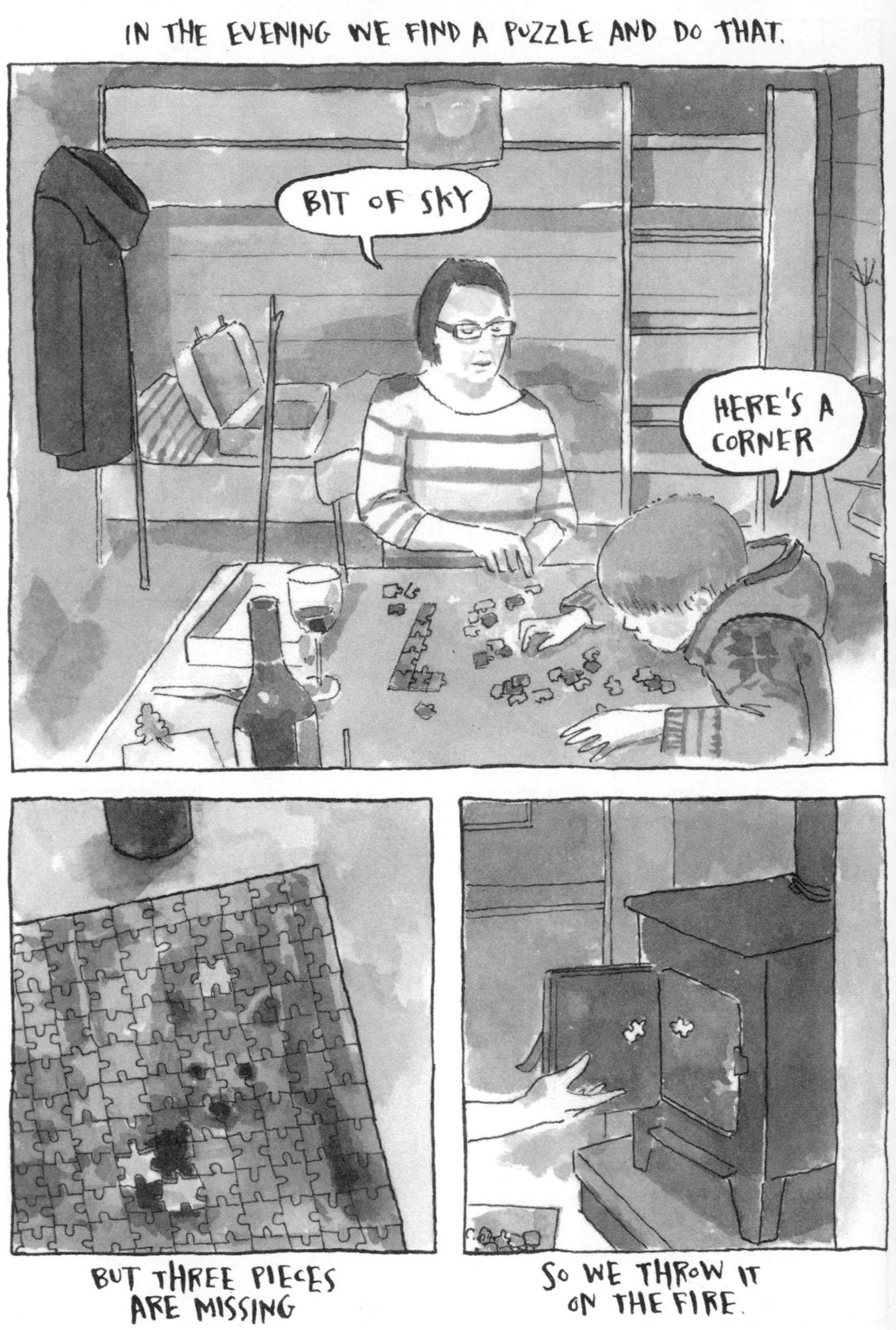
IN THE EVENING WE FIND A PUZZLE AND DO THAT.
BIT OF SKY
HERE'S A CORNER
BUT THREE PIECES ARE MISSING
SO WE THROW IT ON THE FIRE.

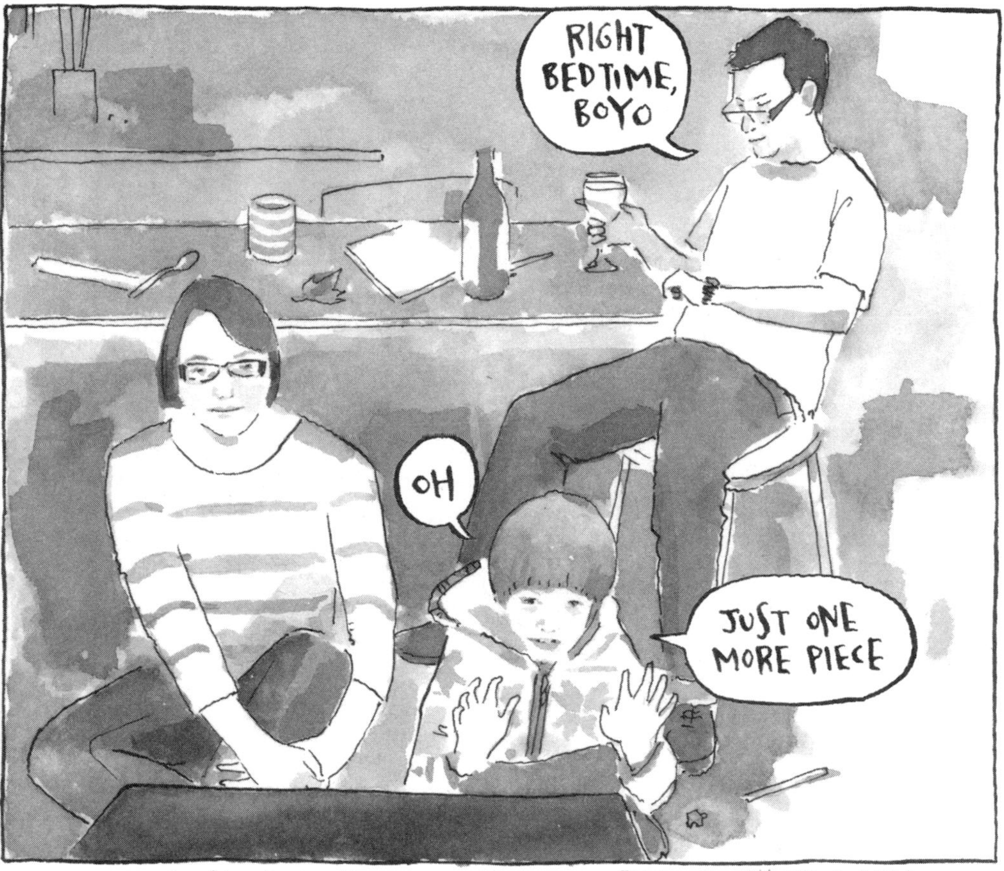
RIGHT BEDTIME, BOYO
OH
JUST ONE MORE PIECE

WATCHING A CRAPPY PUZZLE BURN IS QUITE LOVELY, I RECOMMEND IT.

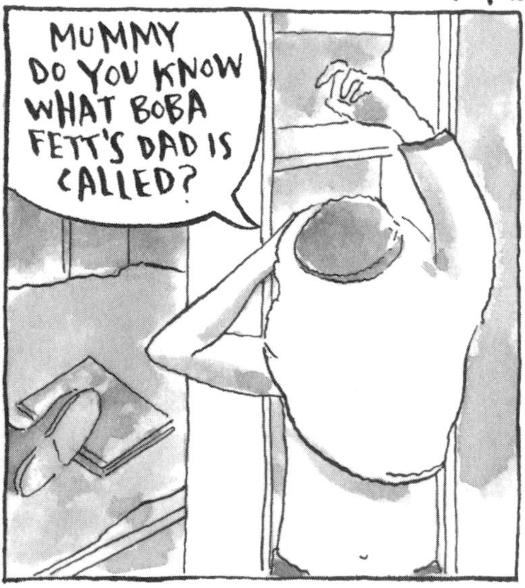
MUMMY DO YOU KNOW WHAT BOBA FETT'S DAD IS CALLED?

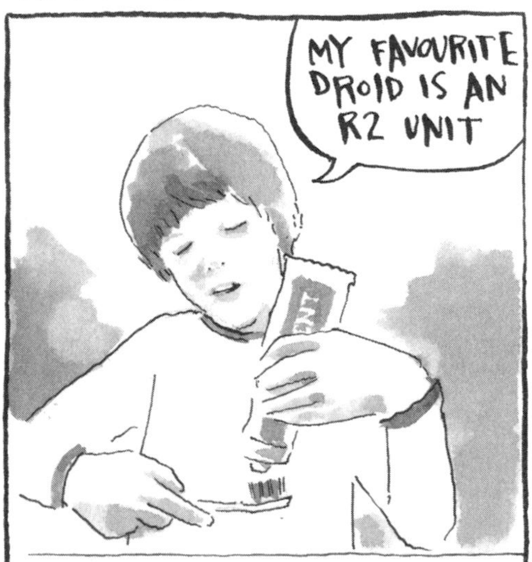
MY FAVOURITE DROID IS AN R2 UNIT

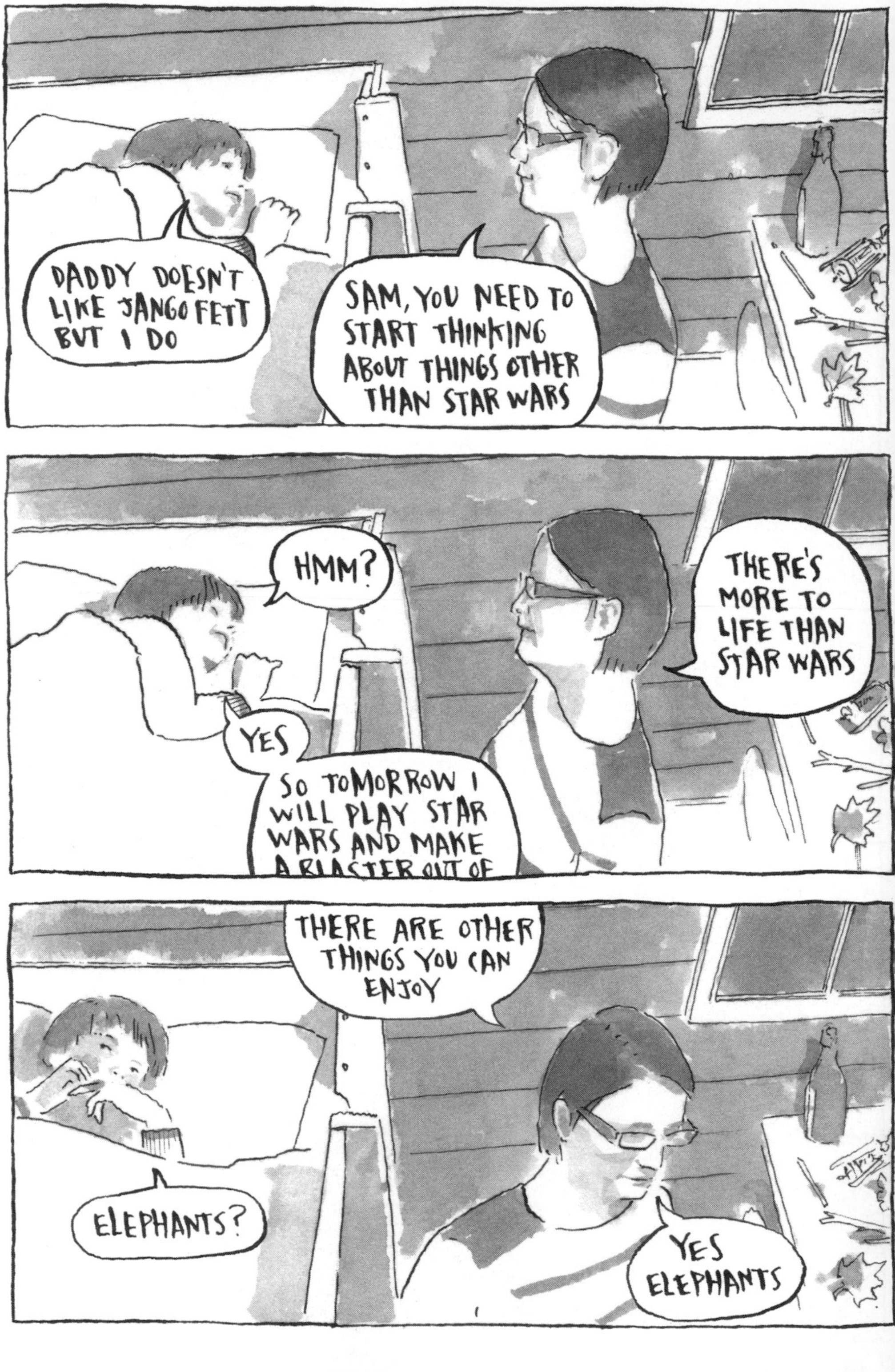
DADDY DOESN'T LIKE JANGO FETT BUT I DO
SAM, YOU NEED TO START THINKING ABOUT THINGS OTHER THAN STAR WARS
HMM?
THERE'S MORE TO LIFE THAN STAR WARS
YES
SO TOMORROW I WILL PLAY STAR WARS AND MAKE A BLASTER OUT OF
THERE ARE OTHER THINGS YOU CAN ENJOY
ELEPHANTS?
YES ELEPHANTS

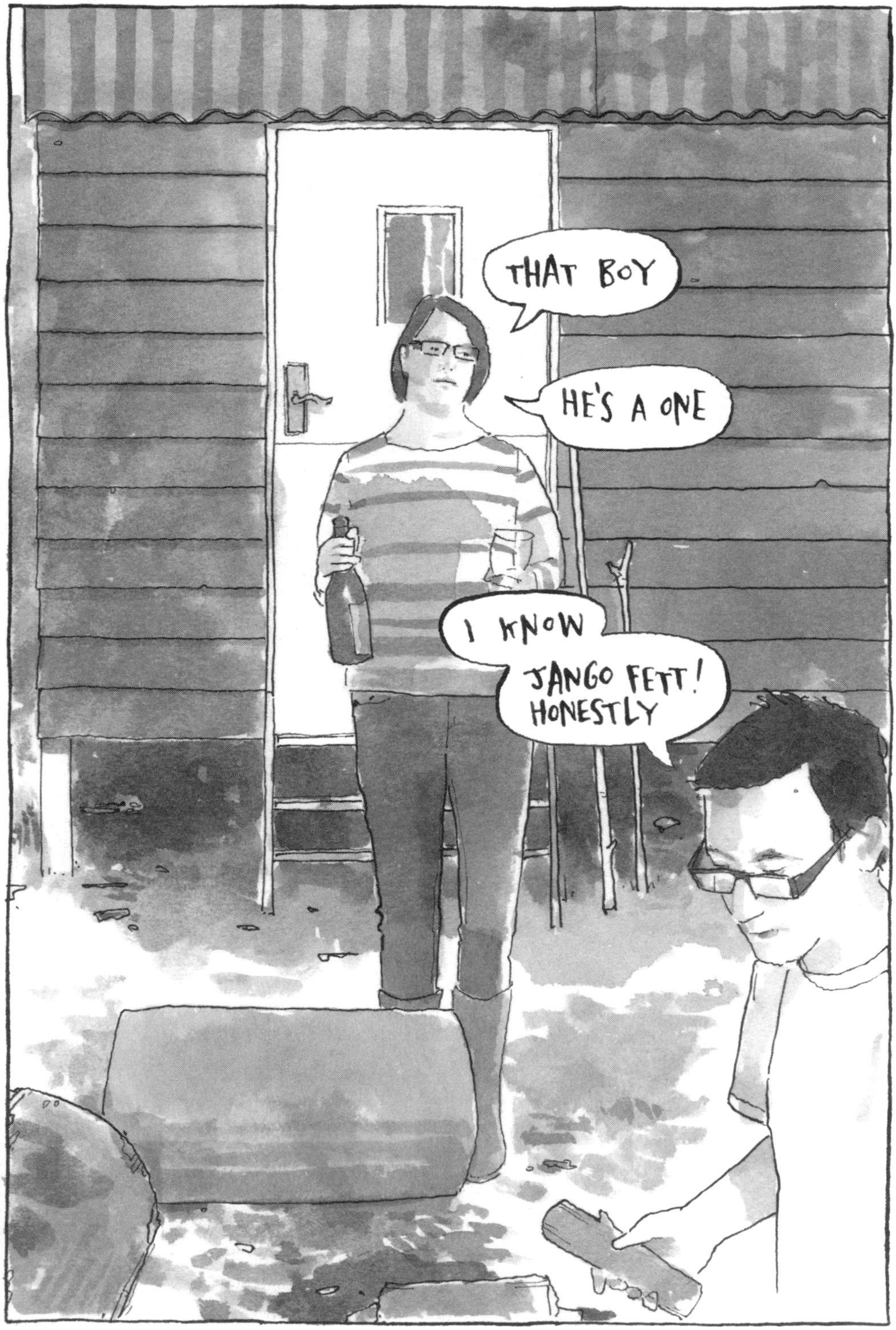
THAT BOY
HE'S A ONE
I KNOW
JANGO FETT! HONESTLY

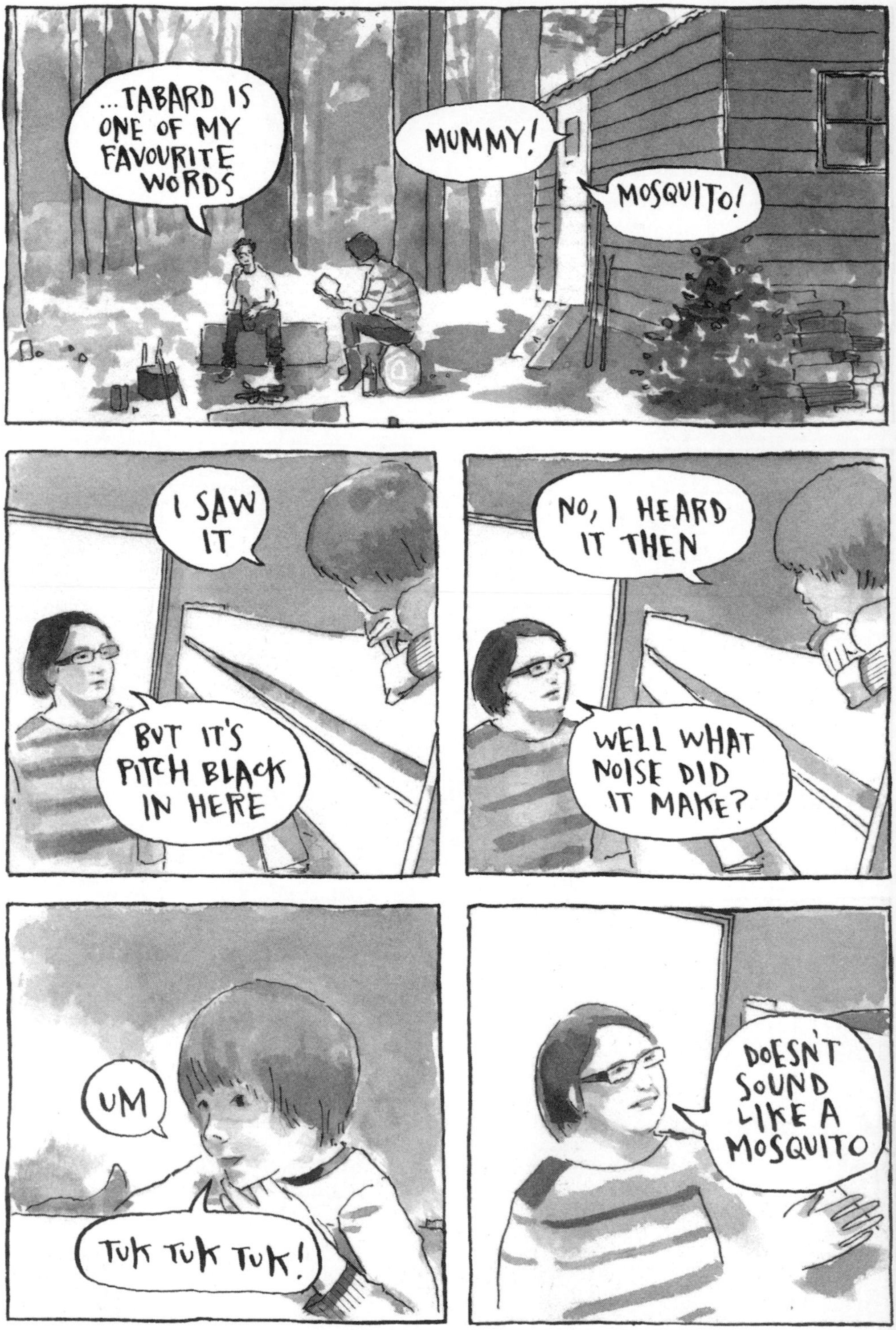
...TABARD IS ONE OF MY FAVOURITE WORDS
MUMMY!
MOSQUITO!
I SAW IT
BUT IT'S PITCH BLACK IN HERE
NO, I HEARD IT THEN
WELL WHAT NOISE DID IT MAKE?
UM
TUK TUK TUK!
DOESN'T SOUND LIKE A MOSQUITO

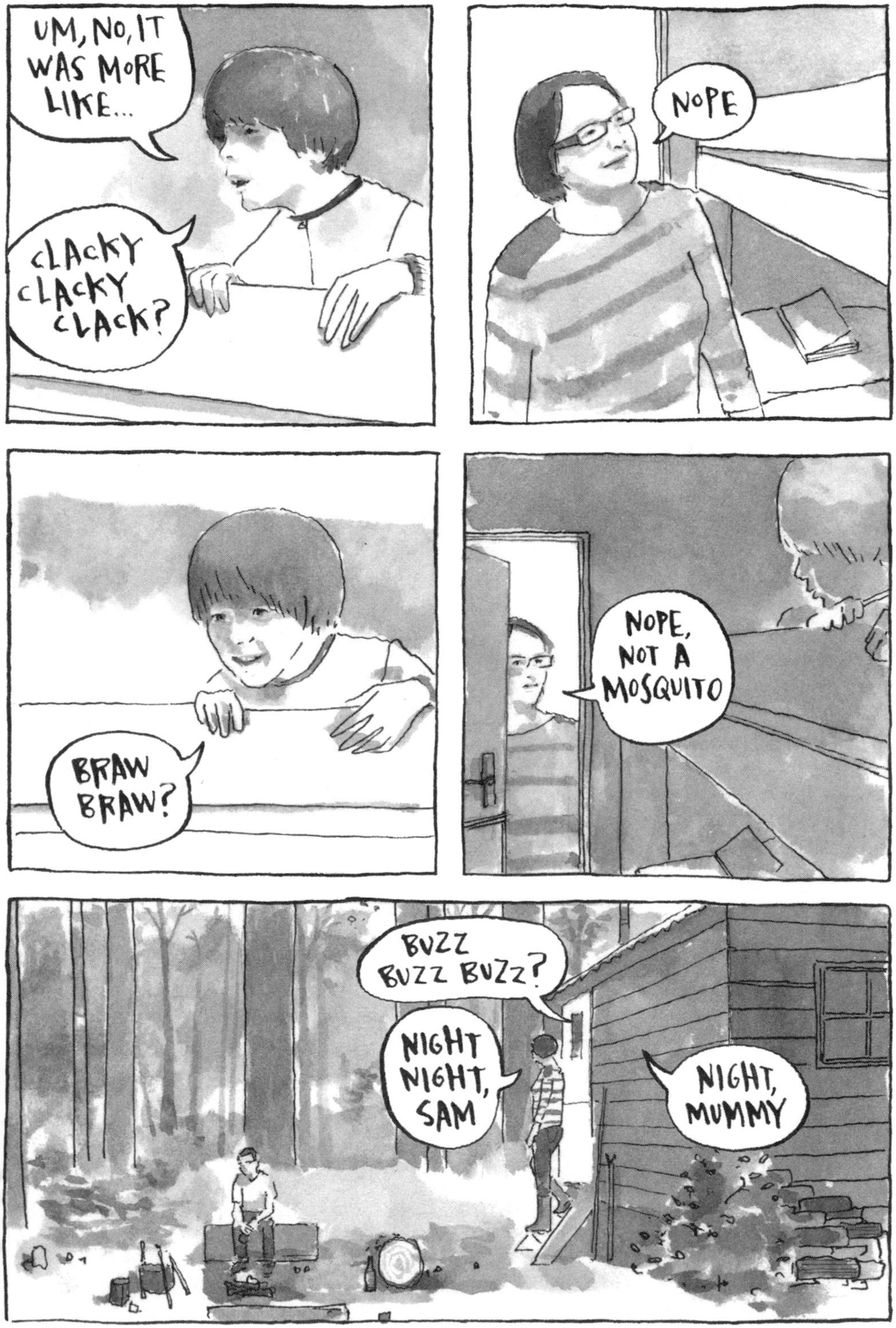
UM, NO, IT WAS MORE LIKE...
CLACKY CLACKY CLACK?
NOPE
BRAW BRAW?
NOPE, NOT A MOSQUITO
BUZZ BUZZ BUZZ?
NIGHT NIGHT, SAM
NIGHT, MUMMY

PEACE AND QUIET. VERY QUIET INDEED.

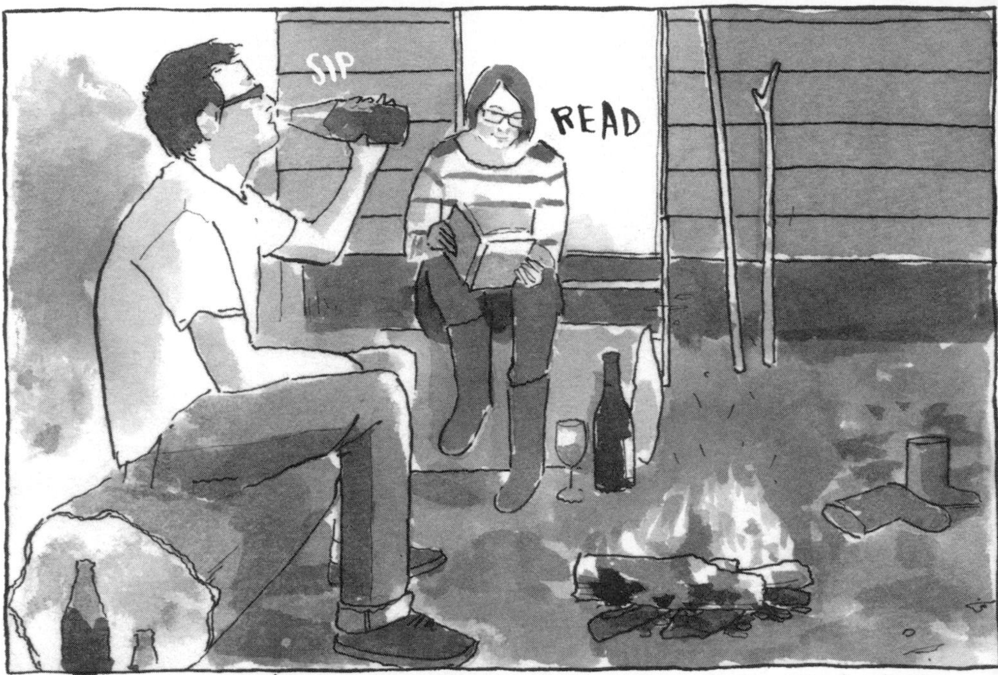
SIP
READ

BUT THEN WITHOUT ELECTRICITY IT GOES AND GETS DARK.
VERY DARK INDEED

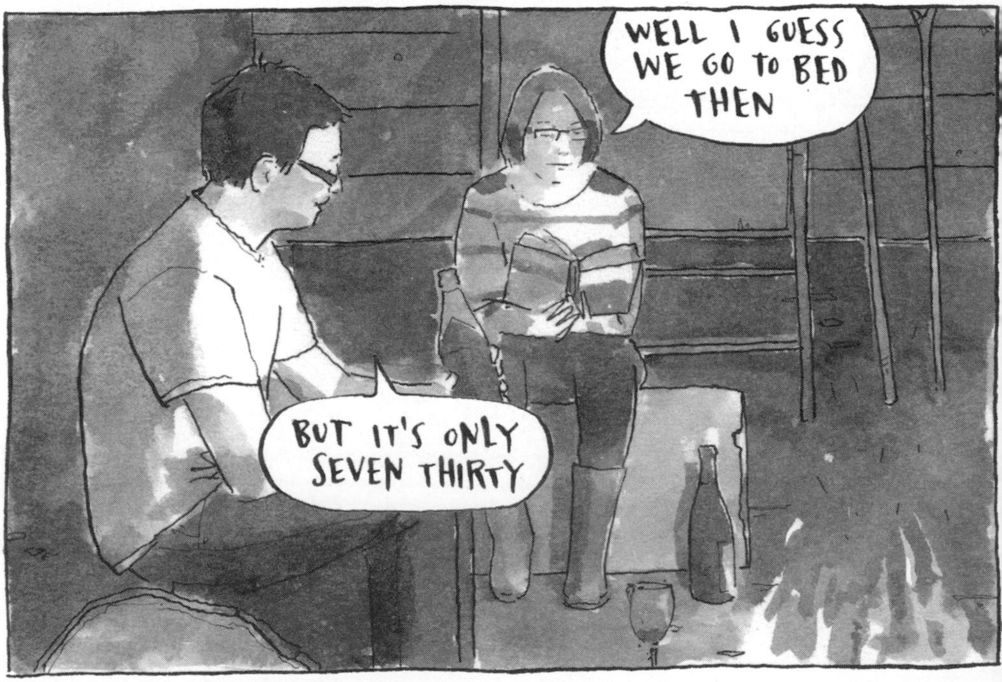
WELL I GUESS WE GO TO BED THEN
BUT IT'S ONLY SEVEN THIRTY

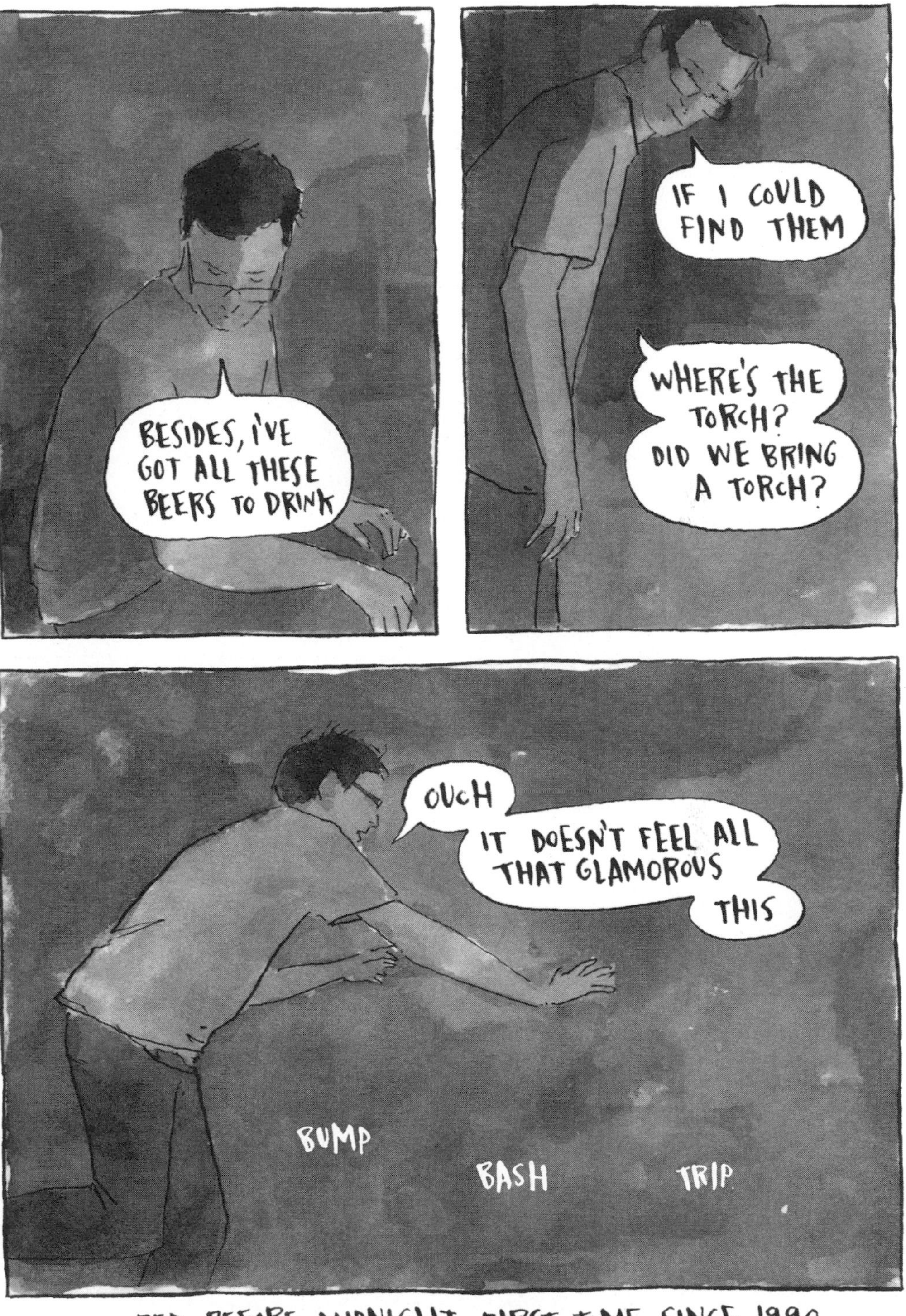
BESIDES, I'VE GOT ALL THESE BEERS TO DRINK
IF I COULD FIND THEM
WHERE'S THE TORCH? DID WE BRING A TORCH?
OUCH
IT DOESN'T FEEL ALL THAT GLAMOROUS
THIS
BUMP
BASH
TRIP

BED BEFORE MIDNIGHT. FIRST TIME SINCE 1990.

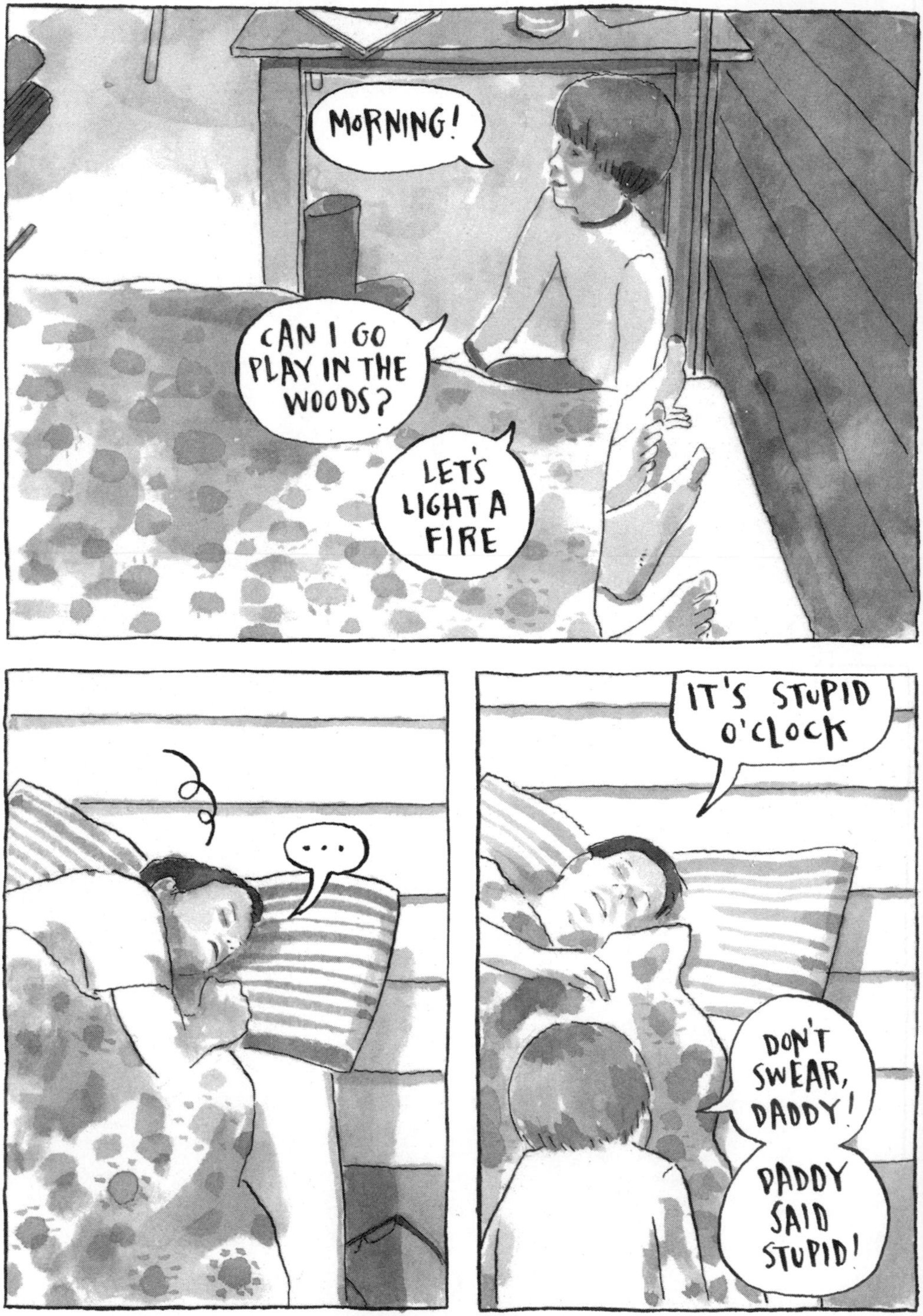
MORNING!
CAN I GO PLAY IN THE WOODS?
LET'S LIGHT A FIRE
...
IT'S STUPID O'CLOCK
DON'T SWEAR, DADDY!
DADDY SAID STUPID!

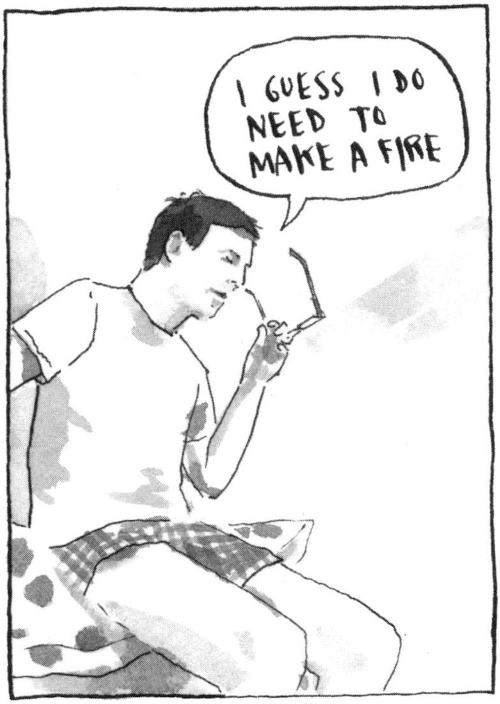
I GUESS I DO NEED TO MAKE A FIRE

NO FIRE
MEANS NO TEA

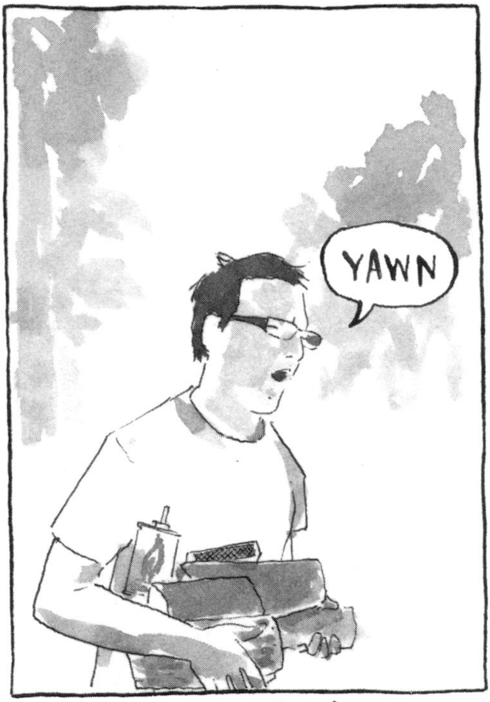
YAWN

AND NO TEA
IS NOT AN OPTION

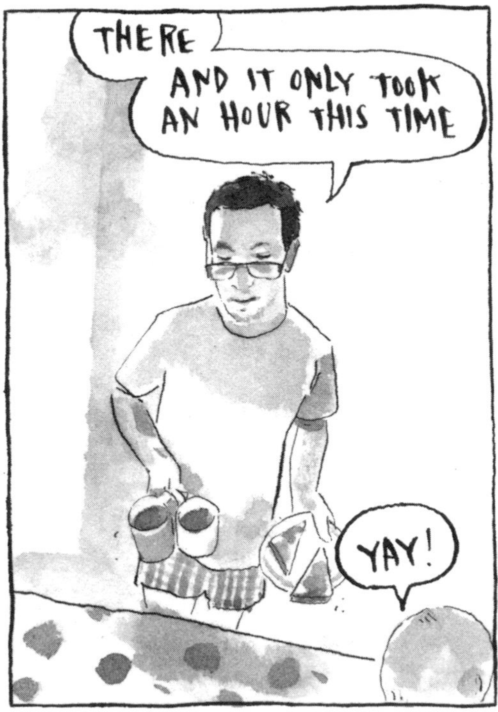
THERE
AND IT ONLY TOOK AN HOUR THIS TIME
YAY!

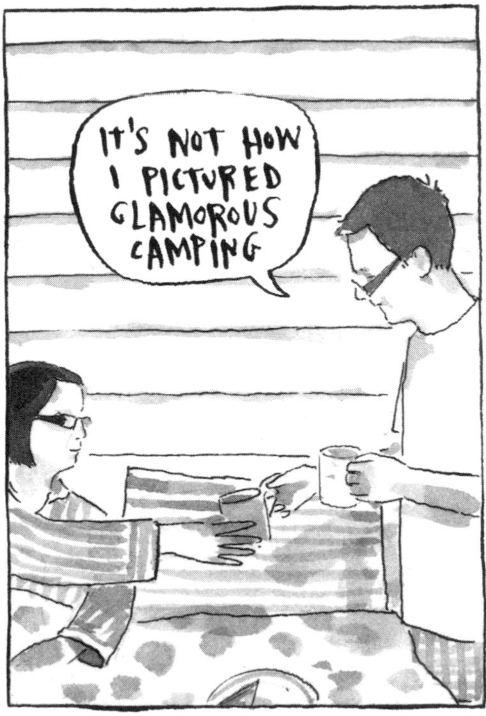
IT'S NOT HOW I PICTURED GLAMOROUS CAMPING

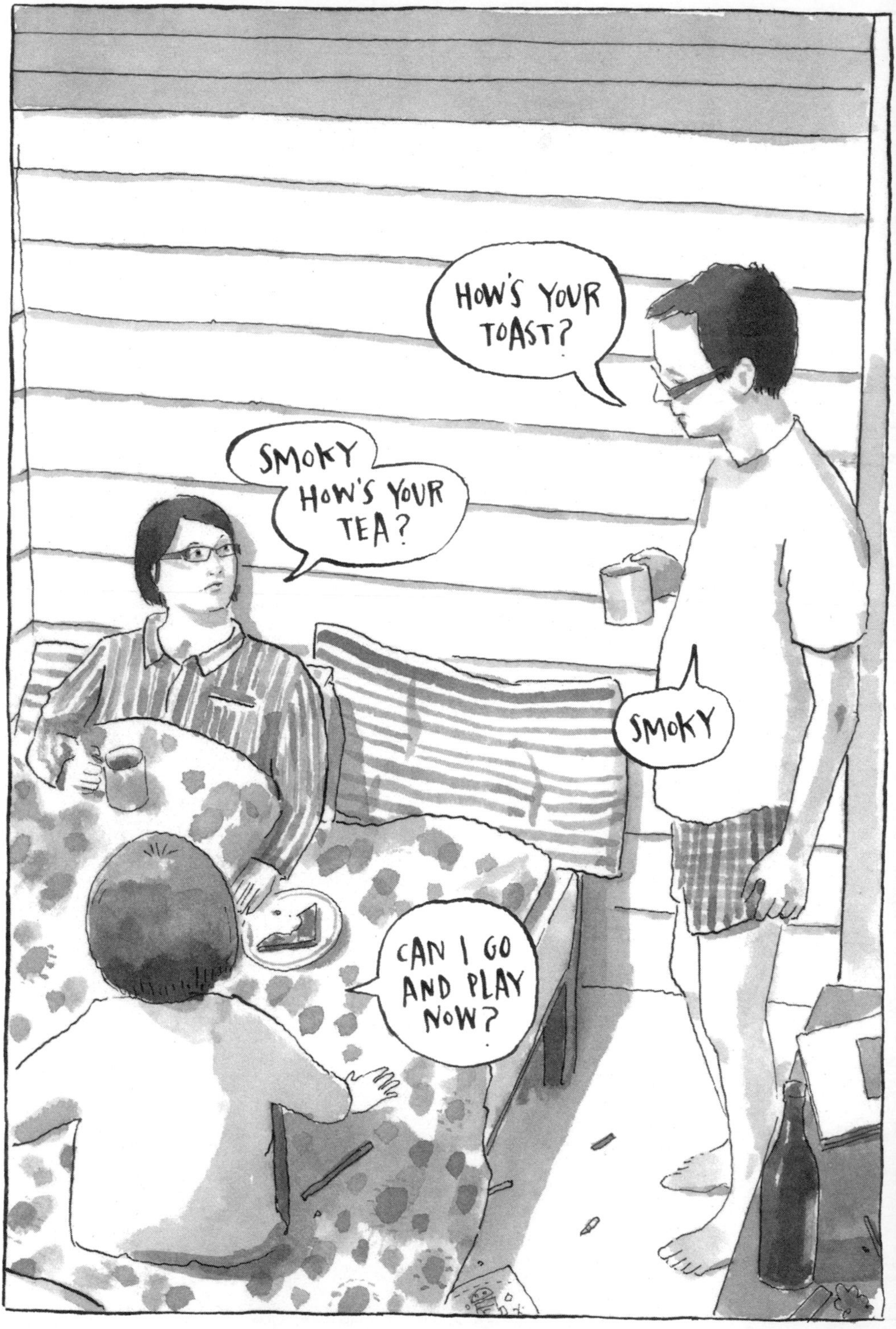
HOW'S YOUR TOAST?
SMOKY HOW'S YOUR TEA?
SMOKY
CAN I GO AND PLAY NOW?

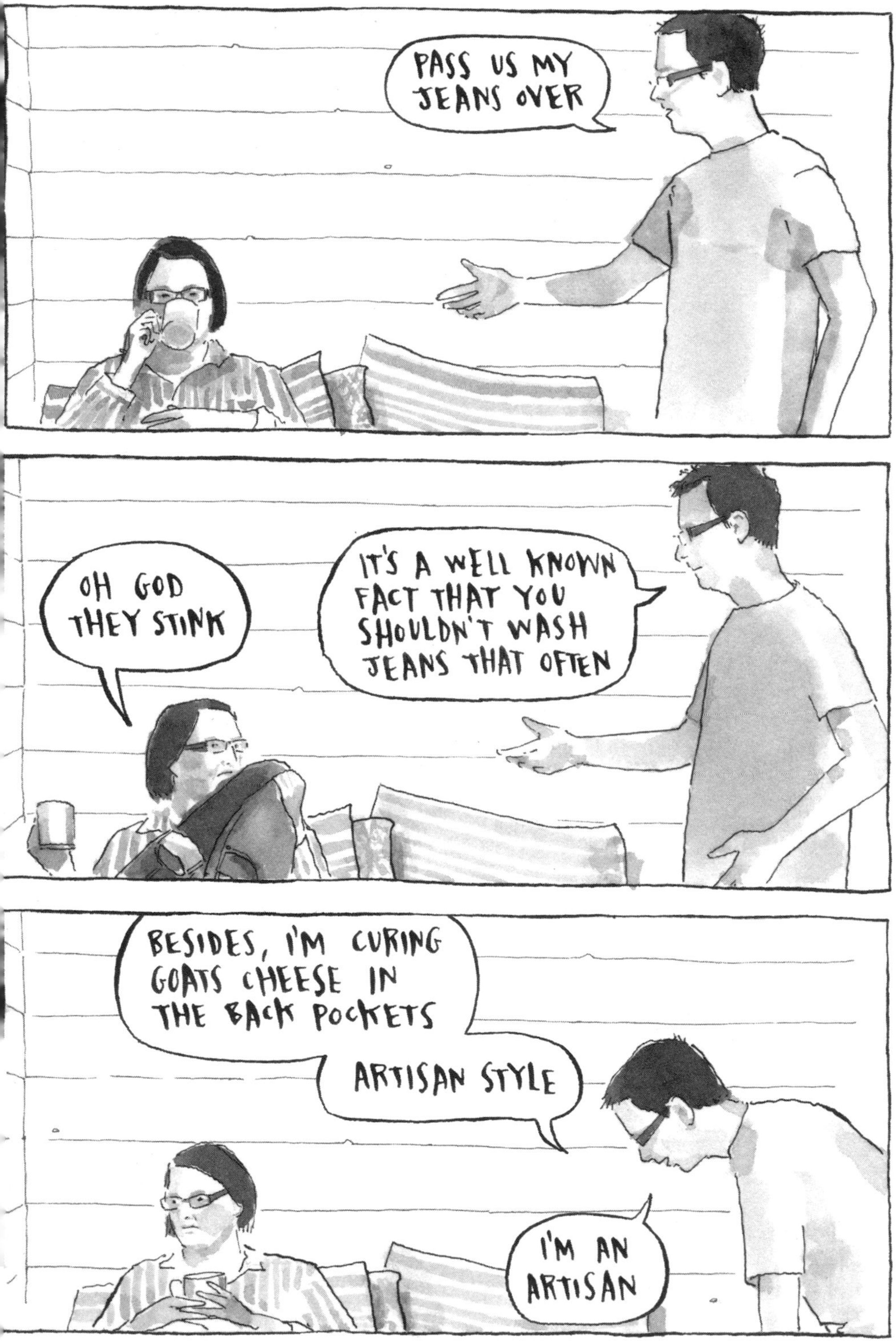
PASS US MY JEANS OVER
OH GOD THEY STINK
IT'S A WELL KNOWN FACT THAT YOU SHOULDN'T WASH JEANS THAT OFTEN
BESIDES, I'M CURING GOATS CHEESE IN THE BACK POCKETS
ARTISAN STYLE
I'M AN ARTISAN

IN OUR FAMILY, WE TRY TO STAY ITCHY.
WE'VE RUN OUT OF SCABIES MITES
AND MY ECZEMA SEEMS TO HAVE CLEARED UP
YOU CAN'T BEAT A GOOD SCRATCH, EH?
WE'LL HAVE TO FIND SOMETHING ELSE
IT'S FINE I'LL FORAGE... HUNT AND GATHER
OOH ANTS
AND POISON OAK
IT'S A HOBBY
A CHEAP HOBBY

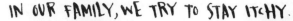

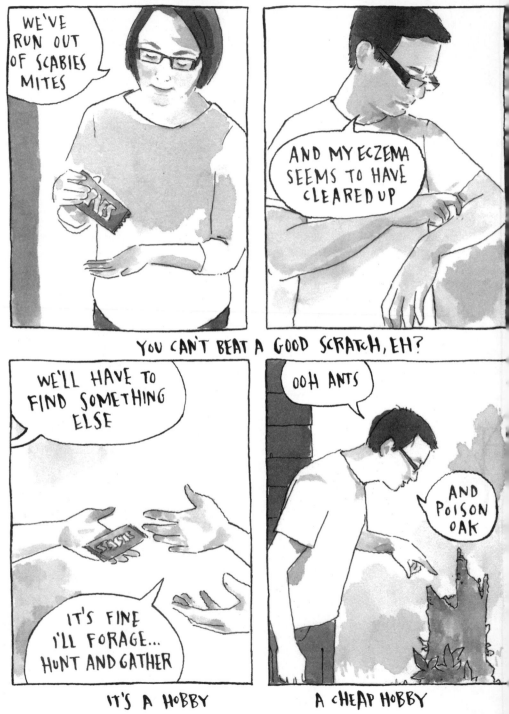

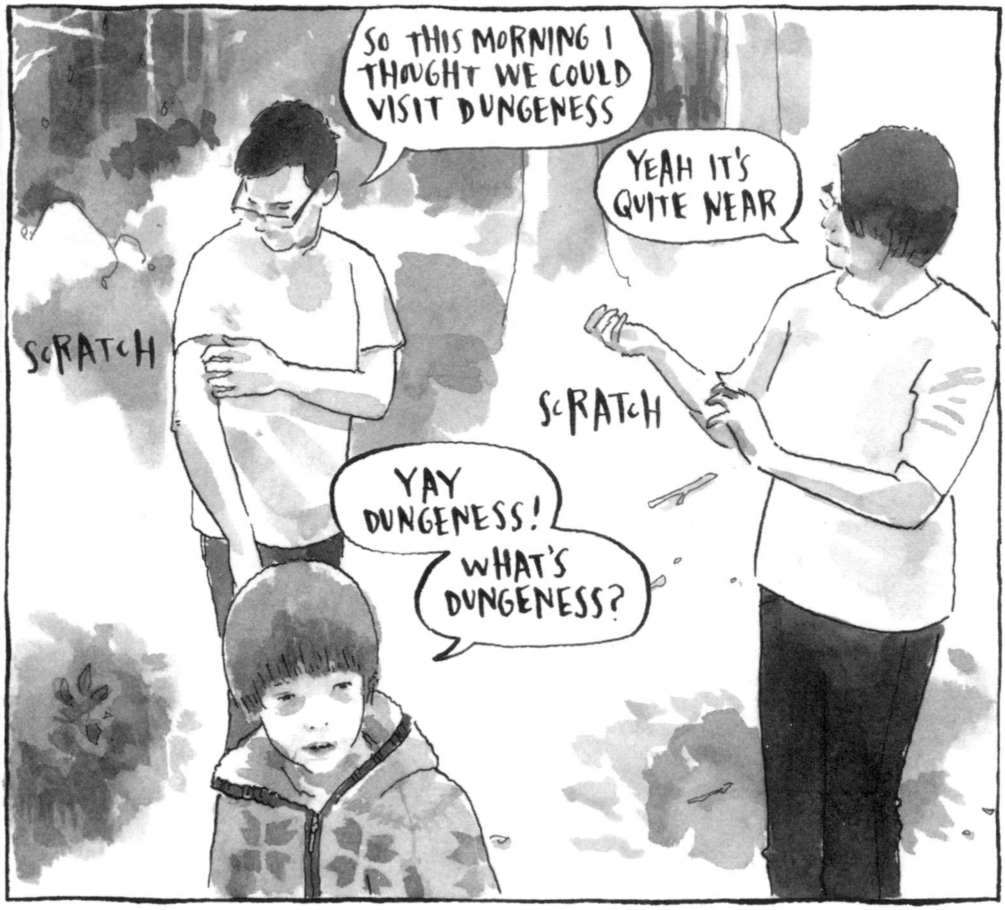
SO THIS MORNING I THOUGHT WE COULD VISIT DUNGENESS
YEAH IT'S QUITE NEAR
SCRATCH
SCRATCH
YAY DUNGENESS!
WHAT'S DUNGENESS?

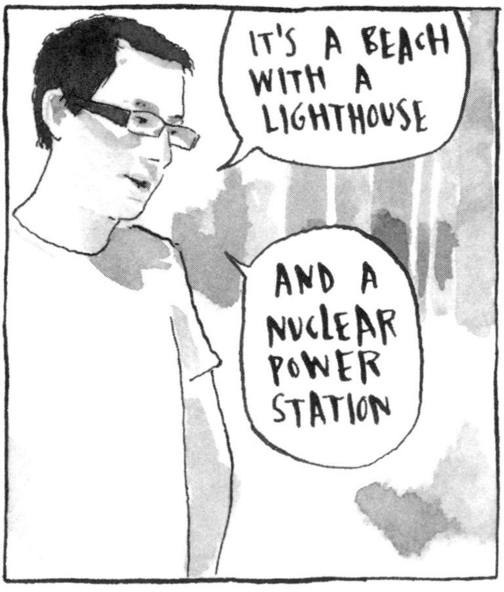
IT'S A BEACH WITH A LIGHTHOUSE
AND A NUCLEAR POWER STATION

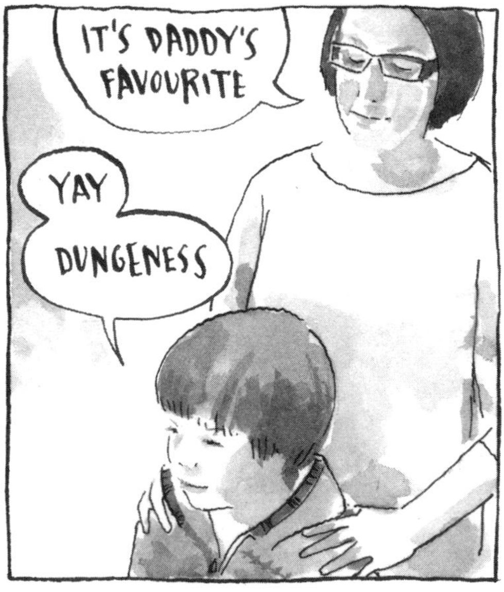
IT'S DADDY'S FAVOURITE
YAY
DUNGENESS

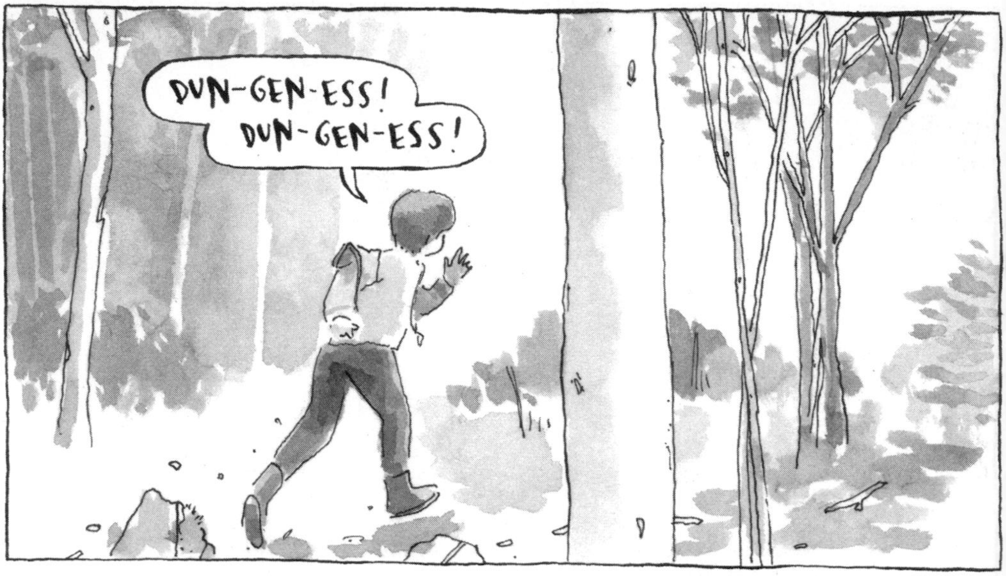
DUN-GEN-ESS! DUN-GEN-ESS!

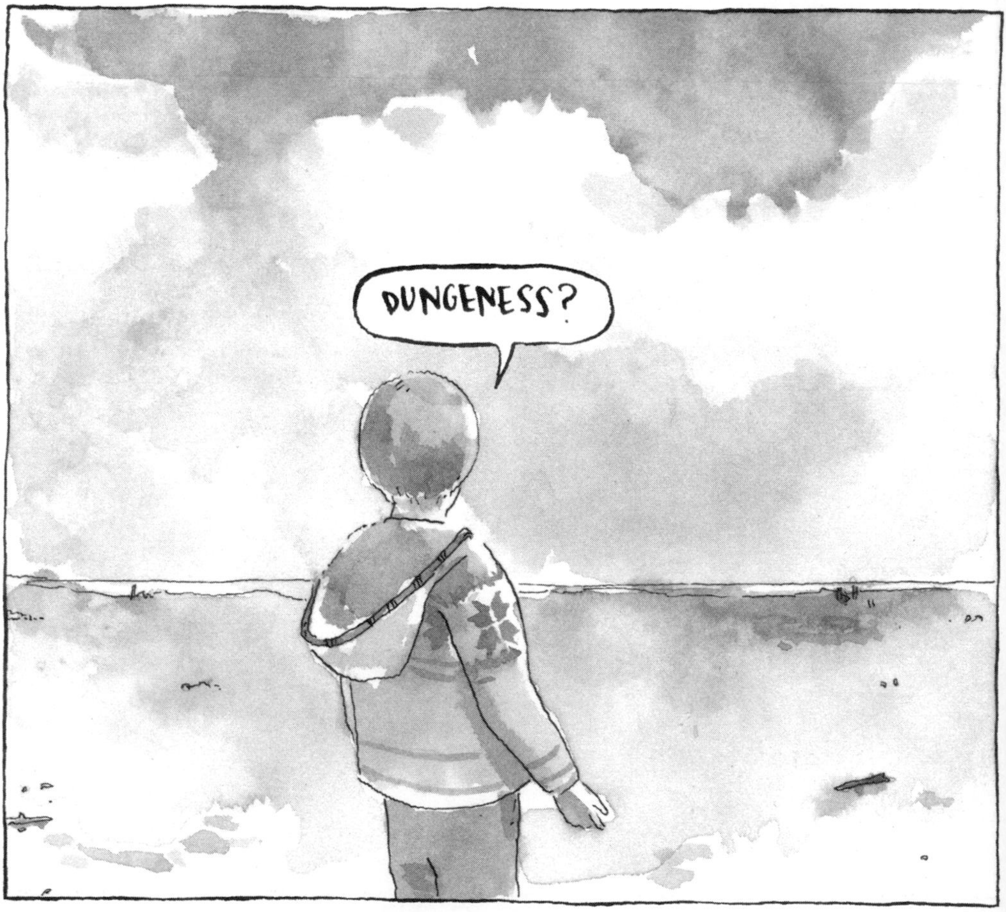
DUNGENESS?

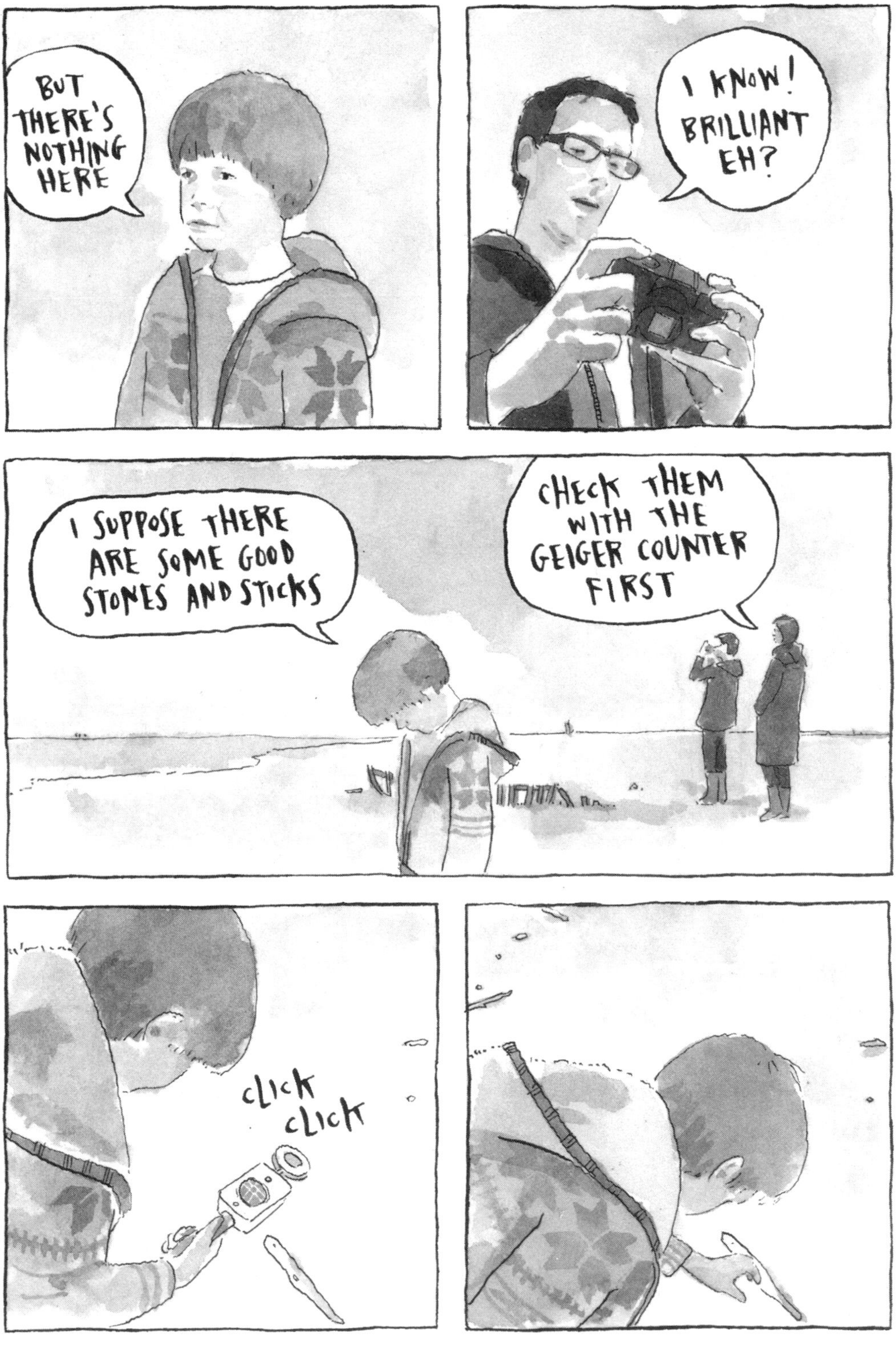
BUT THERE'S NOTHING HERE
I KNOW! BRILLIANT EH?
I SUPPOSE THERE ARE SOME GOOD STONES AND STICKS
CHECK THEM WITH THE GEIGER COUNTER FIRST
CLICK CLICK

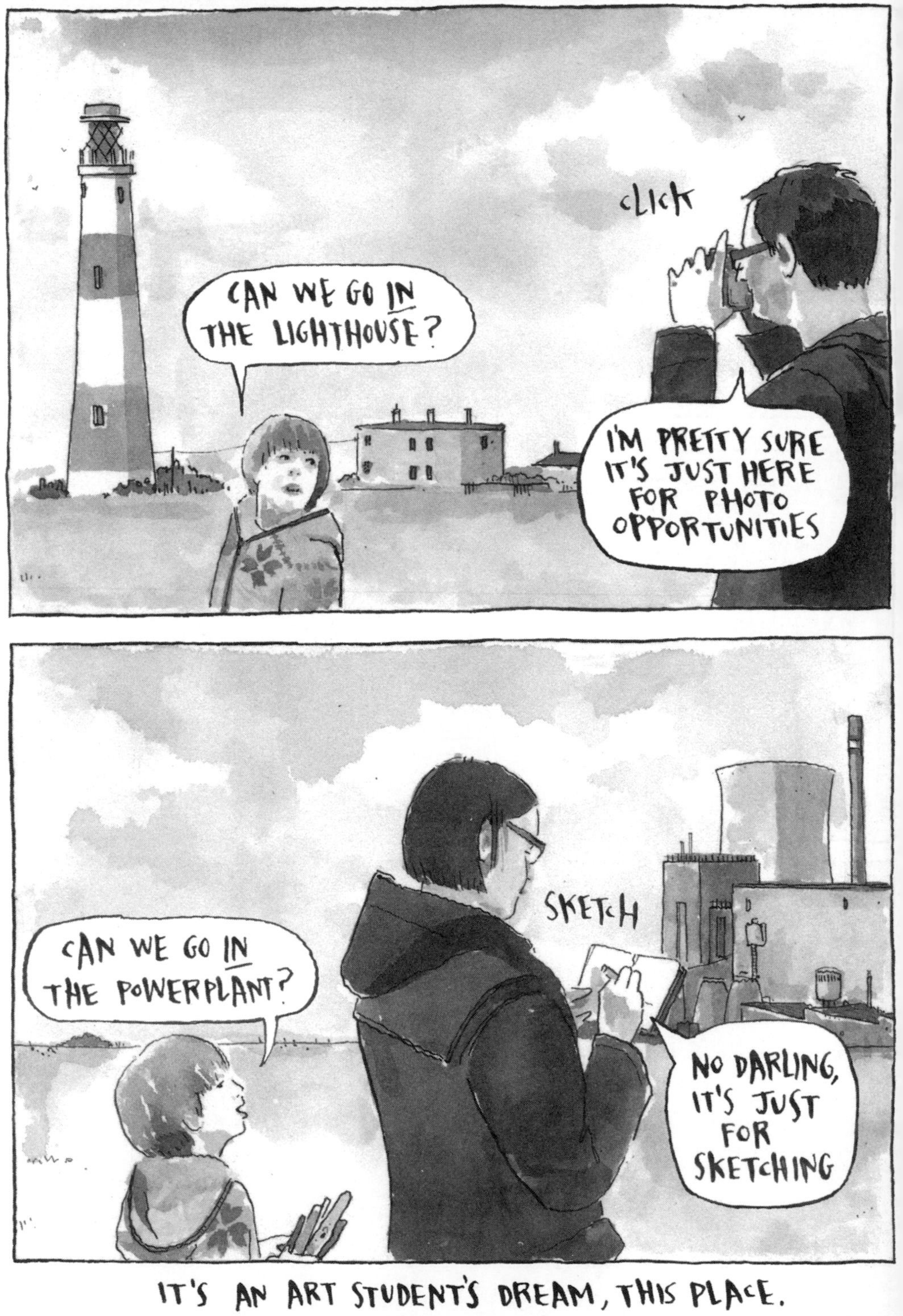
CAN WE GO IN THE LIGHTHOUSE?
CLICK
I'M PRETTY SURE IT'S JUST HERE FOR PHOTO OPPORTUNITIES
SKETCH
CAN WE GO IN THE POWERPLANT?
NO DARLING, IT'S JUST FOR SKETCHING

IT'S AN ART STUDENT'S DREAM, THIS PLACE.

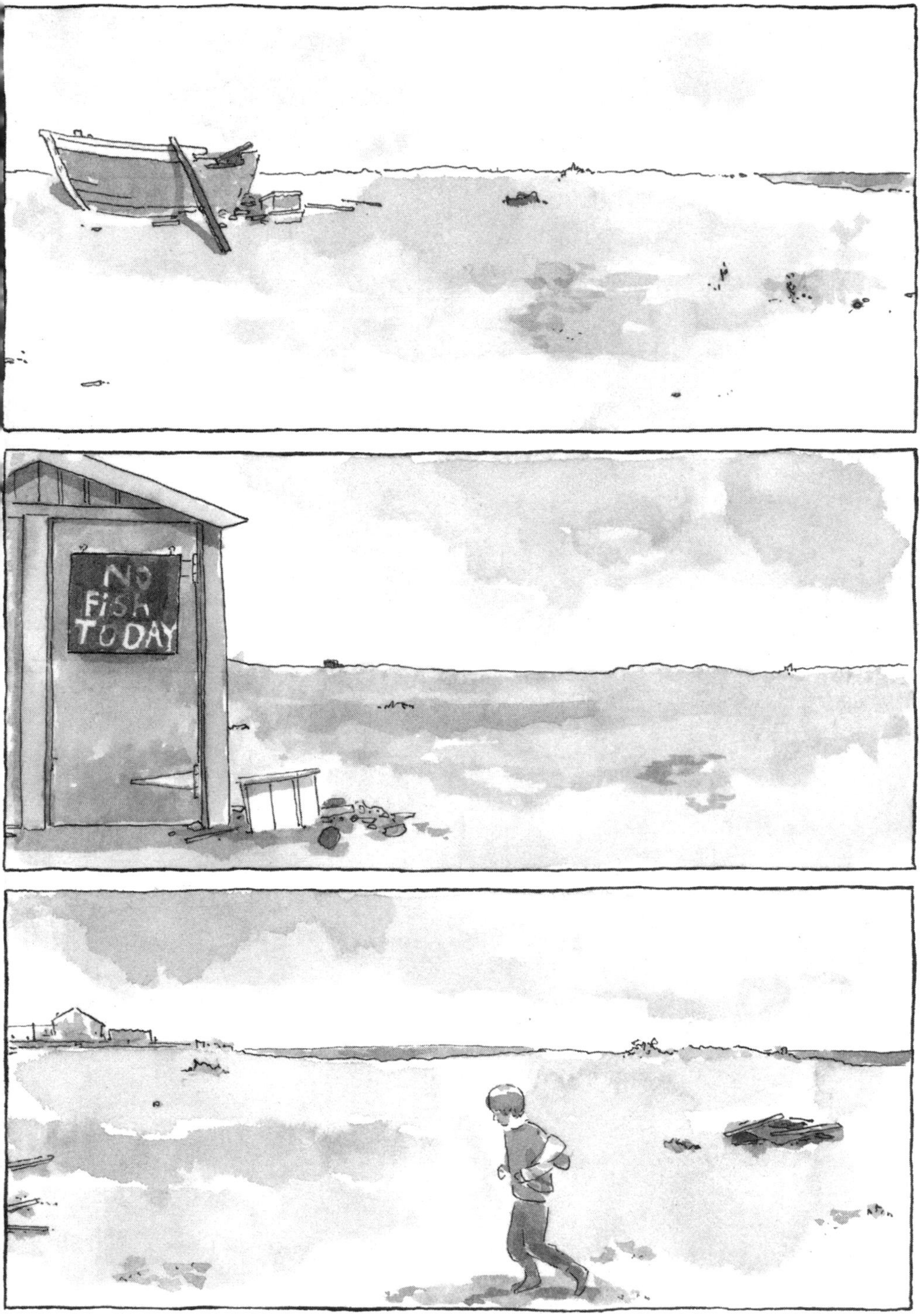
NO FISH TODAY

YOU SHOULD GOOGLE IT

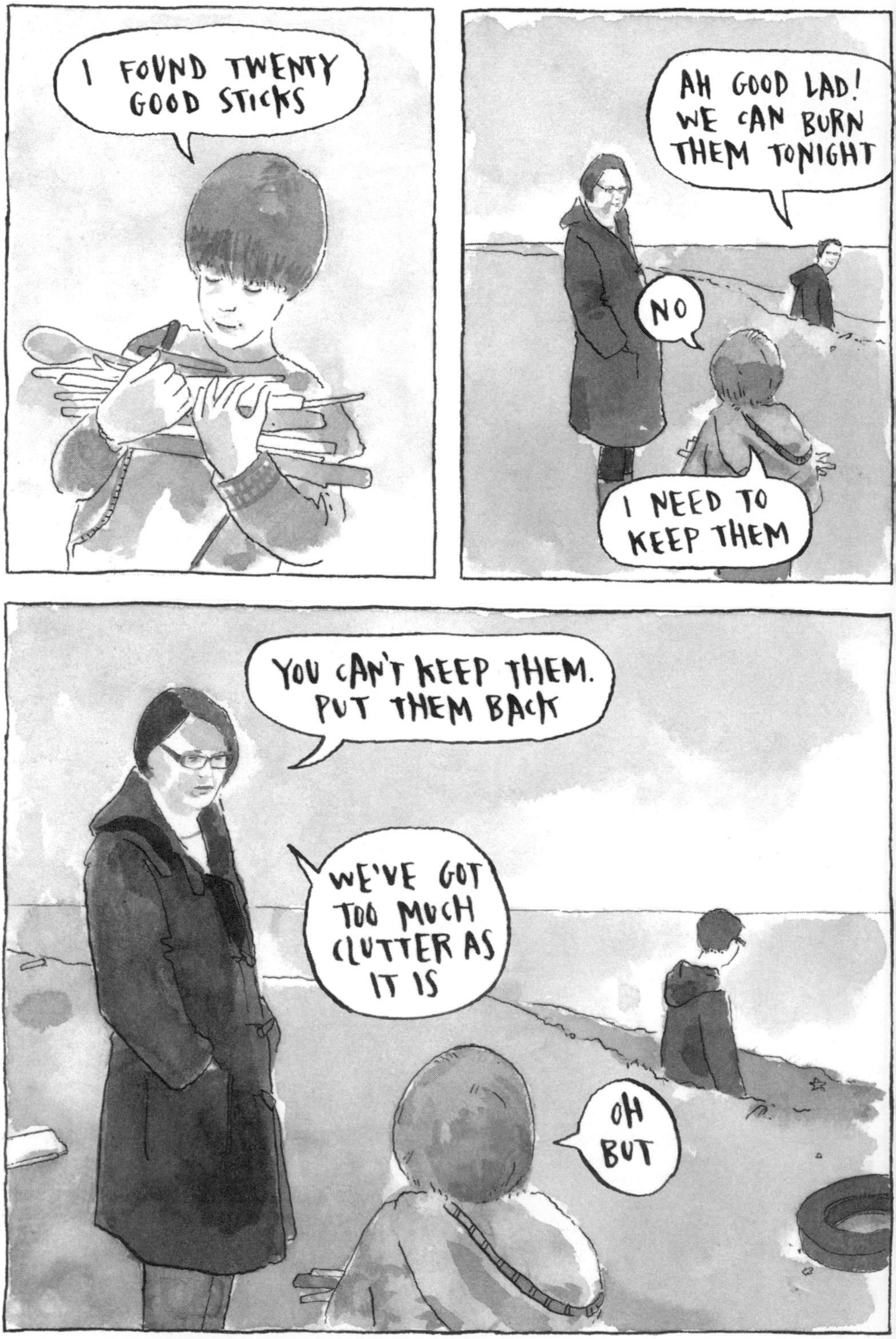
I FOUND TWENTY GOOD STICKS
AH GOOD LAD! WE CAN BURN THEM TONIGHT
NO
I NEED TO KEEP THEM
YOU CAN'T KEEP THEM. PUT THEM BACK
WE'VE GOT TOO MUCH CLUTTER AS IT IS
OH BUT

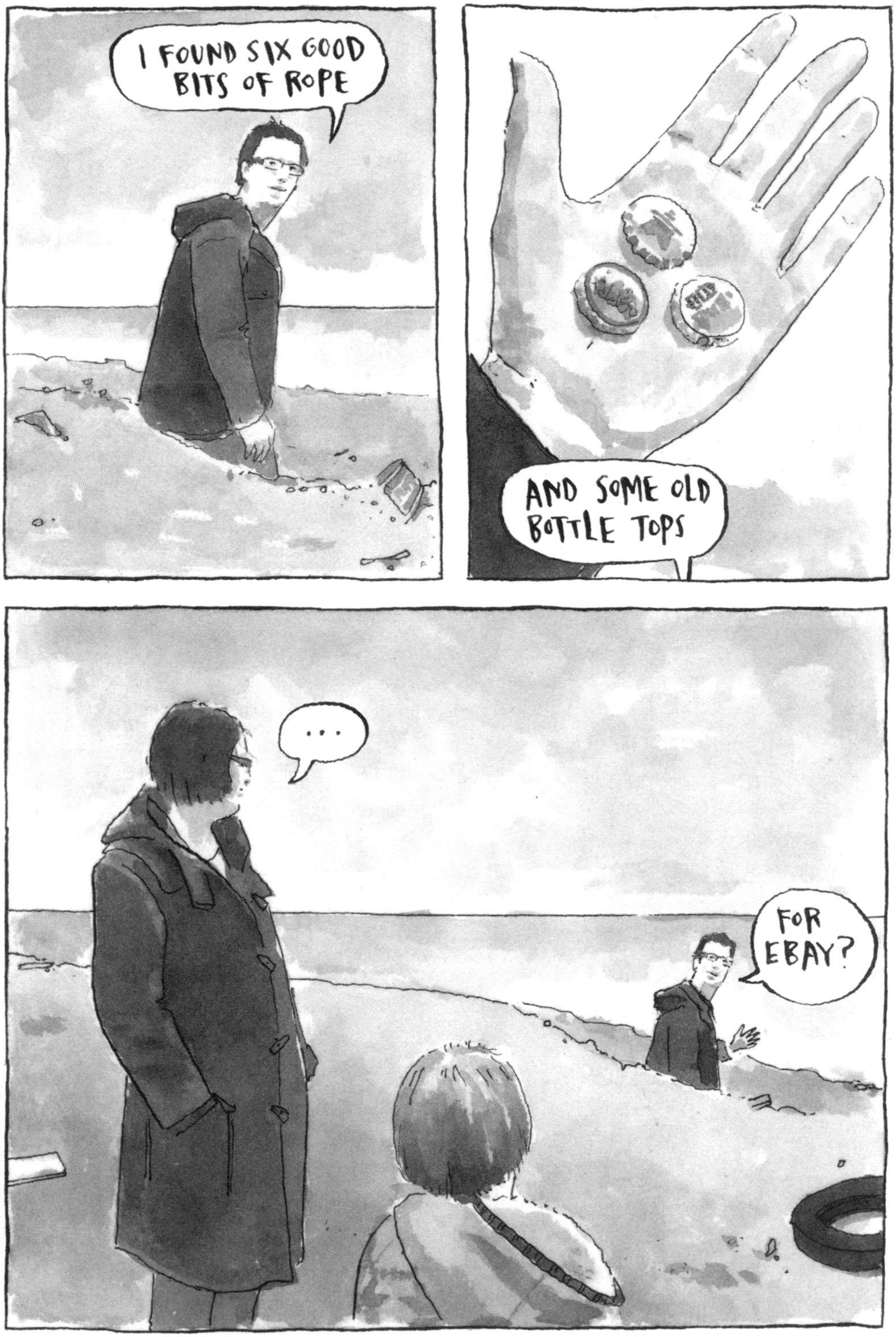
I FOUND SIX GOOD BITS OF ROPE
AND SOME OLD BOTTLE TOPS
...
FOR EBAY?

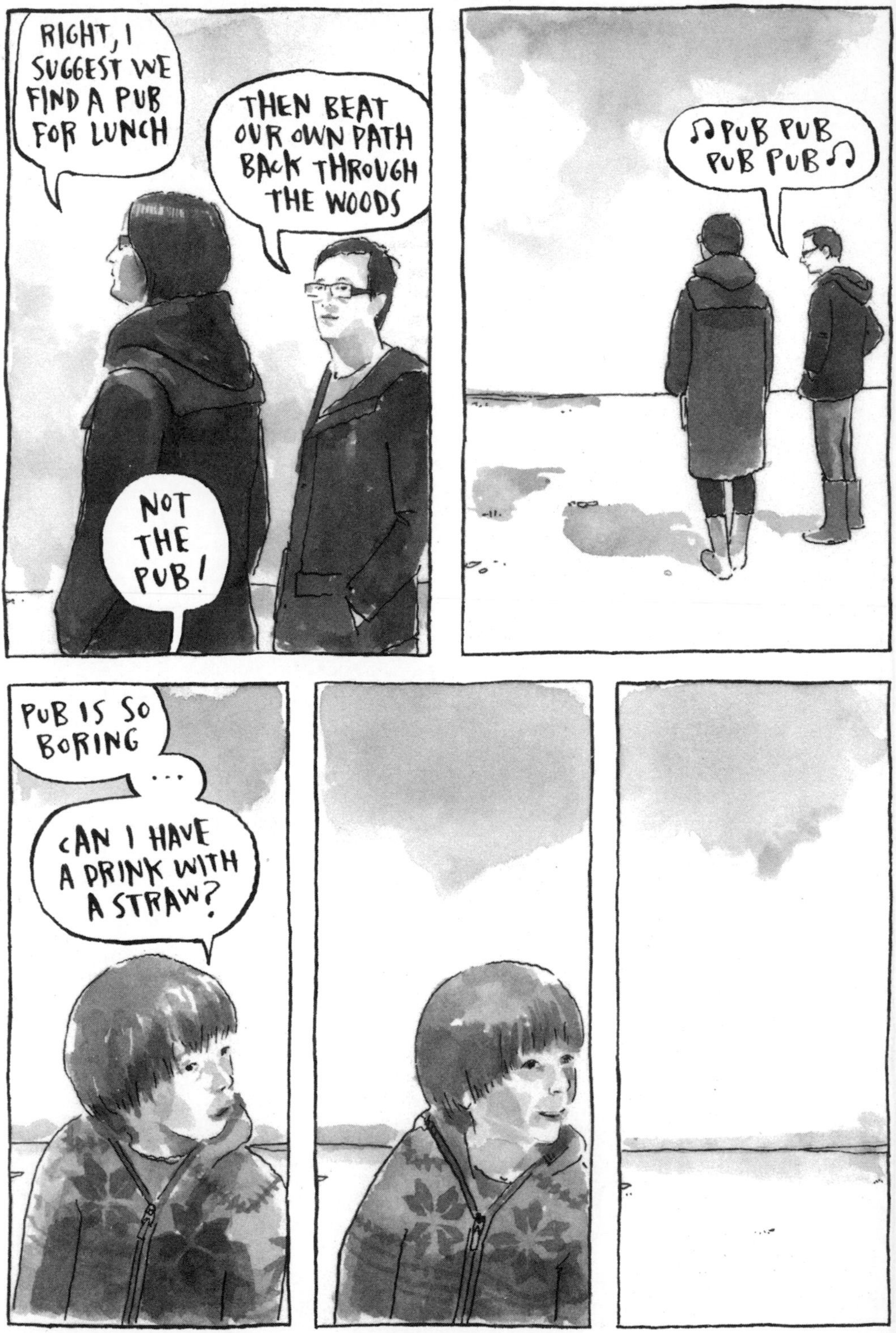
RIGHT, I SUGGEST WE FIND A PUB FOR LUNCH
THEN BEAT OUR OWN PATH BACK THROUGH THE WOODS
NOT THE PUB!
♫ PUB PUB PUB PUB ♫
PUB IS SO BORING
...
CAN I HAVE A DRINK WITH A STRAW?

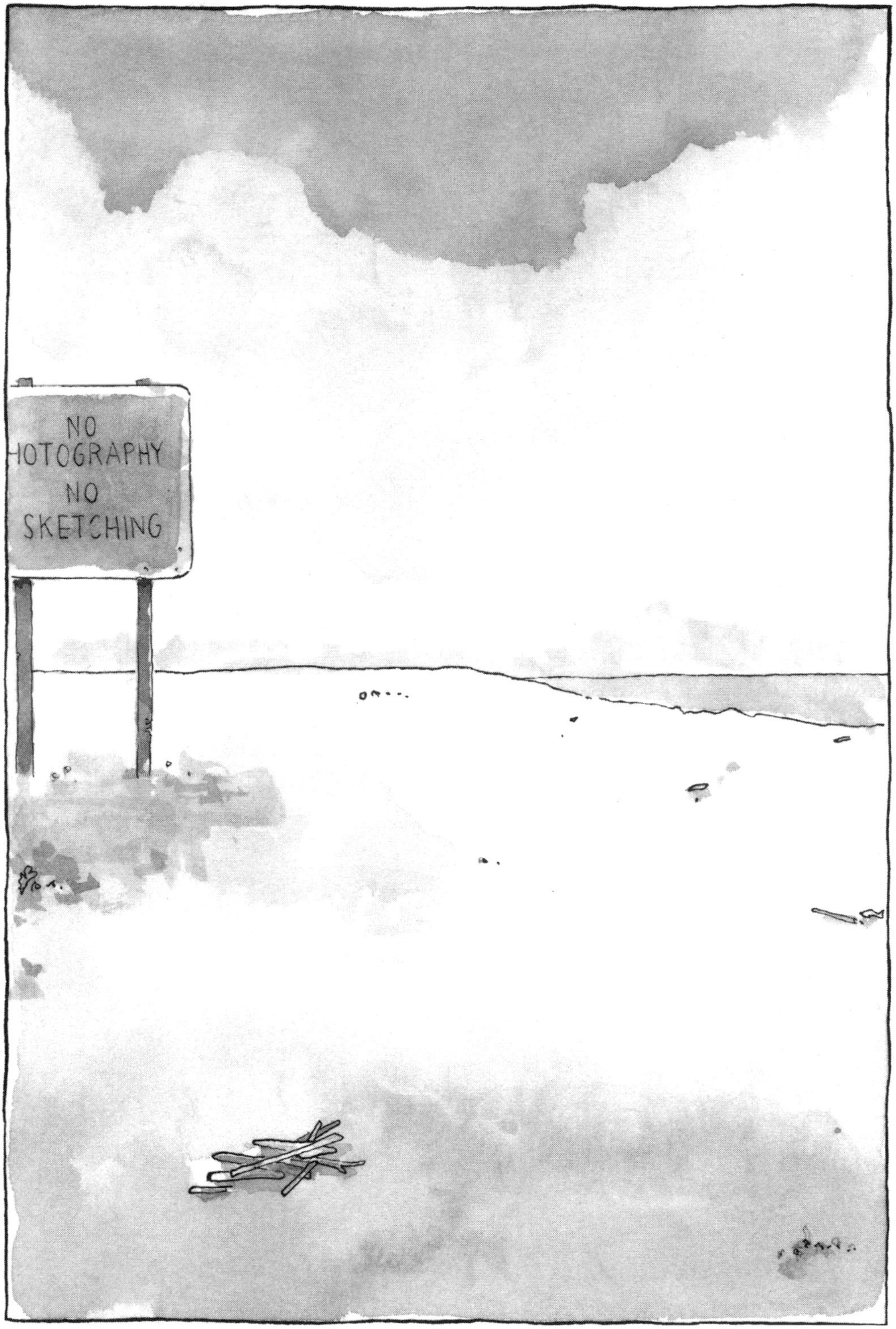
NO
HOTOGRAPHY
NO
SKETCHING

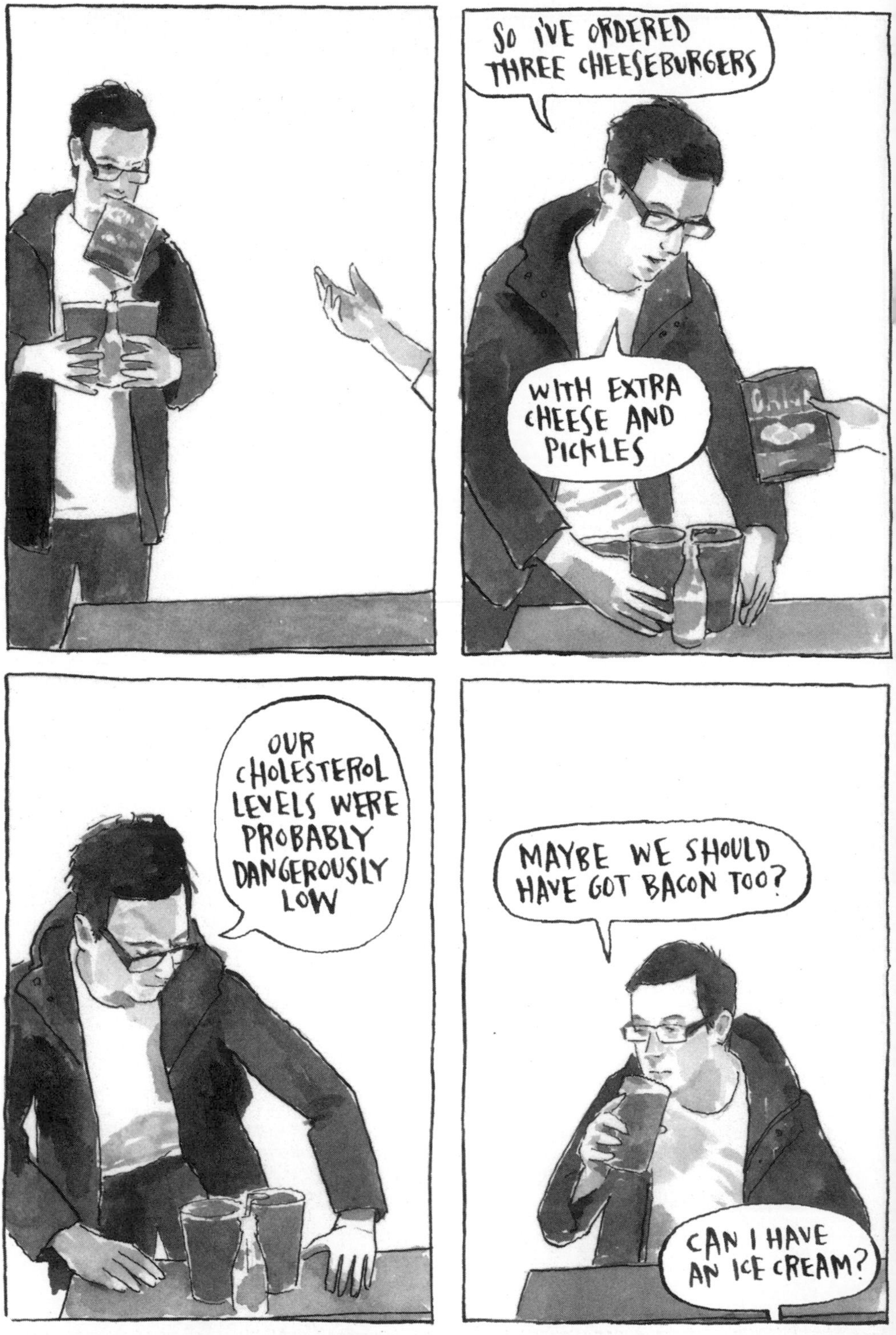
SO I'VE ORDERED THREE CHEESEBURGERS
WITH EXTRA CHEESE AND PICKLES
OUR CHOLESTEROL LEVELS WERE PROBABLY DANGEROUSLY LOW
MAYBE WE SHOULD HAVE GOT BACON TOO?
CAN I HAVE AN ICE CREAM?

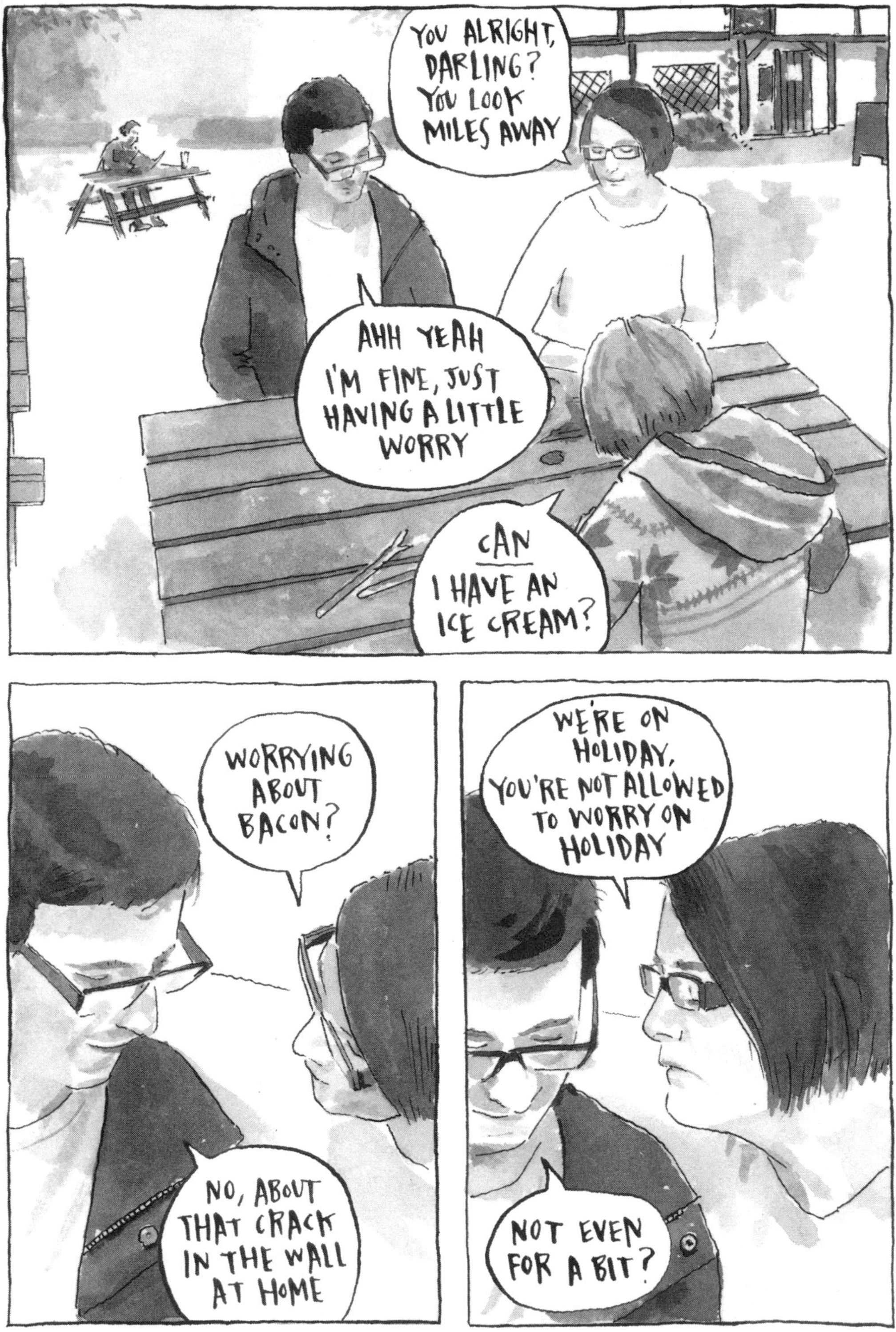
YOU ALRIGHT, DARLING? YOU LOOK MILES AWAY
AHH YEAH I'M FINE, JUST HAVING A LITTLE WORRY
CAN I HAVE AN ICE CREAM?
WORRYING ABOUT BACON?
NO, ABOUT THAT CRACK IN THE WALL AT HOME
WE'RE ON HOLIDAY, YOU'RE NOT ALLOWED TO WORRY ON HOLIDAY
NOT EVEN FOR A BIT?

I'M VERY GOOD AT WORRYING.
I CAN TURN A LITTLE WORRY INTO A MONSTER IN MERE MOMENTS.

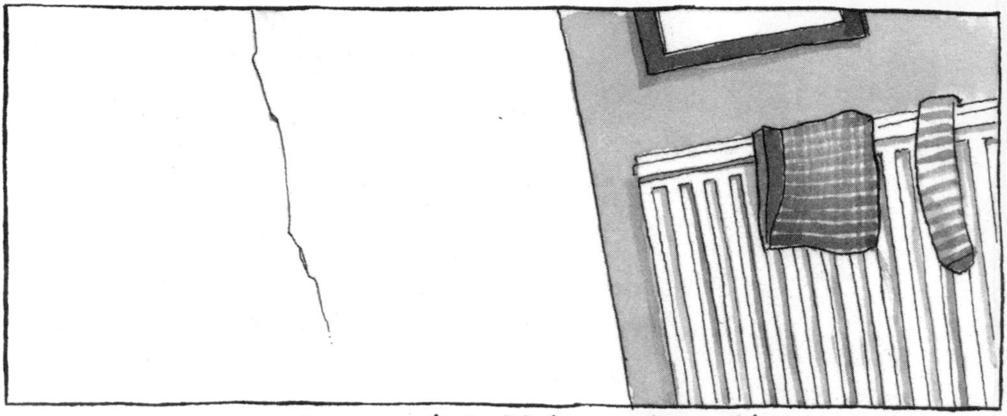

FOR INSTANCE, THIS CRACK IN THE WALL...

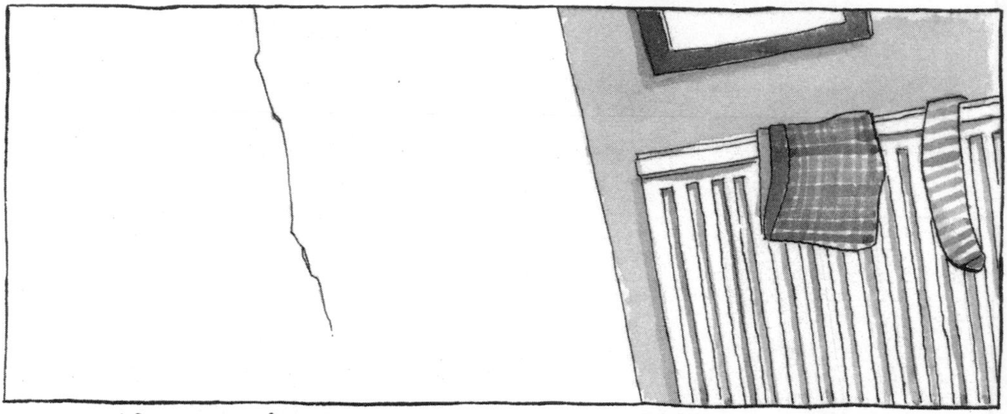

...IT'S BEEN THERE FOR YEARS. IT'S PROBABLY NOTHING.

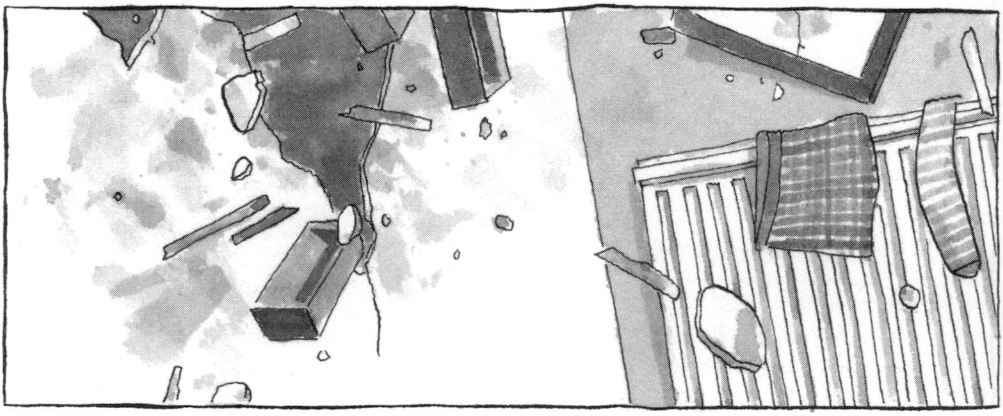

BUT WHAT IF IT'S NOT?

IT'S EASY, I'M AN EXPERT AT IT.

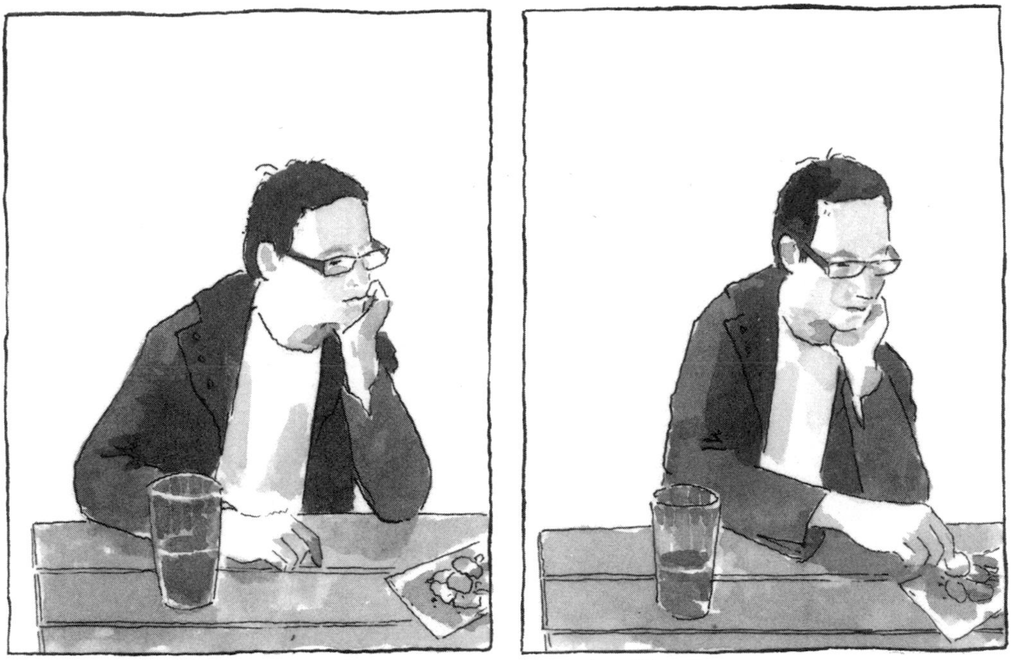

YOU SHOULD GIVE IT A TRY.

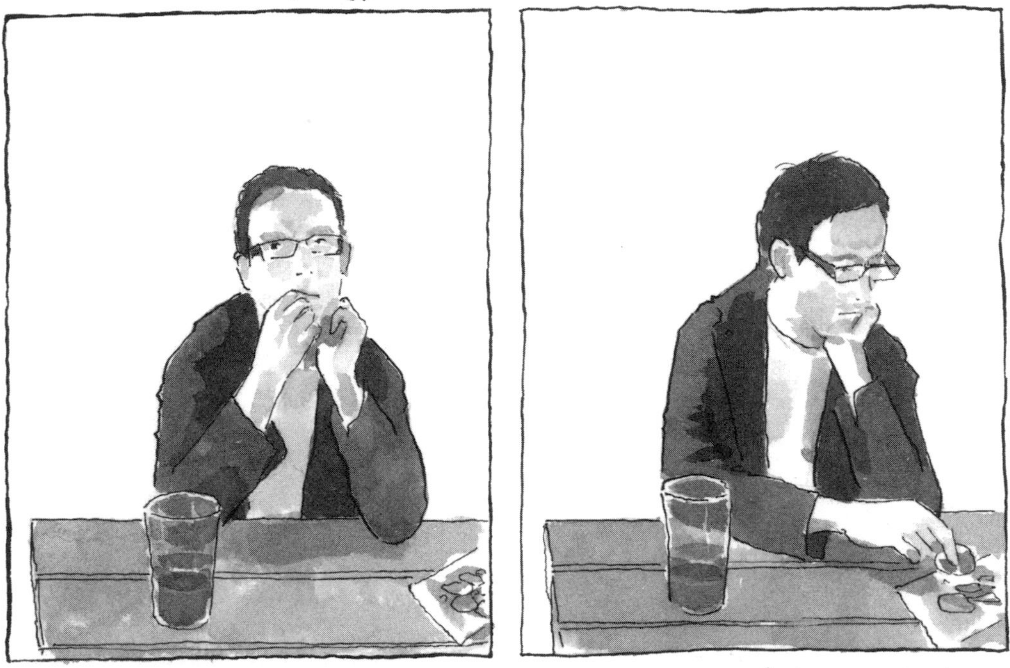

STOP READING THIS FOR A BIT, AND HAVE A GO, HAVE A WORRY.

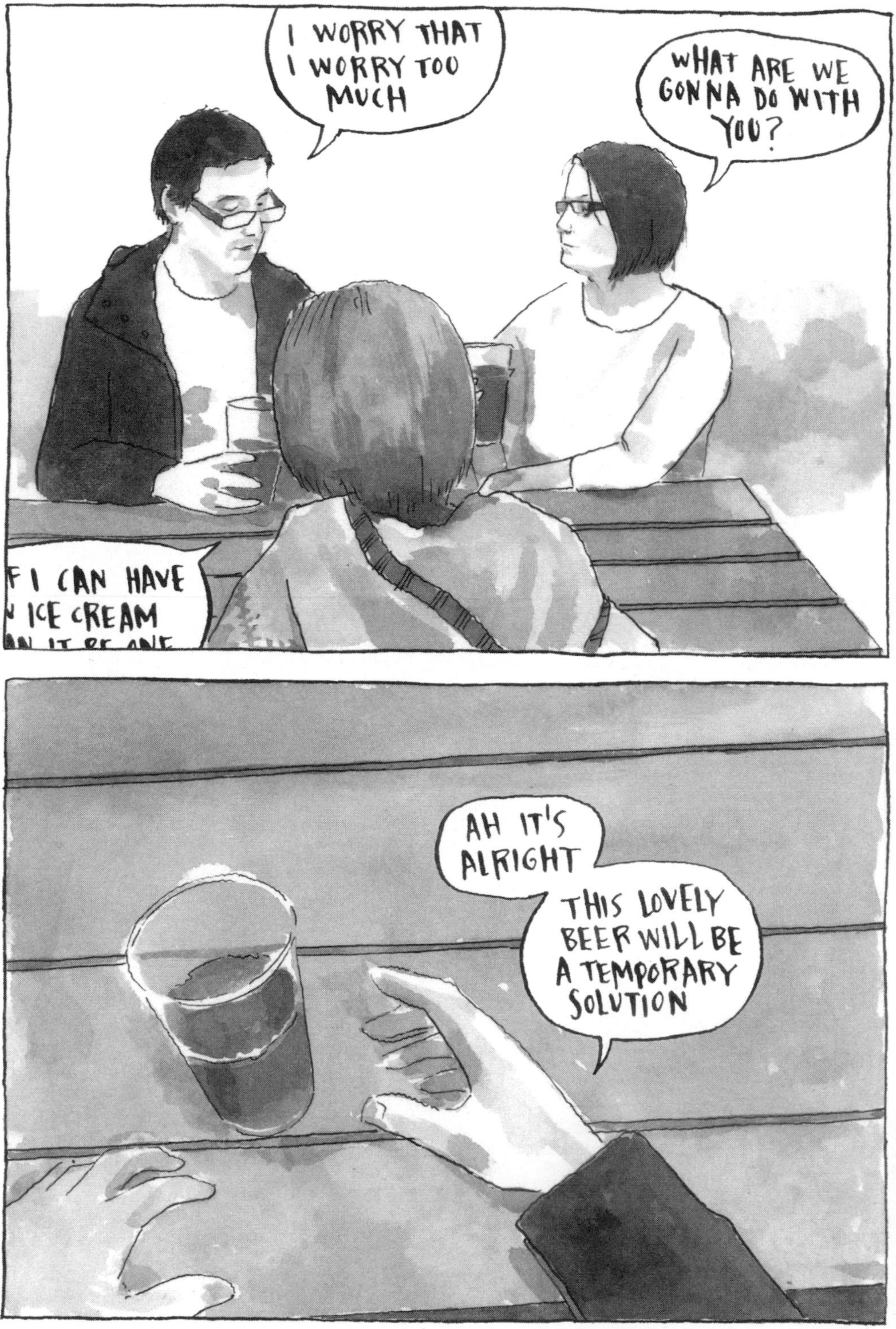
I WORRY THAT I WORRY TOO MUCH
WHAT ARE WE GONNA DO WITH YOU?
F I CAN HAVE
N ICE CREAM
AH IT'S ALRIGHT
THIS LOVELY BEER WILL BE A TEMPORARY SOLUTION

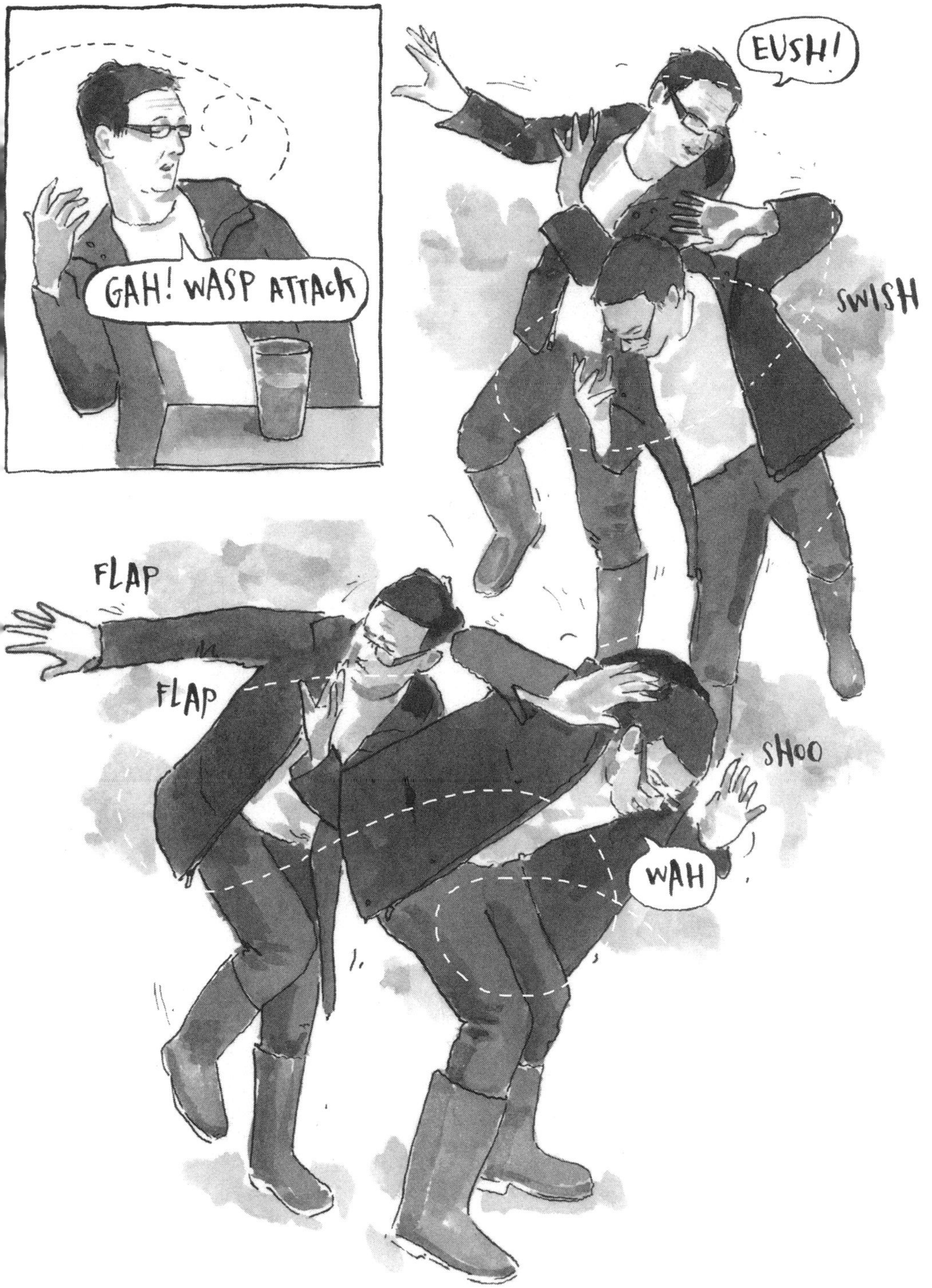
GAH! WASP ATTACK
EUSH!
SWISH
FLAP
FLAP
SHOO
WAH

THE DANCE OF THE WASP ATTACK

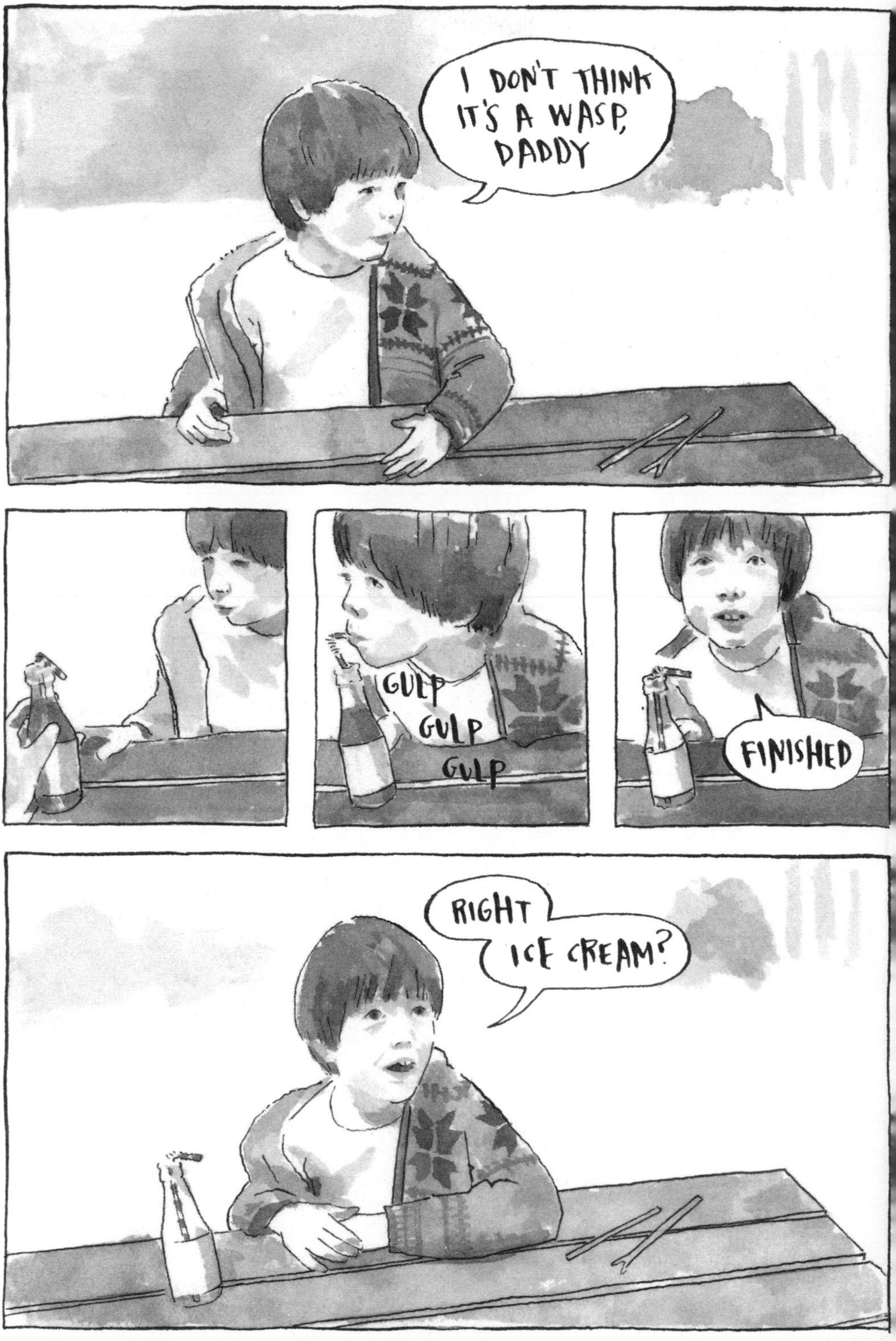
I DON'T THINK IT'S A WASP, DADDY
GULP
GULP
GULP
FINISHED
RIGHT
ICE CREAM?

AND SO...

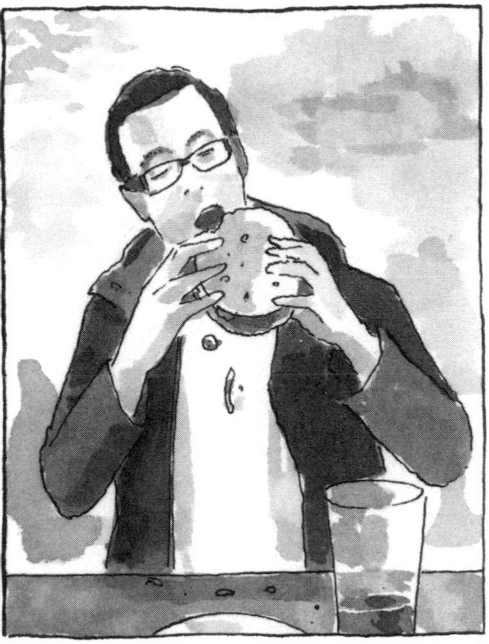

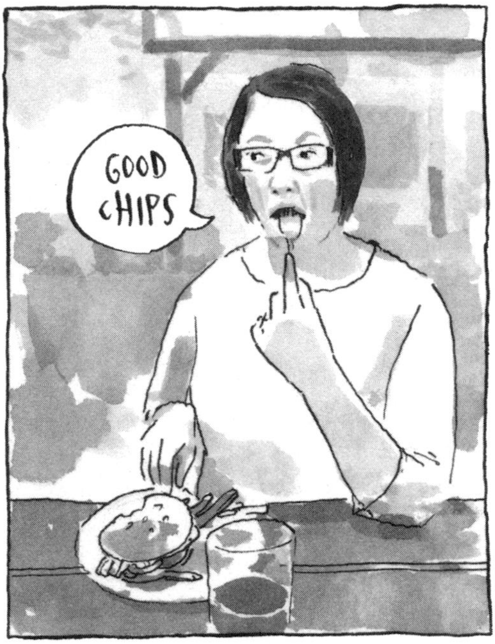
GOOD CHIPS

OH, HOW WAS YOUR WORRYING? DID YOU MANAGE TO MAKE A MOUNTAIN OUT OF A MOLE HILL? AMAZING, EH?

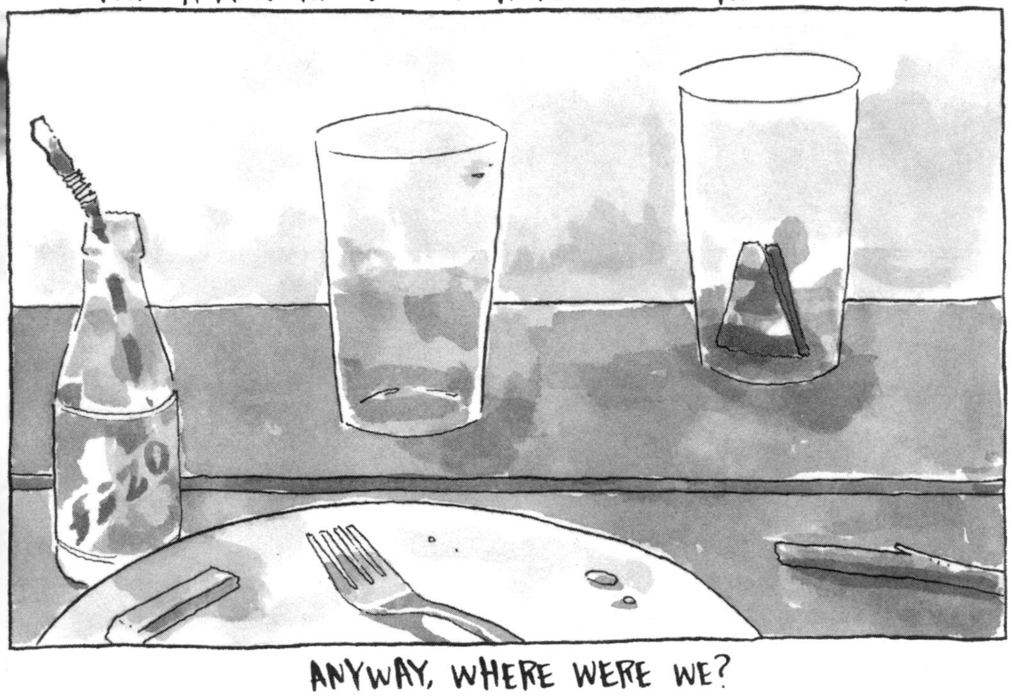

ANYWAY, WHERE WERE WE?

HEADING BACK TO THE WOODS I SUPPOSE.

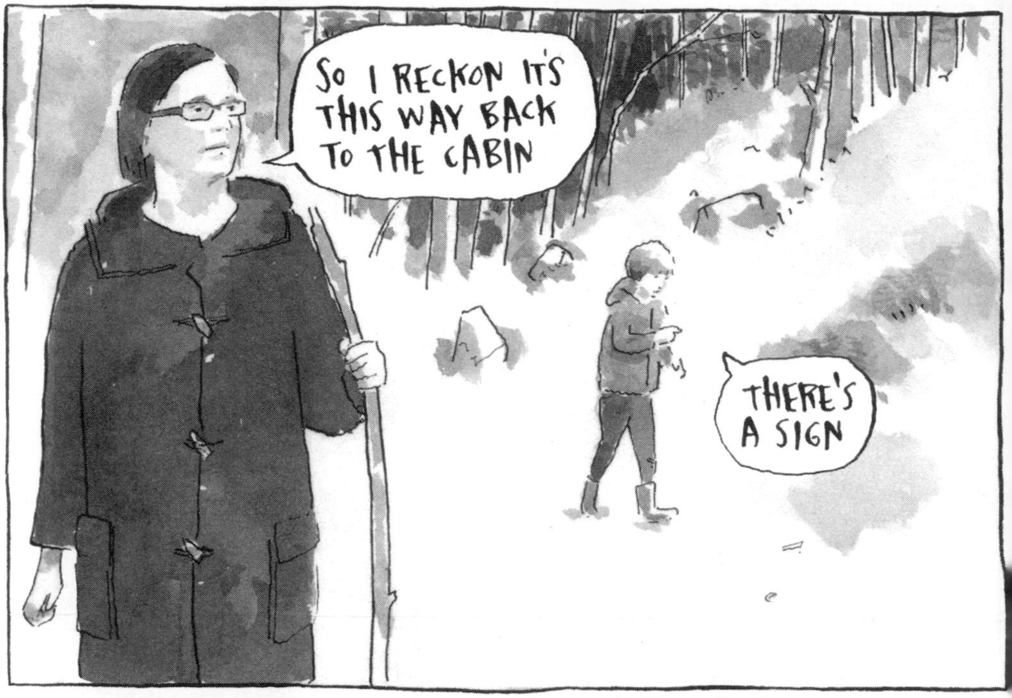
SO I RECKON IT'S THIS WAY BACK TO THE CABIN
THERE'S A SIGN

THE BOY, HE GRAVITATES TOWARDS DANGER.

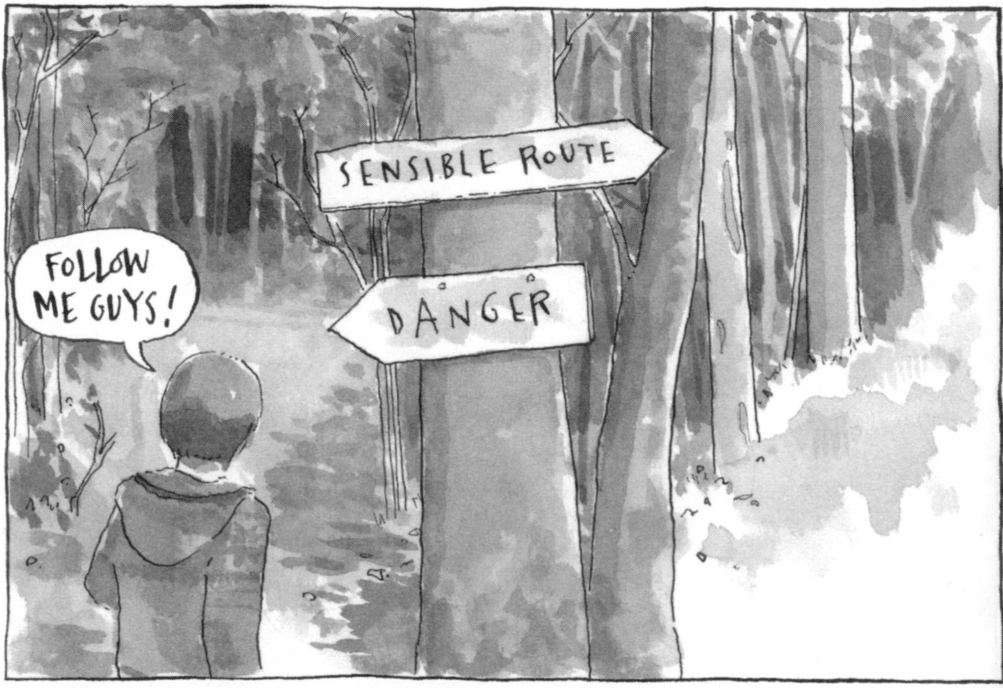
FOLLOW ME GUYS!
SENSIBLE ROUTE
DANGER

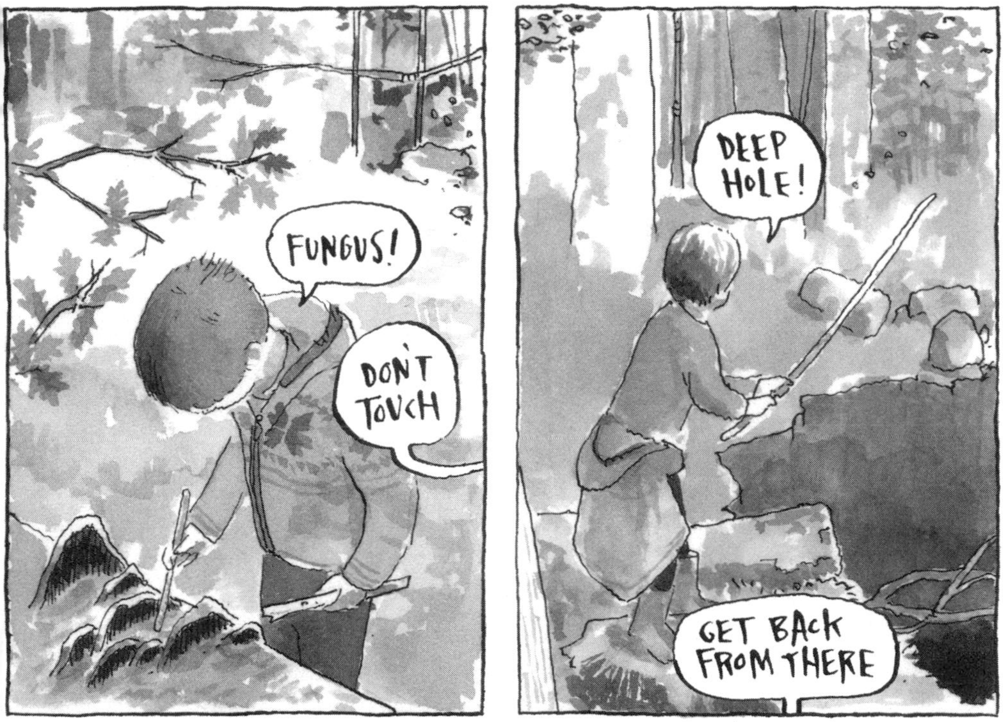
FUNGUS!
DON'T TOUCH
DEEP HOLE!
GET BACK FROM THERE

YOU NEED TO ANTICIPATE HIS EVERY MOVE.

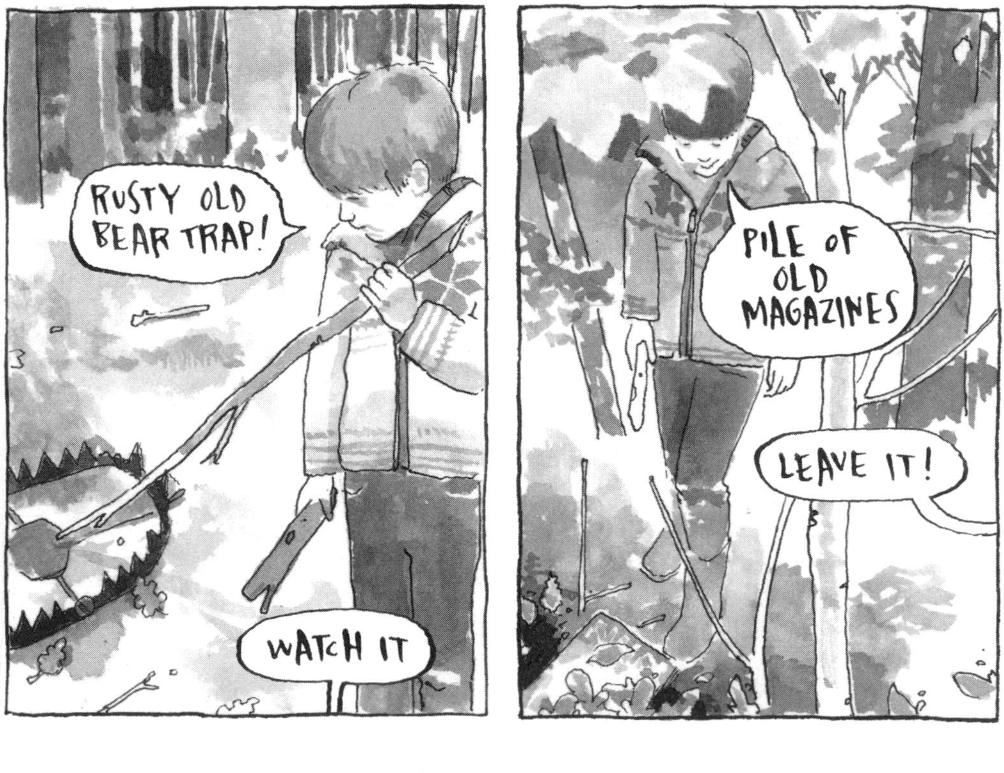
RUSTY OLD BEAR TRAP!
WATCH IT
PILE OF OLD MAGAZINES
LEAVE IT!

HOWEVER, HE'S EASILY OCCUPIED SINGING THEME TUNES.

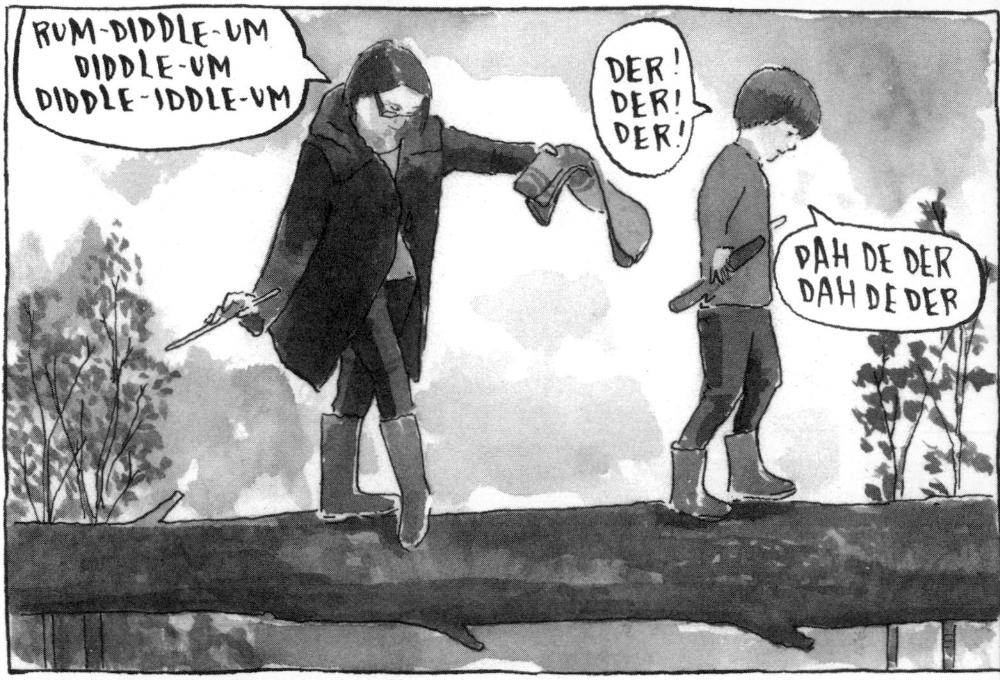
RUM-DIDDLE-UM DIDDLE-UM DIDDLE-IDDLE-UM
DER! DER! DER!
DAH DE DER DAH DE DER

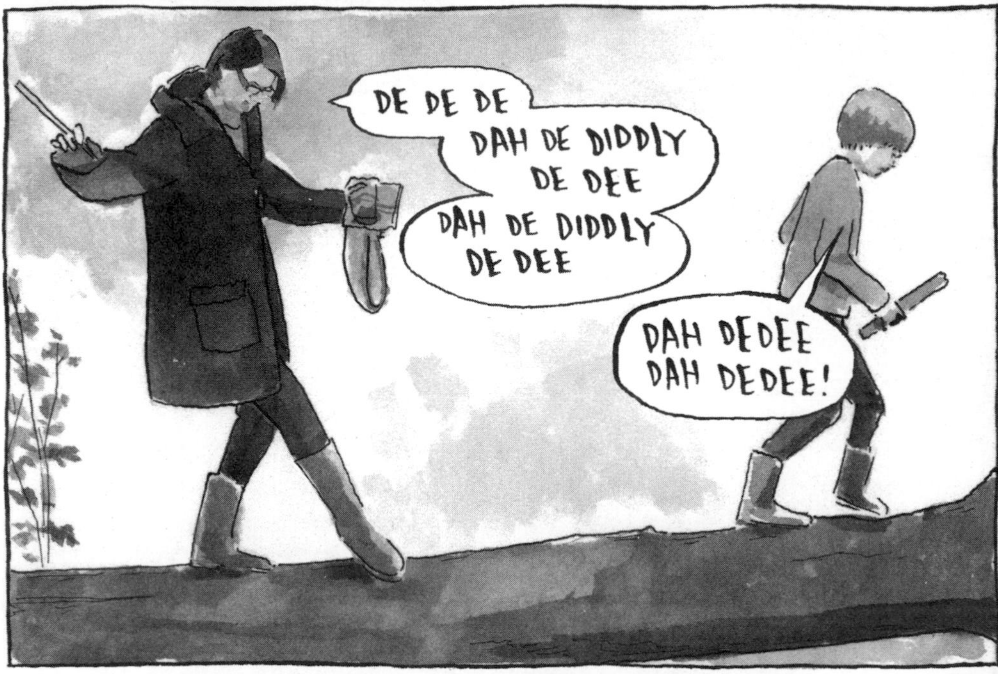
DE DE DE DAH DE DIDDLY DE DEE DAH DE DIDDLY DE DEE
DAH DEDEE DAH DEDEE!

FIVE POINTS IF YOU CAN NAME THAT TUNE.

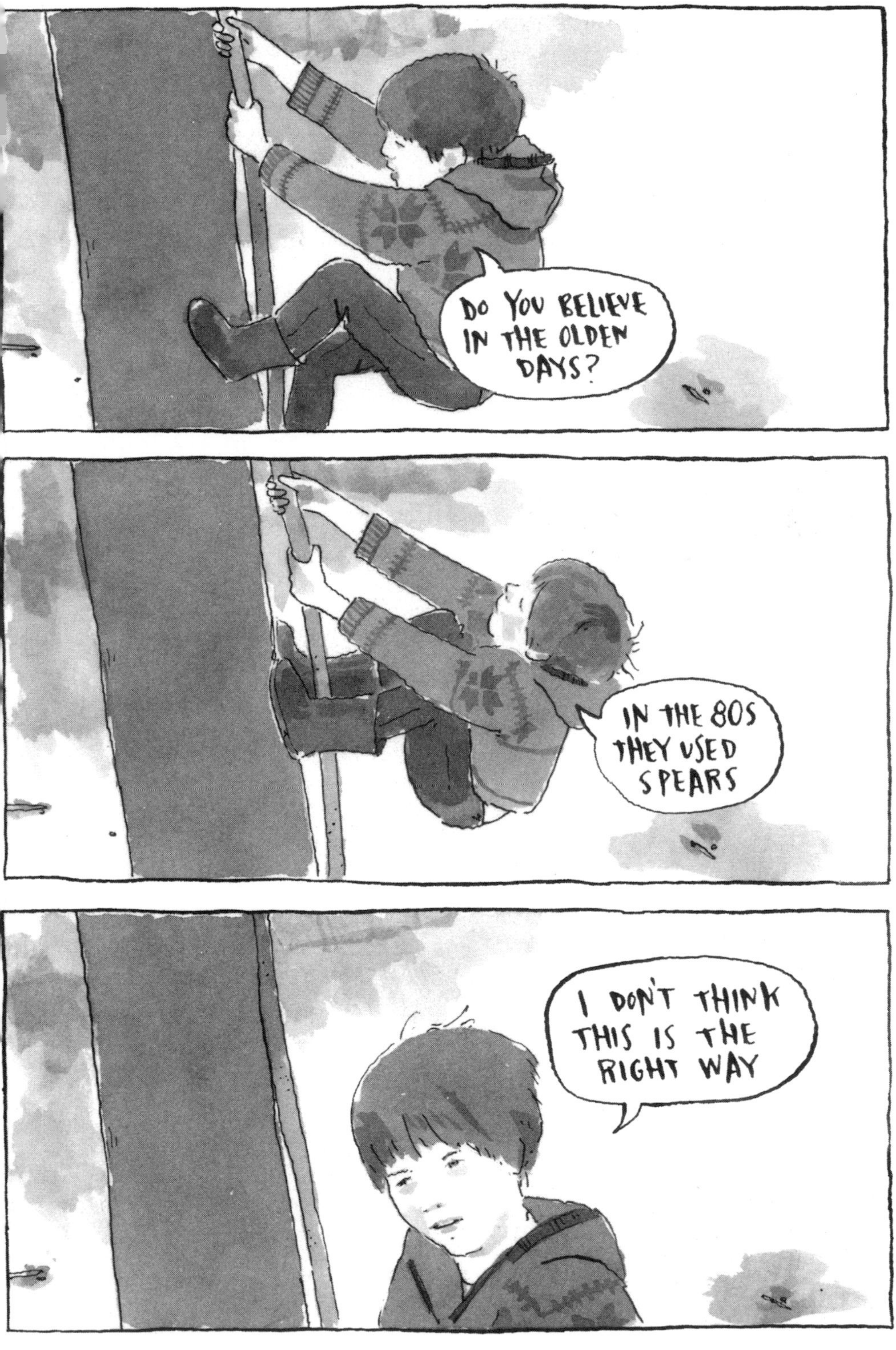
DO YOU BELIEVE IN THE OLDEN DAYS?
IN THE 80S THEY USED SPEARS
I DON'T THINK THIS IS THE RIGHT WAY

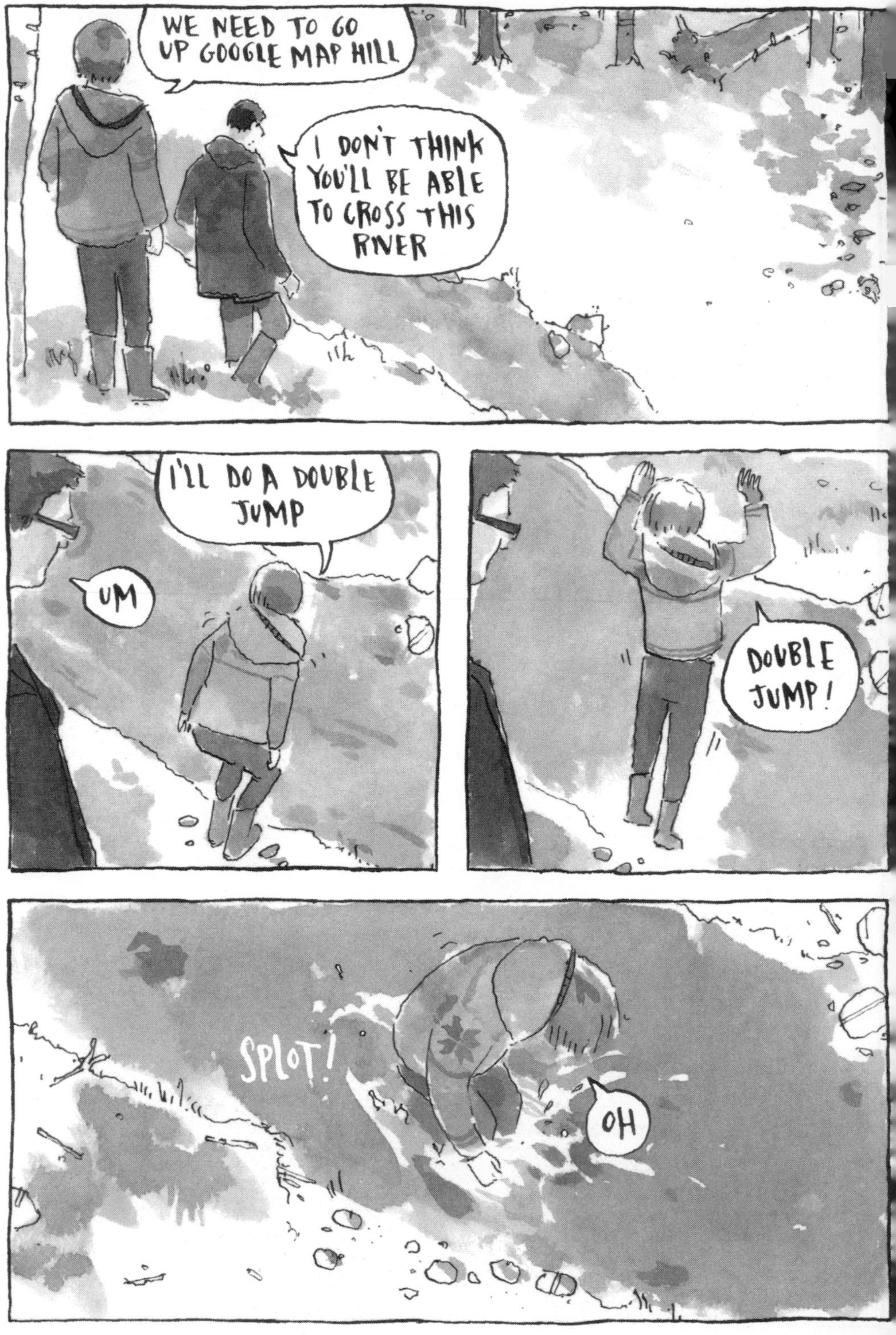
WE NEED TO GO UP GOOGLE MAP HILL
I DON'T THINK YOU'LL BE ABLE TO CROSS THIS RIVER
I'LL DO A DOUBLE JUMP
UM
DOUBLE JUMP!
SPLOT!
OH

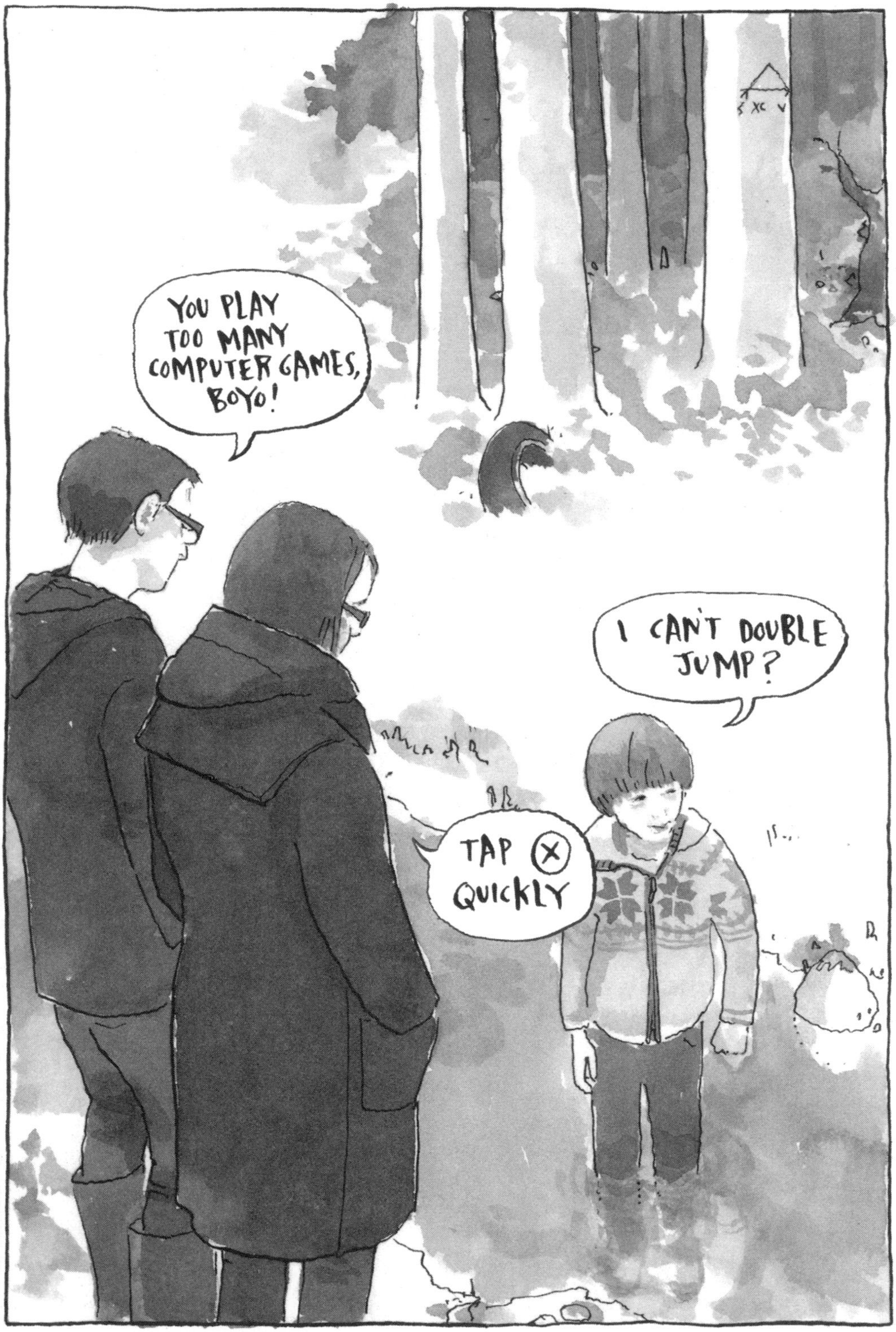
YOU PLAY TOO MANY COMPUTER GAMES, BOYO!
I CAN'T DOUBLE JUMP?
TAP ⊗ QUICKLY

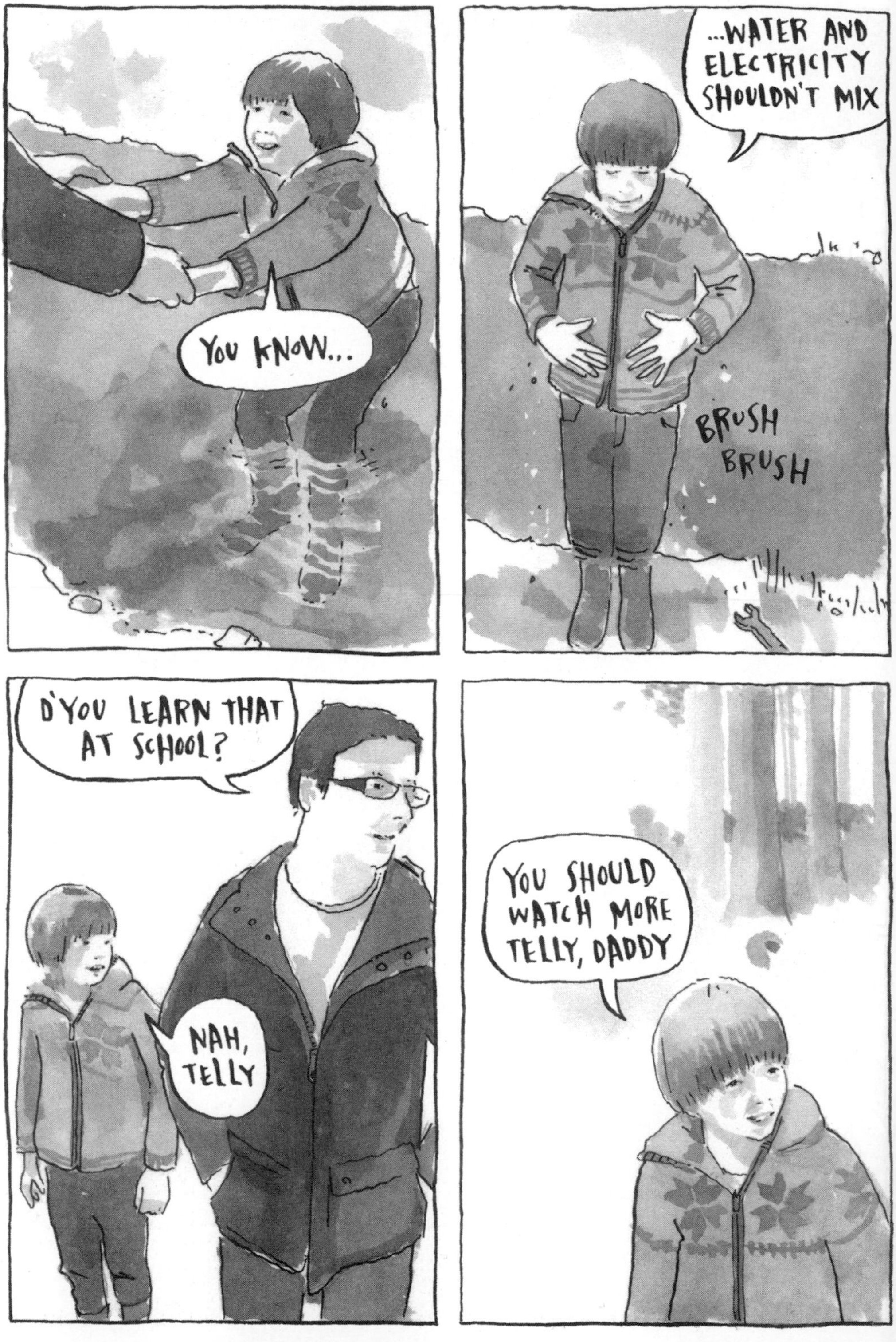
YOU KNOW...
...WATER AND ELECTRICITY SHOULDN'T MIX
BRUSH BRUSH
D'YOU LEARN THAT AT SCHOOL?
NAH, TELLY
YOU SHOULD WATCH MORE TELLY, DADDY

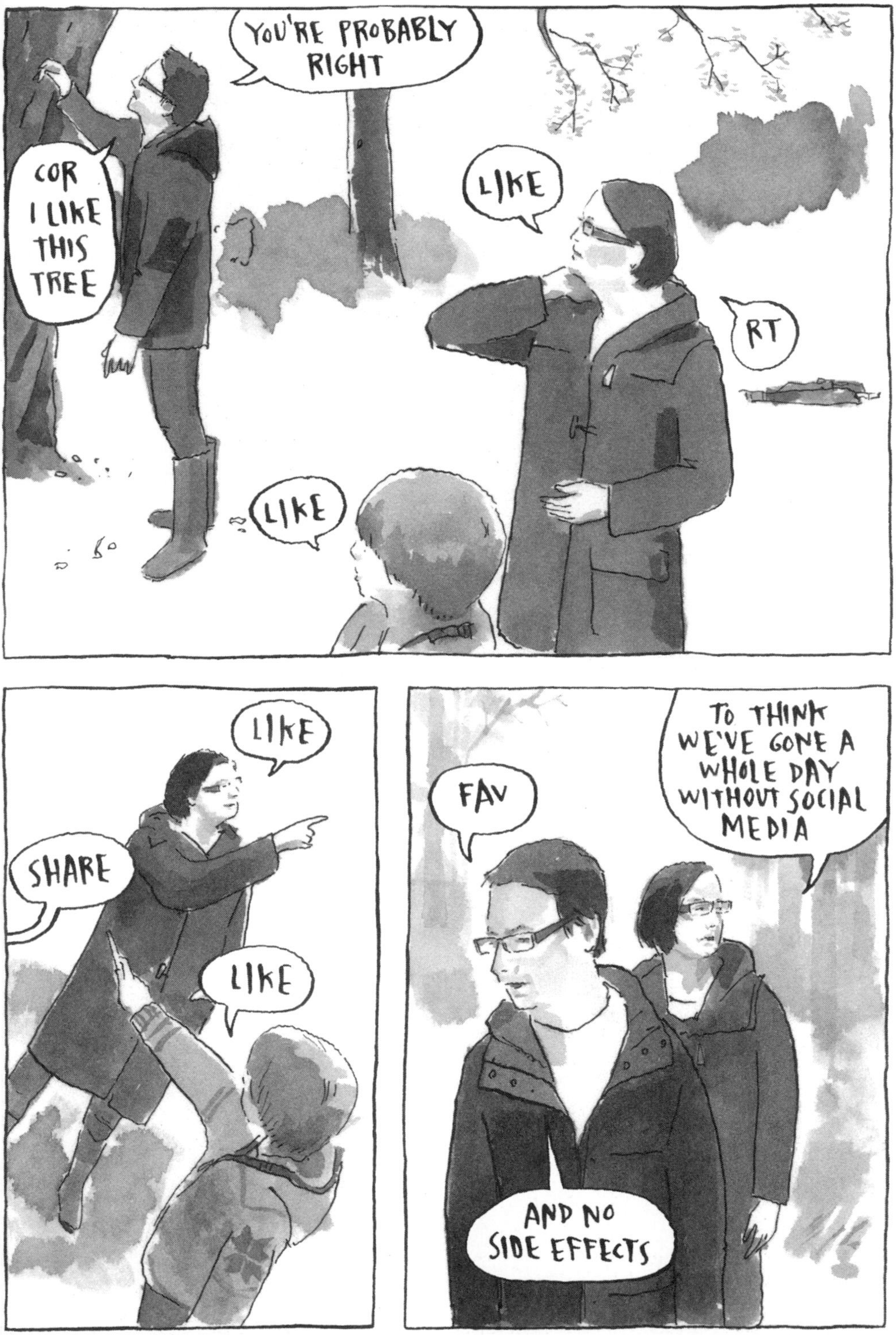
COR I LIKE THIS TREE
YOU'RE PROBABLY RIGHT
LIKE
RT
LIKE
LIKE
SHARE
LIKE
FAV
TO THINK WE'VE GONE A WHOLE DAY WITHOUT SOCIAL MEDIA
AND NO SIDE EFFECTS

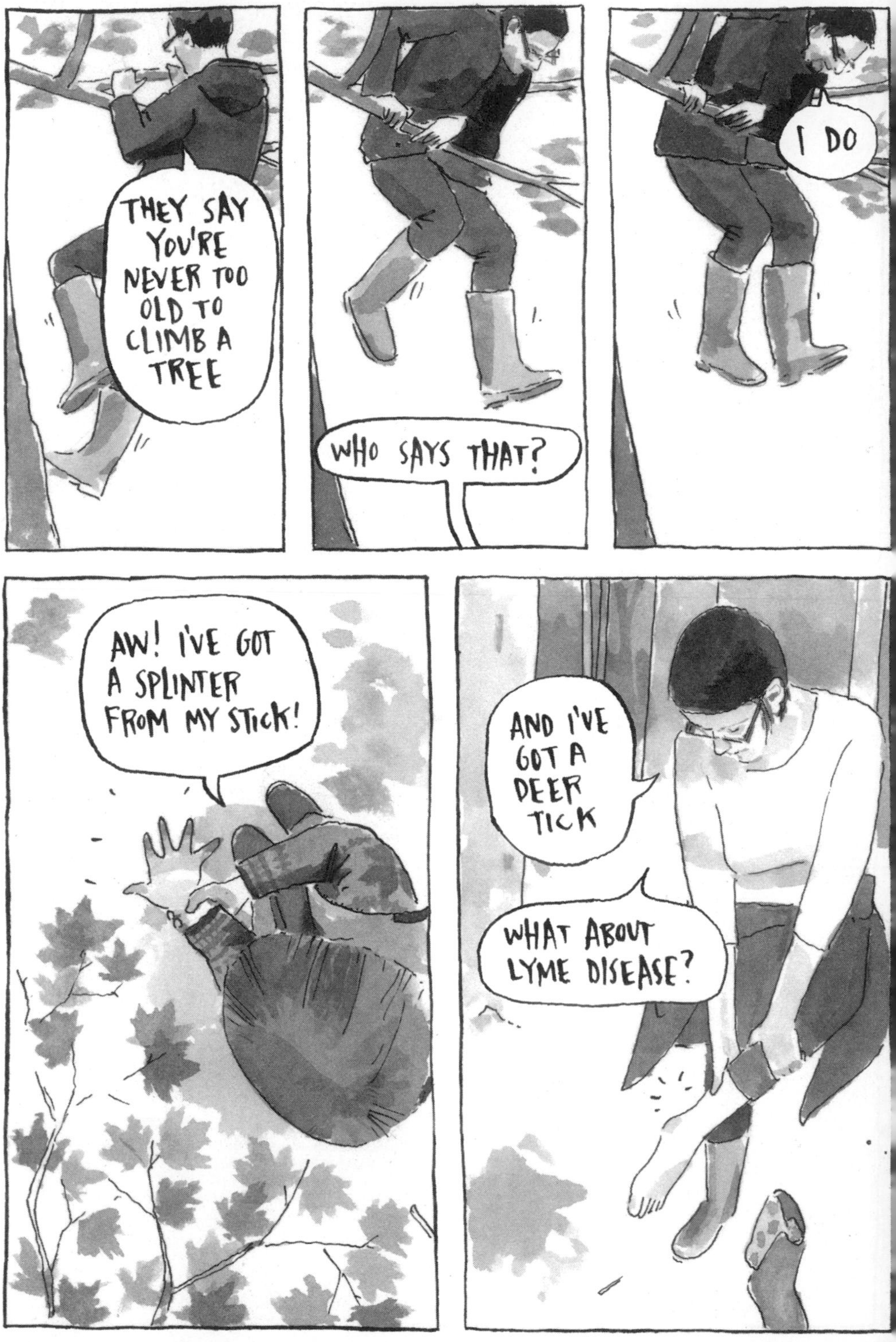
THEY SAY YOU'RE NEVER TOO OLD TO CLIMB A TREE
WHO SAYS THAT?
I DO
AW! I'VE GOT A SPLINTER FROM MY STICK!
AND I'VE GOT A DEER TICK
WHAT ABOUT LYME DISEASE?

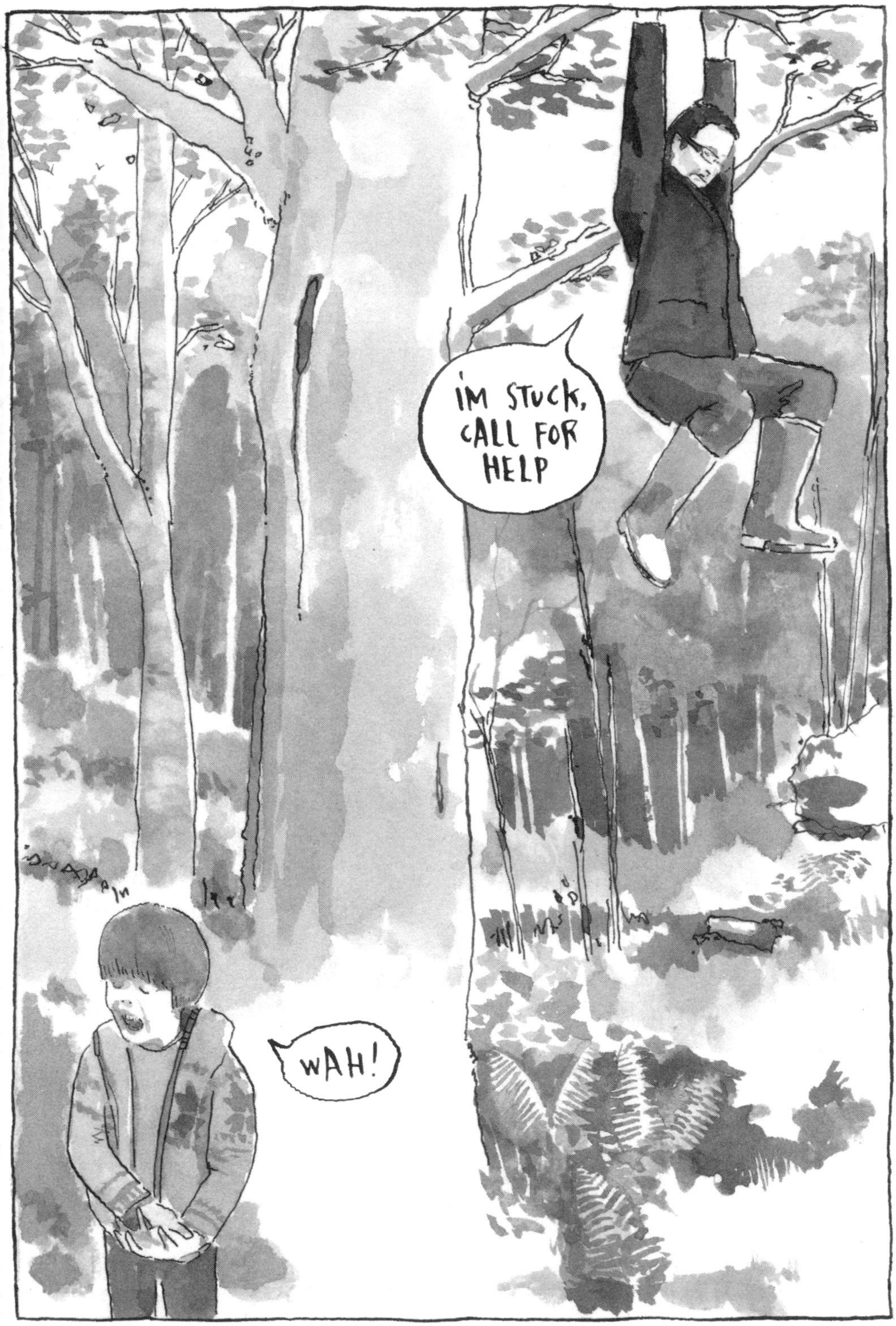
IM STUCK, CALL FOR HELP
WAH!

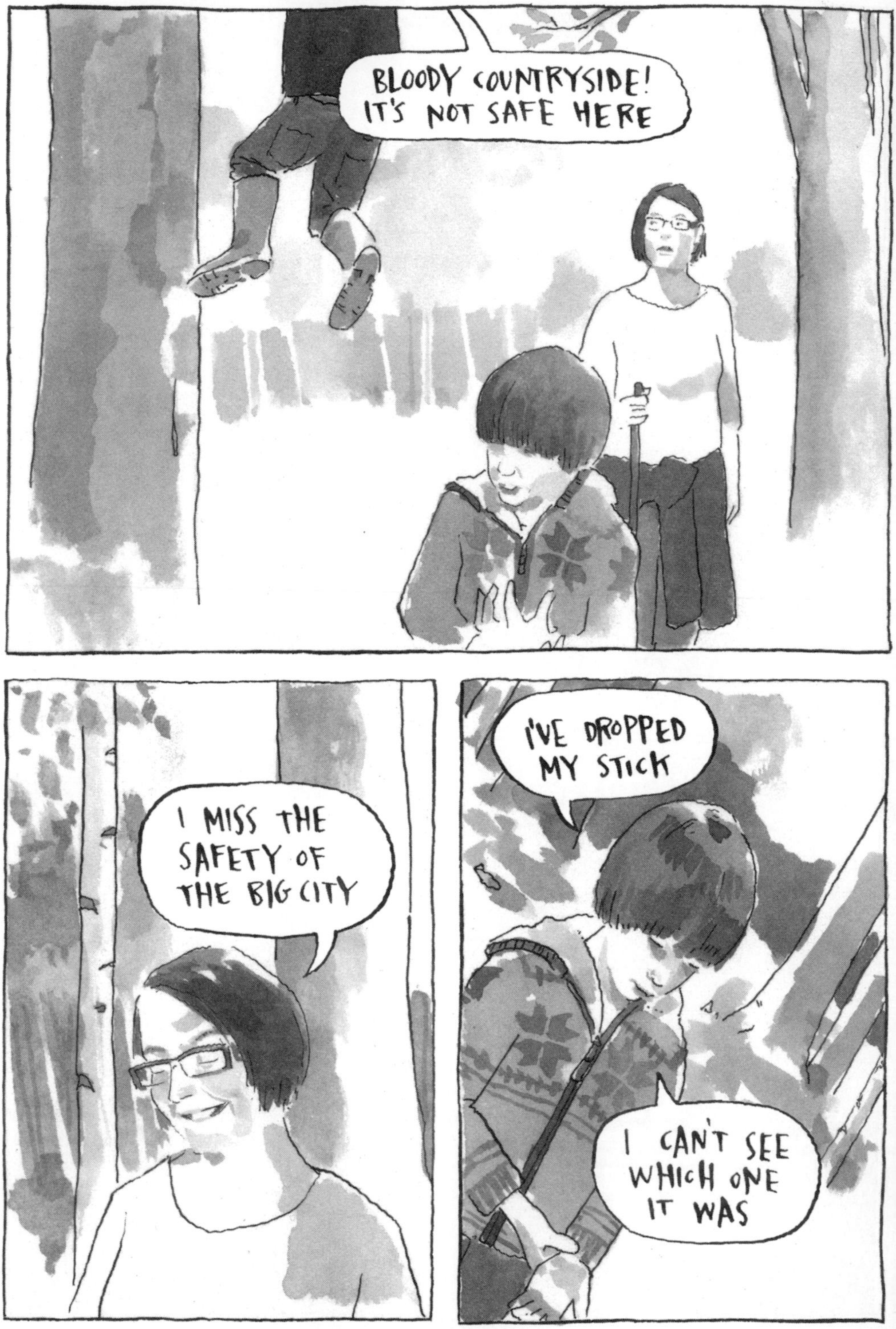

BLOODY COUNTRYSIDE! IT'S NOT SAFE HERE
I MISS THE SAFETY OF THE BIG CITY
I'VE DROPPED MY STICK
I CAN'T SEE WHICH ONE IT WAS

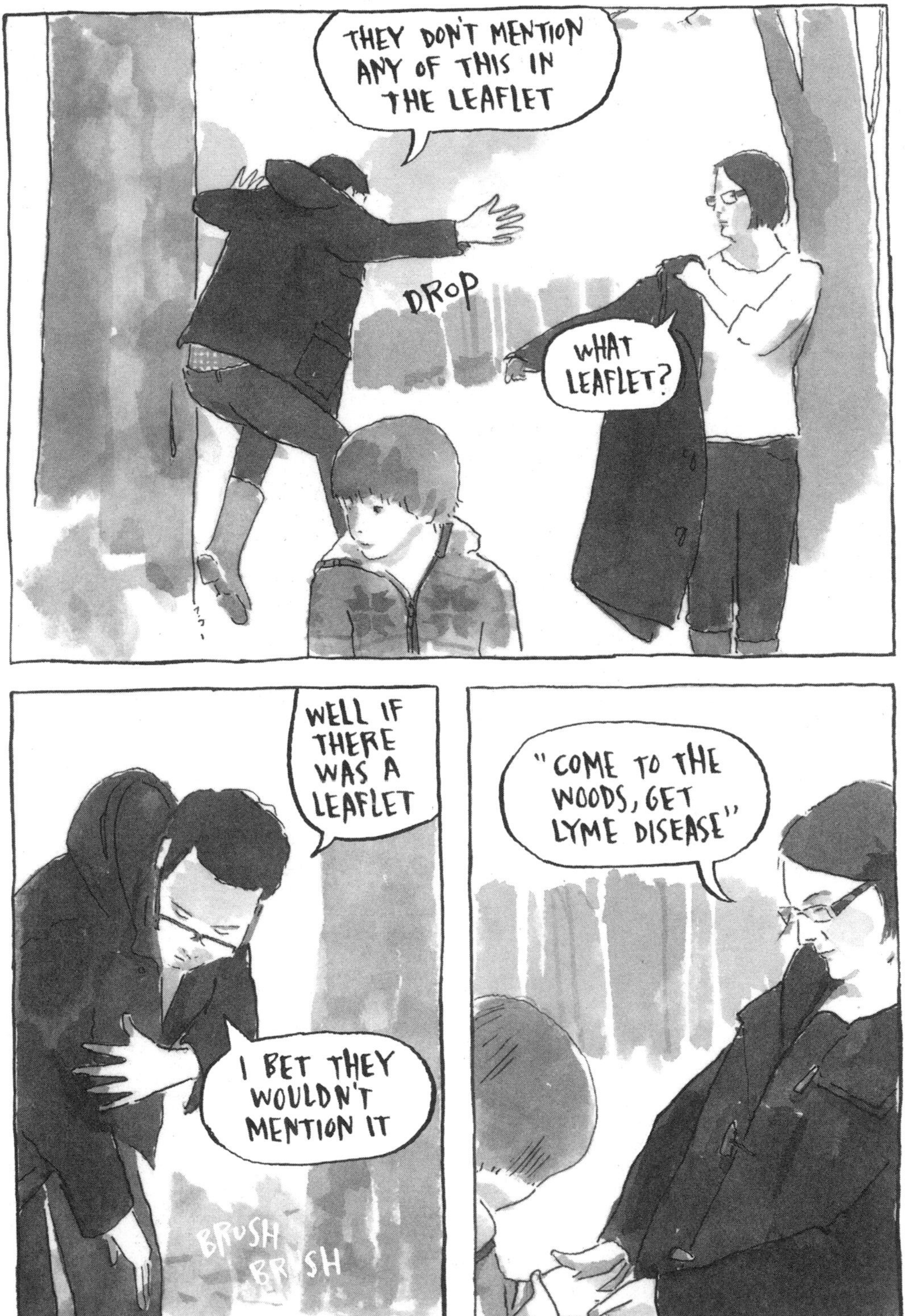
THEY DON'T MENTION ANY OF THIS IN THE LEAFLET
DROP
WHAT LEAFLET?
WELL IF THERE WAS A LEAFLET
I BET THEY WOULDN'T MENTION IT
BRUSH
BRUSH
"COME TO THE WOODS, GET LYME DISEASE"

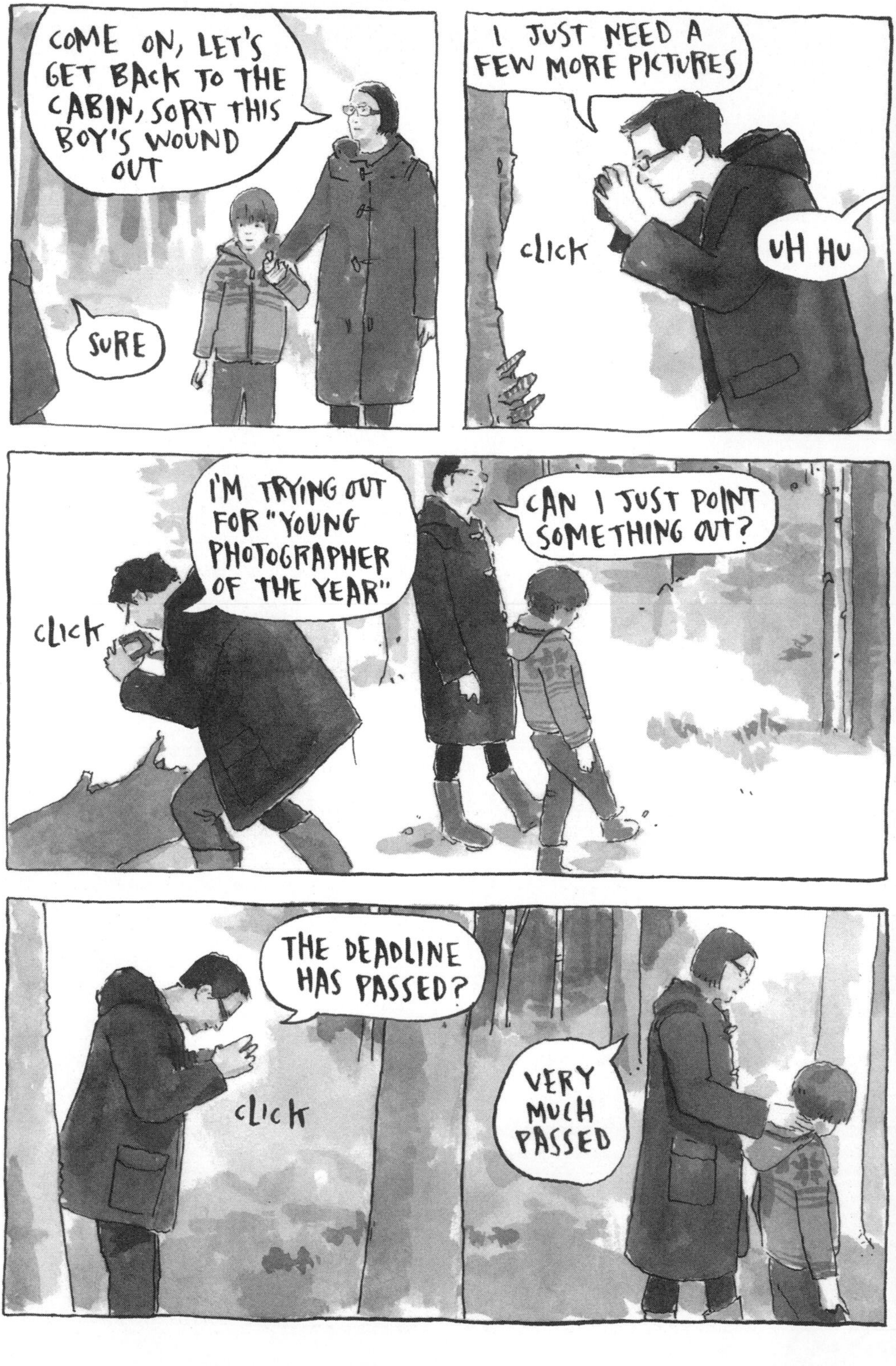
COME ON, LET'S GET BACK TO THE CABIN, SORT THIS BOY'S WOUND OUT
SURE
I JUST NEED A FEW MORE PICTURES
CLICK
UH HU
I'M TRYING OUT FOR "YOUNG PHOTOGRAPHER OF THE YEAR"
CLICK
CAN I JUST POINT SOMETHING OUT?
THE DEADLINE HAS PASSED?
CLICK
VERY MUCH PASSED

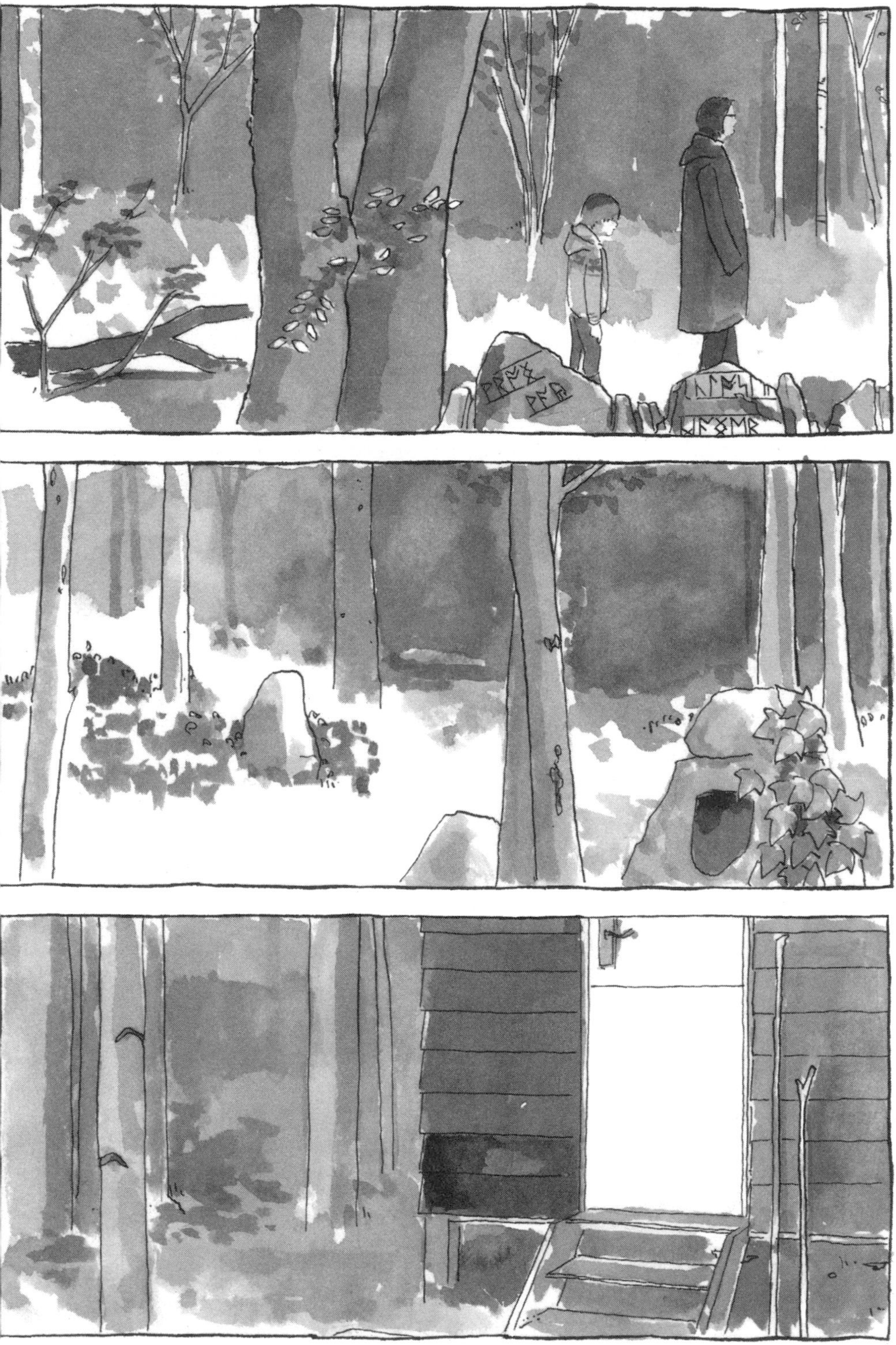

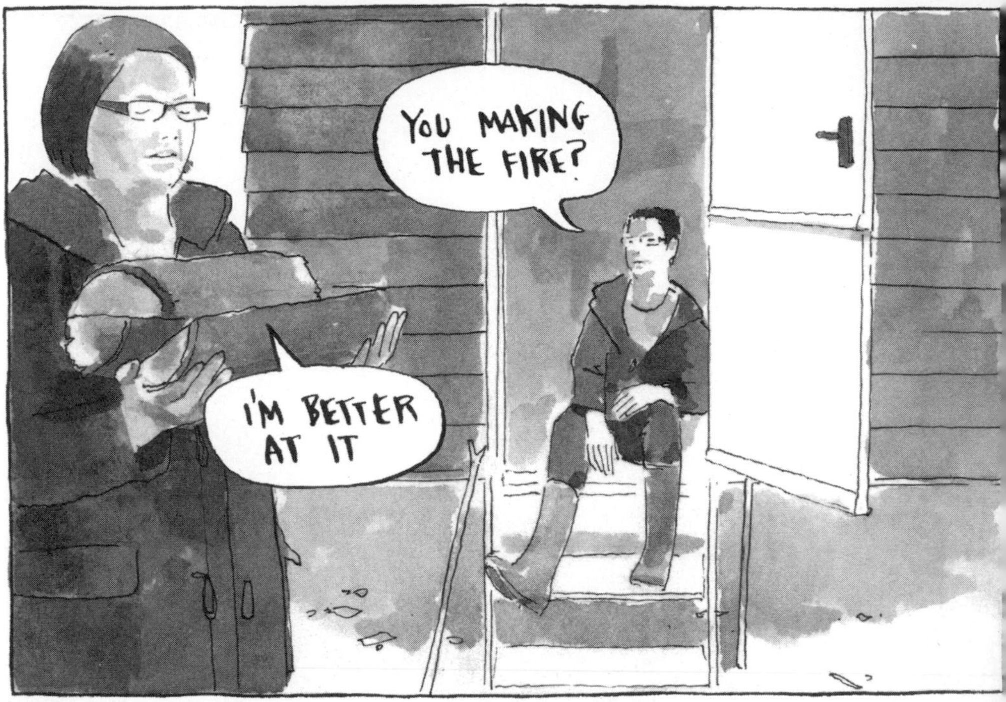
YOU MAKING THE FIRE?
I'M BETTER AT IT

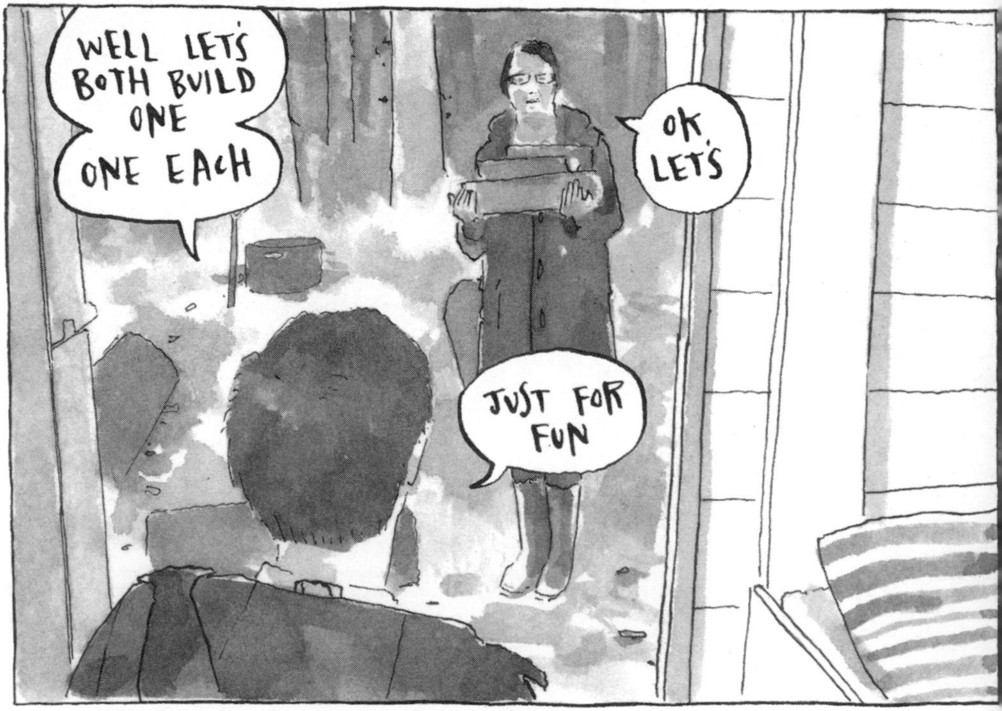
WELL LET'S BOTH BUILD ONE
ONE EACH
OK LET'S
JUST FOR FUN

(I'M NOT COMPETITIVE)

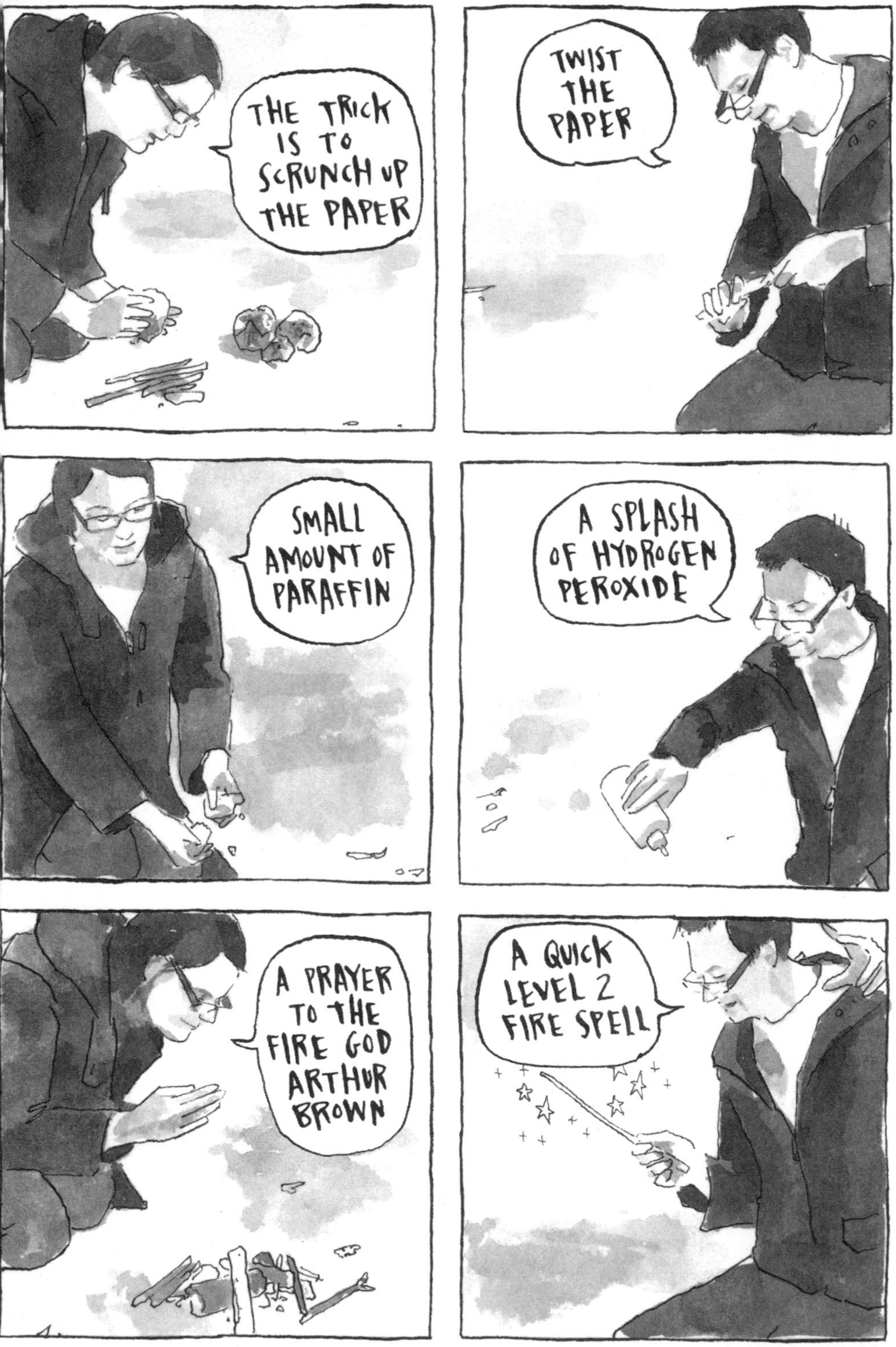
THE TRICK IS TO SCRUNCH UP THE PAPER
TWIST THE PAPER
SMALL AMOUNT OF PARAFFIN
A SPLASH OF HYDROGEN PEROXIDE
A PRAYER TO THE FIRE GOD ARTHUR BROWN
A QUICK LEVEL 2 FIRE SPELL

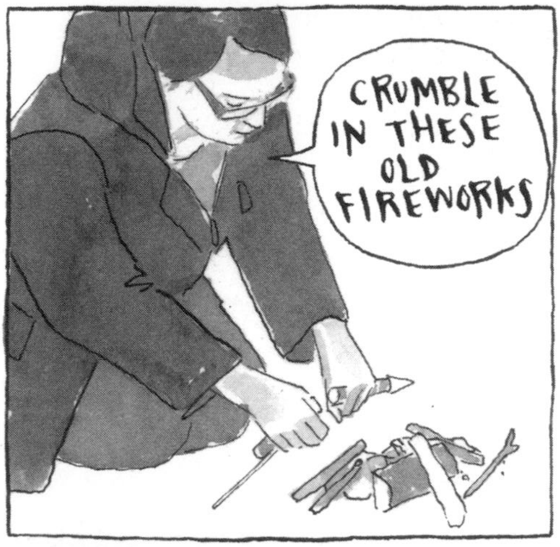
CRUMBLE IN THESE OLD FIREWORKS

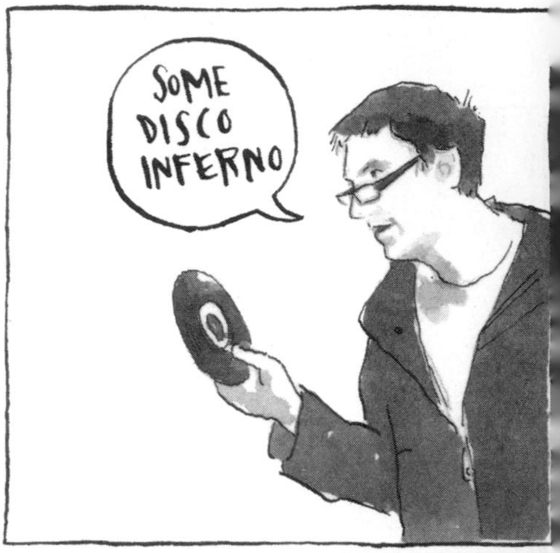
SOME DISCO INFERNO

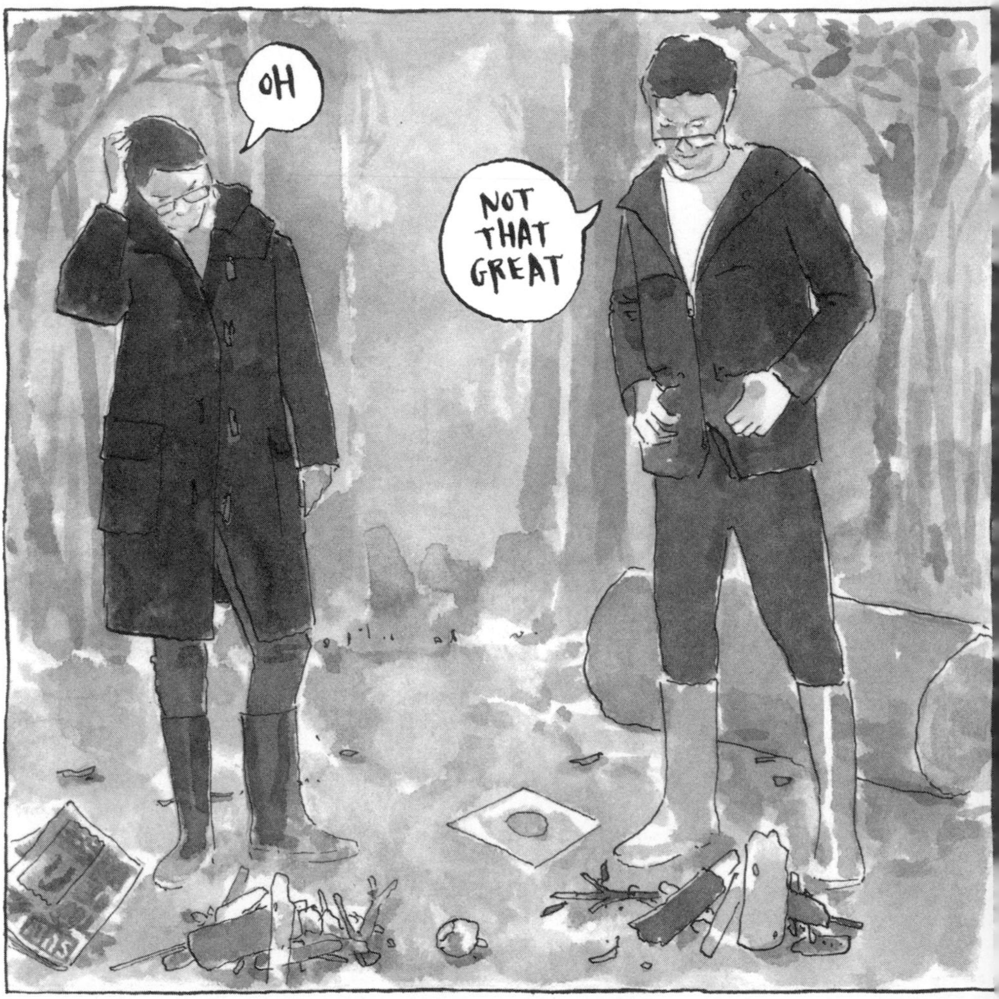
OH
NOT THAT GREAT

TWO UNSUCCESSFUL FIRES CAN BE COMBINED TO MAKE ONE SEMI-SUCCESSFUL FIRE.

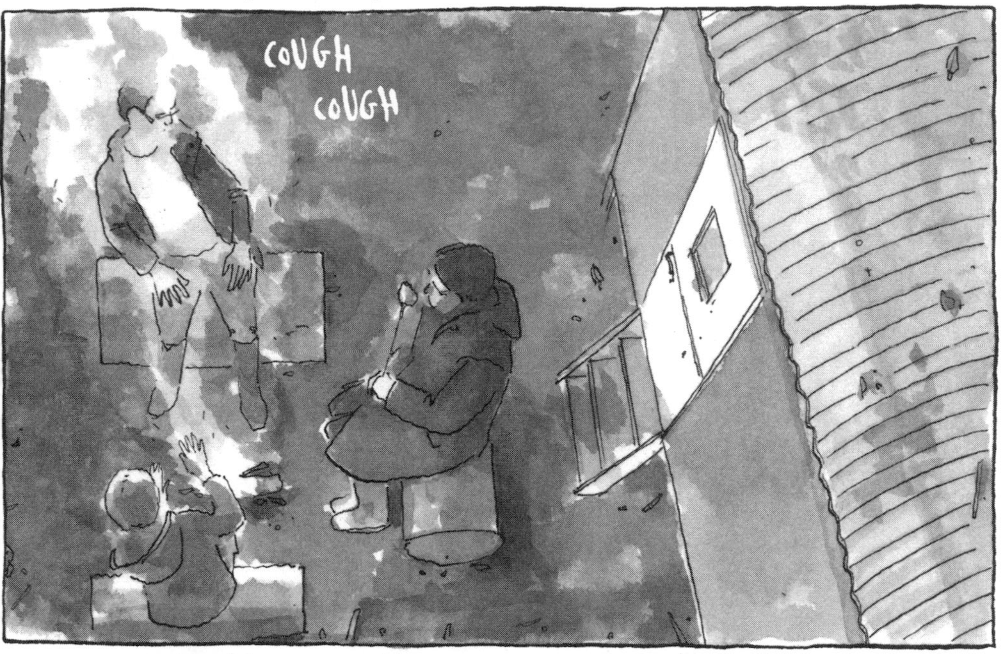
COUGH
COUGH

ALTHOUGH IT'S MORE SMOKE THAN FIRE.

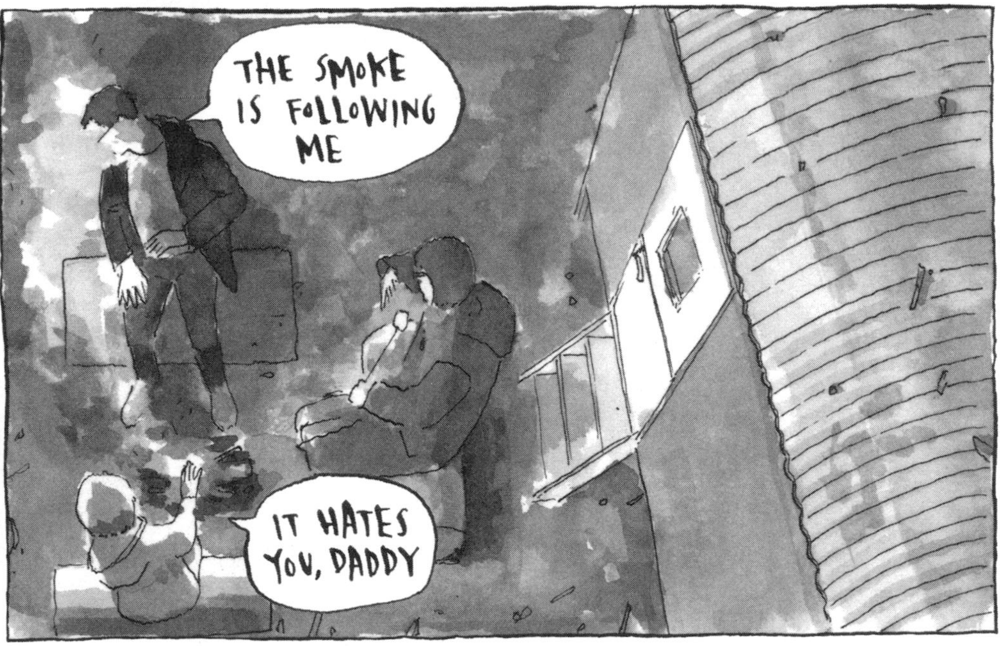
THE SMOKE IS FOLLOWING ME
IT HATES YOU, DADDY

AND I'M A SMOKE MAGNET, IT SEEMS.

WE TOAST MARSHMALLOWS IN THE FLAMES

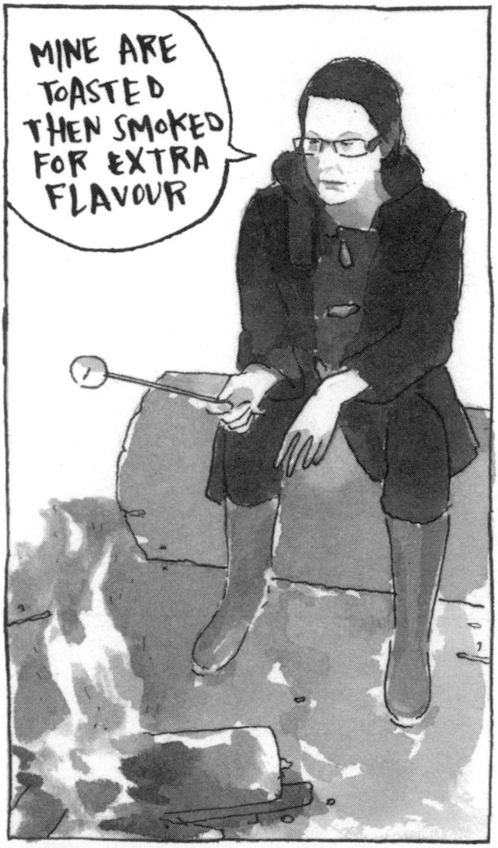
MINE ARE TOASTED THEN SMOKED FOR EXTRA FLAVOUR

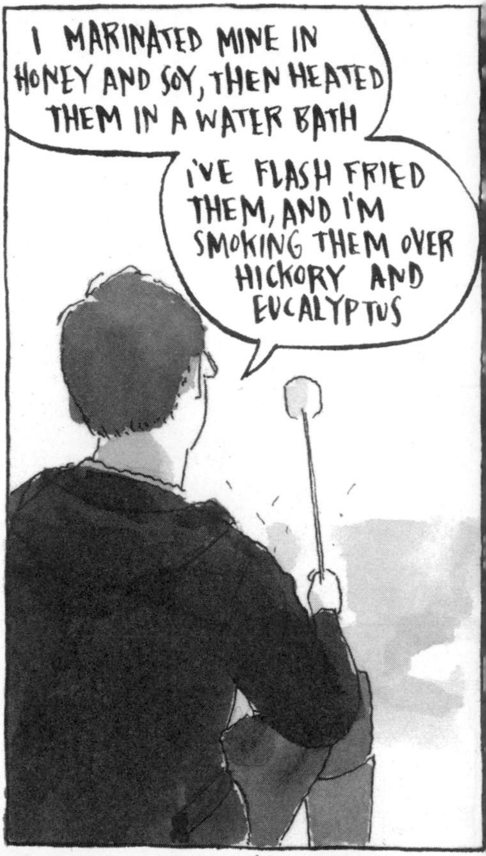
I MARINATED MINE IN HONEY AND SOY, THEN HEATED THEM IN A WATER BATH
I'VE FLASH FRIED THEM, AND I'M SMOKING THEM OVER HICKORY AND EUCALYPTUS

A NUTRITIOUS MEAL, SERVED WITH WINE FROM THE BOTTLE.

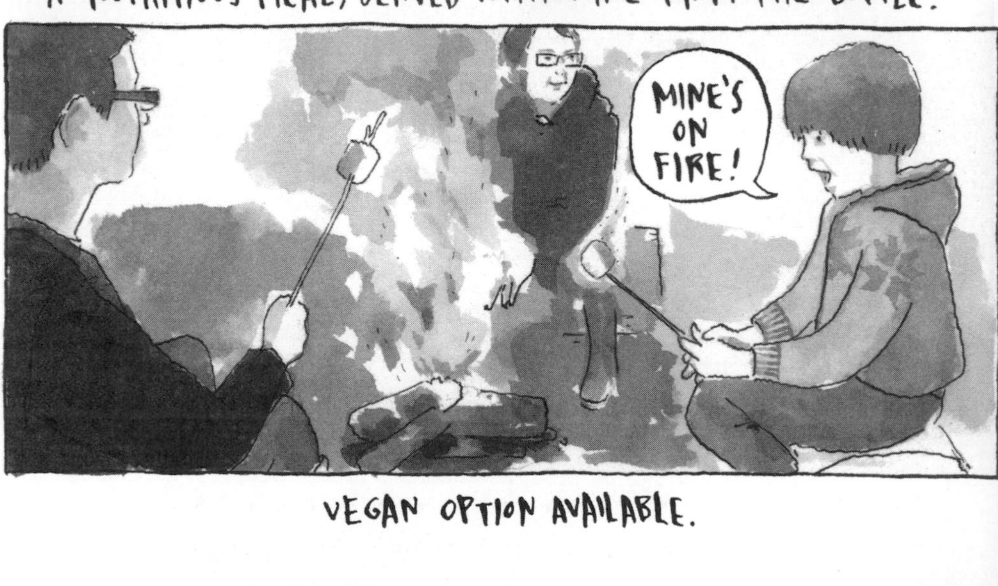
MINE'S ON FIRE!

VEGAN OPTION AVAILABLE.

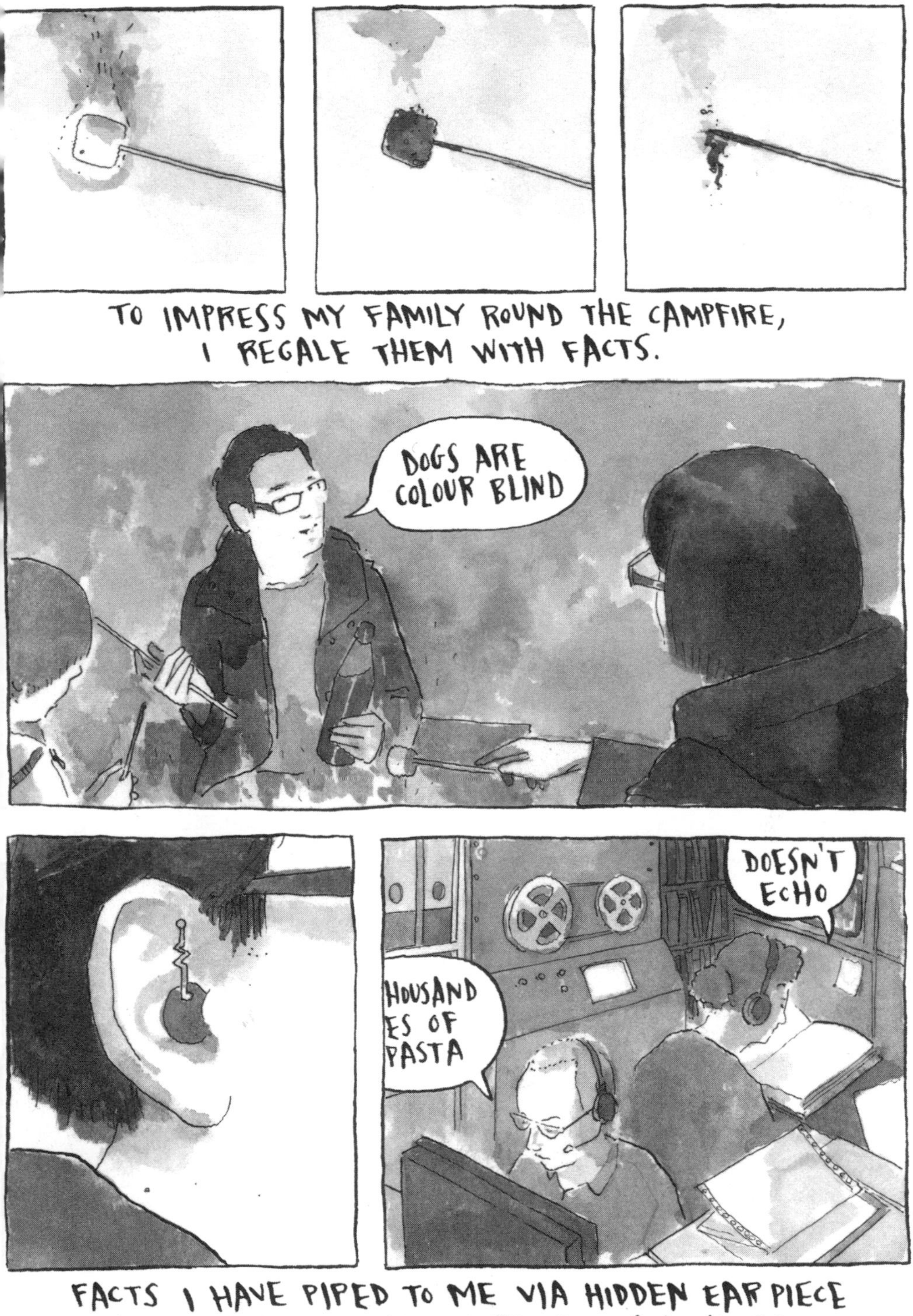
TO IMPRESS MY FAMILY ROUND THE CAMPFIRE, I REGALE THEM WITH FACTS.
DOGS ARE COLOUR BLIND
DOESN'T ECHO
HOUSAND ES OF PASTA
FACTS I HAVE PIPED TO ME VIA HIDDEN EAR PIECE BY A TEAM OF WELL-INFORMED RESEARCHERS.

STRANGELY, MY FACTS DO LITTLE TO HOLD THE ATTENTION OF THE BOY

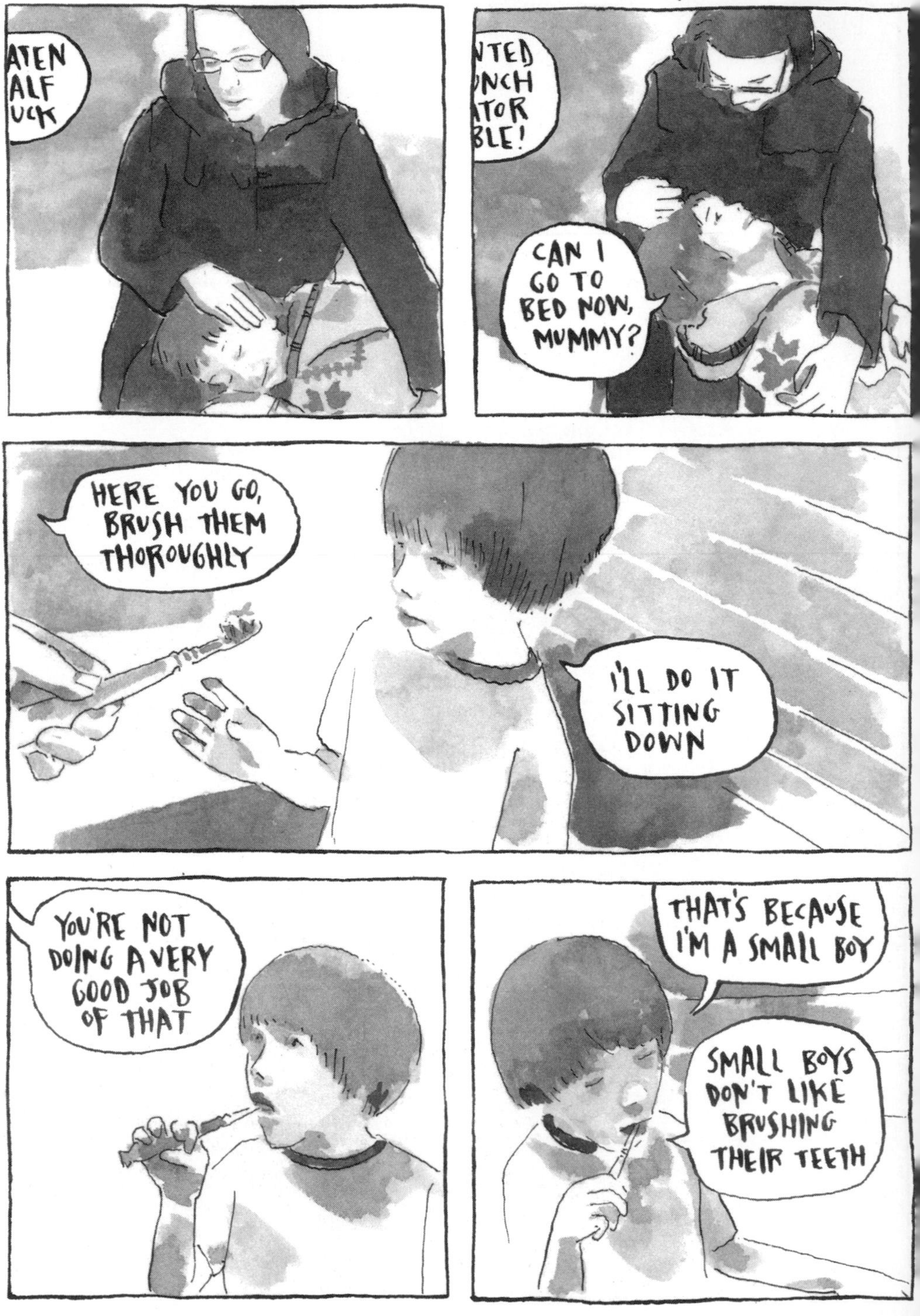

ATEN ALF UCK
NTED UNCH ATOR BLE!
CAN I GO TO BED NOW, MUMMY?
HERE YOU GO, BRUSH THEM THOROUGHLY
I'LL DO IT SITTING DOWN
YOU'RE NOT DOING A VERY GOOD JOB OF THAT
THAT'S BECAUSE I'M A SMALL BOY
SMALL BOYS DON'T LIKE BRUSHING THEIR TEETH

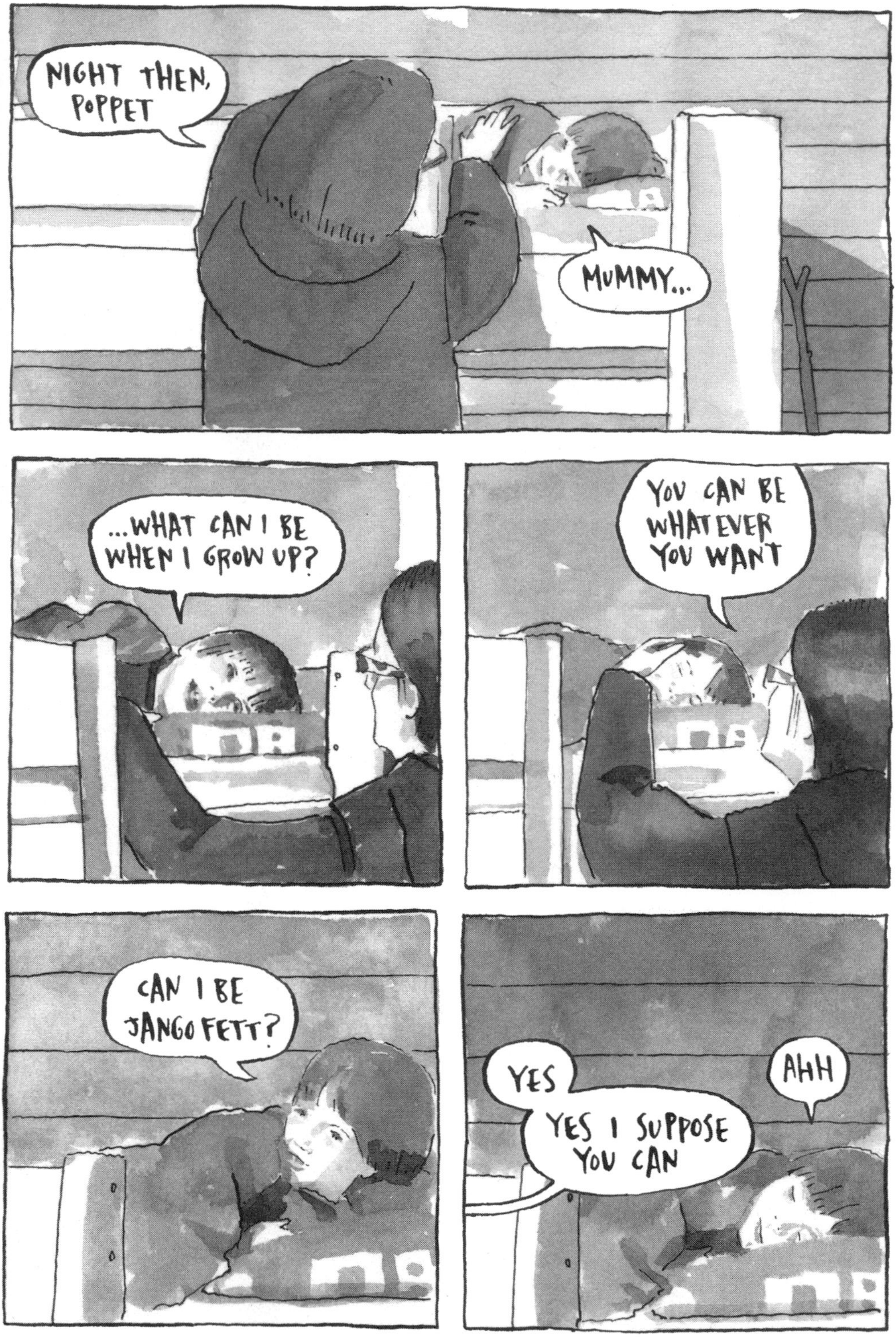
NIGHT THEN, POPPET
MUMMY...
...WHAT CAN I BE WHEN I GROW UP?
YOU CAN BE WHATEVER YOU WANT
CAN I BE JANGO FETT?
YES
AHH
YES I SUPPOSE YOU CAN

AS THE NIGHT DRAWS IN, CONVERSATION TURNS MORE HIGHBROW.

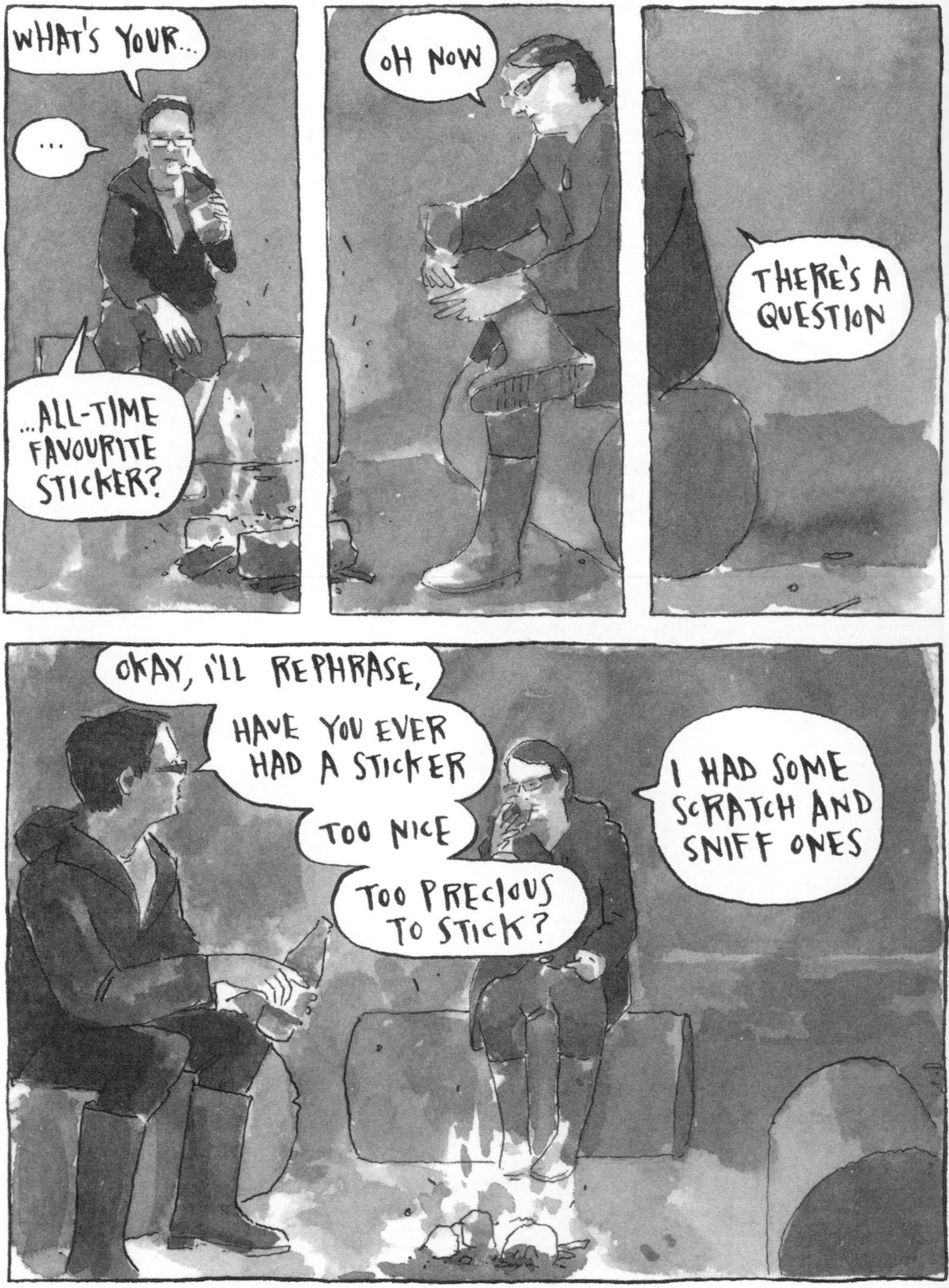
WHAT'S YOUR...
...
...ALL-TIME FAVOURITE STICKER?
OH NOW
THERE'S A QUESTION
OKAY, I'LL REPHRASE,
HAVE YOU EVER HAD A STICKER
TOO NICE
TOO PRECIOUS TO STICK?
I HAD SOME SCRATCH AND SNIFF ONES

I'VE HAD A FEW UNSTICKABLE STICKERS.

IT'S TRICKY BECAUSE A STICKER'S LIFESPAN IS DEFINED BY THE THING IT'S STUCK TO.

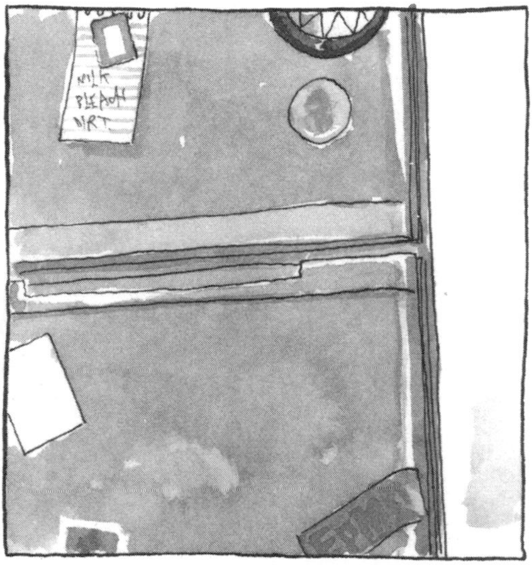

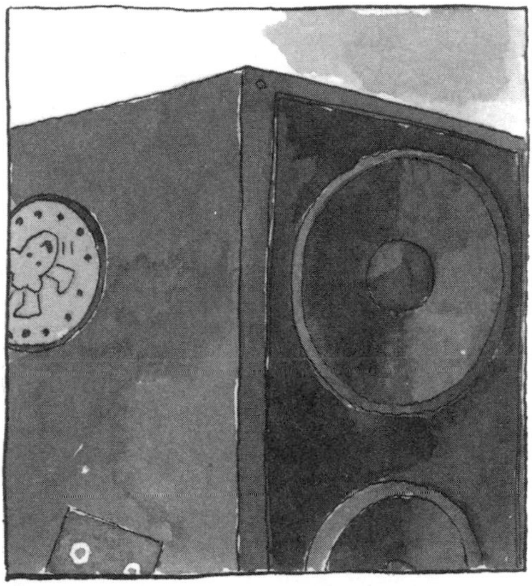

AND REFRIGERATORS DON'T LAST FOR EVER.

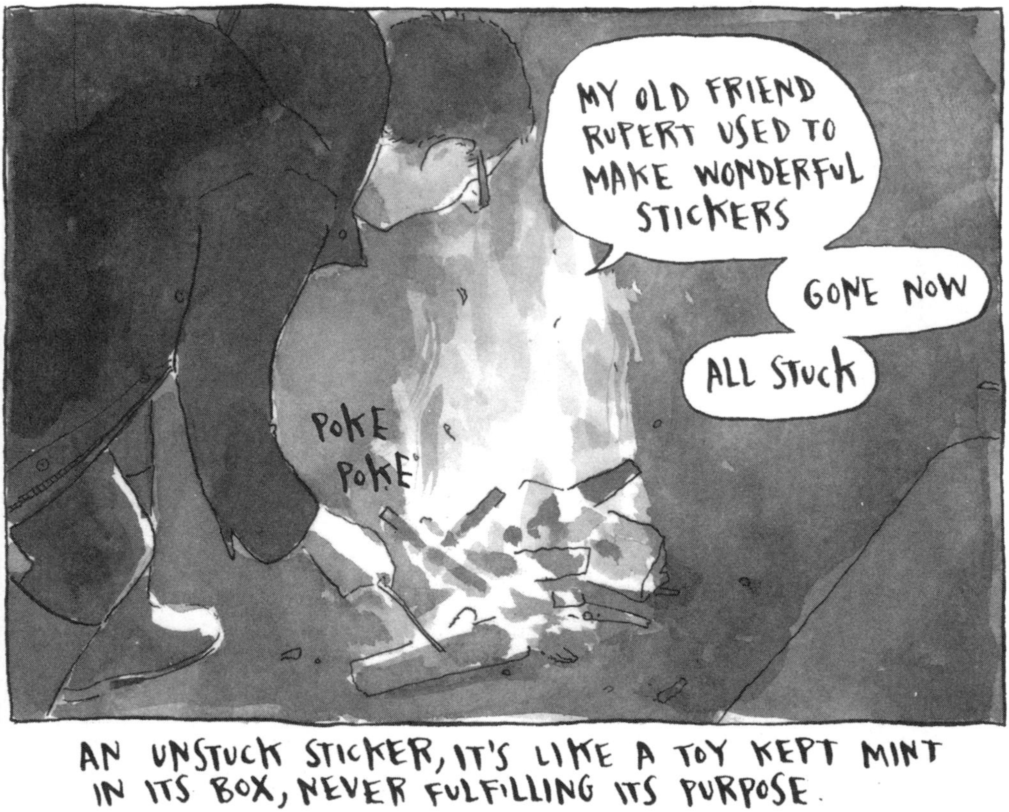
MY OLD FRIEND RUPERT USED TO MAKE WONDERFUL STICKERS
GONE NOW
ALL STUCK
POKE POKE

AN UNSTUCK STICKER, IT'S LIKE A TOY KEPT MINT IN ITS BOX, NEVER FULFILLING ITS PURPOSE.

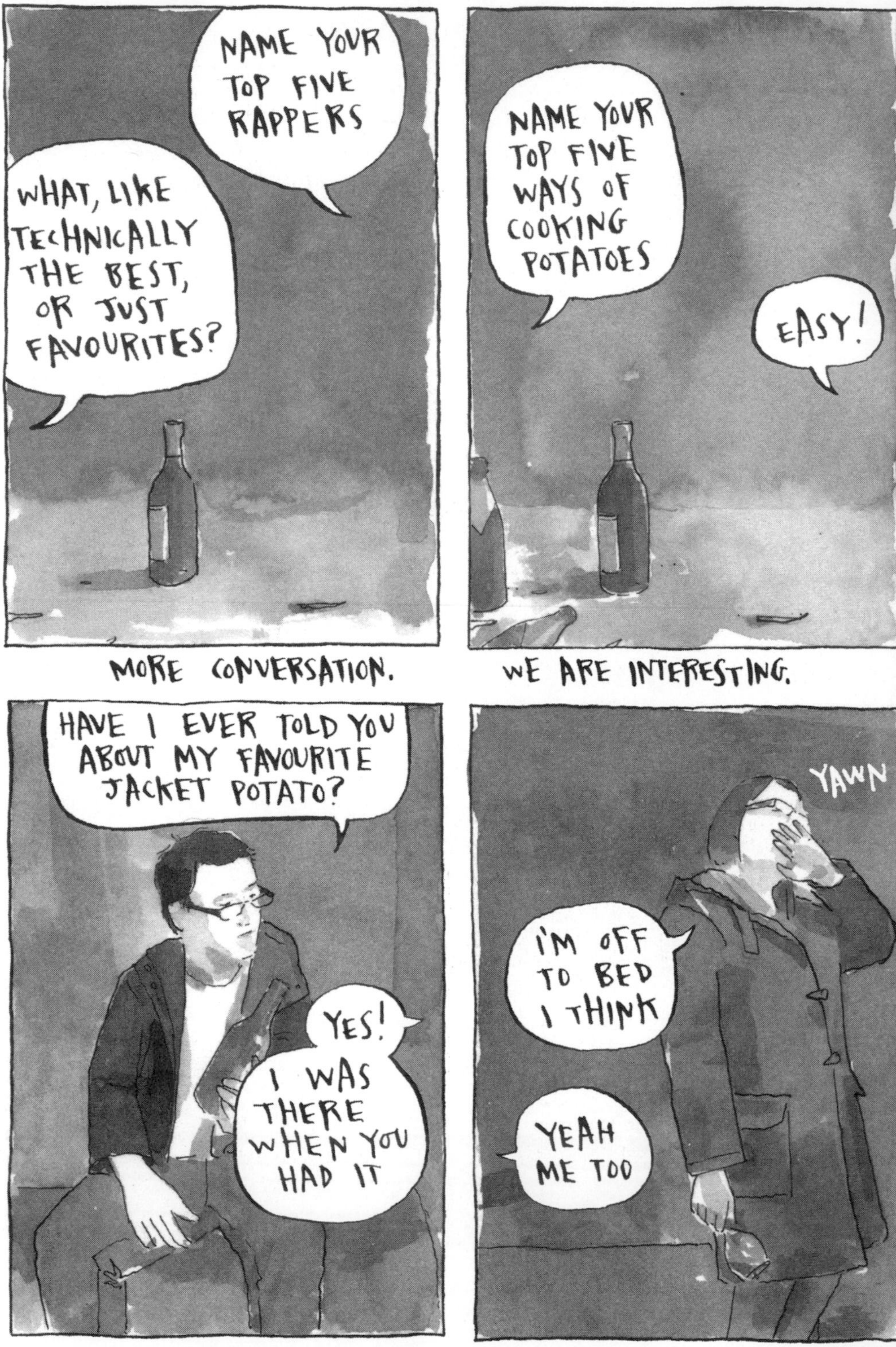
NAME YOUR TOP FIVE RAPPERS
WHAT, LIKE TECHNICALLY THE BEST, OR JUST FAVOURITES?
MORE CONVERSATION.
NAME YOUR TOP FIVE WAYS OF COOKING POTATOES
EASY!
WE ARE INTERESTING.
HAVE I EVER TOLD YOU ABOUT MY FAVOURITE JACKET POTATO?
YES!
I WAS THERE WHEN YOU HAD IT
YAWN
I'M OFF TO BED I THINK
YEAH ME TOO

BUT BEFORE I TURN IN, I HAVE TO...

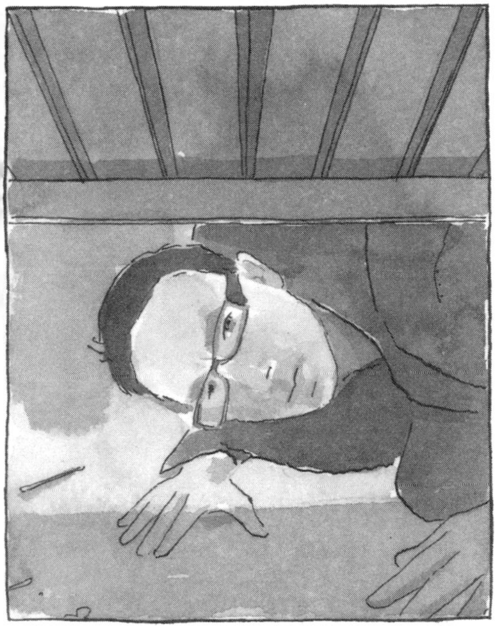

...SPEND 20 MINUTES CHECKING FOR SPIDERS...

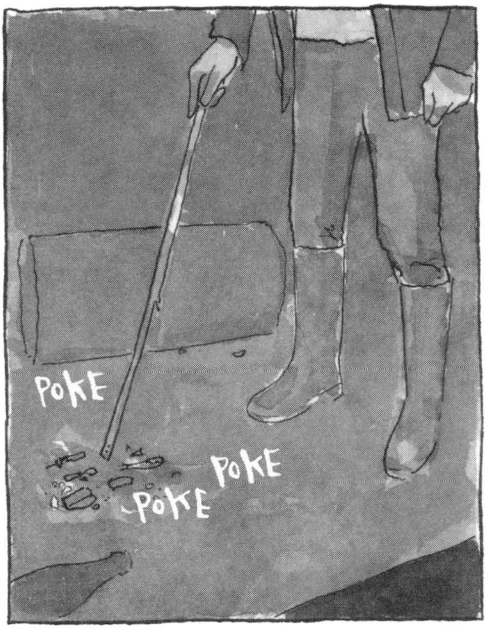
POKE
POKE
POKE

...10 MINUTES WORRYING ABOUT EMBERS FROM THE FIRE...

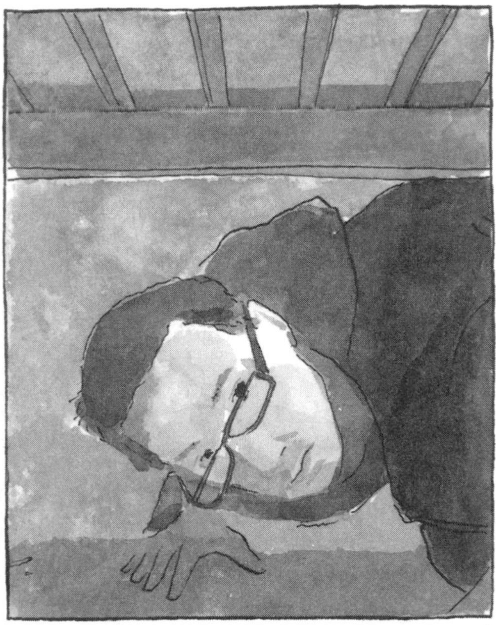

... 10 MINUTES DOUBLE CHECKING FOR UNSEEN SPIDERS...

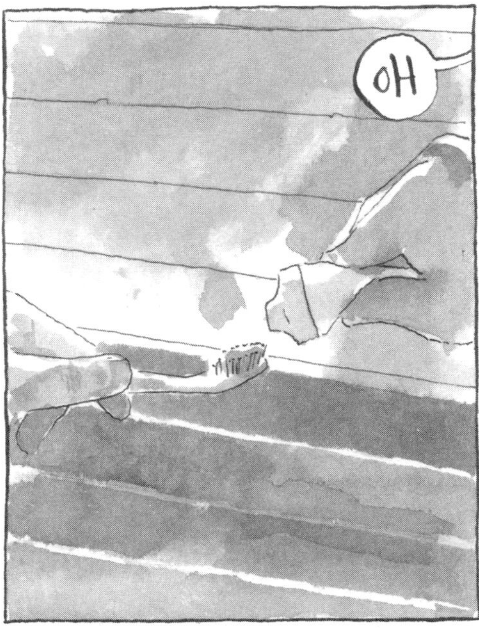
OH

...THEN FINALLY, BRUSH MY TEETH (2 MINUTES)

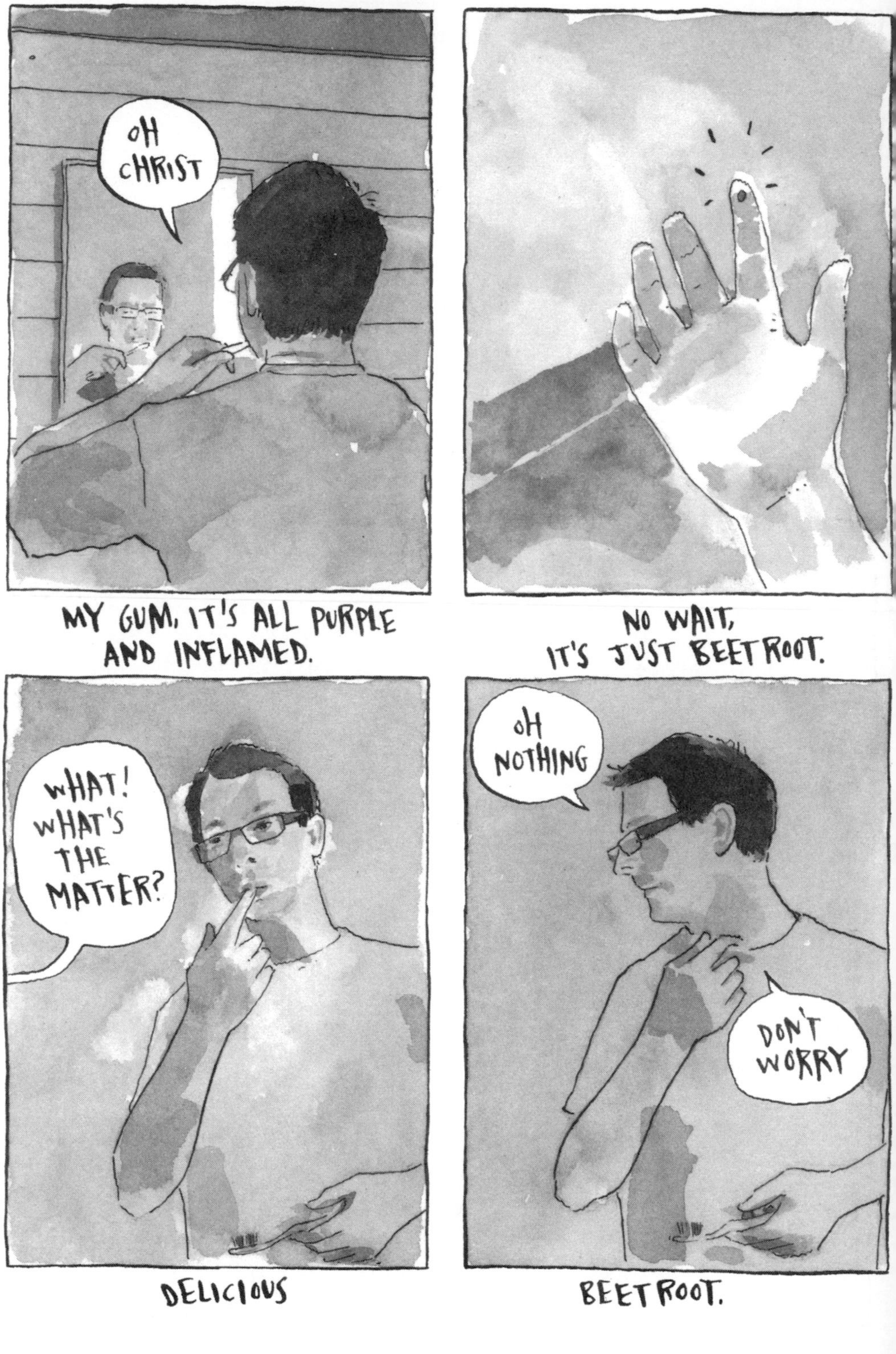
OH CHRIST
MY GUM, IT'S ALL PURPLE AND INFLAMED.
NO WAIT, IT'S JUST BEETROOT.
WHAT! WHAT'S THE MATTER?
DELICIOUS
OH NOTHING
DON'T WORRY
BEETROOT.

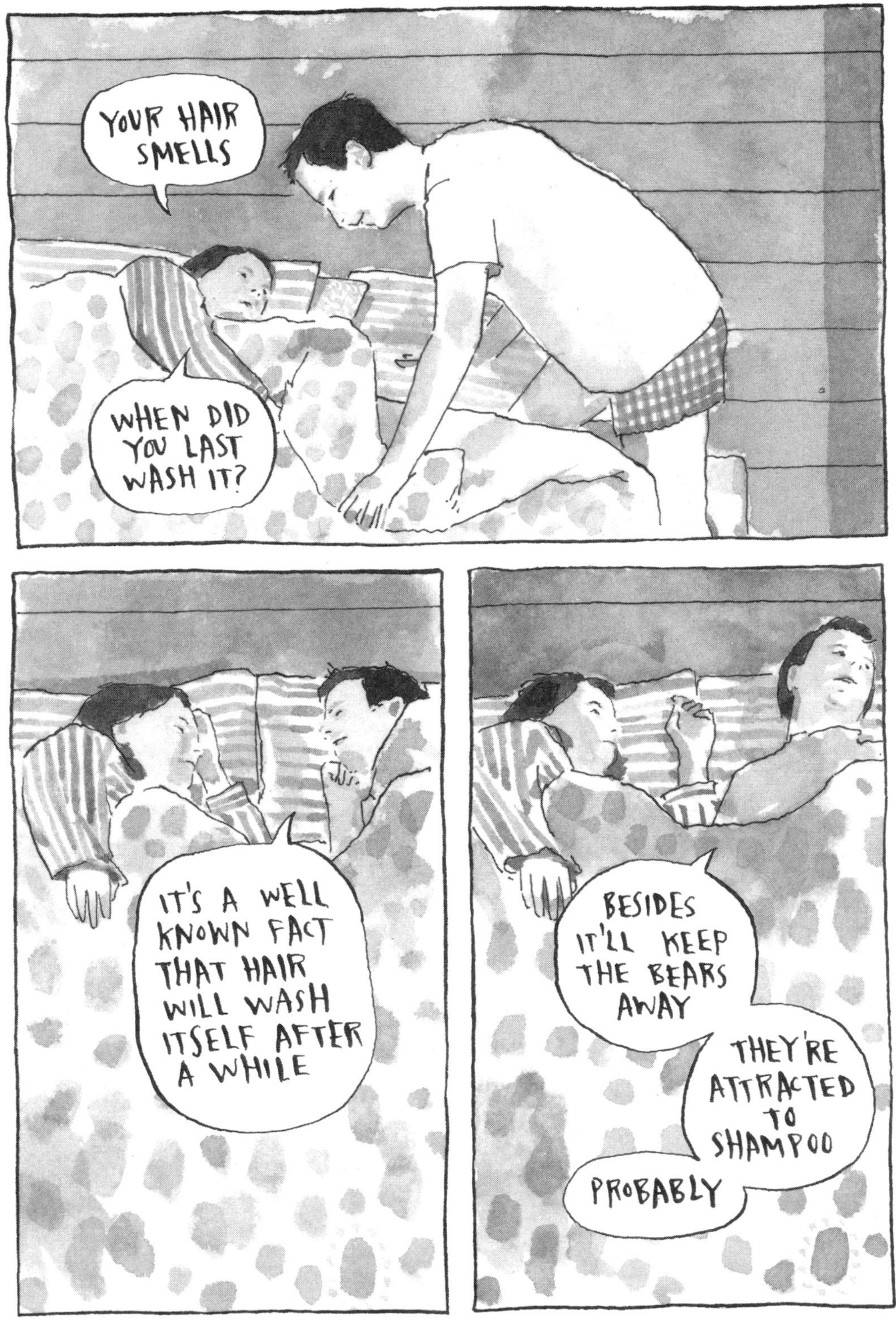
YOUR HAIR SMELLS
WHEN DID YOU LAST WASH IT?
IT'S A WELL KNOWN FACT THAT HAIR WILL WASH ITSELF AFTER A WHILE
BESIDES IT'LL KEEP THE BEARS AWAY
THEY'RE ATTRACTED TO SHAMPOO
PROBABLY

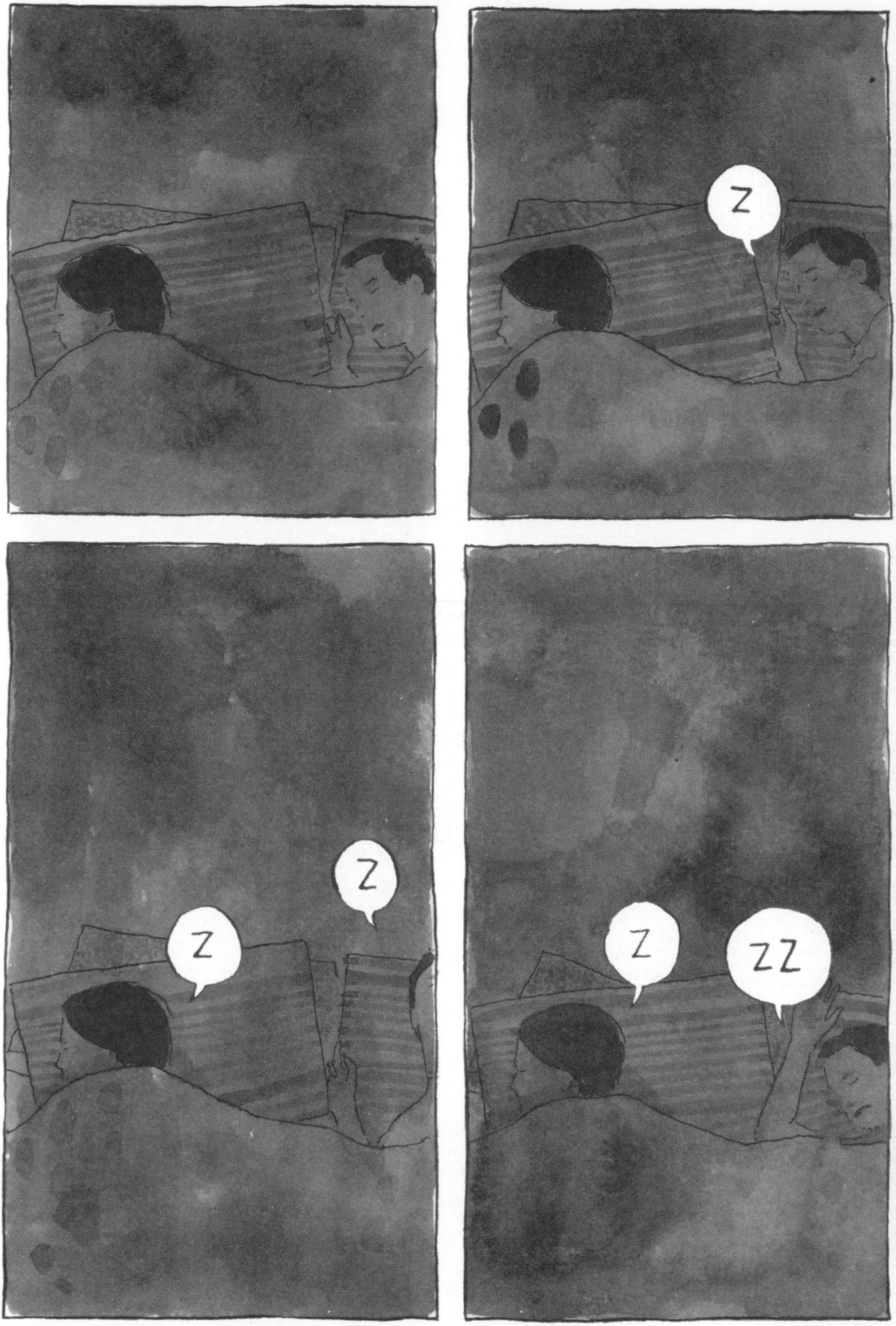
Z
Z
Z
Z
ZZ

2 AM...

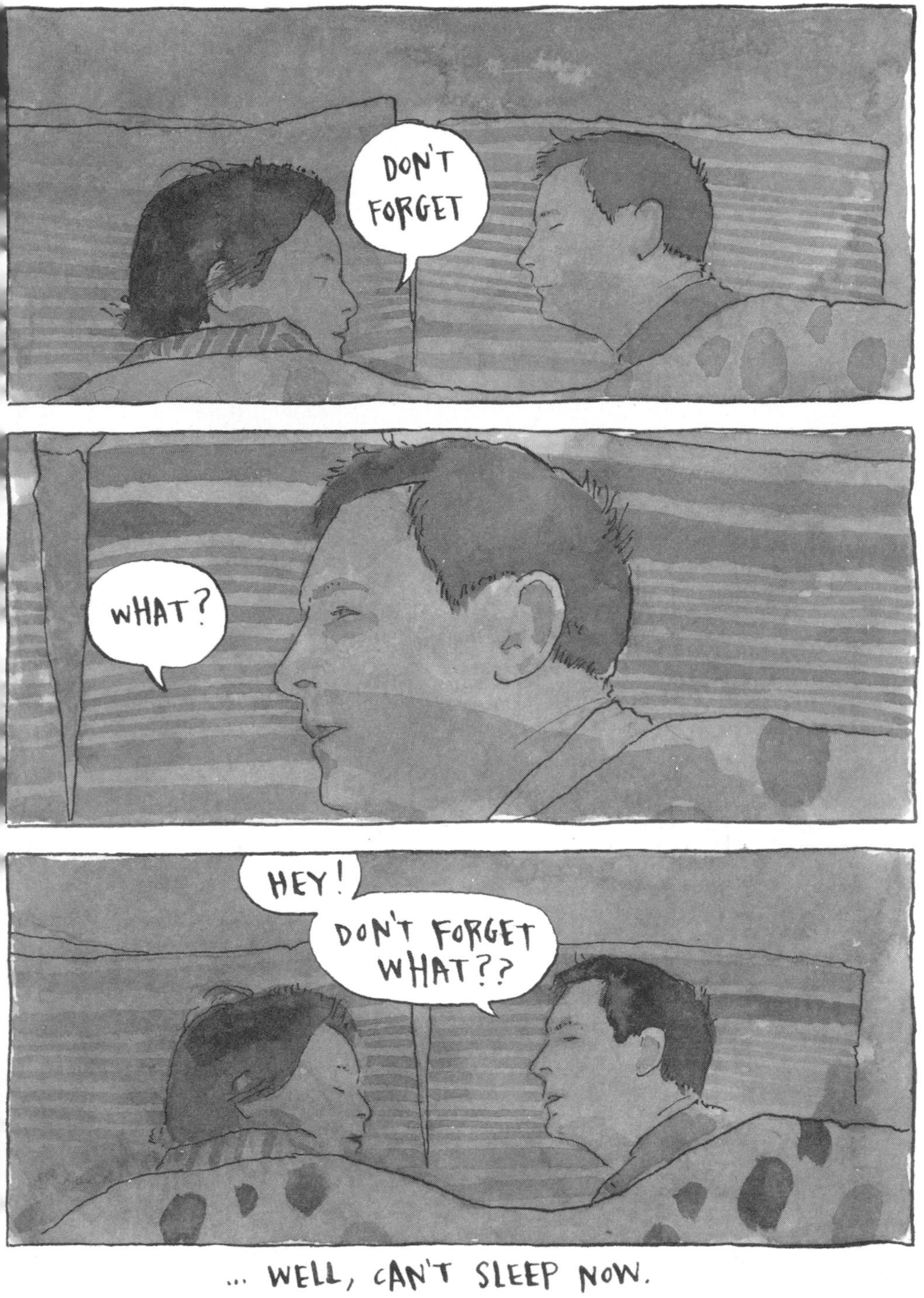
DON'T FORGET
WHAT?
HEY!
DON'T FORGET WHAT??

... WELL, CAN'T SLEEP NOW.

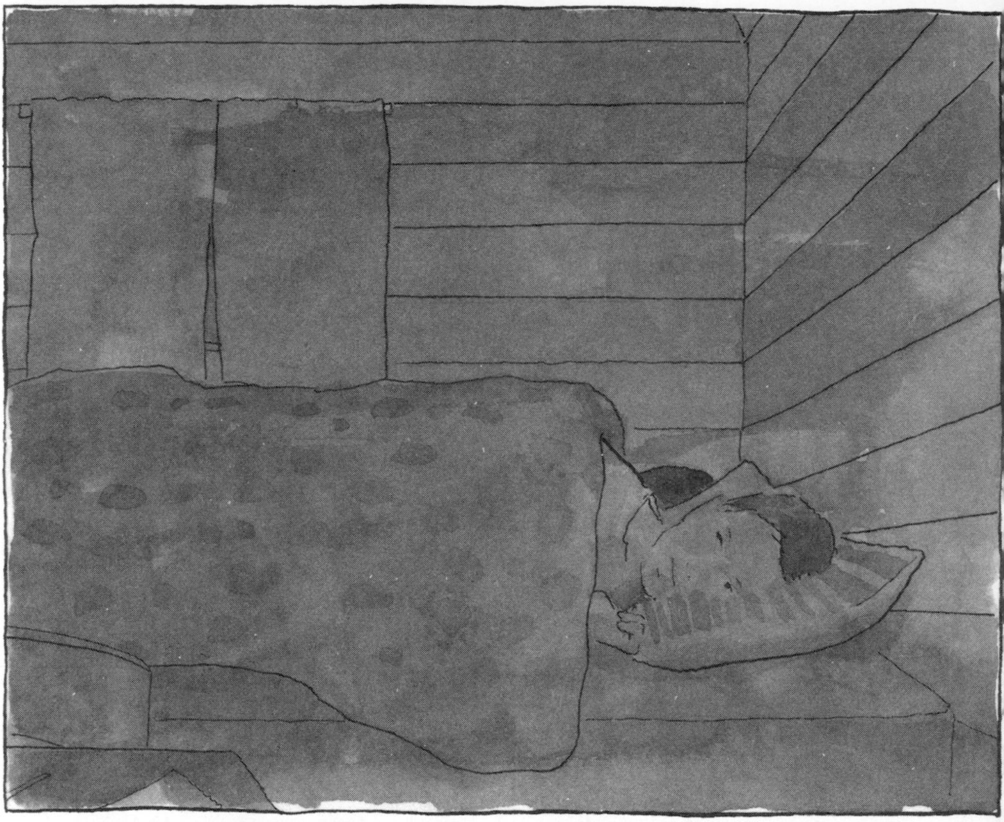

IT'S TIMES LIKE THESE WHEN LITTLE WORRIES CAN GET THE BETTER OF YOU.

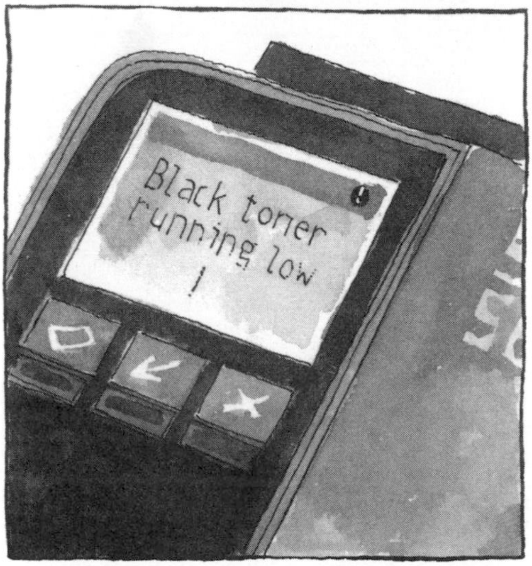
Black toner
running low
!

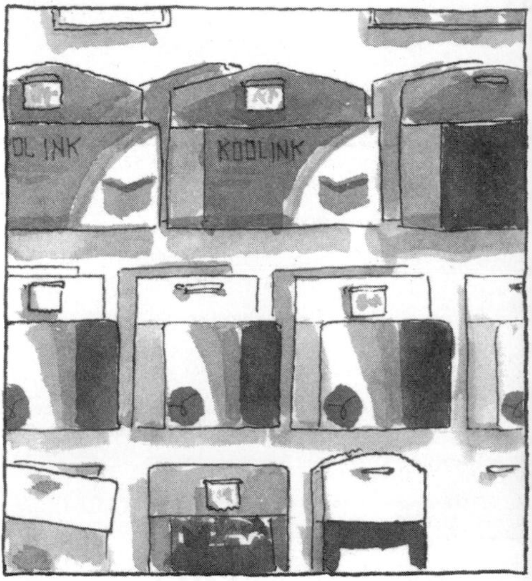
KOOLINK

WORRIES LIKE THE COST OF REPLACEMENT PRINTER INK.

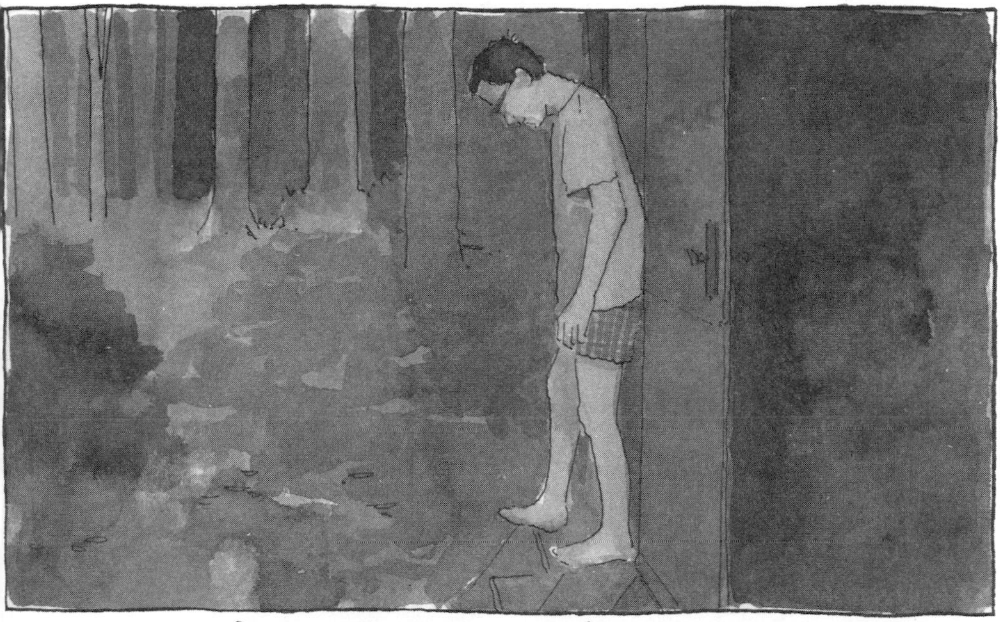

GO OUTSIDE FOR A BIT. CLEAR MY MIND.

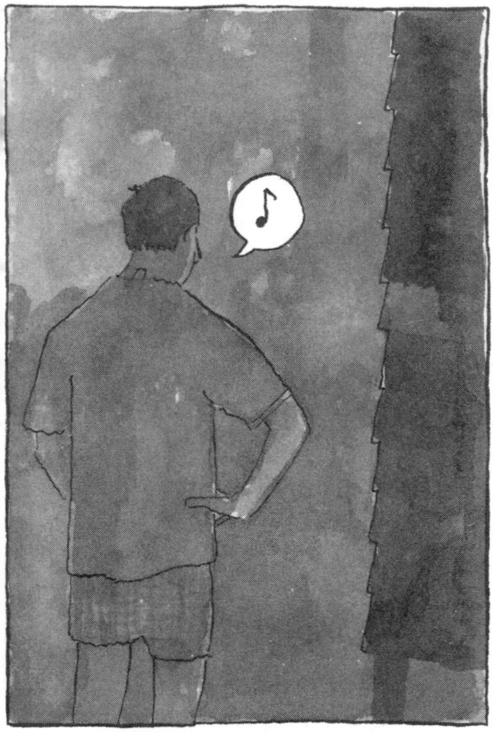

NOTHING BEATS A GOOD DARK NIGHT

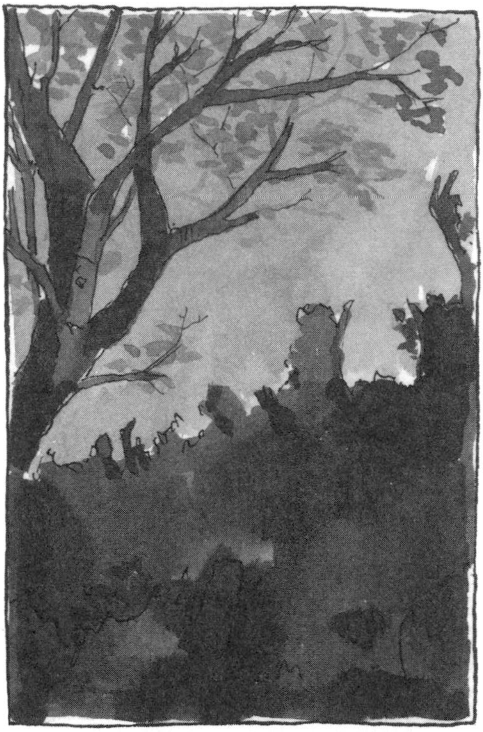

AND SILHOUETTES, EVERYONE LOVES A SILHOUETTE.

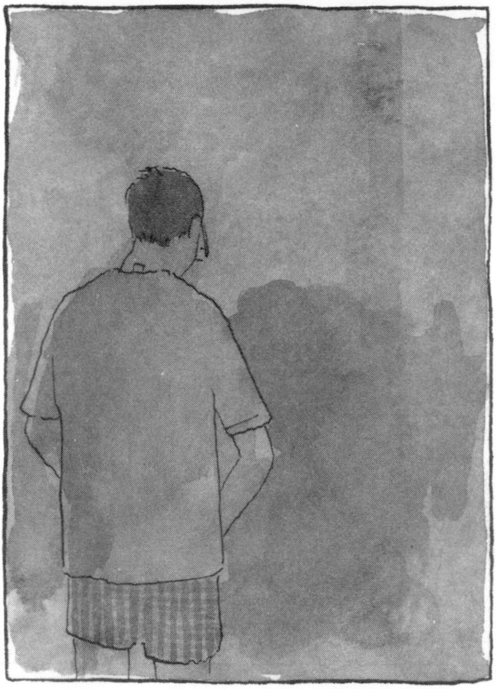

WEE INTO THE ABYSS

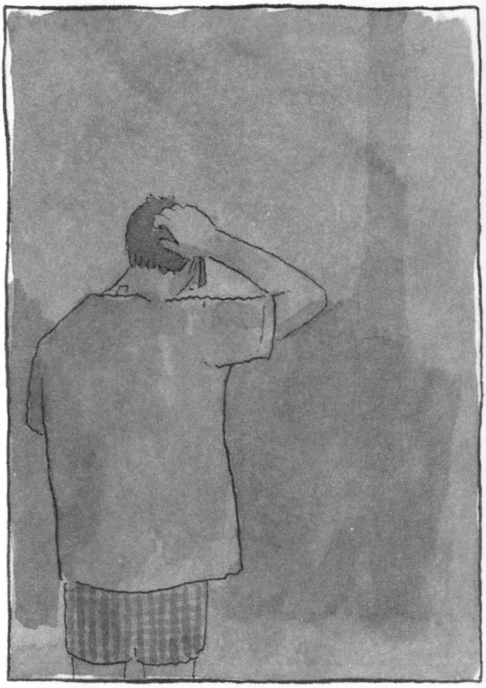

LISTEN TO THE SILENCE

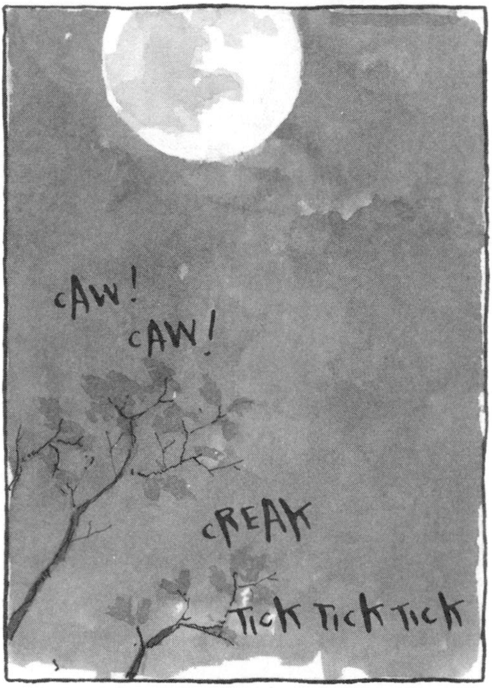
CAW!
CAW!
CREAK
TICK TICK TICK

ANYWAY,

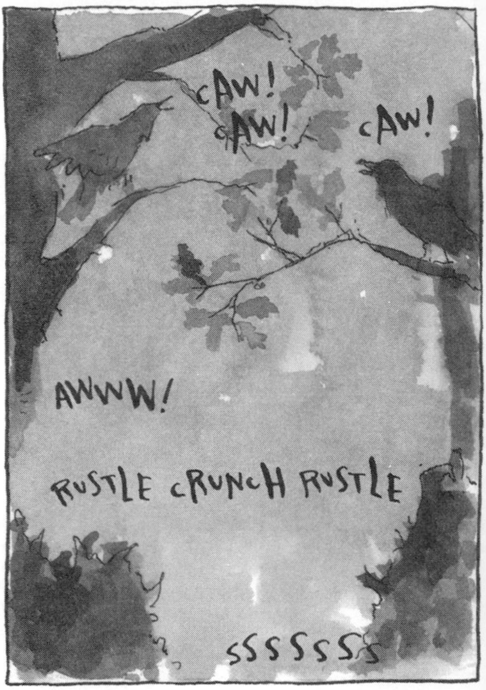
CAW!
CAW!
CAW!
AWWW!
RUSTLE CRUNCH RUSTLE
SSSSSSS

IT'S GETTING A BIT COLD

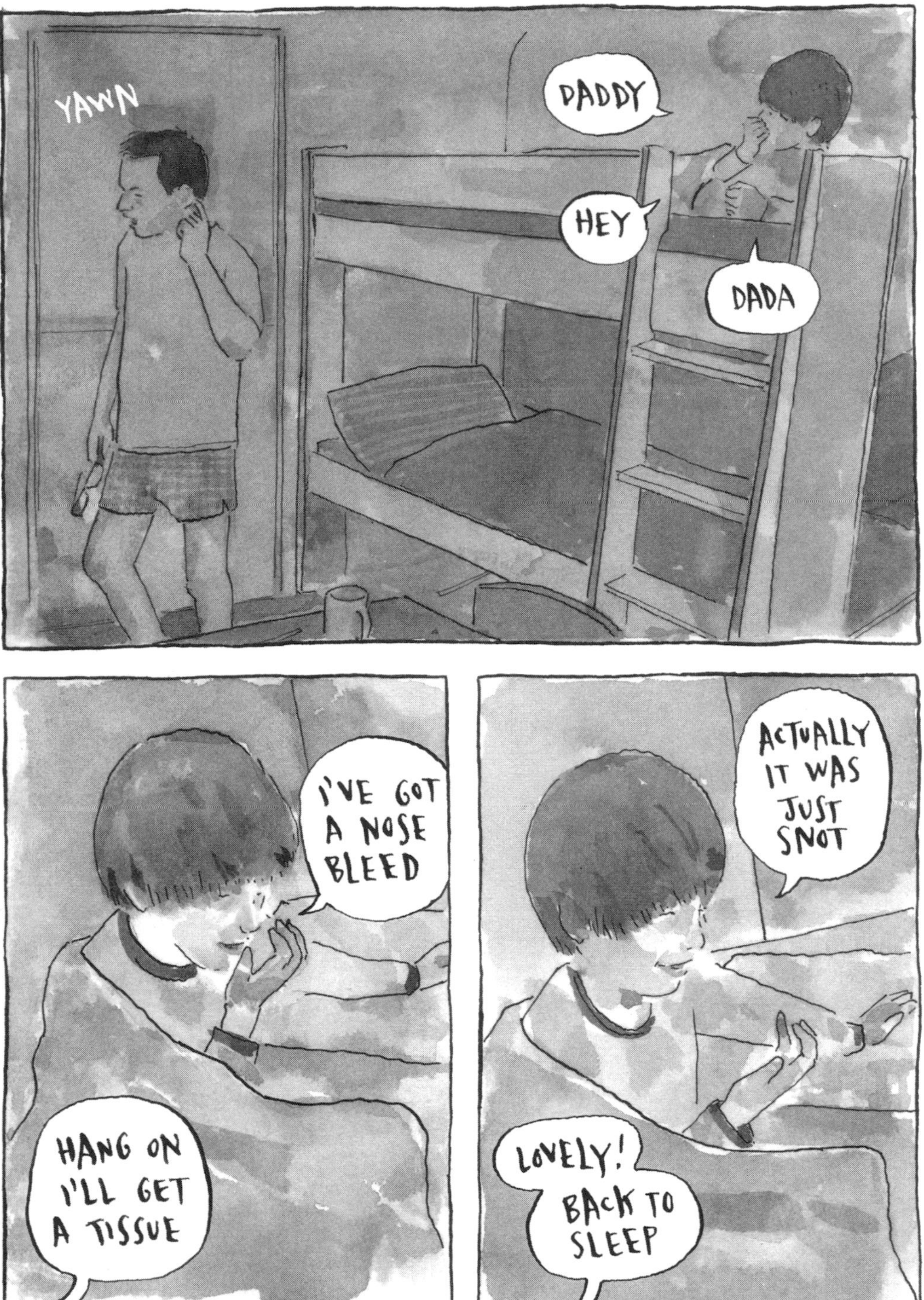
YAWN
DADDY
HEY
DADA
I'VE GOT A NOSE BLEED
HANG ON I'LL GET A TISSUE
ACTUALLY IT WAS JUST SNOT
LOVELY! BACK TO SLEEP

BY THREE A.M WE ARE ALL ASLEEP.

DAWN COMES ABOUT FOUR A.M.
MORNING HAS BROKEN. BROKEN ME.

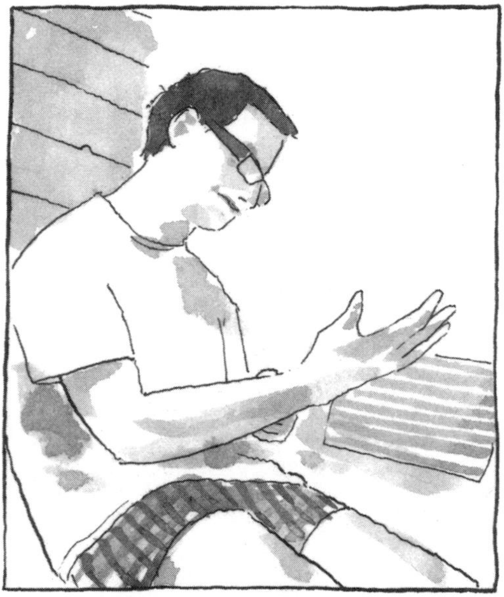

I'VE GOT SMALL BITES
ON MY HAND

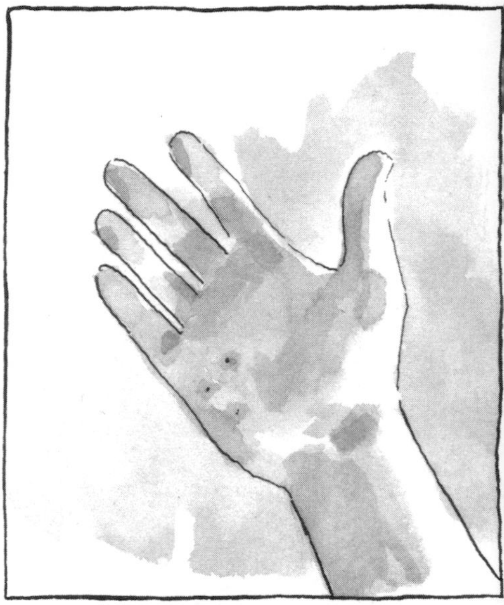

PROBABLY
MOSQUITO BITES

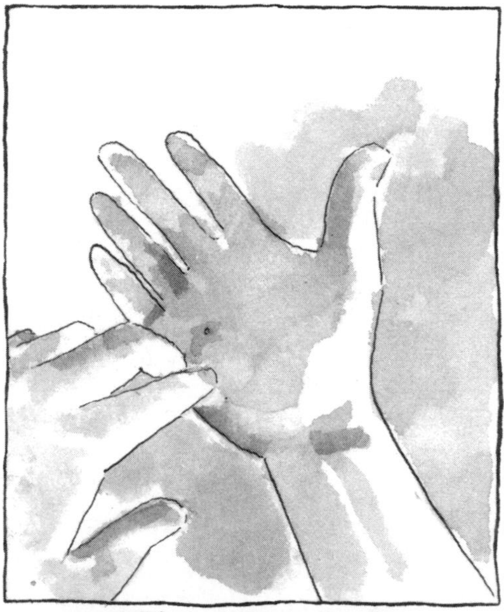

PROBABLY NOT A STRANGE
TROPICAL PARASITE THAT'S
LAID EGGS UNDER MY SKIN.

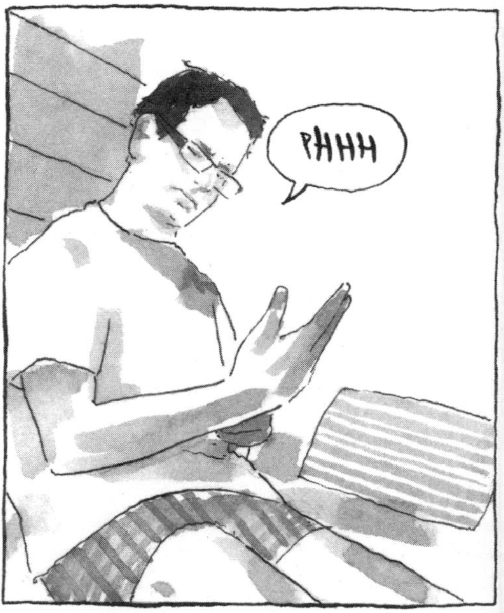
PHHH

PROBABLY NOT.

TO TREAT THE BITES I USE AN "ALL IN" METHOD. MIXING WHATEVER PHARMACEUTICALS I HAVE TO HAND.

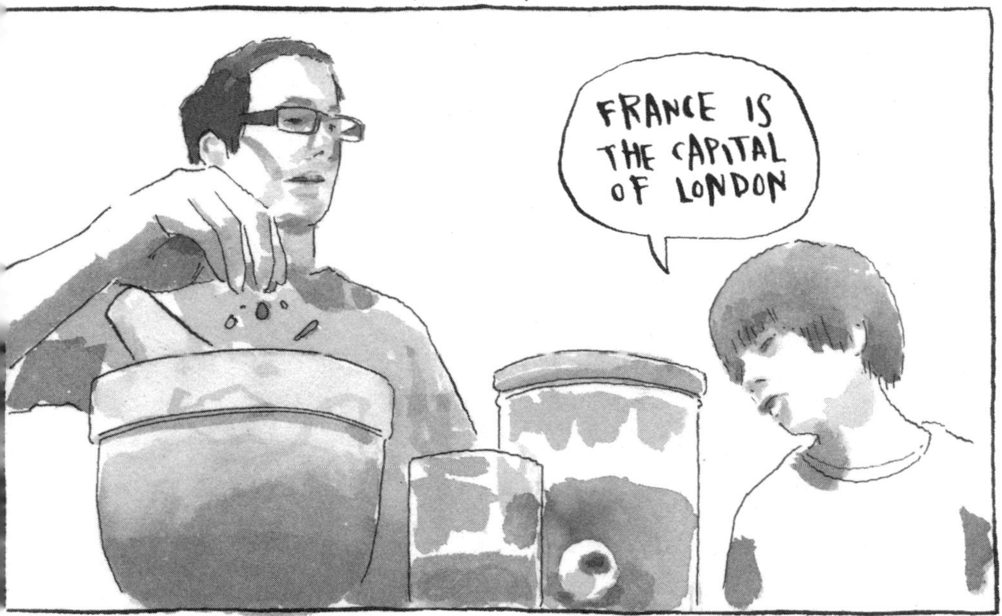
FRANCE IS THE CAPITAL OF LONDON

ANTIBIOTICS, TIGER BALM, HYDROCORTISONE, MORPHINE AND SOME HOMEOPATHIC PILLS, JUST FOR FUN.

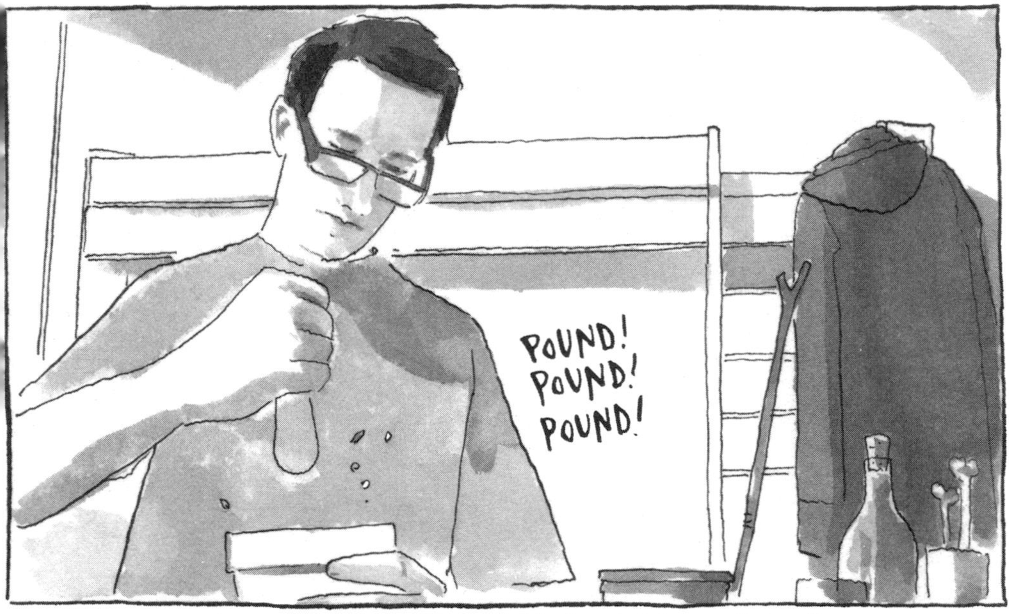
POUND! POUND! POUND!

LEAVE IT ON THE WOUND UNTIL IT BURNS. EVERY IDIOT KNOWS "NO PAIN, NO GAIN".

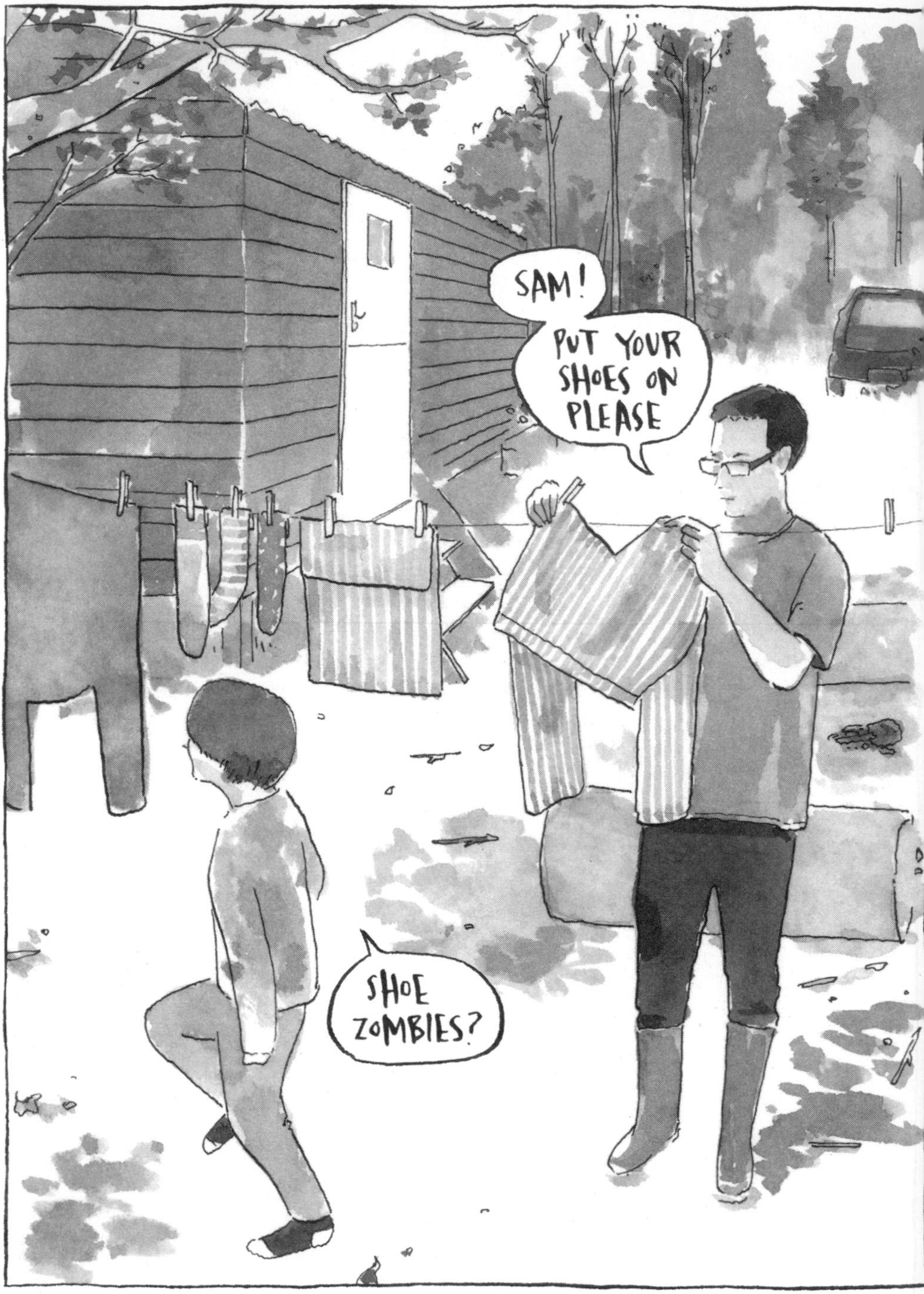
SAM!
PUT YOUR SHOES ON PLEASE
SHOE ZOMBIES?

I'M NOT A GAMBLING MAN,
BUT THE RISKS WHEN HANGING OUT WASHING ARE QUITE HIGH...

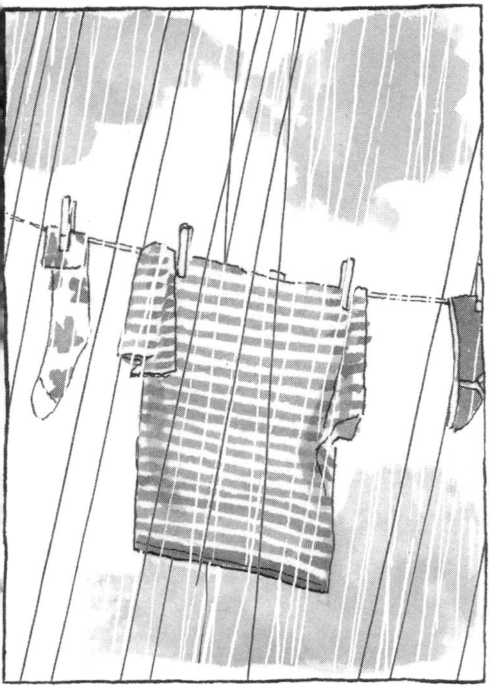

3/1 CHANCE OF RAIN

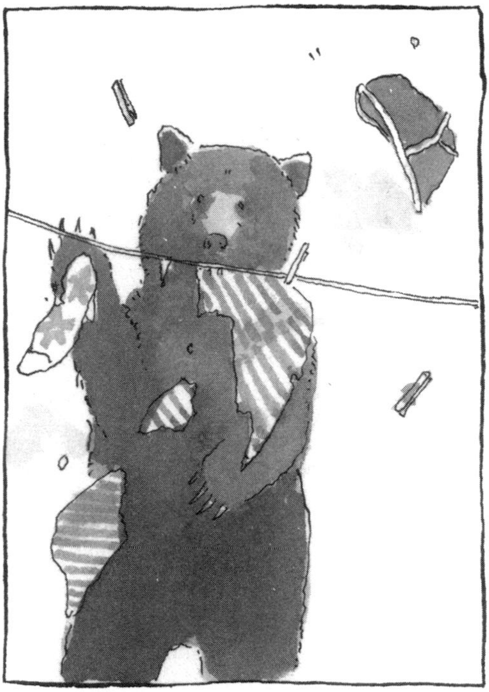

4/1 EATEN BY BEARS

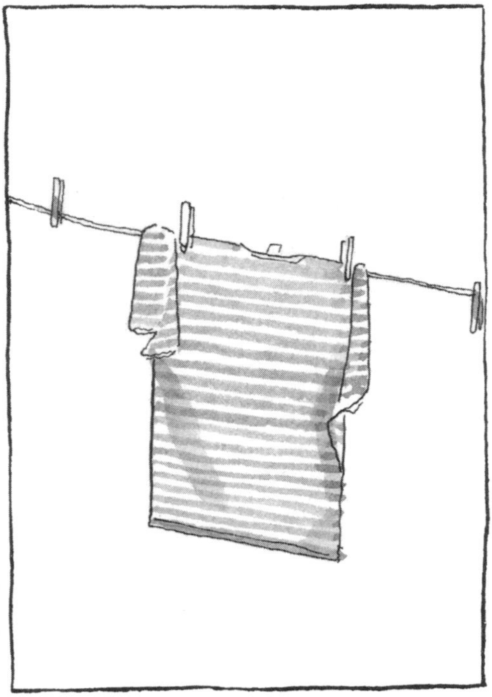

20/1 UNDERWEAR STOLEN

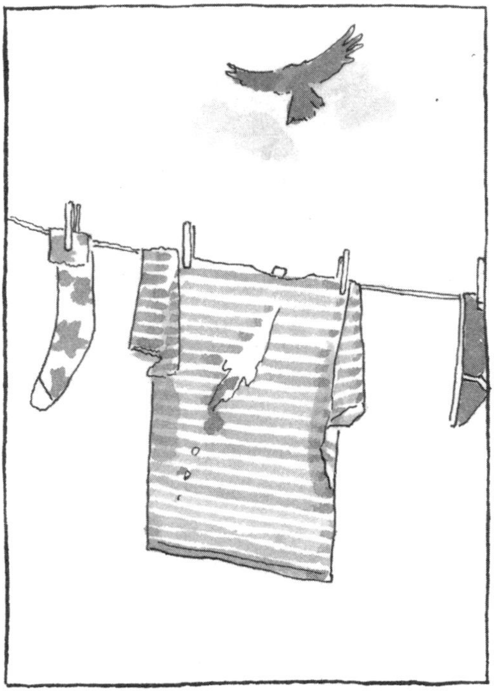

ODDS ON :- BIRD POO

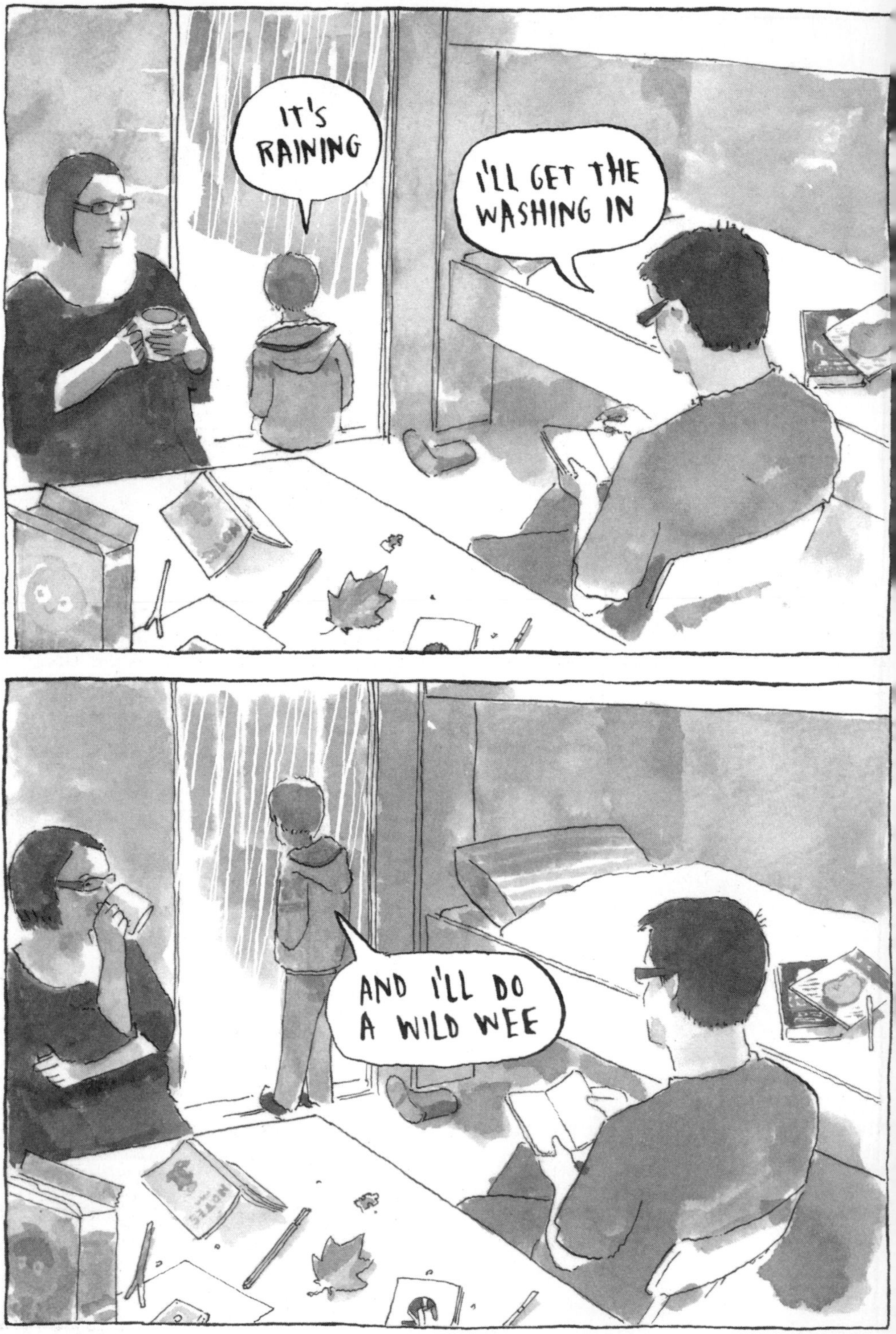
IT'S RAINING
I'LL GET THE WASHING IN
AND I'LL DO A WILD WEE

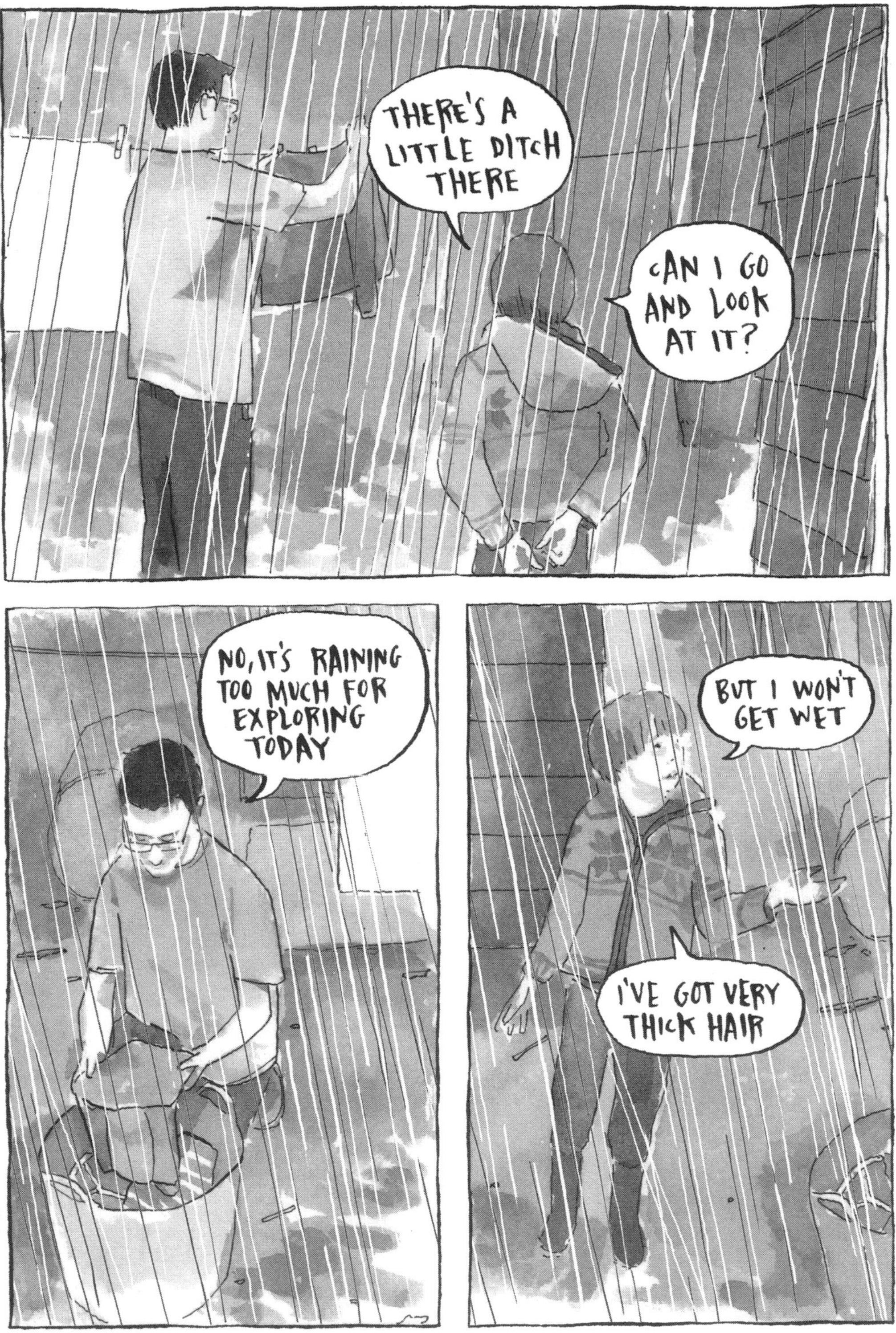
THERE'S A LITTLE DITCH THERE
CAN I GO AND LOOK AT IT?
NO, IT'S RAINING TOO MUCH FOR EXPLORING TODAY
BUT I WON'T GET WET
I'VE GOT VERY THICK HAIR

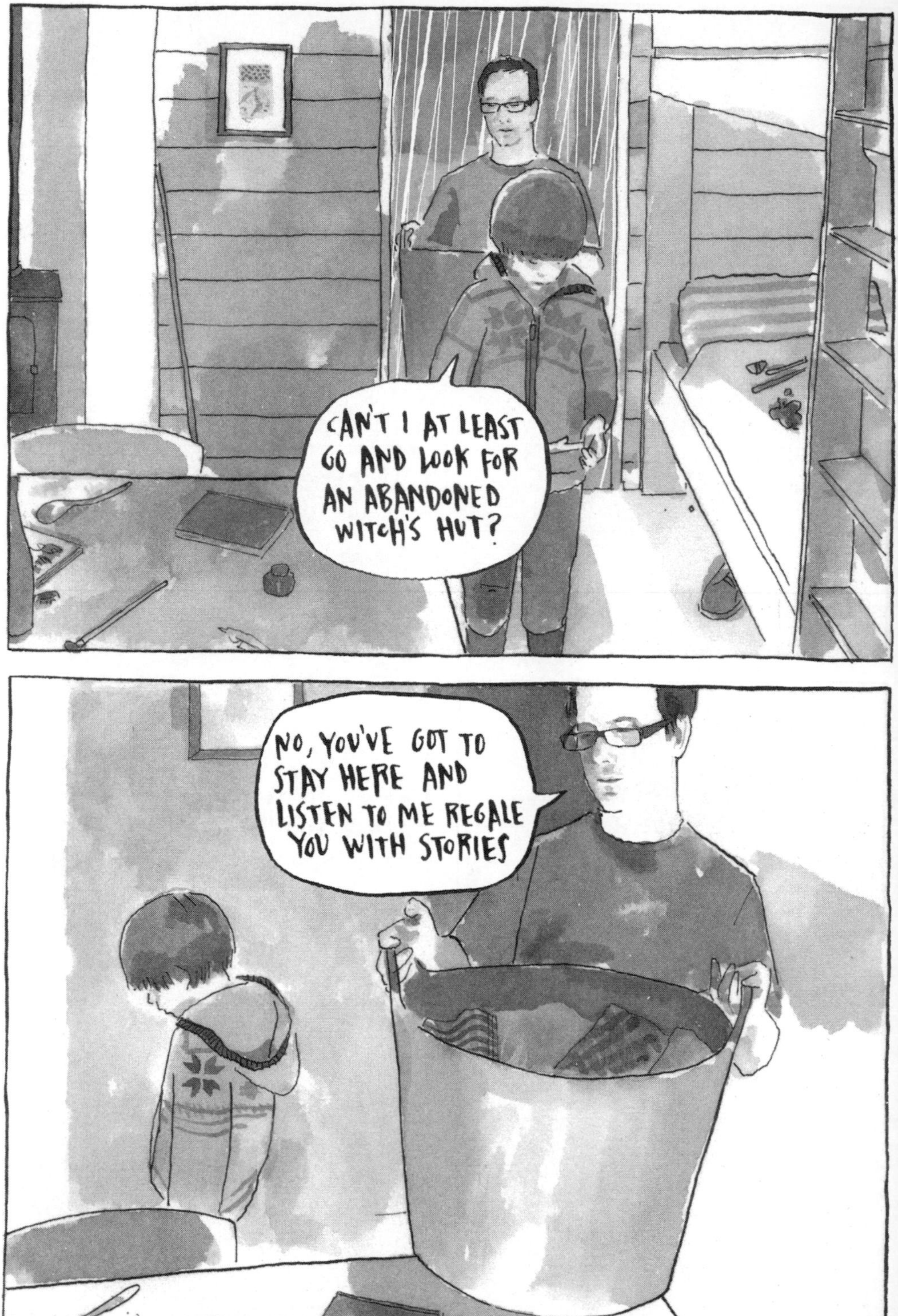
CAN'T I AT LEAST GO AND LOOK FOR AN ABANDONED WITCH'S HUT?
NO, YOU'VE GOT TO STAY HERE AND LISTEN TO ME REGALE YOU WITH STORIES

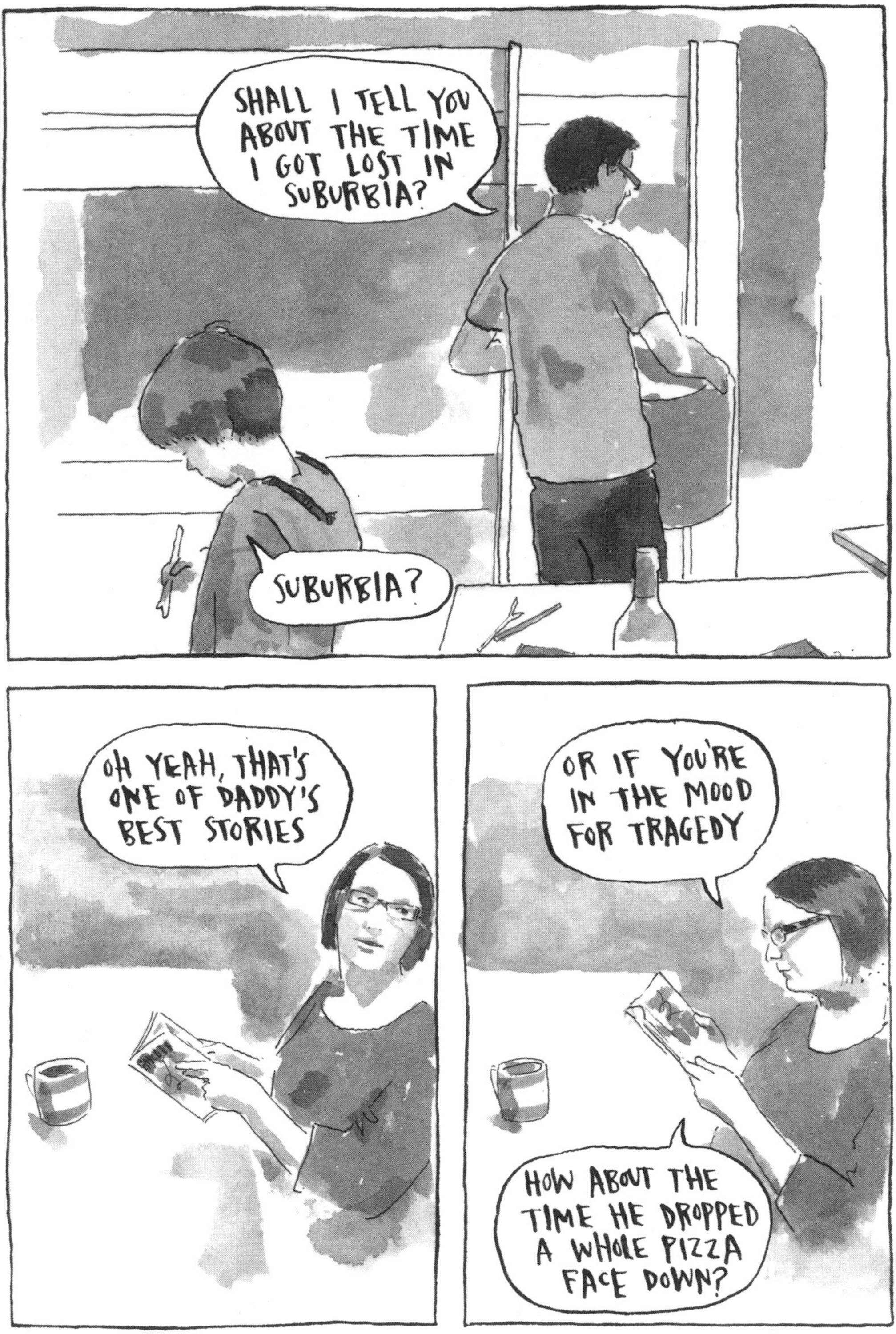
SHALL I TELL YOU ABOUT THE TIME I GOT LOST IN SUBURBIA?
SUBURBIA?
OH YEAH, THAT'S ONE OF DADDY'S BEST STORIES
OR IF YOU'RE IN THE MOOD FOR TRAGEDY
HOW ABOUT THE TIME HE DROPPED A WHOLE PIZZA FACE DOWN?

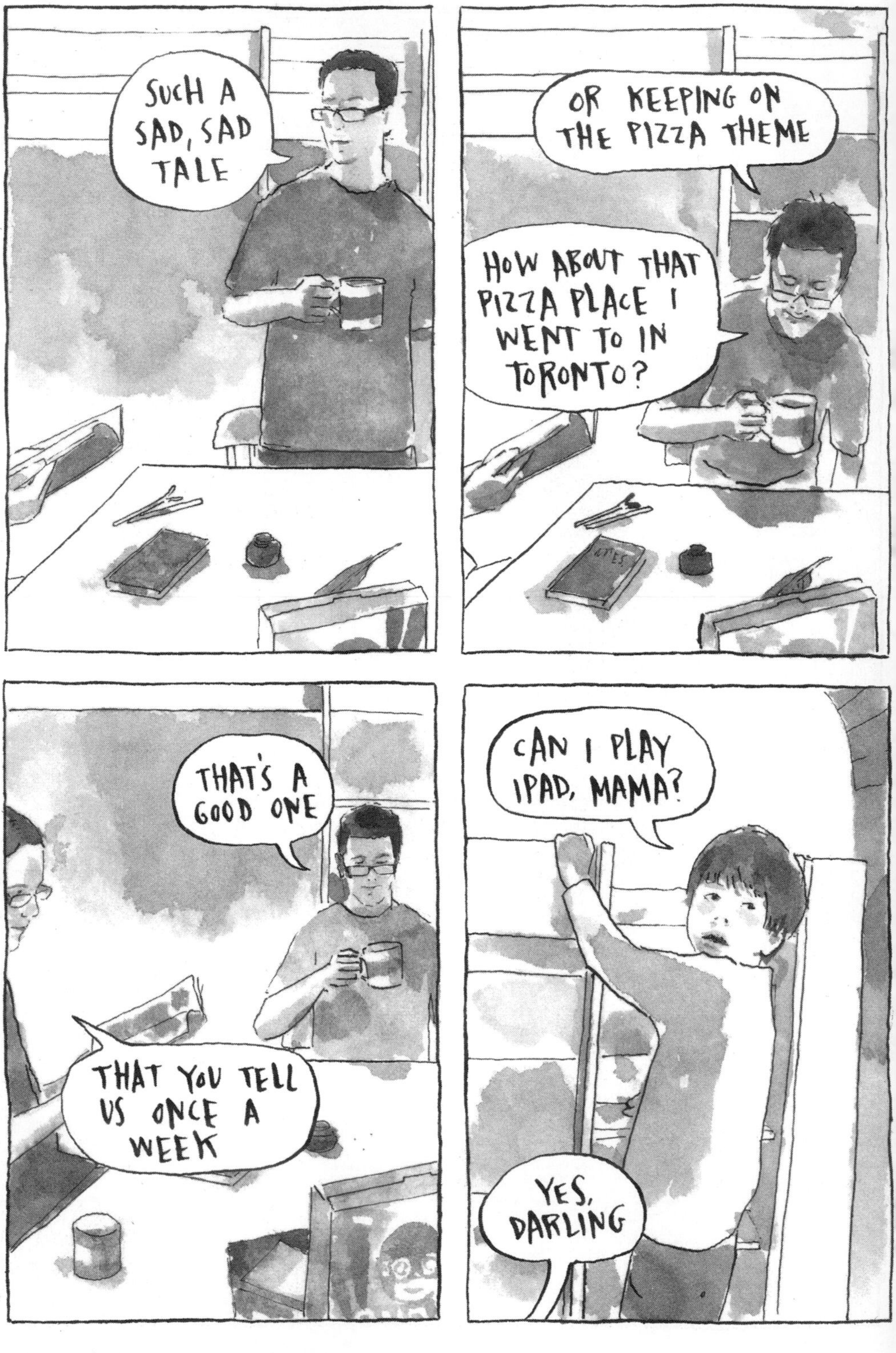
SUCH A SAD, SAD TALE
OR KEEPING ON THE PIZZA THEME
HOW ABOUT THAT PIZZA PLACE I WENT TO IN TORONTO?
THAT'S A GOOD ONE
THAT YOU TELL US ONCE A WEEK
CAN I PLAY IPAD, MAMA?
YES, DARLING

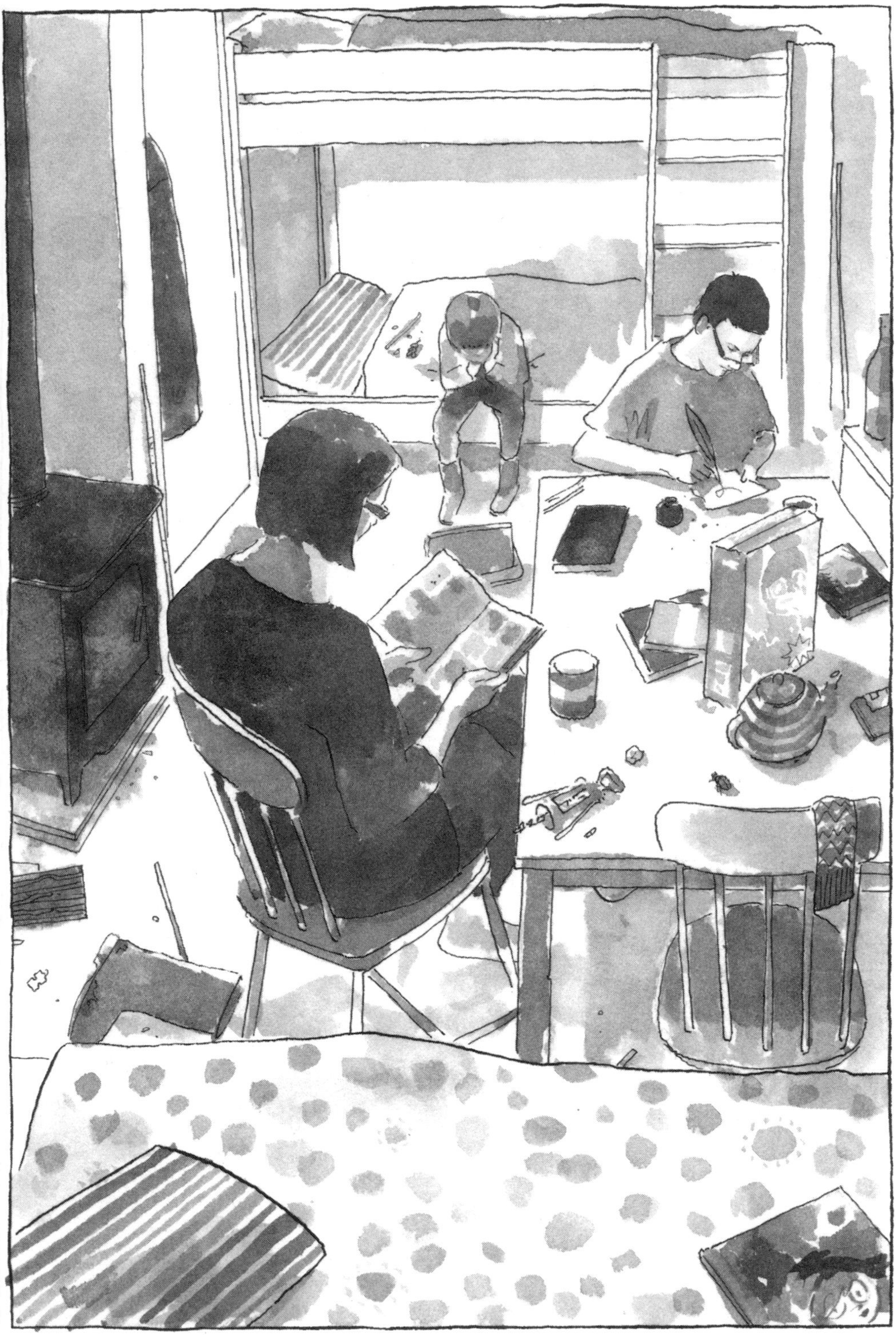

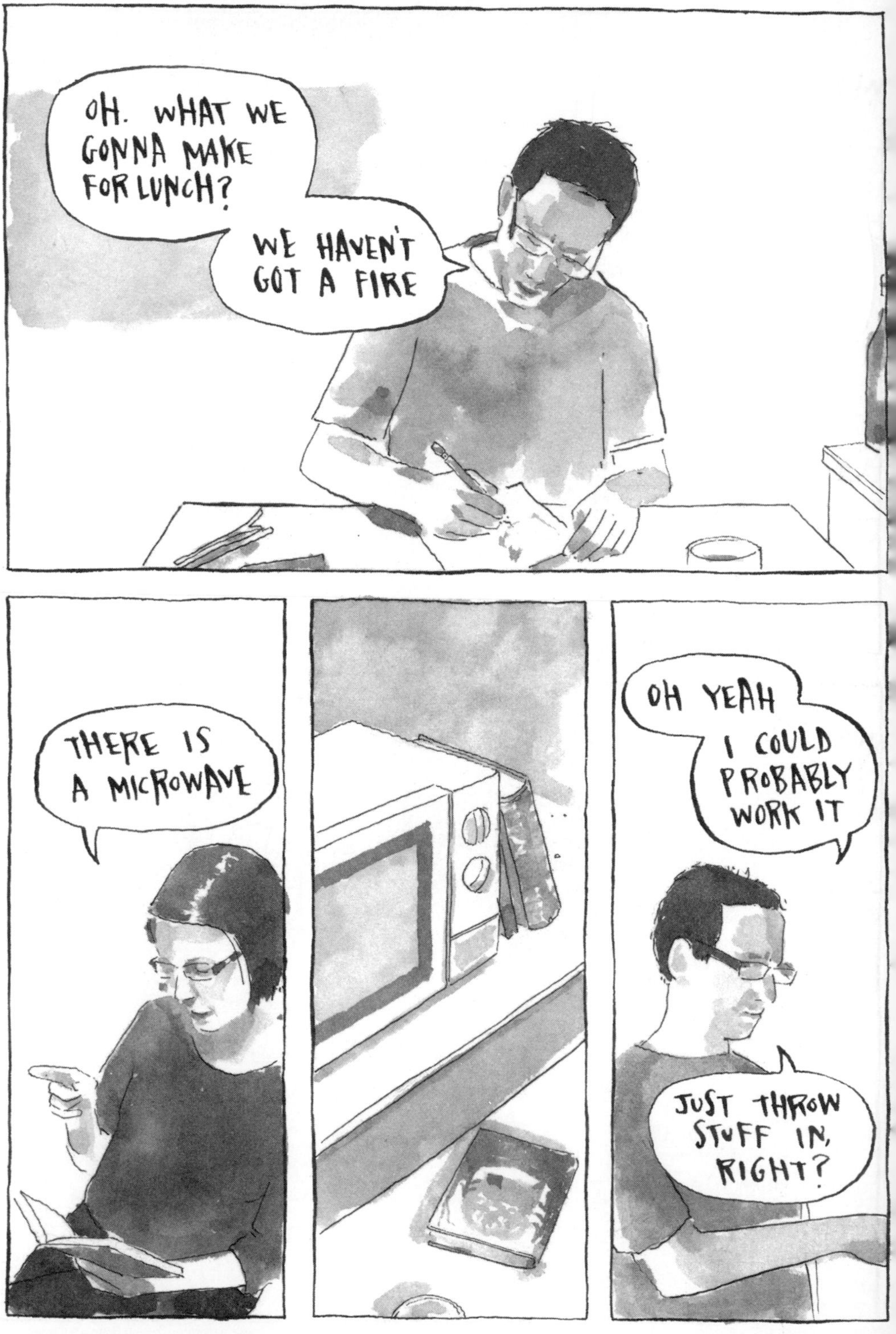
OH. WHAT WE GONNA MAKE FOR LUNCH?
WE HAVEN'T GOT A FIRE
THERE IS A MICROWAVE
OH YEAH
I COULD PROBABLY WORK IT
JUST THROW STUFF IN, RIGHT?

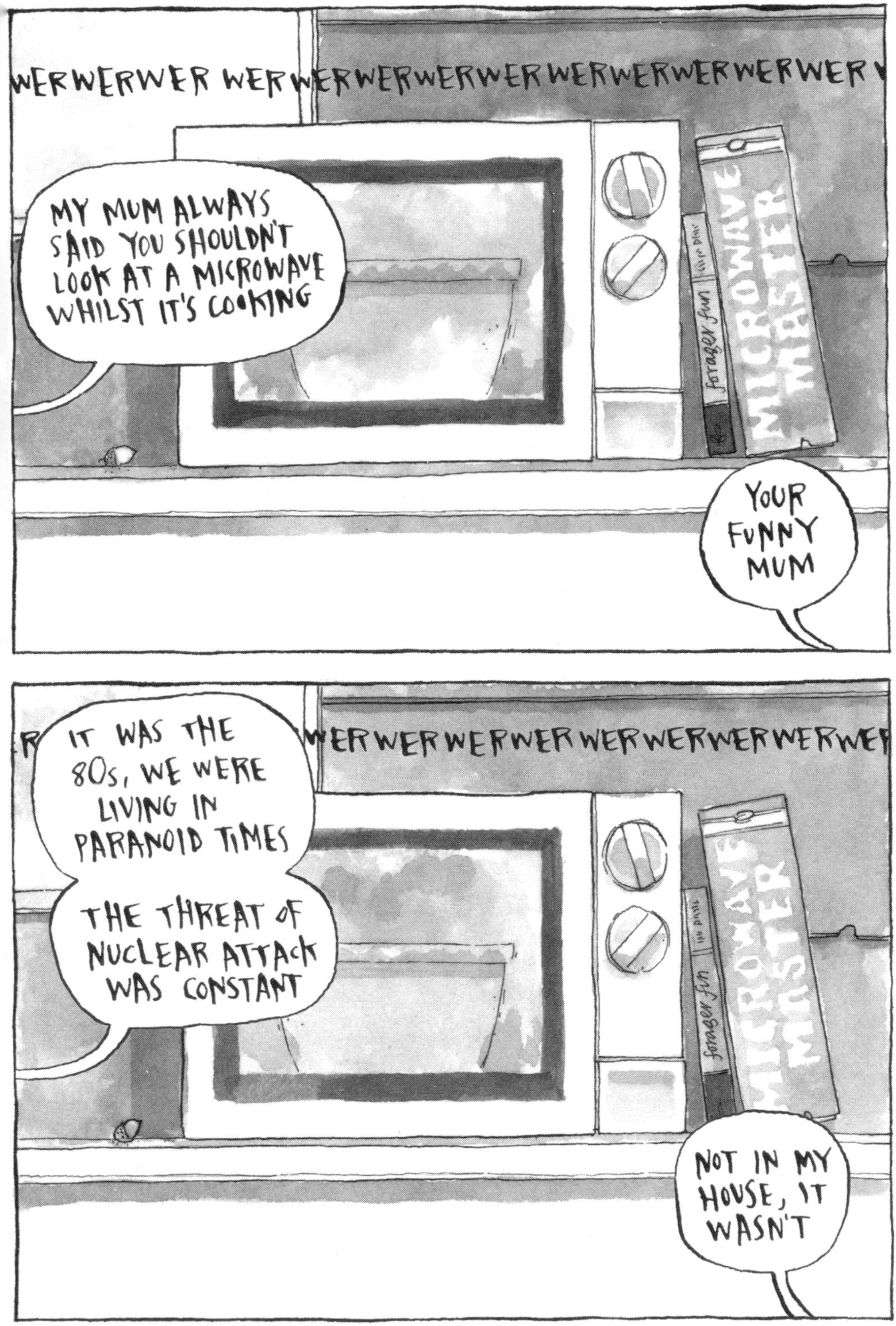
WERWERWER WERWERWERWERWERWERWERWERWERWER
MY MUM ALWAYS SAID YOU SHOULDN'T LOOK AT A MICROWAVE WHILST IT'S COOKING
forager fun
MICROWAVE MASTER
YOUR FUNNY MUM
WERWERWERWERWERWERWERWERWERWER
IT WAS THE 80s, WE WERE LIVING IN PARANOID TIMES
THE THREAT OF NUCLEAR ATTACK WAS CONSTANT
forager fun
MICROWAVE MASTER
NOT IN MY HOUSE, IT WASN'T

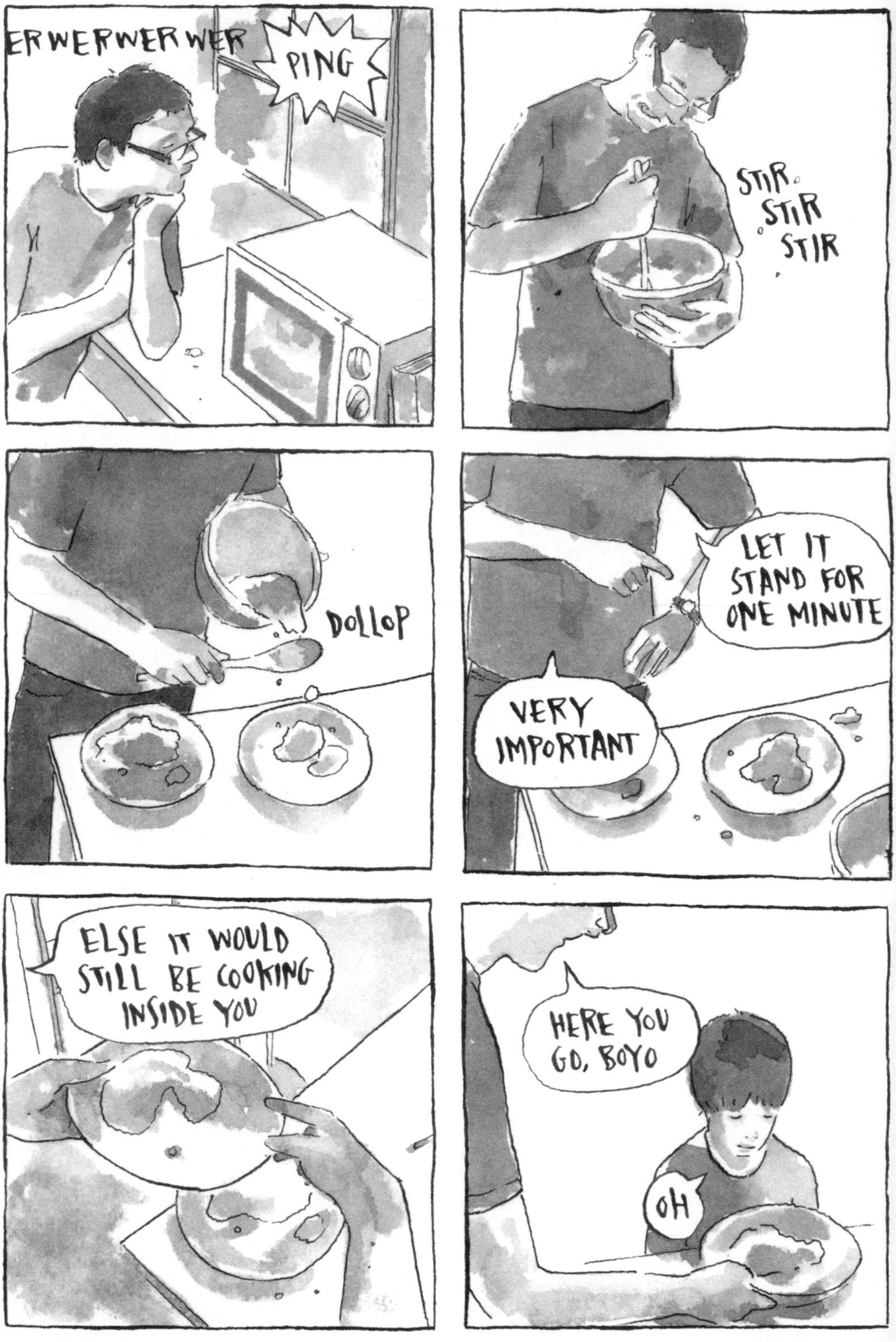
ERWERWERWER
PING
STIR
STIR
STIR
DOLLOP
LET IT STAND FOR ONE MINUTE
VERY IMPORTANT
ELSE IT WOULD STILL BE COOKING INSIDE YOU
HERE YOU GO, BOYO
OH

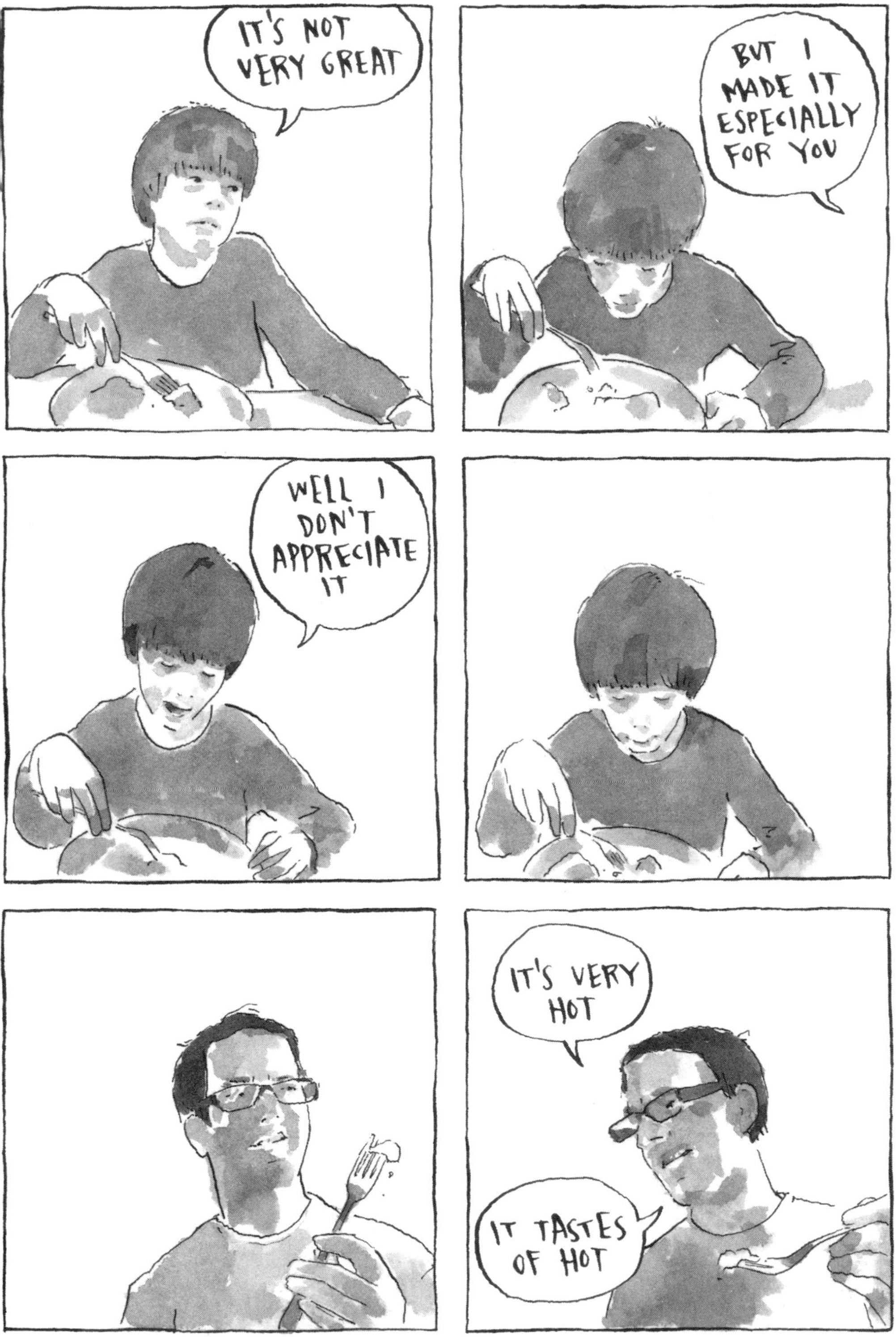
IT'S NOT VERY GREAT
BUT I MADE IT ESPECIALLY FOR YOU
WELL I DON'T APPRECIATE IT
IT'S VERY HOT
IT TASTES OF HOT

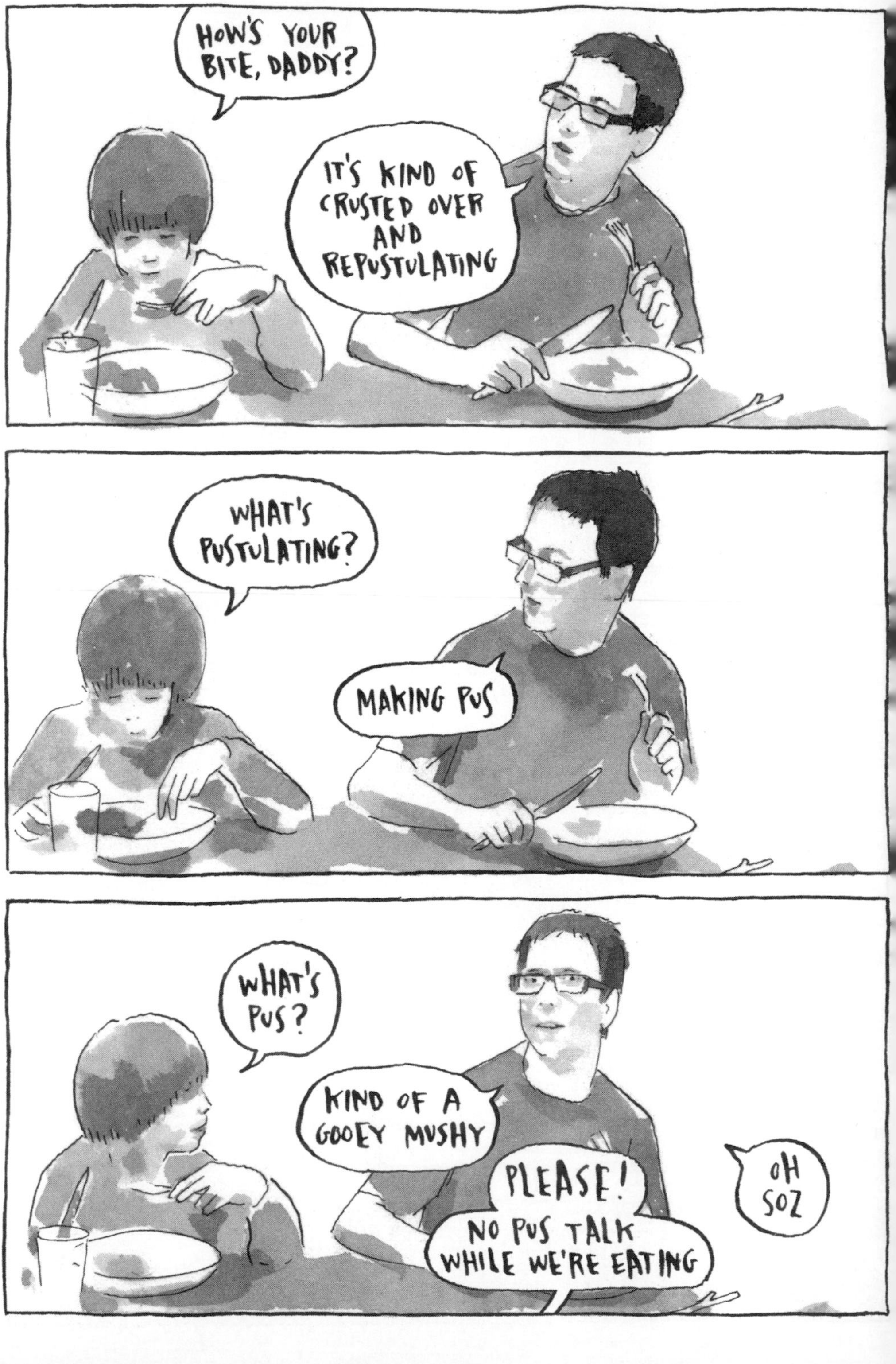
HOW'S YOUR BITE, DADDY?
IT'S KIND OF CRUSTED OVER AND REPUSTULATING
WHAT'S PUSTULATING?
MAKING PUS
WHAT'S PUS?
KIND OF A GOOEY MUSHY
PLEASE!
NO PUS TALK WHILE WE'RE EATING
OH SOZ

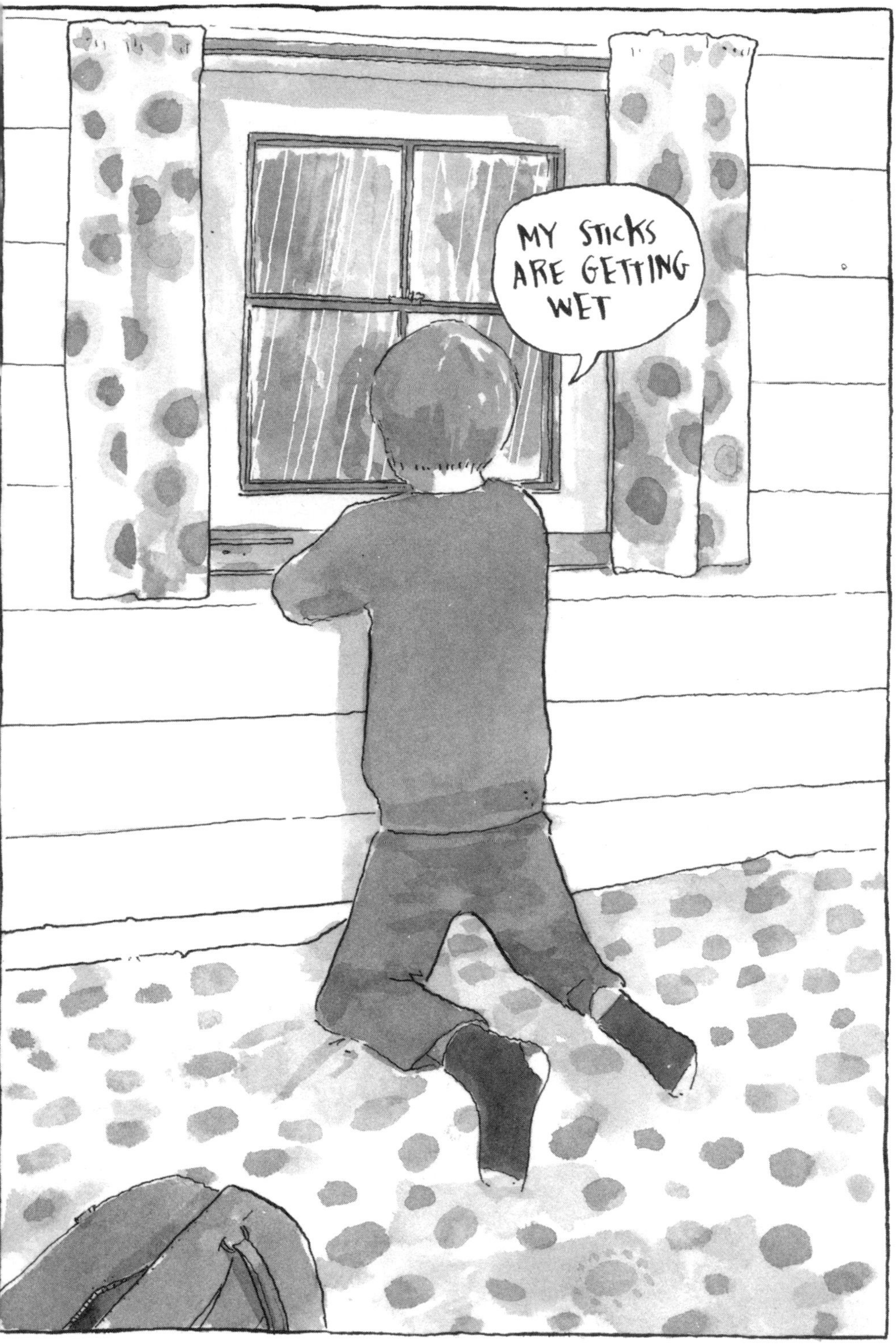
MY STICKS ARE GETTING WET

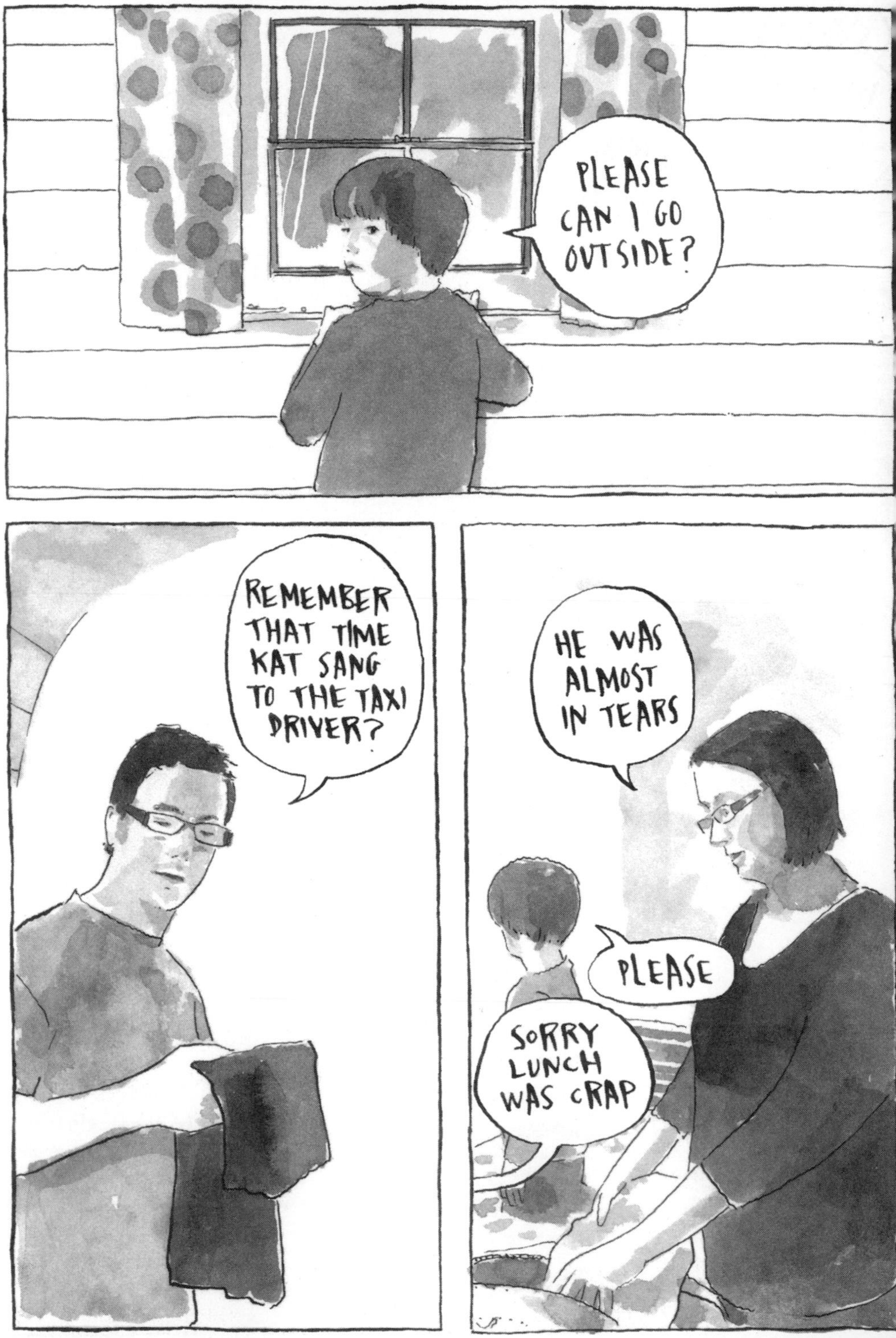
PLEASE CAN I GO OUTSIDE?
REMEMBER THAT TIME KAT SANG TO THE TAXI DRIVER?
HE WAS ALMOST IN TEARS
PLEASE
SORRY LUNCH WAS CRAP

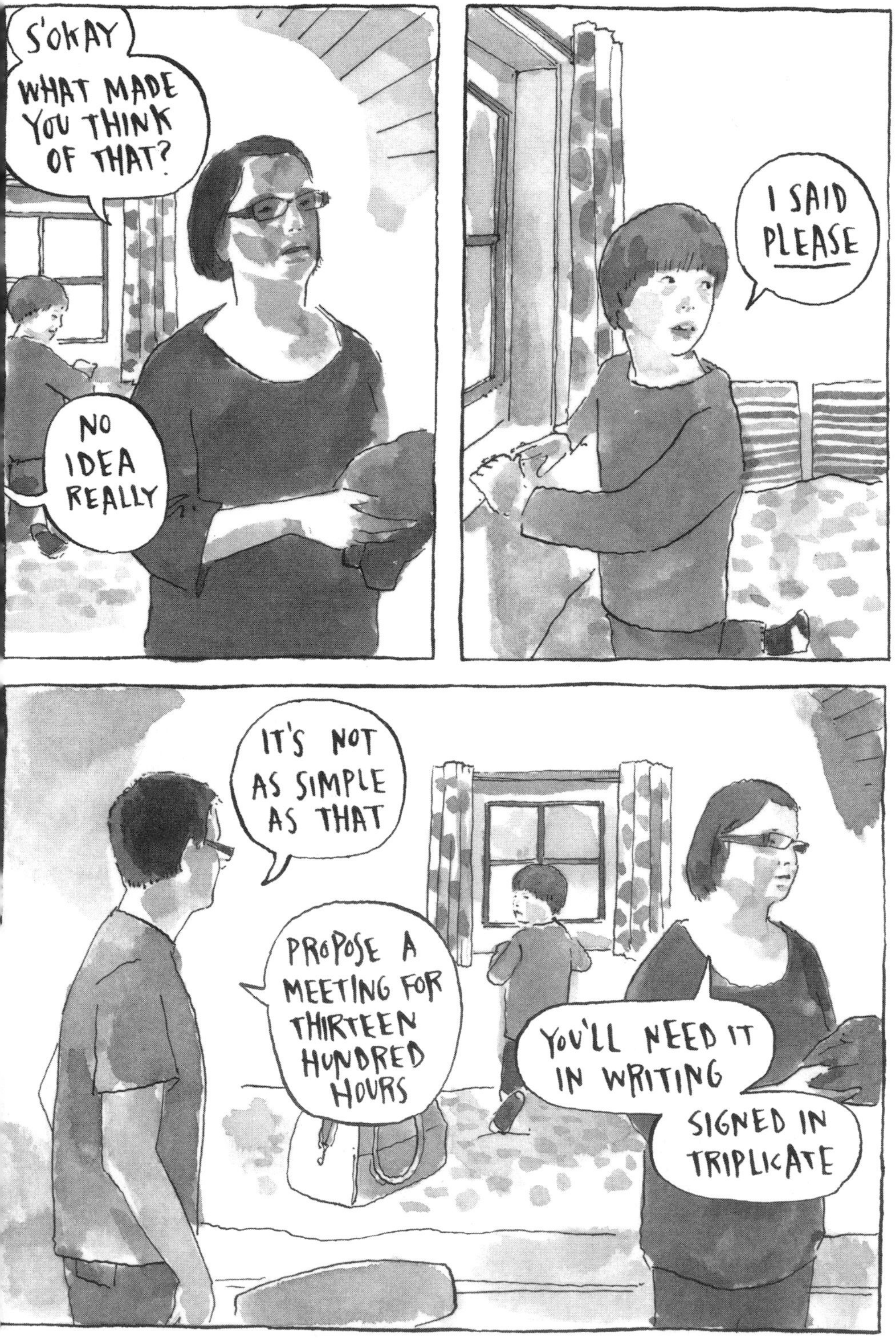
S'OKAY
WHAT MADE YOU THINK OF THAT?
NO IDEA REALLY
I SAID PLEASE
IT'S NOT AS SIMPLE AS THAT
PROPOSE A MEETING FOR THIRTEEN HUNDRED HOURS
YOU'LL NEED IT IN WRITING
SIGNED IN TRIPLICATE

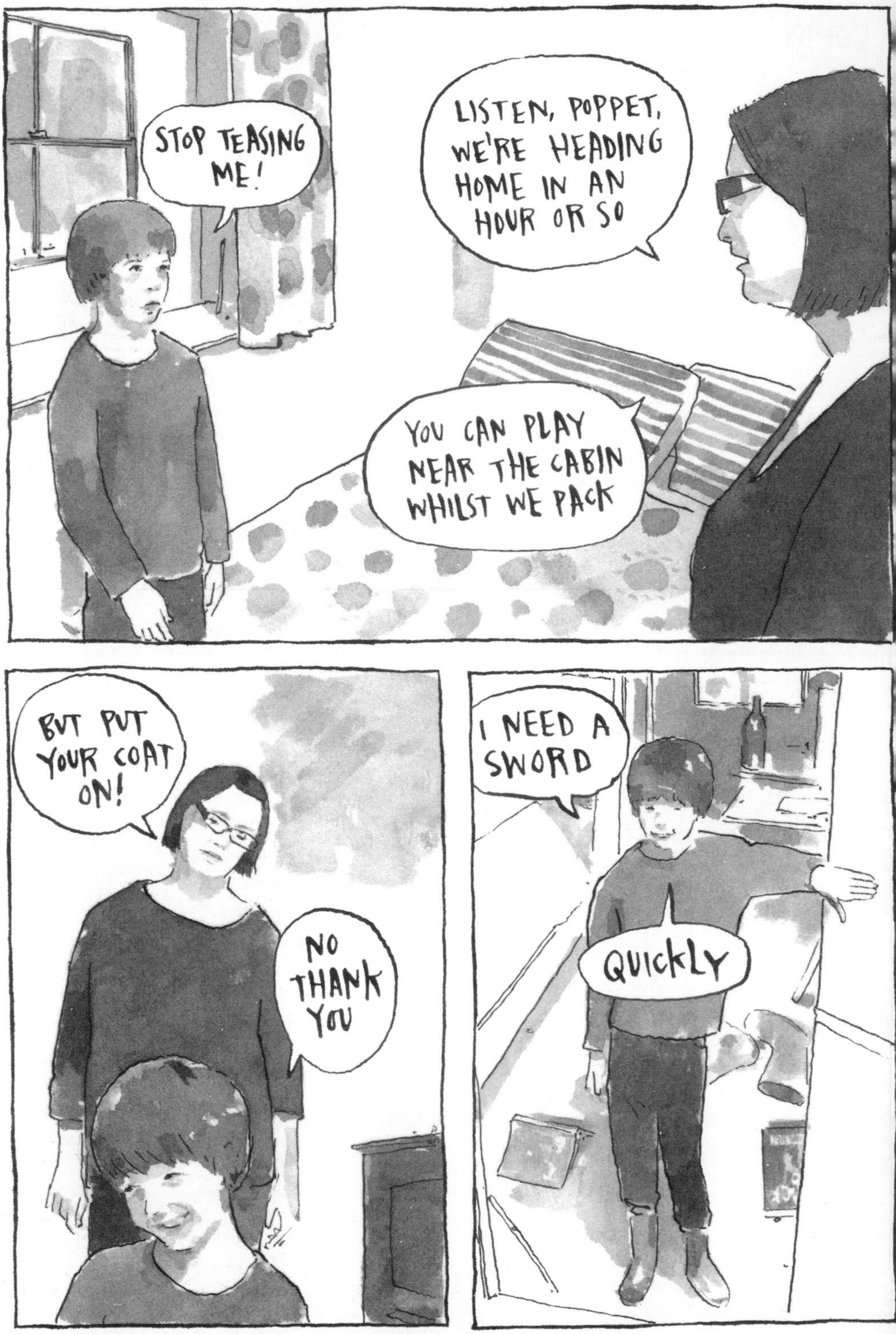
STOP TEASING ME!
LISTEN, POPPET, WE'RE HEADING HOME IN AN HOUR OR SO
YOU CAN PLAY NEAR THE CABIN WHILST WE PACK
BUT PUT YOUR COAT ON!
NO THANK YOU
I NEED A SWORD
QUICKLY

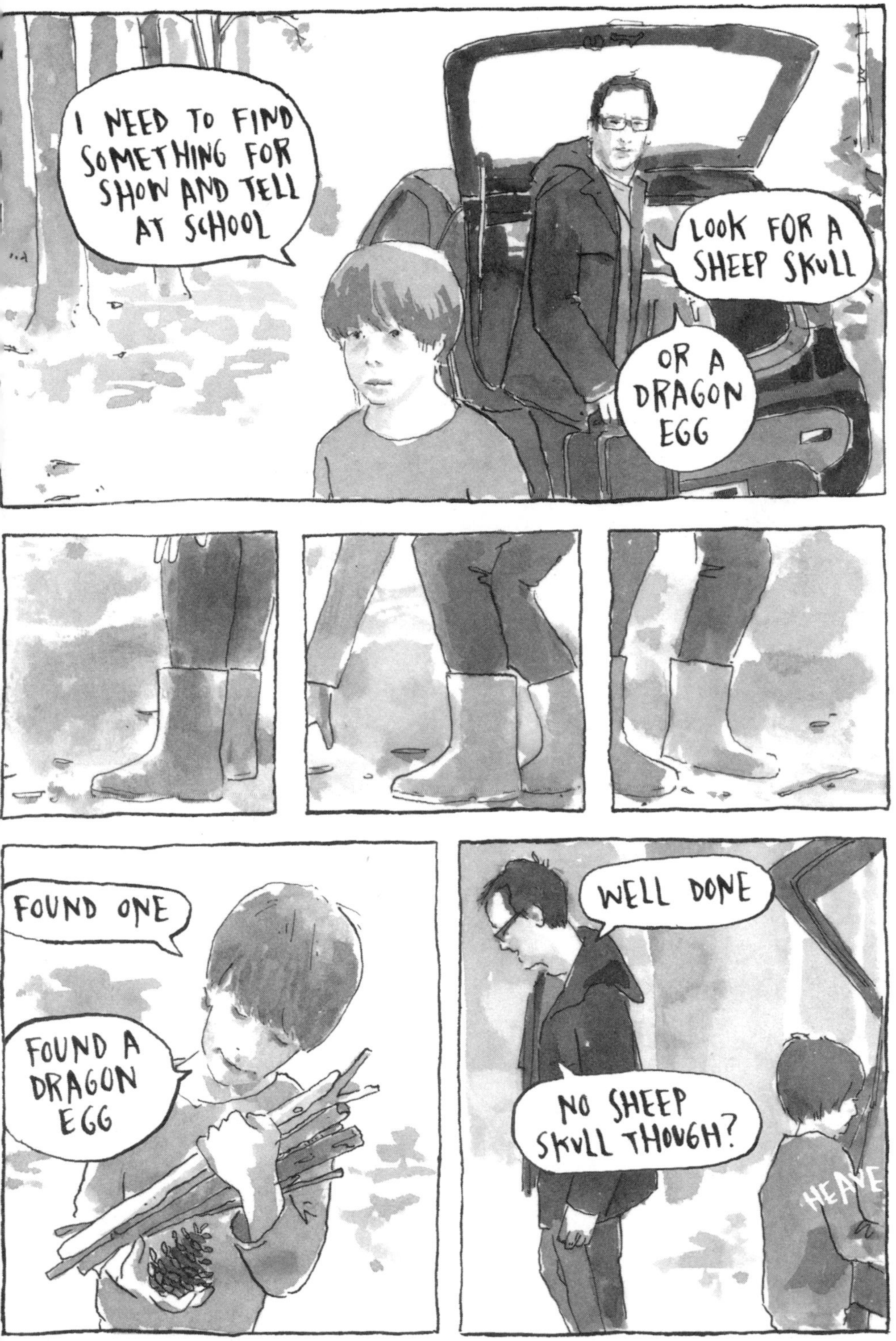
I NEED TO FIND SOMETHING FOR SHOW AND TELL AT SCHOOL
LOOK FOR A SHEEP SKULL
OR A DRAGON EGG
FOUND ONE
FOUND A DRAGON EGG
WELL DONE
NO SHEEP SKULL THOUGH?
HEAVE

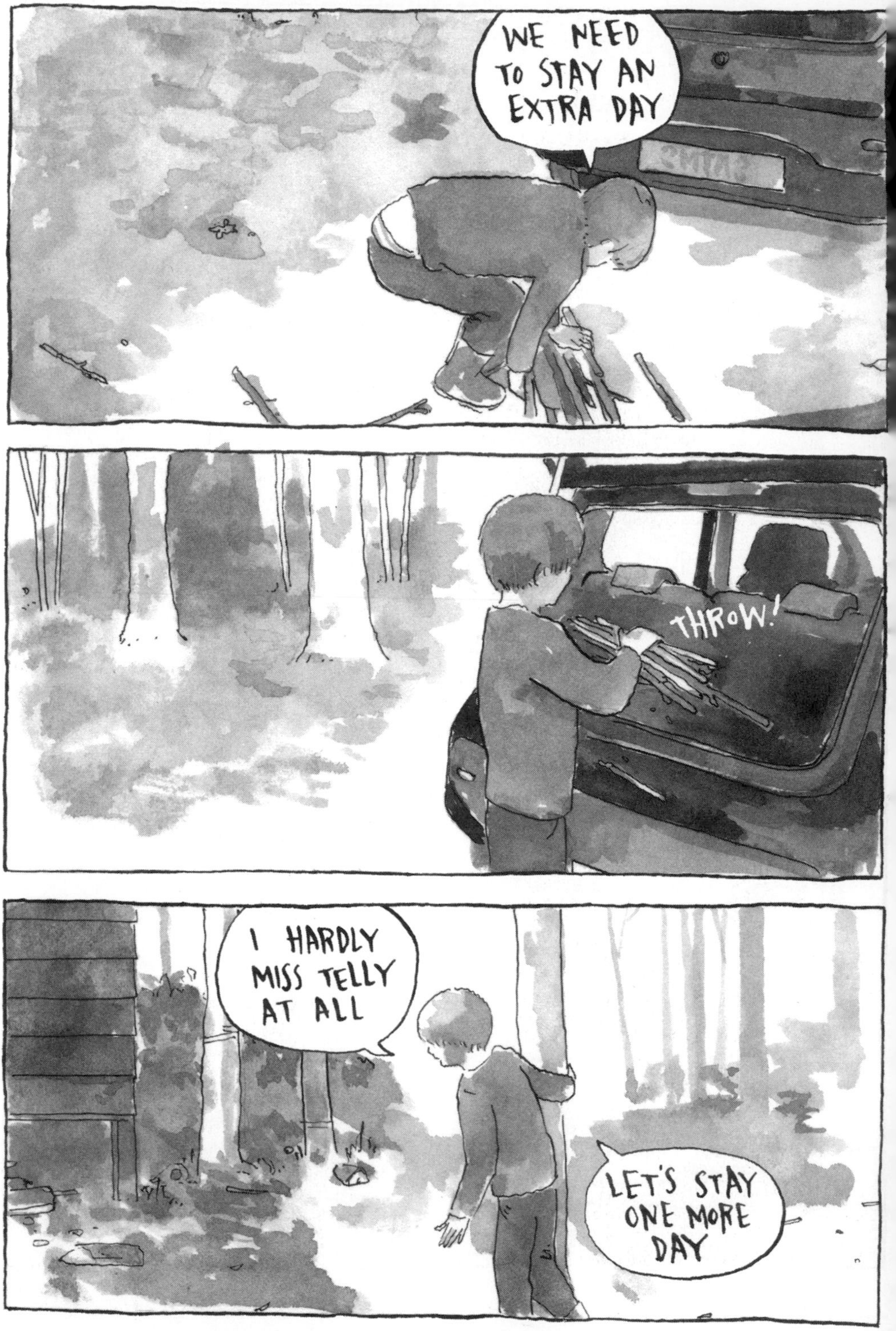
WE NEED TO STAY AN EXTRA DAY
THROW!
I HARDLY MISS TELLY AT ALL
LET'S STAY ONE MORE DAY

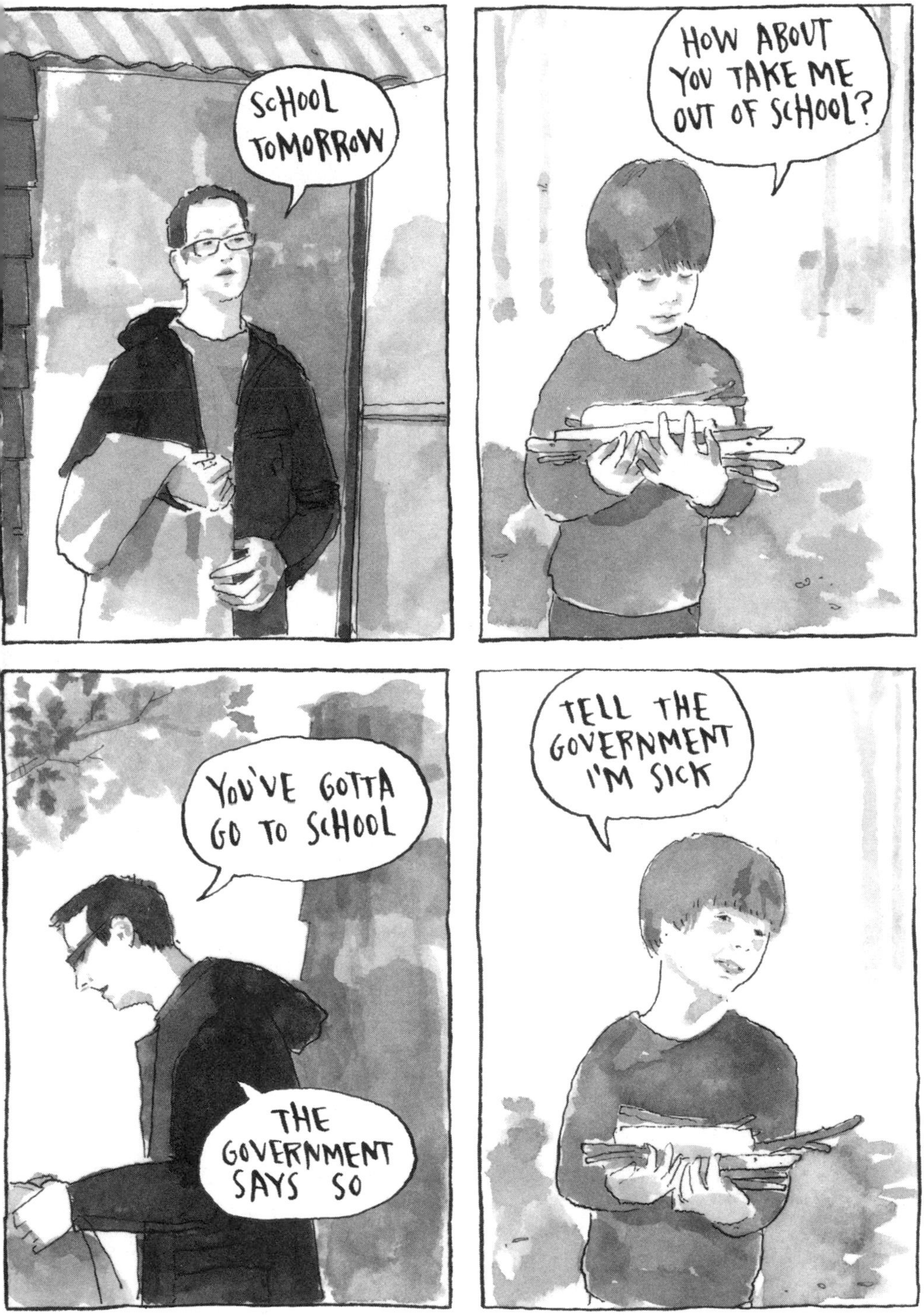
SCHOOL TOMORROW
HOW ABOUT YOU TAKE ME OUT OF SCHOOL?
YOU'VE GOTTA GO TO SCHOOL
THE GOVERNMENT SAYS SO
TELL THE GOVERNMENT I'M SICK

REBEL REBEL!

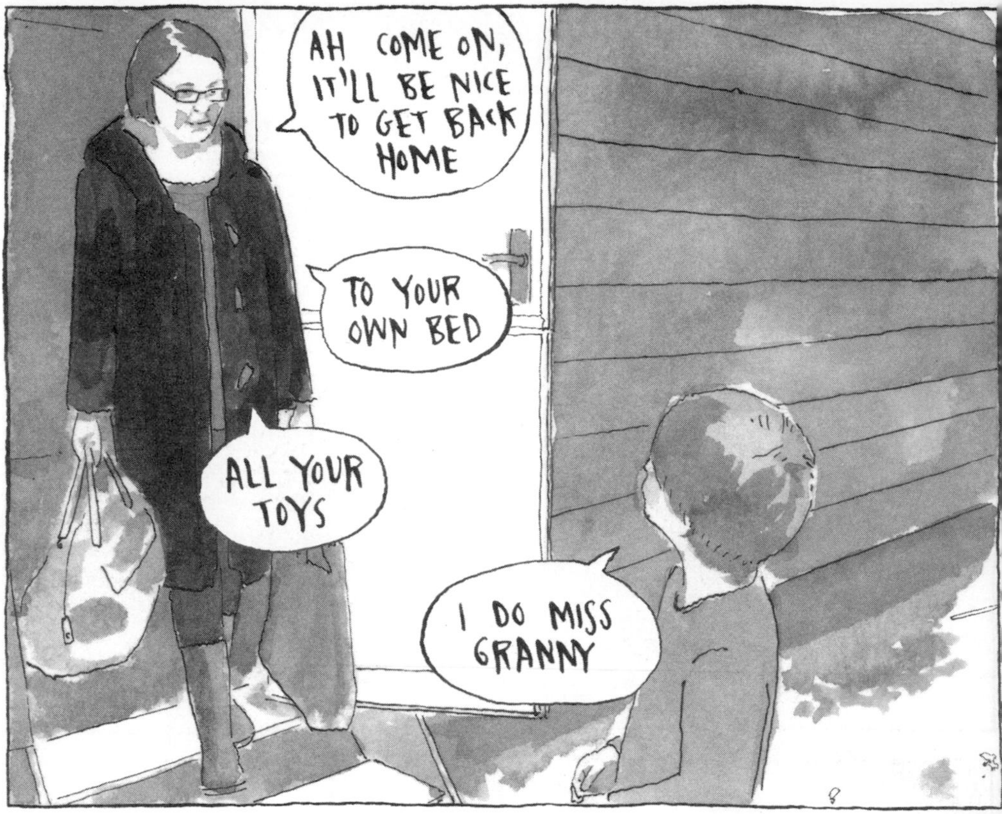
AH COME ON, IT'LL BE NICE TO GET BACK HOME
TO YOUR OWN BED
ALL YOUR TOYS
I DO MISS GRANNY

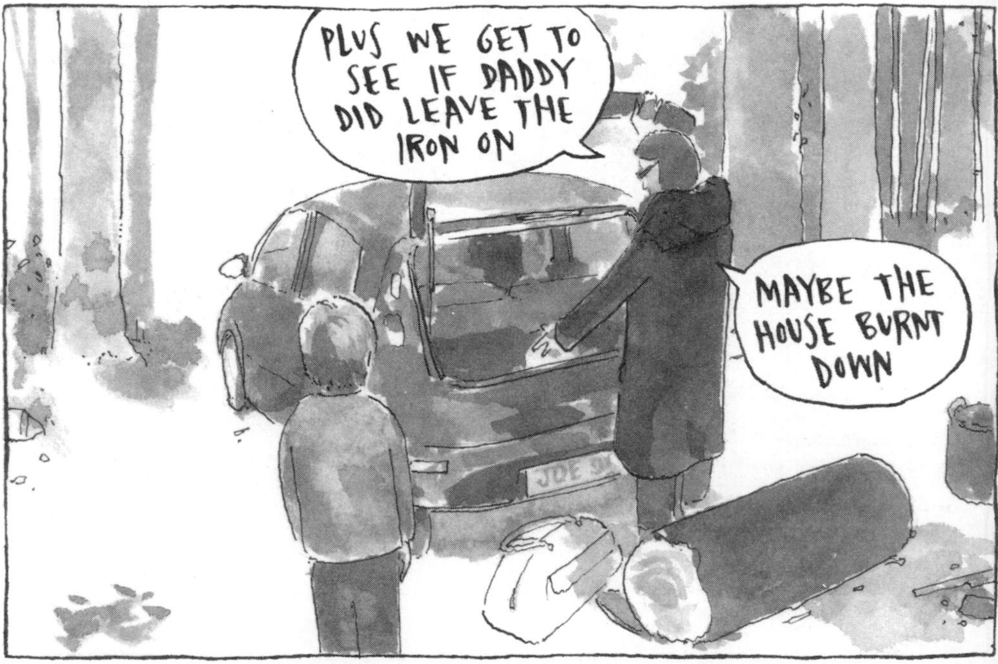
PLUS WE GET TO SEE IF DADDY DID LEAVE THE IRON ON
MAYBE THE HOUSE BURNT DOWN

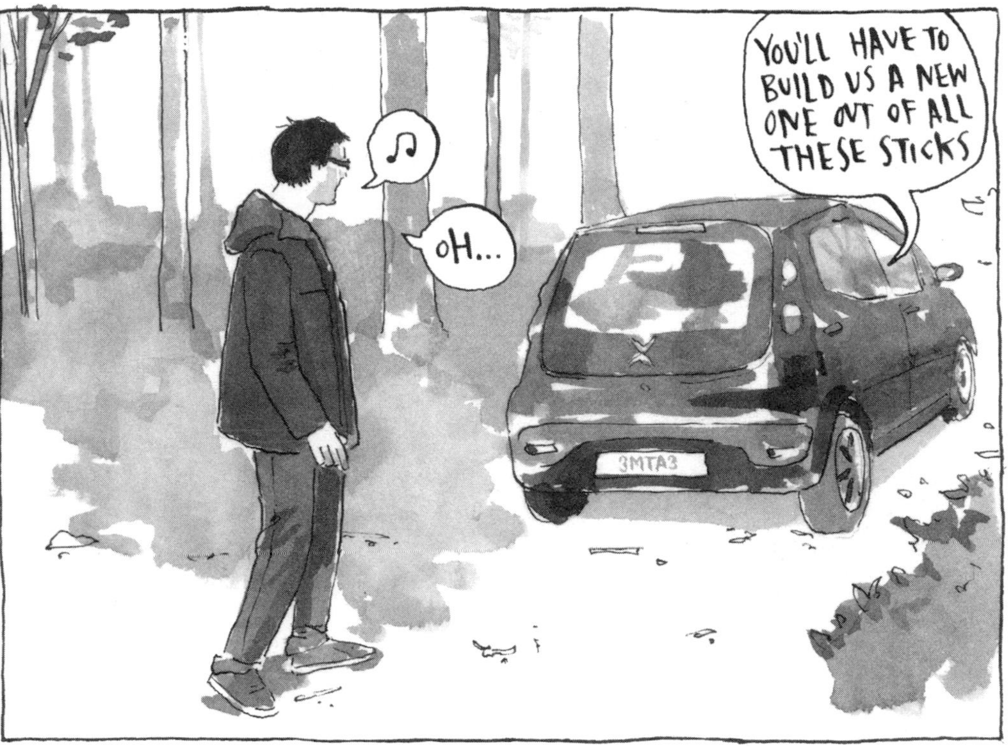
♫
OH...
YOU'LL HAVE TO BUILD US A NEW ONE OUT OF ALL THESE STICKS
3MTA3

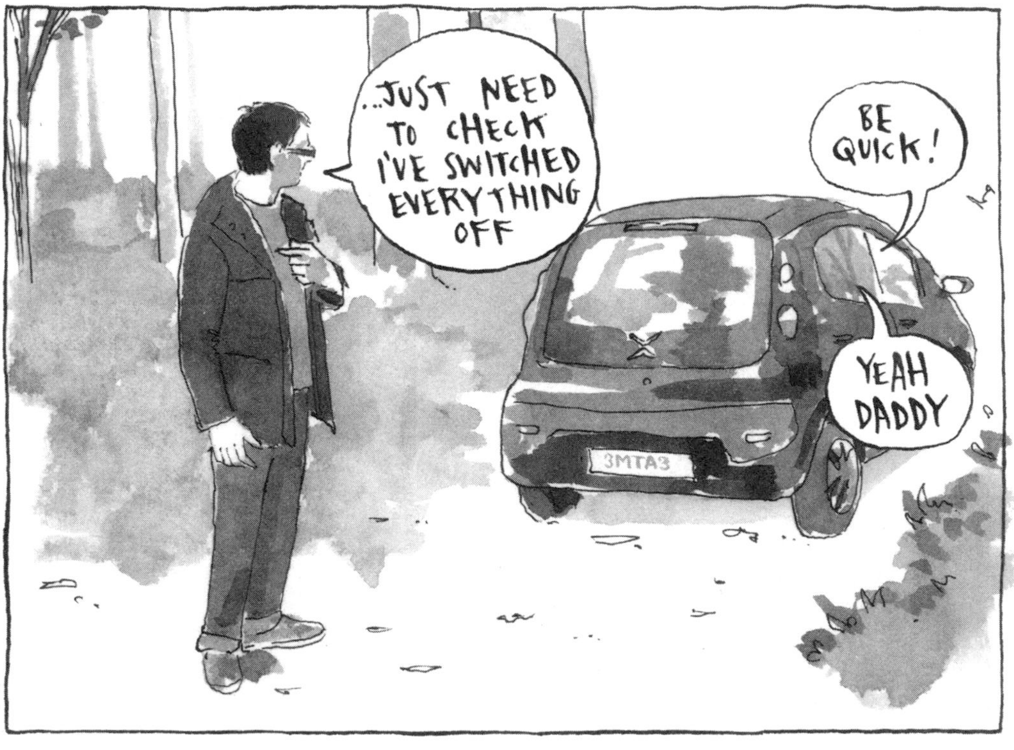
...JUST NEED TO CHECK I'VE SWITCHED EVERYTHING OFF
BE QUICK!
YEAH DADDY
3MTA3

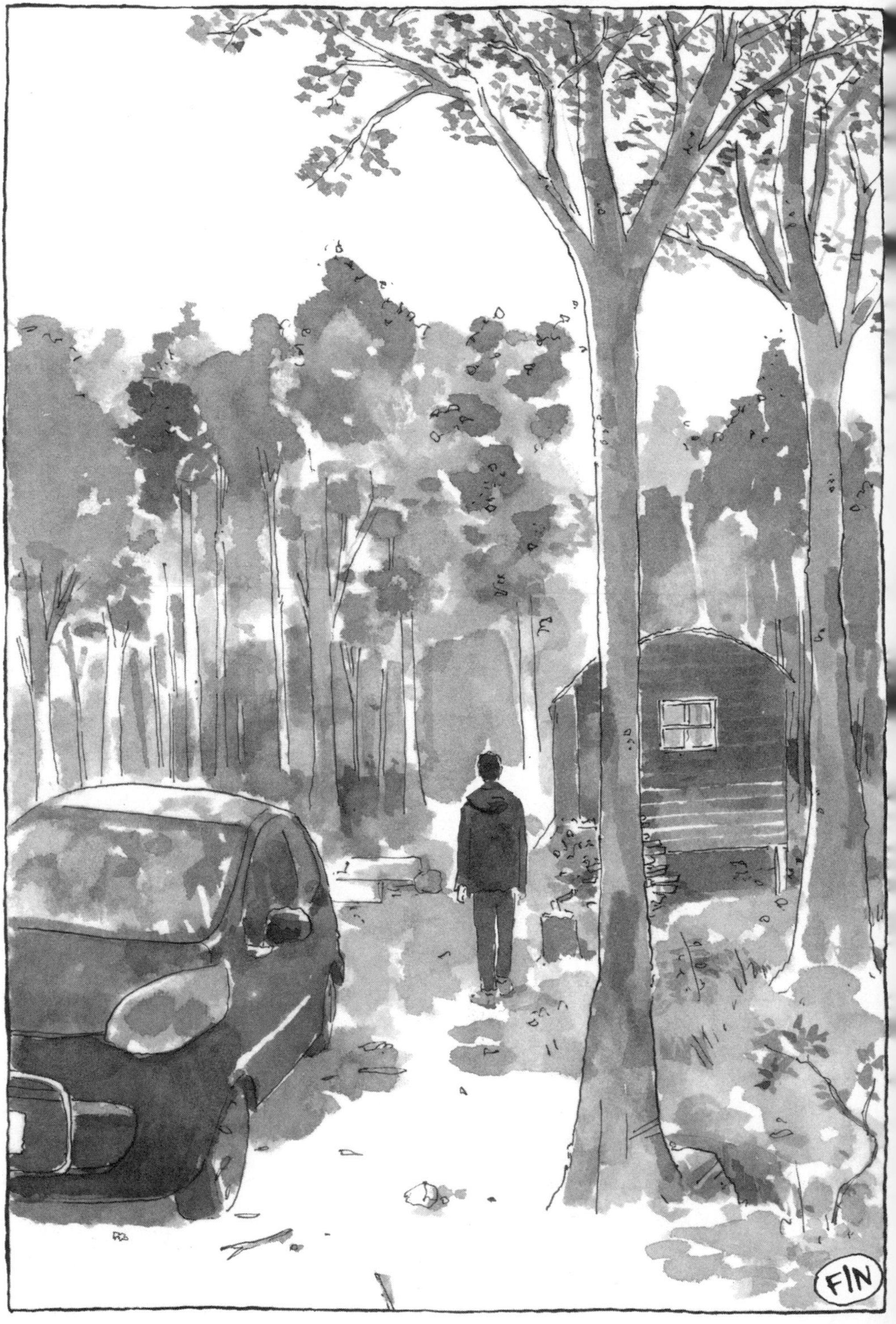
FIN

EPILOGUE

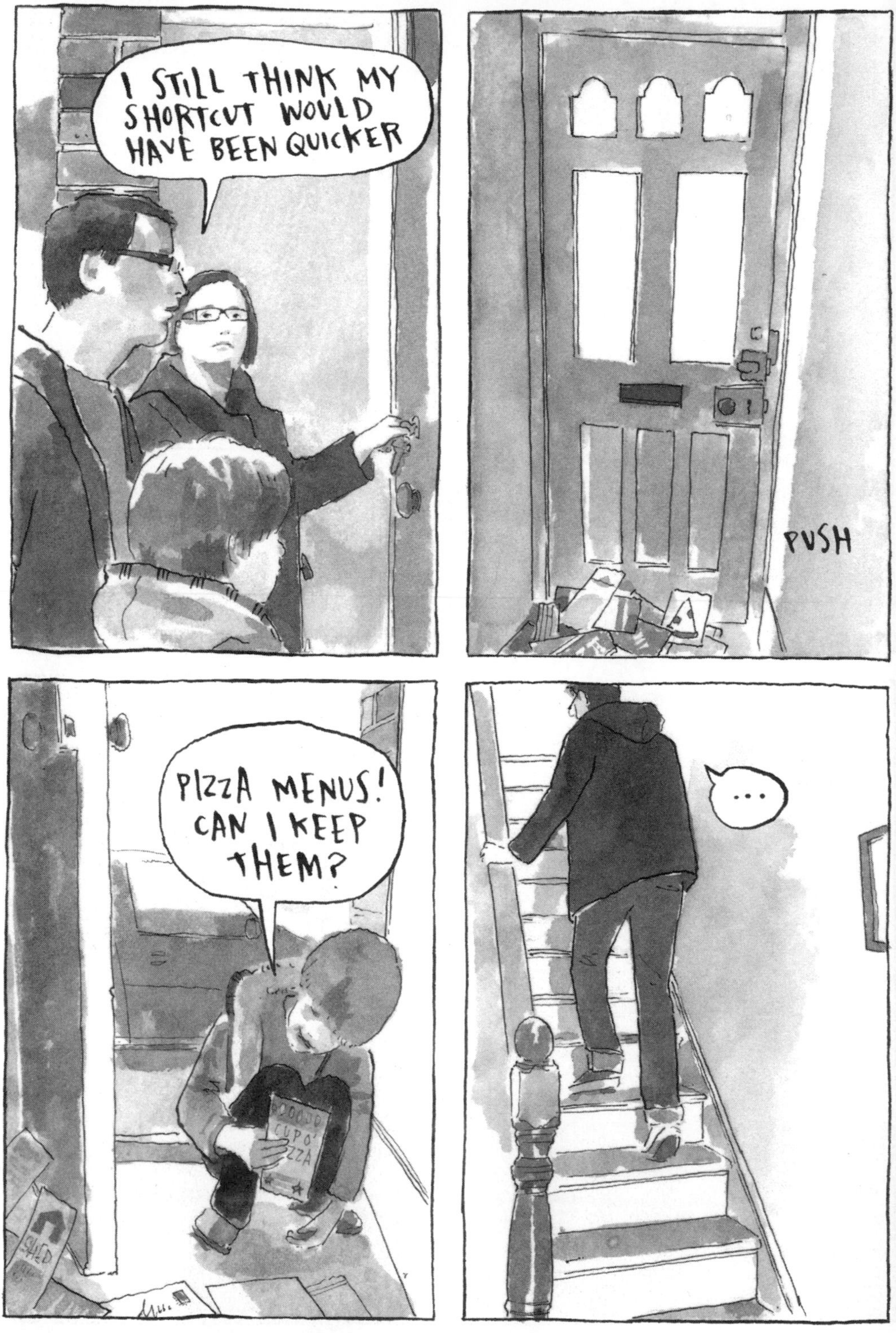
I STILL THINK MY SHORTCUT WOULD HAVE BEEN QUICKER
PUSH
PIZZA MENUS! CAN I KEEP THEM?
...

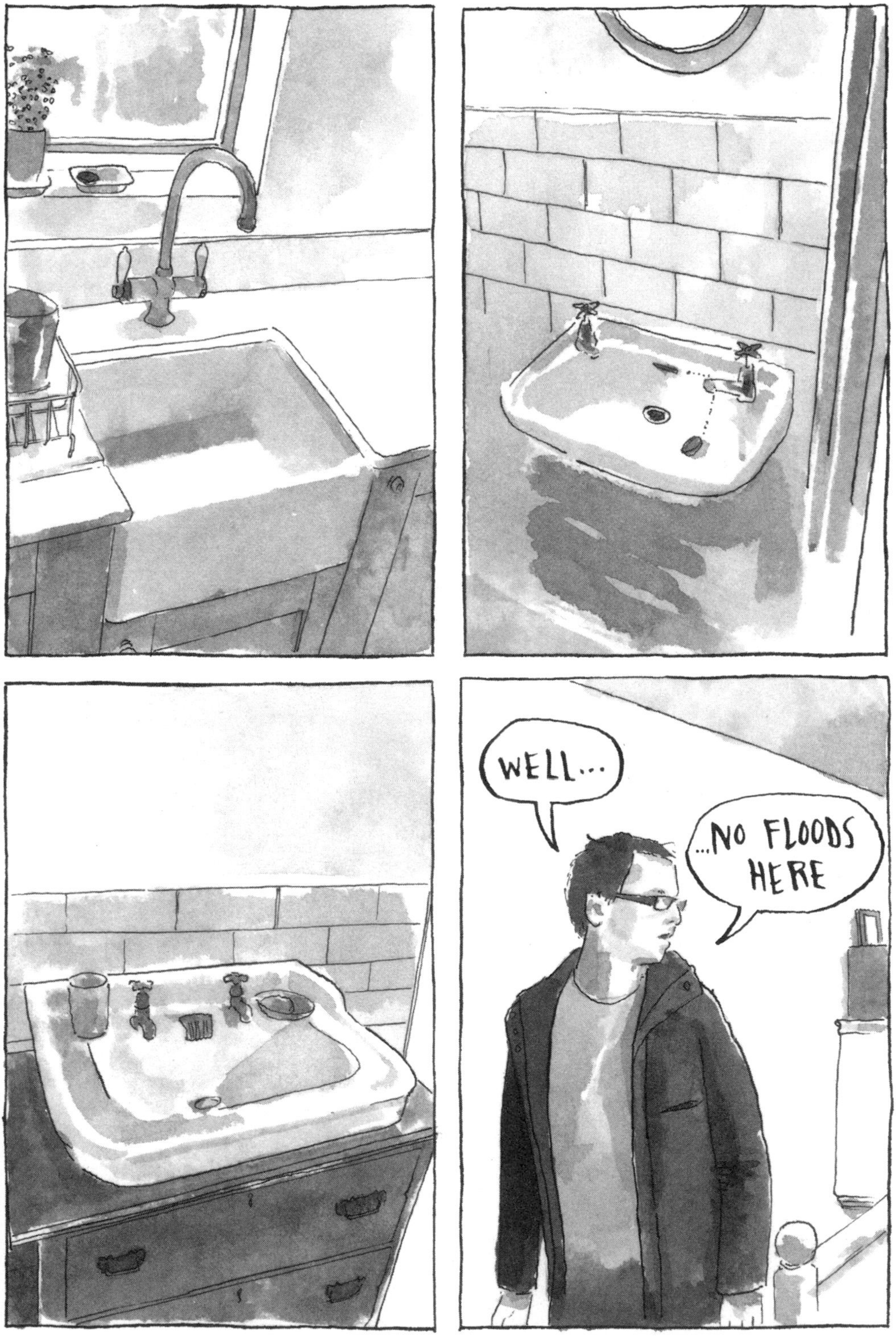
WELL...
...NO FLOODS HERE

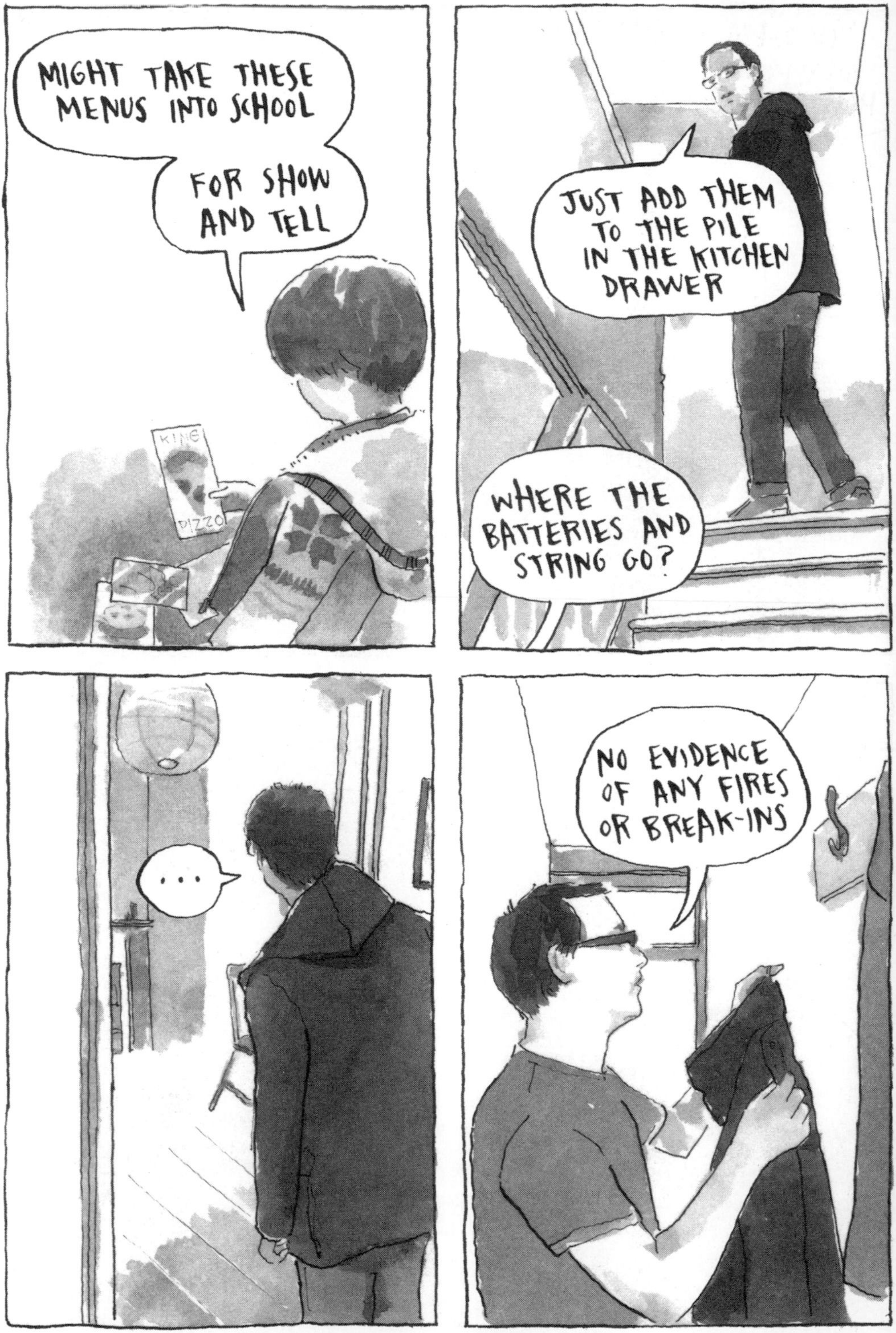
MIGHT TAKE THESE MENUS INTO SCHOOL
FOR SHOW AND TELL
KING
PIZZA
JUST ADD THEM TO THE PILE IN THE KITCHEN DRAWER
WHERE THE BATTERIES AND STRING GO?
...
NO EVIDENCE OF ANY FIRES OR BREAK-INS

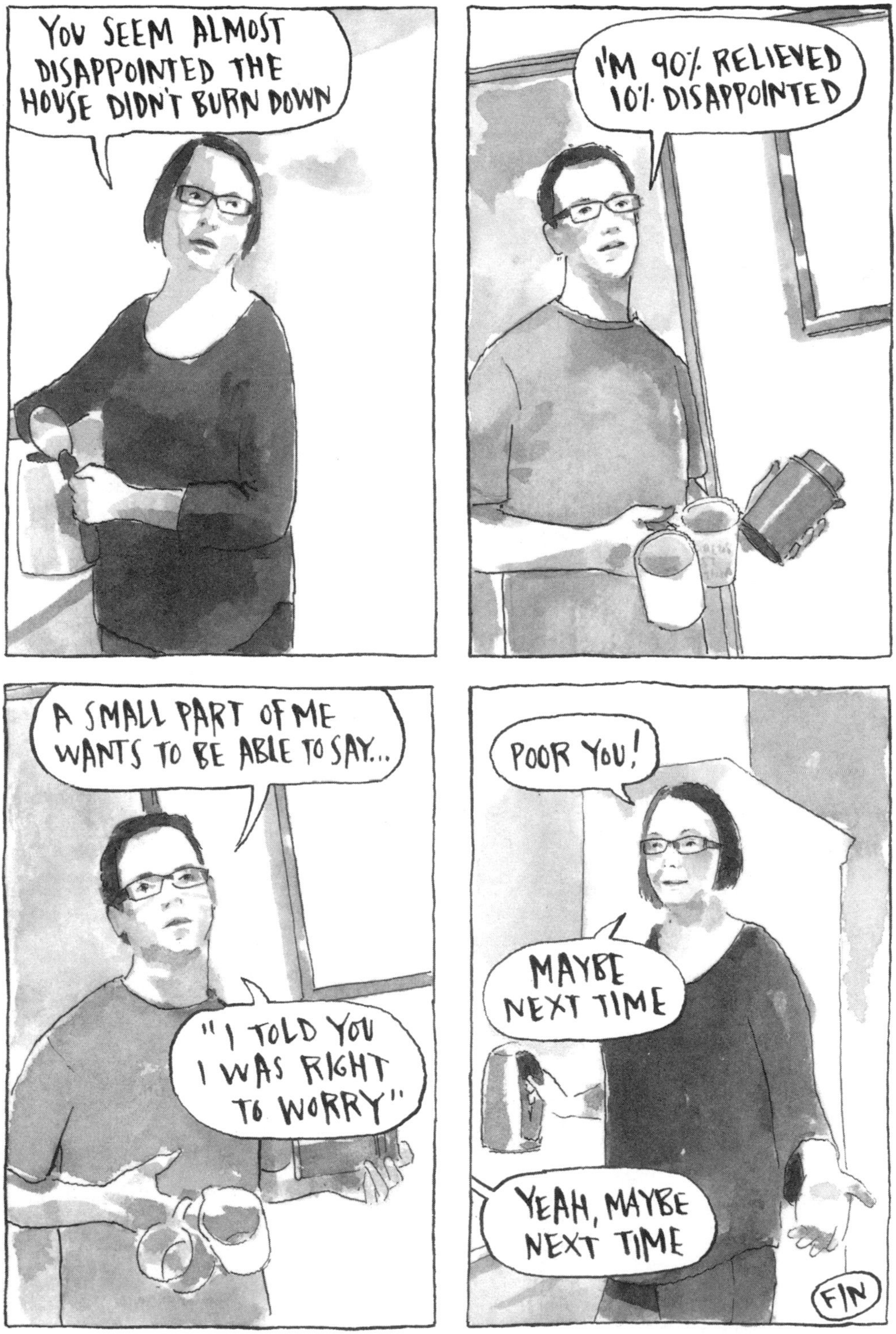
YOU SEEM ALMOST DISAPPOINTED THE HOUSE DIDN'T BURN DOWN
I'M 90% RELIEVED 10% DISAPPOINTED
A SMALL PART OF ME WANTS TO BE ABLE TO SAY...
"I TOLD YOU I WAS RIGHT TO WORRY"
POOR YOU!
MAYBE NEXT TIME
YEAH, MAYBE NEXT TIME
FIN

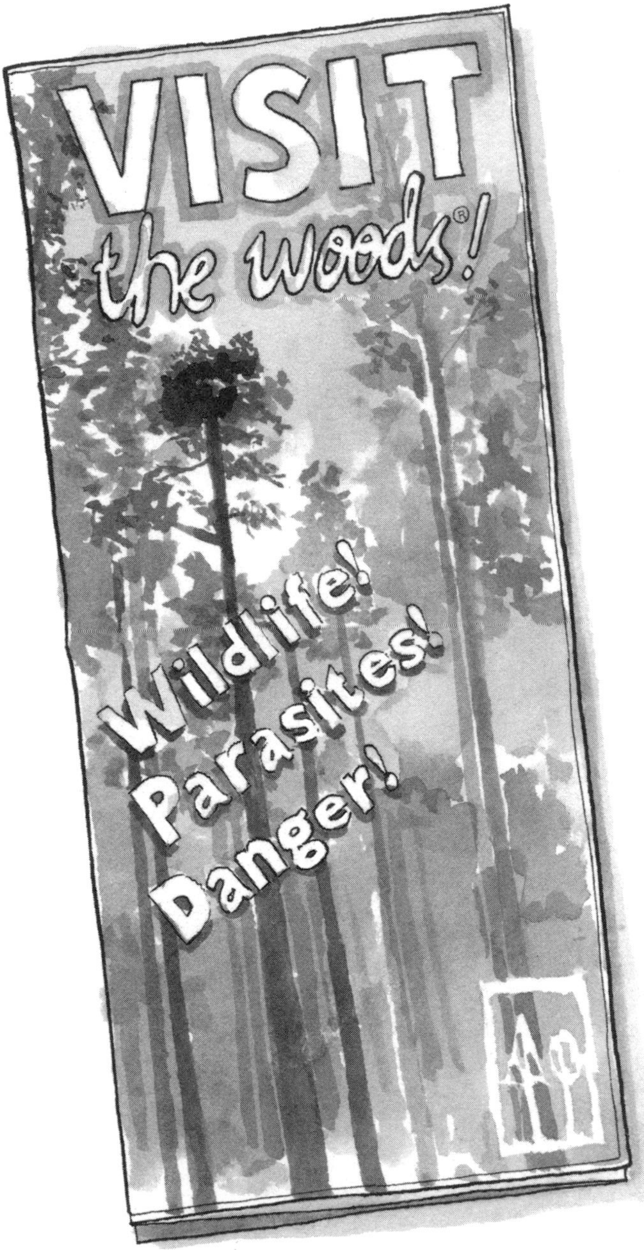
VISIT
the woods®!
Wildlife!
Parasites!
Danger!

1 3 5 7 9 10 8 6 4 2

JONATHAN CAPE, AN IMPRINT OF VINTAGE PUBLISHING,
20 VAUXHALL BRIDGE ROAD, LONDON SW1V 2SA

JONATHAN CAPE IS PART OF THE PENGUIN RANDOM HOUSE GROUP
OF COMPANIES WHOSE ADDRESSES CAN BE FOUND AT
global.penguinrandomhouse.com.

FIRST PUBLISHED IN 2017 BY JONATHAN CAPE

www.vintage-books.co.uk

A CIP CATALOGUE RECORD FOR THIS BOOK IS AVAILABLE FROM THE
BRITISH LIBRARY

ISBN 9781910702734

PRINTED AND BOUND IN INDIA BY REPLIKA PRESS PVT LTD

PENGUIN RANDOM HOUSE IS COMMITTED TO A SUSTAINABLE FUTURE
FOR OUR BUSINESS, OUR READERS AND OUR PLANET. THIS BOOK IS
MADE FROM FOREST STEWARDSHIP COUNCIL ® CERTIFIED PAPER.

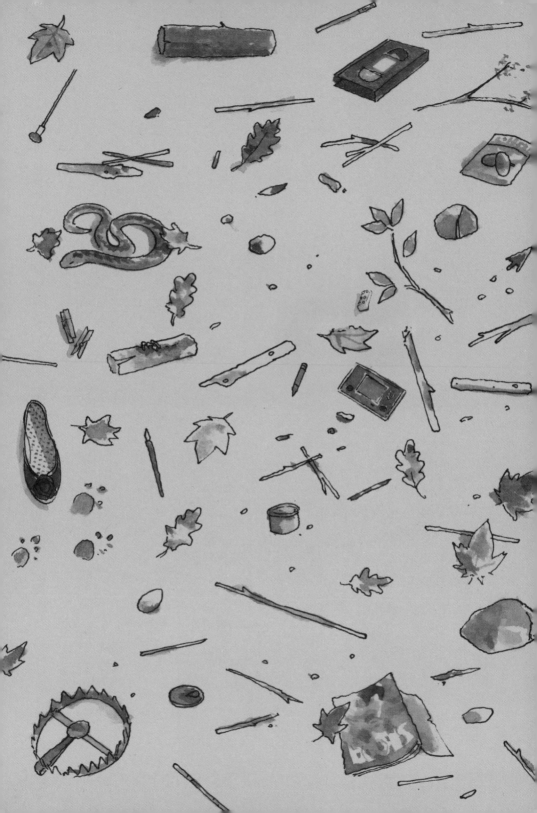